## More Advance Praise for
## *All Is Beauty Now*

"A deft, kaleidoscopic chronicle of a family's grief, *All Is Beauty Now* is an unflinching look at the pervasive effect of secreted mental illness. Like the brilliant swirl of Carnival, the Maurer family's story possesses multiple layers of both splendour and affliction. I lost myself in its white sands, birds of paradise, and madness."

—Anne Korkeakivi, author of *Shining Sea*

"At once an intimate family portrait, a mystery, a romance, and a stylistic tour de force. Think Alice Munro's *Lives of Girls and Women*, Virginia Woolf's *The Waves*, Michael Ondaatje's *Running in the Family*, and Alejandro Jodorowsky's *The Dance of Reality* in a gloriously refreshing mash-up."

—Johanna Skibsrud, author of *The Sentimentalists*,
winner of the Scotiabank Giller Prize

"For the reader, beauty illuminates every page, the loveliness of Faber's prose bringing light to even the darkest turns and twists of the Maurers' story, like stars across the night sky. A magnificent, compassionate, and beguiling novel from a great new talent."

—Rebecca Silver Slayter, author of *In the Land of Birdfishes*

# ALL
# IS
# BEAUTY
# NOW

SARAH FABER

*McClelland & Stewart*

Library and Archives Canada Cataloguing in Publication is available upon request

ISBN: 978-0-7710-0933-4
ebook ISBN: 978-0-7710-0934-1

Book design by Kelly Hill
Cover art: girl underwater © Getty Images/WIN-Initiative
Cover and interior flower art courtesy of The Miriam and Ira D. Wallach Division of Art, Prints and Photographs: Print Collection, The New York Public Library. New York Public Library Digital Collections. Both accessed February 3, 2017. "Végétaux des forêts vierges du Brésil." http://digitalcollections.nypl.org/items/510d47df-7774-a3d9-e040-e00a18064a99 "Végétation des forêts vierges." http://digitalcollections.nypl.org/items/510d47df-777b-a3d9-e040-e00a18064a99

Typeset in Sabon by M&S, Toronto
Printed and bound in the USA

This is a work of fiction. Names, characters, places, and incidents either are the products of the author's imagination or are used fictitiously.

McClelland & Stewart,
a division of Penguin Random House Canada Limited,
a Penguin Random House Company
www.penguinrandomhouse.ca

1   2   3   4   5      21   20   19   18   17

*For Oisín, Fianan, and Neva,*
*my three great loves*

I lost two cities, lovely ones. And, vaster,
some realms I owned, two rivers, a continent.
I miss them, but it wasn't a disaster.
—ELIZABETH BISHOP, from "ONE ART"

Her many sins have been forgiven, for she loved much.
—LUKE 7:47

OUTSIDE RIO DE JANEIRO

MARCH 1962

The day Luiza disappeared was as bright and hot as any other that summer, and although most of us were at the beach, no one saw anything, even if many of us would later claim we had. Such a curious thing—everybody wanting to be a part of it. We thought she was swimming out awfully far, and said so to one another afterwards. We were sure we heard splashing. Why didn't we do anything at the time? She was such a strong swimmer, and it was so calm. She was twenty years old, no longer a girl. We thought—

The air changed, became heavier, suspending the gulls above us. Water roared in our ears, muffling the sound of someone calling out. This is what we would say, most of us, whenever we told the story. Even the sky was different. Not storm clouds, grey-gathered in warning, but silver, brighter than any of us could remember, flashing off the water almost painfully. Mist reflecting the white sun. We squinted against it and finally made out a voice, more insistent—her youngest sister, Evie, calling out again from the rock pools, the stick she held still jammed in the sand, and she ran toward us, pointing. We all followed the child's gaze out to sea, then had to turn our eyes away, blinded briefly by the scattered light.

But there's no one there! someone said finally.

I can't see a thing.

My god. She's right. Luiza's not there.

Some of us waded out into the water, then swam toward the empty horizon, while the rest stood on the beach, unsure of what to do. Evie ran to those still asleep on towels and bleached beach chairs, fell into a crouch, and shook them awake, still calling her sister's name. It was strange to hear her voice, so loud and piercing, because she was the shy one, always lost in her own little world. She soon gave up on us and sprinted back to the rocks, crying out for her other sister, Magda, sharp and angular, always scowling.

Luiza's not there anymore!

Magda leapt down from the boulder, spraying sand. Soon they were both crying. A few of us ran the length of beach to see if maybe Luiza had been pulled along by the current. We stared out over the water, imposing a tiny dark shape onto the brilliant haze, the arc of diminutive arms. But there was nothing, just empty, dazzling space.

Eventually, her parents arrived and Hugo fell to his knees, his great body heaving in the sand. Dora remained standing, resting her hand on his shoulder; we always said she was his buttress against himself. In the hours that followed, she stayed calm and asked questions, but her lovely face was warped by fear. Then the police and an ambulance came, just in case. And us, murmuring, hearts thudding, shaking sand from our towels to cover their warm, trembling arms.

Later, someone would say they saw a vulture circling in the distant sky.

We sent our maids with food to the family's home in Villa Confederação, and we visited for a time, embracing them and clasping their hands. But then we stayed away—surely, we whispered, they needed time alone. But the truth was that Hugo frightened us. His tall, wasting body, his feral stare. Yet we continued to drive past their house, surrounded like our own by eight-foot stone walls embedded with broken glass and barbed wire; its gate locked, doors bolted, the windows with bars, decorative and invulnerable, because like us, they had once found footprints in the flower beds outside their bedrooms.

We imagine walking through their gardens as we had at their parties so many times before, and there we see Luiza leaning against the trunk of a schefflera. We follow her, weaving through firs, hibiscus, the pink-studded branches of the silkfloss tree. She was always a bit odd, too serious—she sometimes seemed to swallow anxiously at nothing, then look around quickly, hoping no one had noticed. Or maybe hoping they had? At parties, she was more comfortable with children, braiding tattered flowers into their hair. So earnest! we said, fatigued by her affectations: her scribbling in journals and her mannered speech, the way she wore her grandmother's ratty white gloves everywhere. But some of us thought we loved her for them. For others, it was Hugo—the handsome Canadian expat, once all limbs and laughter—whom we loved for his easy charm and inextinguishable energy, whipped up and transmitted through us like light. Others among us have loved Dora all our lives, and admired her proud beauty, even as she drove around the neighbourhood in that noisy little Simca. She was one of us, a descendant of the *Confederados*, who fled in defeat from Alabama after the American Civil War to Brazil, where they licked their wounds and prospered. Our ancestors, Baptists and Methodists, brought clean churches to this superstitious place and woke the echoes with their hymns. Peasants here farm with ploughs now, which they never would have had in this backward country if not for our people.

Together, Hugo and Dora were the golden ones in our small community. Ever since those early years when they wore nothing but white and danced at the Copacabana, Hugo pulling her up onto the tabletops to join him, and Dora shaking confetti from her hair while we watched them dance aloft. Him, laughing easily, his fist crammed with bills won from the Jockey Club. Her at the beach, lacquered nails against the lichen of craggy seaside rocks, looking out at the white sea shedding haze. He brought out the best in her, warm flickers of joy, and somehow it mattered to us that she stayed with him through everything, haughtily selfless. That remarkable family. Not so golden anymore.

They had been scheduled to sail for Canada within days when Luiza disappeared. Would Dora still move her family away? Theirs had been the life—such a life! Until the vultures circled the shore, and seeing something, they dove . . .

—Why say such an unkind thing?

—Yes, stop that! Why must we always try to make stories about dead girls into something lurid.

—It was a terrible accident, nothing more.

—But was it really? An accident? My maid swears she saw her all alone on the tram. And this was the day of their good-bye party. And she was crying!

—Oh, everyone but her parents knew she was up to something.

—It's true. Such troubled people.

—What a dreadful thing. What awful people we are.

But some of us can't stop ourselves. We say it's retribution for too much shine, too many flowers. So much fruit. We heard Luiza was ashamed of us. All her mother's money from diamond mines and sugar plantations, and *her* ashamed of *us*! Drunk once at a party (her parents had always indulged her), she said we might as well still be slaveholders for what little we paid them—our chauffeurs and maids, the *babás* who raised our children—as though condemning herself as well made it all right. Her mother, embarrassed, apologized and took her home. But things soon got worse. She gets it from him, we whispered. It was bound to happen. When people are that beautiful, the rot is on the inside.

And yet sometimes we walk along the beach, searching for a sign, imagining we will be the ones to find her. Each time, we are frightened and a little hopeful that maybe we could ease their pain. We pity them, wondering which hell is worse—knowing, or not knowing. Finding, or not finding.

We loved them—we still do. But they've long been lost to us. They stepped outside themselves for a time, just long enough to let us in, to subdue our bristling need, before retreating back into their family's embrace, and behind their walls. We were not enough for them. Fallen, they are still our betters.

And if we found Luiza, would she be bloated and blue, face eaten away by sea animals? Or by now would she be nothing but a bleached heap of frail bones, sun-stripped? Who among us could stomach it, to wrap some part of her in fine cloth and take her home? Something to lay to rest, we would say in hushed, ragged tones. We couldn't bear it, to be the ones to mark the end of their age. But then we could truly embrace them, even the men among us, because we do that here. We feel that much.

Yes, they belong *here*, with us: the embodiment of our brightest selves flashing in the night. If they go, we dim and grow smaller. And they become mortal after all.

— I —

# FEBRUARY 1963

# DORA

T here has been no funeral because there is no body. The police searched and telephoned and apologized and were kind, but no trace was ever found. And yet Dora needs to bury something, some object of Luiza's, so they'll have a place to return to someday, to clutch at the soil and pretend she is there, beneath them.

Now, finally, almost a year later, she and Hugo stand on one side of the empty grave while everyone else stands on the other, facing them, as though they might have some idea of what to do next. Evie and Magda are with the maids, who have come—of course they have!—despite being given the day off. And yet Dora finds herself staring meaningfully at Maricota, who is openly weeping, too upset to notice how Evie, seeming so much younger than her twelve years, is peeling apart the lily she was given to hold for the ceremony. She rubs the petals between her thumb and forefinger, then holds them up to the sun, peering through their crushed, now-translucent segments.

How much will they suffer? Please, not too much. Evie in particular, with her clear, deep feelings, has been afflicted in some ineffable way. Already dishevelled though it's not yet midday, with her plaits too loose, dirty fingernails, legs mottled with different-hued bruises. Reckless, like Luiza. Always feathery and odd, lately she's been running off, looking almost hunted as she disappears into hidden corners of the garden and creeps along its walled perimeter. She's virtually skinless, inchoate; her little magpie heart still seeking out something shiny in this sad place. She might ache forever, Dora supposes. Yes, she will suffer the most.

Though a year older, Magda is shorter than Evie, and compact, muscular. Neatly dressed and rigid as a cadet, she moves only occasionally and deftly to snatch some inappropriate diversion from Evie—the macerated lily, a thread pulled from her hem. Dora knows Magda will suffer too; she is unyielding, and hasn't yet learned to pretend for others' sake. She doesn't permit even well-meaning lies. She's difficult for adults to like, though children usually fear her, which is something. At thirteen, she is all switches and thorns. And she's the better for it.

But Hugo—he feels more than all of them.

Dora stands beneath the canopy of palm trees and soft-needled pines, vaguely grateful for their shade, her eyes skimming over the complicated root network of a nearby fig tree. Luiza would have said it was like something out of a fairy tale. Off to the side, rows of weathered grey tombstones in marble and soapstone, sprouting moss and etched with names like McKnight, Thomas, Baird. An anemic ceremony at the Campinas Cemetery, even though Hugo thinks it's meaningless because they don't go to church, and shouldn't God disdain those who only seek him out in times of grief?

And it's true that even Dora has never cared for this cemetery, for its annual festival when descendants of the *Confederados* come dressed in hoop skirts and Confederate uniforms to gaze out upon the sugarcane fields and rows of tombstones, disgorge some dour Revival hymn, then lay out dishes of fried chicken and cornbread, peach pie and sweet tea, conjuring Alabama. Regret, nostalgia—so much longing for a place that never was.

'Why?' Hugo asked a few days before when she had announced her plans for the ceremony, and he had objected, with almost mechanical disdain, to the location. 'We don't believe in all that nonsense, and Luiza certainly didn't. That place is poisoned.' He couldn't even look at her, his long body seeming prematurely caved in, readied for blows.

She knows that the ceremony means little to him, that a few graveside hymns won't change anything: he hasn't accepted that Luiza is gone. None of them has. But there has to be somewhere to put all this confusion, still unexpressed. Inexpressible. A ritual that can give it shape. Maybe the ceremony will ignite in her the strength she needs to unshutter her family, gather them up, take them away. They had been so close to leaving for Canada last year, and then—. Now, for the second time, Dora must organize useless items into meaningless piles, contact old friends, arrange more goodbye parties, get on a ship at last. Go. For his sake. For all their sakes. Still, Luiza presses in upon their every thought, whispering in their ears. They have to have a place to put her. To find her.

No one actually saw Luiza disappear in the water, even though there were several people at the beach: the McMullans, the Dawseys, the dentist and his sister visiting from Santarém. The Dawsey boy said that Luiza had helped him bury his father in the sand and laughed when he added 'girl parts.' Someone else said she ate half a sandwich quickly, then offered up the rest. She read a few pages of her book but told the kind dentist that she couldn't get into it.

'Tacitus,' she said rather sadly, he thought. But then she laughed. 'Who wants to think about Rome burning in this heat?'

Soon after that, she drifted off to sleep while Evie and Magda turned their attention toward her, entombing her twitching feet again and again. She started a little when she woke, smiled at them, and thanked her sisters for being so good, for not going in the water alone as they'd promised. She caught the eye of Mrs. Buchanan, who winked and said, 'I'll watch them, *querida*.'

Dora knows all this even though she wasn't there. (Why wasn't she there?) Others have described the scene to her and Hugo over and over, as though it were some mystery that could be solved through repetition. As though perhaps Luiza had simply drifted away, carried out by the tide and all these stories. For months, Dora collected these varying accounts, telling herself that maybe the details would accrete, eventually shaping a whole story. Tell them where Luiza would wash up. She might be exhausted from fighting the tide and trying to swim back in, maybe a little bruised from tumbling ashore, the crotch of her swimsuit filled with sand the way it used to when she was a girl. But Luiza would come back to them with the waves that broke on the shore, terrified but otherwise unharmed.

Blood roars in her ears now. At least, Dora tells herself, it all happened quickly. She's heard that drowning is a peaceful death, once you let go. (But how could that be? And who would know? And who would ever really let go? *Not* Luiza.) But something else plagues her. Had there been signs, unusual behaviour? Dora sometimes thought so. Luiza grimacing as she pored over new books, as though hoping to extract something vital. Going out more often and alone, then shutting herself in her room for hours. Was she worried about the move? Lonely? Or maybe the opposite—was there a boyfriend? Boys often called the house for her, but she always told Dora she was bored by them, that they were too immature. It hurts too much to think of her being lonely. Alone in the water. *No. Push it away.*

They had been about to leave Brazil—did any of them need excuses to be unsettled? It was her daughter's temperament to be dreamy, distracted. How many times had Luiza forgotten the kettle until it boiled dry, or left a bathtub to overflow? She lived in a near-constant reverie, so careless with herself. Only because she was so beautiful did people fail to notice, or pretend not to: torn stockings, missing buttons. Two holes in the back collar of her dresses from where she'd hastily torn out the labels, rather than simply asking one of the maids to use the seam ripper. Thoughtless, headstrong girl. But Dora had been grateful, in some ways, for her daughter's pretenses, her solemn air and lost buttons. She was too beautiful and the awkwardness tempered it a little, put men off.

And yet, for years, Dora's stomach contracted, bathed in acid, waiting for the injuries, the ruination of Luiza's lovely body: the fall off a cliff's edge when she had wanted to smell the sea air; the car crash after something roadside and gleaming had caught her eye. She was that kind of person. Surely it was just a terrible accident.

Dora has to once again hold back images of Luiza afraid, choking on water, reaching out. She knows her eldest daughter tried to be responsible that day, catching Mrs. Buchanan's eye, making sure someone was watching the girls. But some days she finds herself almost blaming Luiza. For being so sure of herself, so cocky, for always swimming too far out even when they called to her from the shore.

*Come back!*

Once, when Luiza was little, Dora slapped her for not listening, for swimming too far. The child stood there with water streaming down her face and over her red cheeks. 'Those aren't tears,' she said. 'I'm not sorry.'

*I am sorry, I am sorry.* The words repeat in Dora's head. Maybe they should have waited for one more day. What if Luiza were to come back today and see that they are trying to bury her? Today might be the day she finds her way home. But that is what Dora has told herself every day for the past eleven months. So her mind practises: *She is not coming back.*

Dora looks at her family, trying to will herself to adjust to Luiza's absence. Whenever they're all together, her mind fills in the ever-widening aperture where Luiza used to be. Unconsciously, she projects Luiza into that space, several inches below Hugo, smiling in a way that Dora recognizes as strained, preoccupied. (Yes, something *was* different before she vanished. Something about her had altered.) Now she struggles to see them as they are, without Luiza: three and not four; a man and two young, graceless girls; the other, most beautiful one erased. But again, the excision fails; her brain won't submit. Luiza is there, in partial shade, indistinct at the edges but not gone.

No, the ceremony must be today because they can't stay here much longer. For years, a great momentum has been building beneath the surface of their lives, pushing them inexorably toward elsewhere. Away. And it had begun long before Luiza disappeared.

In some corner of her mind, a petulant voice asserts that anyone not here today will be scratched off any future list of invitees. But when she scans the blurred faces in front of her (oh, she is nearly crying again!), she realizes they have all come. Even Carmichael, who she hasn't seen in almost a year. And they've all dressed beautifully, and brought flowers.

'Having an English mother has conditioned you to expect too little from people,' Hugo used to tell her. And it's true that Brazilians—warm and demonstrative—still surprise her. Cab drivers will weep upon hearing your sad story, servants will embrace (and chastise) you. Even in this transplanted, anglophone community, people are good and affectionate and kind. This community of friends and neighbours who have all come to offer up their memories, clasp hands, embrace them. Even a few satellite acquaintances, like the dentist from Santarém who held Dora's hand when he told her what Luiza had said about the Romans and how she kissed Evie on the forehead before she went in the water. This is what they'll be leaving behind when they move to Canada.

The truth is, Dora knows that Luiza would never have wanted to be buried here at Campinas Cemetery; she said it was a hate-filled place, marked by suffering.

'Well, it *is* a graveyard,' Dora had said, barely suppressing the vague, ironic smile that she knew incited Luiza's accusations of condescension.

'No, not just illness and death. *Murder*—' Then, once again, Luiza told the story of Colonel Asa Thompson Oliver as though she alone had safeguarded it these hundred years: how his wife died after the journey over from America, his two daughters soon after from tuberculosis, and then Oliver himself, bludgeoned with a shovel by a slave he caught stealing potatoes. In revenge, three *Confederados* loyal to Thompson lynched the slave and left him hanging from a tree on the property for days. A warning.

'And they're all buried there, in that horrible place where you make us take flowers. Except the slave, I'm sure.'

'A place can't be everything it ever was forever and ever,' Dora argued as she always did. 'It's a symbol. It can mean something else to us than it did to them. It's just a place to remind us where we came from.'

'But what if I don't want to remember?'

And yet here in a foot-deep hole, among the graves of the Confederate settlers and their descendants, Dora places a wooden box with some of Luiza's things, some cheap trinkets because her sisters should be given the better things: a pair of broken earrings, some photos. The snapshots of Luiza are all small, blurry: as a girl, next to Mother's birdcages, awkward in a white sunbonnet. Luiza hanging upside down by her knees from a swing in their old backyard on Colonial Drive. As an infant, pliant and pale and alien. (Dora had been happiest then, when Luiza nursed all day, it seemed, sending currents of heat through Dora's breasts.) On her sixteenth birthday, her nose buried in the journal written by her grandmother, frowning even though Dora warned her the crease between her eyes would become permanent, like her own. Now they begin to sing. Dora forgot she had asked for some hymns, knowing they'll be mostly Baptist, but she also requested one from her Catholic school days. She told the minister it was Luiza's favourite, though really it's hers.

*Star of the sea, pray for the wanderer. Pray for me.* As Dora had tried to snap the photo—'Look up, darling, look up!'—Luiza asked, unsmiling, 'What do you think it does to a person, to be owned by someone?' 'I'm sure I couldn't presume to know. Look up, my love. You're so much prettier when you smile!' 'Then what does it do to the person who owns them?' 'Oh, do stop scowling!' *Oh, gentle chaste and spotless maid. Virgin most pure, star of the sea. Pray for the mourner, pray for me.* Dora has to wrench her gaze away, count the trees, read the tombstones—anything to keep from crying. Luiza would be so angry, her things mixed in among the bodies of soldiers; even the inscriptions on their tombstones are martial and defiant: *Soldier rest! Thy warfare over. Once a rebel, twice a rebel and forever a rebel! Died in perfect peace.*

How had Luiza become so distant from her? While the girl forgave Hugo everything.

The maids had taken over Luiza's care when she was still so young. *Dearest links are rent in twain. But in heaven, no throb of pain.* It occurs to her now that Luiza grew up alongside her, maybe in spite of her. *Meet me there.* They fed and washed her and read to her, but Dora still lifted her sleeping from her cot and brought her into bed with her at night. All those times Hugo was away; Dora hated being alone, though she'd always taken pains to hide it. *Are your garments spotless? Are they white as snow?* If her daughter were still here, she would be almost the same age as Dora was then. Luiza would have begun to understand. *Are you washed in the blood of the lamb?* Understand how hard it was to be so young and alone, with a husband you sometimes couldn't recognize. Maybe. If she were still here. *Pray for the children, pray for me.* An awful sound rises over the hymns, hoarse and deep, like wailing. Her throat strains, her chest vibrates. Why? she wonders. Why does her body ache? Because the sound is coming from her.

Afterwards, there is no reception. Everything was planned so quickly, she tells their friends, and the house is still half packed from the last time they were about to move. But soon, she promises, soon there will be a party.

'We'll do something to kick off Carnival, like we always do, and then a proper goodbye party at the Copacabana too!'

She tries to sound gay, then blushes—false cheer and talk of parties at a funeral. Surely it's improper. She promises to let them know. They kiss her cheeks and clutch her hands, these friends she's known most of her life. Of course, they say. *Tchau, tchauzinho.*

In the car, on the way home, Hugo is mostly silent, the skin over his knuckles tight and translucent against the black leather of the steering wheel. She tries to say something, ask what the matter is, but nothing comes. Ridiculous question. Finally, Hugo says, 'We'll have our own ceremony.'

When they arrive home, the house is empty. She had allowed the maids to go home to their families for the night. Now she wishes they were here to make Evie change her clothes, which were dirty before they even left the house earlier that morning. Dora had literally trembled with rage when she found her playing out in the garden in her best dress before they were meant to leave. She led Evie to her bedroom, her hand a talon fixed on the child's shoulder, and commanded, absurdly: 'You stay in there and think about how you want to treat your things!'

She then went to the bar in the dining room, made herself a Scotch and soda, and drank it down in two swallows. She went back to Evie's room a few minutes later. Her youngest child was red-faced, splotchy about the neck (that tender ginger complexion), and bleary-eyed, but already recovered and undressing an old china doll.

'Come here,' she said, and when Evie came Dora kneeled before her and clutched her waist. She let Evie play with her hair for several seconds before standing and straightening both their dresses. 'You have to change your dress.'

'I like *this* dress.'

'Fine. Rinse your hem in the sink.' Better wet than dirty. Better weak than cruel. Dora was becoming the kind of mother who lets her children go to funerals in dirty clothes.

When Magda comes to her now to say that Evie won't eat her bologna sandwich, Dora sighs and again looks around, waiting uselessly for the maids to appear. And Evie used to be the easiest of the girls, the dreamy and docile one. The Nice One.

'Just take her outside and help your father,' Dora says, suddenly desperate to lie down.

Later, when she goes out into the garden, Hugo is still cutting flowers and placing the long stems across Evie's outstretched arms. Then Magda takes the flowers and places them into a bucket filled with water. They are a grim little assembly line, but they are together, and soon three buckets overflow with all of Luiza's favourites: gladioli, birds of paradise, lilies. Finally, Hugo decides there are enough and binds together four large bouquets with some old fishing line from the garage.

'So many,' Dora says when he hands her an enormous bouquet, careful to inflect the comment so that it's a statement rather than a question, and to sound pleased. In truth, the flowers verge on obscene—everything too tall, too much. This is who he is: excess.

Hugo gives both Evie and Magda a bouquet to carry, hands his own to Dora, then leads the girls by their free hands along the winding dirt road toward the beach. Dora follows closely behind, watching the girls struggle to hold their flowers with just one arm, though neither wants to let go of their father's hand. None of them has been back to this beach, or any other, since Luiza disappeared; Dora and Hugo have not been able, and they forbade the girls from going near the water by themselves. There's no prayer by the water, no poem or elegy, which is unlike him. Hugo always has some scrap of verse he's committed to memory, ready to recite. But today he remains quiet, clutching the bouquet she handed him, and all of a sudden Dora feels his sadness more acutely than her own. She studies him closely, maybe for the first time in months, and sees his face has somehow contracted: deeper lines, new hollows. Now, with an awkward, jerky movement, he flings the flowers into the surf. They land just a foot or so in front of him, then catch in the sand, carried ashore by an abject little wave. If they were in a film, he would gather up the wet stalks, his tie flapping behind him in the breeze, and walk into the waves fully dressed. The sea would swallow up the blooms like it swallowed Luiza, and some dreary circle would be complete. Then he would walk out of the ocean drenched and severe-looking, and lead the girls back home by their hands. But instead he turns away, leaves the flowers mashed in the sand, and crouches. He gathers the girls to him and sobs into Magda's hair until Dora worries he might choke. Evie, always eager for affection, seizes him back, grabbing the fabric of his suit jacket in her pale, dirt-streaked hands. Magda stiffens and leans away at first, but then she too melts into him, and Dora is struck by how seldom she sees the body of her stern, middle daughter—normally taut, hyper-vigilant—relax in this way.

As much as he can sometimes tire people out, his gift is that he can always draw them back in.

'Angel! She will be our angel.' Part of Dora wants to break up this embarrassing infliction on the girls, realizing that Evie has now had both parents prostrate before her in one day. But their small grey faces brighten as he speaks. 'No, no—*angel* is too maudlin, too common. She will be our seraph. And who has that? Who has their very own seraph to watch over and protect and listen to them? Not just some sentimental wisp from a painting but a real girl, a girl we know with a face and voice we'll remember, and who will be loving but mighty also, with six wings instead of two, like the highest order of supernatural beings from . . . '

As if losing energy, he trails off, which is a relief. She knows she should listen closely to his monologues, remain watchful for the signs. But today she's grateful to Hugo for rearranging the moment, giving it order and grace. Giving them all a fragment of God. Maybe in Canada she could love him again like she once did.

And yet she suddenly feels ill. She can't possibly endure for another minute such sweet, ridiculous notions as heaven and angels. She once envied those with unambiguous ideas about the afterlife, who imagine their dead in tender, pastoral settings, still themselves but in shades of only grey and white, unspoiled by loneliness or decay. But it all seems mawkish and insufficient to her now. She drops her flowers to the sand, unzips the back of her dress, scratches imaginary sandflies in her hair.

Hugo removes his shoes and walks into the water, not bothering to roll up the cuffs of his pants. The girls, of course, do the same, and soon they are all standing in knee-deep water, staring out at the sea. The ocean is always there, so vast and so close, and standing at its edge for the first time in almost a year, Dora's heart hammers her ribs. He could so easily continue out into the sea, toward Luiza. Walk underwater until his clothes were too heavy and his body too tired and his lungs too full. If he believes in an afterlife, an actual place where he could find Luiza, what's to stop him from wanting to join her there?

Sometimes she tries to imagine Hugo and Luiza together in some airborne place, drained of vibrancy, like clothes left too long in the sun. But she sees them mostly as heat, an exchange of thrumming atoms, confusion, vibration. Maybe their consciousness would dissolve altogether and become taut cords of fear. Or maybe they will end up somewhere together but not know it, and still feel lonely and afraid. And when she dies, will Dora be the connecting thread, or will she, too, be scattered, confused, disembodied and without thoughts, just remnants of these worst days?

The sun is setting behind them now, and though the air remains hot, they all seem to shiver on the dull sand. Dora picks up her bouquet from the sand and carries it to the water's edge. She tries to say *goodbye*, but it feels false and lodges in her throat, so she takes a few steps into the sea and lays her bouquet on the surface of the shallow water. Then she walks back to her family—diminished, tractable—and turns them toward home.

# EVIE

On her way to the garden, Evie passes her mother lighting a cigarette as she reads on the veranda. Mama's hair is curled and pinned up on top of her head, and she's wearing a smart, straight skirt and a blouse that ties in the front. Even though she often complains about how she's getting old (almost forty-five), people still speak about how beautiful she is, which makes Evie proud. Mama is so pretty, so elegant, thinks Evie, whereas there is a stain on her shirt from when she drank her pink lemonade too quickly, the juice flowing in thin rivers down her cheeks. The stain is edged in red and touches some dried jam; that's from looking out the window when she ought to have been paying attention to her breakfast, but as she bit into her toast a thrush clattered through the branches and landed, and its head turned this way and that and its breast heaved, and Evie wondered, Had it just come from America where their cousins live? So eating was forgotten and the jelly slid from toast to shirt, from shirt to table.

'Soak it right away,' Maricota had said, going into the laundry room. 'So the stain doesn't set.'

Three times she called this to Evie and three times Evie called back, 'I'm just about to!'

But there was a honeybee trapped on the windowsill, its wings glinting in the sun, and she wanted so badly to set it free but couldn't think how without getting close enough for it to sting her, until she remembered how Papa does it with a glass and something to slide underneath (though Mama just swats them with a rolled-up newspaper). By the time she finished running all over the kitchen to find a glass, Maricota had come back in the room and started crying. She said it was because the stain had set, but she stared and stared at the glass in Evie's hand. Evie couldn't understand why she'd cry over a dusty old glass with a flower design until she realized it was Luiza's glass. A fist gripped inside her stomach and she peeled off her shirt as fast as she could right there in front of Maricota, but she was right. It was too late.

Now, Evie walks along the borders of the brick wall that surrounds their property—*over an acre!* her mother used to say proudly. Evie doesn't know how large that is, but she understands it's more than anyone else on their street has. Ivy brushes the back of her neck, and she wonders once again if she's safe in here. Luiza used to promise that anyone who tried to get over that wall—with all that broken glass and barbed wire—would be torn to ribbons, and Evie always imagined an intruder's head atop lengths of bloody string and hanging red rags. But then, wouldn't it be the same for someone trying to get out?

She leans back and feels the points of her shoulder blades touch the concrete wall first, before any other part of her body, which according to Magda means Evie has bad posture. When Luiza comes back, she thinks, everything will go back to normal. But it will have to be very soon. Just the other day, after the ceremony, Mama came into the bedroom where Evie and Magda were listening to music and told them, without even sitting down, that it was time to start getting their things together again: now that they had 'said goodbye,' they would be leaving for Canada in a month. She didn't hold their hands or kiss their cheeks afterwards like she had when she told them they would be holding a funeral for Luiza. She just turned and left. Evie and Magda looked at each other but said nothing; though they couldn't put it into words, they shared the sense that more things were slipping away. They were all being ripped up by the roots and set adrift, like the armfuls of flowers they had dropped in the sea the day before.

But she wants to be done with worrying and crying for today, done with feeling sad, so she sprints across the lawn, past the garden to the edge of the clearing at the back of their property, untucking her shirt from her waistband with one hand and loosening her left plait with the other as she runs. The awkward movements cause her to stumble, but she doesn't care. Grass-stained, unfastened—this is how she wants to be. Her hair is often messy these days because she almost always pulls out her plaits. Now that Luiza's gone, Mama lets Magda braid her hair: French and tight. She's very good at it and has fast, strong fingers that pull the plaits into two very neat, even rows. But at twelve, Evie thinks she's too old for plaits and she knows Magda hates braiding hair—she hates many of the things she's good at but does them anyway, and sometimes she hates Evie for not doing any of the things she dislikes. For not caring.

She liked it better when Luiza used to braid her hair. Evie would sit out on the stones of their patio, Luiza in a chair behind her, brushing out Evie's fine, red hair. But Evie's favourite time with her sister was during the early winter mornings at their country house, when it was still cold and she would run to Luiza's room upon waking and climb into bed with her, and they would lie, interlaced, keeping each other warm. One morning, Luiza had come to Evie's bedside first and whispered to her to come see, then led her by the hand back to her room.

'Look!' she whispered, pointing to the open window, where white fog spilled through. 'A cloud is coming in the window!'

'Close it, close it!' Evie cried, and Luiza slid the window closed again before they hurried back into bed, their feet reaching uselessly for the limp, tepid water bottle from the night before.

'Tell me a story,' Evie begged Luiza then, as she so often did when they were alone together.

'Okay, but it has to be from a book,' she said, yawning. 'I'm too tired to make something up.'

Once upon a time there was a miller's daughter who was smart and brave and beautiful and loved books more than anything. One day the devil came and promised her father riches for whatever stood behind his mill. The man thought he was losing nothing more than a crooked, old apple tree. But on that day, the girl sat reading beneath it, and so her father had signed her away. When the devil came to collect her, she was so free of sin the devil couldn't touch her. He swore then he'd take the miller instead, unless he chopped off his daughter's hands, which he agreed to do.

'But then she cried so hard, her stumps were washed clean and the devil was thwarted once again.'

There was more to the story than Evie can remember now, so she had thought it had a happy ending. But Luiza shook her head, and stared out the window for a moment before finishing.

'She can't touch anything now. She can try, and people will feel something, but they won't really have been touched by *her*. She'll always be separate from them.'

Evie hadn't liked the story, and still doesn't understand it, but she wishes she could hear it one more time. This time she would understand. But there are no more stories or soft hair brushes. Just jam on an old shirt and Magda's rage seeping into her braids, which she's sure she feels leaking into her skull, so she must keep pulling out her plaits, mussing the strands all around her face, and take off again. A disgrace on the run.

Suddenly, Magda is coming across the clearing toward her; she is on the hunt, her own blond rage-plaits flying behind her. Evie keeps running.

'What are you *doing*?' Magda keeps shouting. 'Stop running around! We have to look tidy to go into the city. Mother says she'll take us shopping as a treat.'

Evie knows that when her sister catches her, she'll pound her for running away, but she can't stop. She wants to run from Magda (angry), from Maricota (heartbroken), from her parents (shattered), from what happened before Luiza disappeared. She runs until the feeling of running inside her is faster than her legs can manage. Once she has built up enough momentum, she leaps, launching herself as hard and as high into the air as she can. When her body hits the ground, she lies still with her limbs splayed, all breath forced out, dazed yet pretending to be dead, moving only to turn onto her back and stare up at the sun.

Every few days for months now, whenever the pressure of everyone's sadness builds up, becomes too much, she does some version of this. She walks calmly by her parents, smiling, until she reaches the edge of the orange grove and climbs up a tree trunk into its canopy. Then she jumps and tries to fly, arms flapping, legs a pinwheel of freckled white until she crumples in a heap on the ground, smelling dirt and azaleas. Luiza gone, Papa still sick, the family getting ready to leave Brazil—when her body can't hold it all in and begins to itch and hum, only moving helps her feel something else. Running, that half-second of flying when she throws herself through a shred of sky (where Luiza might be) to the earth (where Luiza might be), and the shock of something cool when her face hits the ground. Sometimes she wonders what her parents would do if they knew, but they never notice anything. Not even when she scrapes her knees and palms, or bruises her elbow as she lands on twisted tree roots.

Evie thinks she knows now why Luiza filled her head with fairy stories, fables, tales about handless maidens. She and Magda sometimes thought Luiza meant to frighten them, keep them tethered to home and inside the walls, just like the maids do. But at last Evie understands: their sister was giving them secret knowledge of where she is. She lives beneath the surface of the water now, black pearls in her hair. She is a ghost, a point of light that hovers always in the corner of their eyes. But Evie doesn't tell anyone this. She doesn't tell any of Luiza's secrets. Like how the day before she disappeared, Luiza had been so angry in the garden, standing under the cassia tree, and Evie couldn't bear to ever see her like that, like a changeling or an ugly witch in one of her stories—Luiza's mouth bent and angry, her lips pinched, eating themselves. But she's not a witch; she's a spirit, and Evie will find a way to tend to her. She won't think about the cassia tree, the way her entire body vibrated afterwards, even her teeth. Inside her ears. Instead she runs quickly in and out of rooms, opens her eyes underwater, peers up at cloudy skies. She whirls around suddenly every time she detects a tremor of light, a ripple among the ferns, a beetle skittering across a rock, and she whispers, 'Luiza?' Her sister told her those stories so she would know how to examine the world more closely. Like this little thing here, lifeless and raw; a baby bird beneath Evie's favourite pine tree.

When Magda finally catches up to her, Evie is crying, hunched over the bird in her cupped hands. 'It must have fallen out of its nest.'

It's bald and alien-looking, like the birds Maricota prepares before they go in the oven, but with a head much too big for its body, and folds of translucent, pimpled skin. As soon as she's close enough, Magda reaches out and knocks the bird out of her hand.

'What are you doing?' Evie drops to the ground to pick the bird back up.

'It's disgusting! It could have a disease.'

'It died of a broken neck.'

'Well, you shouldn't touch it.'

'I'm going to bury it.'

And so they have to go through the entire ritual, just as Luiza showed them whenever they inevitably found the wretchedly appealing corpses of tiny animals: mice killed by the neighbourhood cats, birds that smashed against windows, their eyes two tiny, sorrowful black lines. All those froglets they accidentally crushed in Florida. An empty matchbox from the maids, a handkerchief to make the box more comfortable, a few amandine flowers from the garden. A cross of two sticks bound together with long grasses. Evie recites the ode of St. Francis, who loved all God's beasts—the same one Luiza always used to recite. 'All praise to you, Oh Lord, for all these brother and sister creatures.' She says it under her breath, as though they're cursing, because she's scared Mama and Papa would be angry if they overheard, even though they're nowhere around.

Before they fill in the hole with dirt, Evie says, 'I want to give him these.' She unclips the double gold hearts from her velvet Mary Janes. Magda fastens them to the outside of the matchbox. They're lovely, gleaming against the dull, grey box.

'You could give him your amethyst ring too,' Magda says.

'I just got it.'

'He *is* going to be all alone in the ground.'

'But I gave him my hearts.'

It's coming again, the buzzing tension, as though somewhere inside her is about to rip open. But it would be rude to run away from the bird's funeral. Tears slide down her cheeks and suddenly Magda looks tired, scratching the backs of her arms. She tells Evie it's okay—she should keep her ring.

'At least this time,' Magda says, 'we have something to bury. And anyway, we barely knew him.'

# HUGO

'Let's go for a walk,' Hugo whispers to Evie and Magda, sprawled and sullen on the veranda floor, playing a weary game of cards.

Evie is already on her feet, but Magda keeps her cards fanned tightly, hidden even from him. 'Where?' she demands.

'Let's just go for a little tour and see where we end up, shall we?'

He forces brightness, but the truth is there are things he needs to understand, things only the girls can tell him. But Dora would not like it, what he's asking of them. She mustn't find out. She must think he was comforted by the ceremony earlier this week, as she was.

The funeral was, after all, for her. Like all of them, the chorus of do-gooders and well-meaners, she wants to *move on*. The ceremony was beautiful, in the way of many lies, and everyone came, which matters only because it matters to Dora. Some even cried, including Hugo's former colleague Carmichael, though he tried to hide it. But when Dora cried, he forgot everyone else, and was ashamed to realize that it surprised him, her animal pain. He wanted to hold her, but she didn't seem to notice when he moved closer, put his arm around her. And the breach between them widened. Then a show of self-control, the rearranging of garments, more psalms. Delicate breezes. For a few hours afterwards, catharsis: the sense they had been somehow purified. Or perhaps it was just a welcome respite from sensation, a kind of emptiness, because for those few hours he focused on shaking hands and accepting condolences. And on the beach after, with the girls and the flowers, that had been real to him at the time. A fugitive moment in which he believed that he could say goodbye, *move on*. But to where? There can be no other place, no life without Luiza. Whatever peace the ceremony gave him, it did not last.

Now he lays his hands gently on the girls' shoulders as he eases them alongside the house, toward the front gate. 'If you're very good, we'll go for ice cream afterwards. It will be our little secret, won't it?'

Magda rolls her eyes.

They walk past all the houses in their neighbourhood, grand and gated like their own, then head down toward the beach, the girls walking ahead of him. They pass the banana grove and the old cottages that smell of wood smoke and hyacinth, brambles tangled around windows, tapping the panes. One cottage has a wooden nameplate: *Shangri-La*. He stops walking once they arrive at the dusty beach parking lot. He needs time to prepare himself for the girls' memories, to ask them the questions they've already answered countless times. Even though they carry their beach buckets, red towels, a folding chair (he told them to bring whatever they had with them on the day Luiza disappeared), there is nothing of their chubby, child bodies left. How big they've grown, how tall and thin Evie's become, while Magda is athletic. They are suddenly grown-up and strong. But so was their sister, and it hadn't saved her.

At the beach, the water is glassy, the sun a blinding disc above the horizon.

'Well?' says Hugo, affecting a detached curiosity as best he can. 'Where did you sit?'

'Over there, by that stump,' says Magda, pointing about fifty yards away.

They head toward the sheltered part of the beach, just before an outcropping of rough rocks that forms the break-water, where they've sat countless times over the years with friends. This afternoon, their section of the beach is empty, and there's nothing on the shore but some weathered logs, stumps—makeshift seating around a few scorched twigs. But Hugo can almost see their old things scattered about—beach balls, rough blankets, their battered, wicker picnic basket. The remembered remnants of past beach evenings, their skin a mottled lavender in the twilight. He lurches inside. It occurs to him that, as many times as Evie and Magda have had to answer these same questions, point out the relevant landmarks, he was never present. He couldn't—Dora, the neighbours who were there that day, the police, even the maids!—they all came back here, looked this way and that, calculated distances, proposed where Luiza might reasonably be expected to swim. Or wash up. But until today, he couldn't bear to come, to picture her last day too clearly.

'Luiza was reading her book,' Evie is saying now, 'so we went over to play by the rocks.'

The girls run ahead to the outcropping, shovels knocking inside their buckets, which is a relief because he doesn't want to arrive at the point of his absence too quickly, when he should have been there, protecting Luiza.

He had always tried to protect her. Like he had when she was little and they stayed at their country house in Petrópolis. Their cottage was primitive at first: a propane camp stove for making tea, wood heat. (*Your Saxon blood!* Dora teased. *It makes you crave cold and privation.*) Winter mornings and evenings were cool there, but it warmed enough to eat outside

in the daytime. There were great hills all around them, rounded
and lushly forested, so unlike the jagged, snow-capped Canadian
mountains he'd seen in his youth, and waterfalls just steps from
the house. And at night, monkeys and owls—both!—calling
from the trees. A place where even the men who worked on the
house used to ask if Luiza was a good baby, how much she ate,
if she slept well at night. There was no country in the world, he
was sure, that loved children better than Brazil. And he thought
gratefully how almost by accident he'd ended up having a family
here, among such peculiar and perfectly sentimental people.

When Luiza was a child, he had led her by the hand, winding around the garden beds until they found night-blooming
angel's trumpets. The flowers were large and white and flared
at the bottom, hanging straight down from their stems like
little pointed hats.

'You must be careful,' he chided gravely. 'Remember that
they have poison.'

'You say that every time, Papa,' Luiza answered, already
wilful. 'You can stop always *saying*.'

'*You* stop saying, you little tyrant!' Laughing, he lifted her
up over his head so she could see the escarpment and the mountains beyond. 'Now, touch the mountains and kiss the sky
goodnight.' And she wriggled about in his arms, performing a
ritual of movement that was always the same, always unseen,
until finally when she fell still and quiet, he would let her drop
down into his arms and carry her to bed.

It wasn't long after that Luiza was twice assaulted by the
insect world in one month. First, she was hit on the head by a
wooden swing at a park and knocked to the ground for several
minutes. The gash on her forehead was easily stitched up, but
soon it swelled, red and angry, its edges white. The doctor
found eggs beneath the skin, a gelatinous mass of gametes laid
in her wound. A week later, she stepped into a shoe hiding a
poisonous spider and was left paralyzed for a month. It was a

sign, he decided, from the animal kingdom that this country, however paradisiacal and lush, was a threat to his family. He dismantled all the wooden swings in all the parks in nearby towns for miles, bought every can of pesticide he could find, sprayed any insect he saw. He filled their shoes with newspaper and turned them upside down. Not even the beautiful, milky blue fireflies Luiza loved were safe. They hovered eerily toward him in the air, still steady in the tropical downpour. He reached for them, each a bright, slow-moving eye in the gloom, easily closing his fist around them. Finally, he pulled up all the angel trumpet flowers by their roots and told Luiza a storm had come in the night. During those early days, he was aware enough to try to hide most of this activity from Dora, and she said again he must be under too much stress. She begged him to get more sleep. But he knew then that even in Petrópolis, their secret haven, Luiza wasn't safe.

'This is where she fell asleep while we buried her,' says Evie now. 'We had to keep doing her feet over and over because she kept moving.'

And suddenly he's vaulted out of paradise and forward in time, and sees Luiza startling awake on the beach that day, rising quickly to her knees and clutching her sisters to her as they protest the destruction of her giant sand-legs. He imagines that as she looked out over the water she was struck all at once by the terrifying and incomprehensible unity of the image. She had told him that this sometimes happened when she was especially tired, that if she saw something quickly, took anything in too abruptly, she became frightened—she was unable to break it down into identifiable parts. He's sure he can see what she saw: three endless bands before her (white, green, blue), massive bloody clots to her left, a large-breasted dead man to her right. Hugo blinks as she must have blinked, his breathing slowing with hers as the images fall into place: sand, water, sky. The girls' red towels, dropped in wet heaps, just as she always told them not to do. And Mr. Dawsey buried up to the neck, fissures in his sand-breasts as he snored. She told him she'd often perceive such distortions, the grotesque in the perfectly banal. She worried it was something malformed in her brain. He falters, wonders: maybe she'd felt it too, that sudden desolation, and it was too much for her—or too little—the way the world could, in an instant, tilt away from the sun, turn cold. Had it come upon her, that swift thrust toward the unconstellated periphery of experience? The terrifying estrangement from oneself. Was that why she didn't fight? Did she suffer, or was slipping underwater a kind of release? *No*, he thinks. It never got that bad for her. He would have known if she felt such vacant loneliness. She was so lively, so much better than him. She would never have wanted to die.

And yet, though he tells no one, the truth is that he wakes in the night, muscles sore, clenched by nightmares, certain he should have known what was coming, should have watched her more closely—surely someone so lovely must be only loaned to them from some other sphere.

'What else?' he asks too loudly and the girls jump. 'What did you do next?'

'Luiza said she wanted to go for a quick swim alone and rinse the sand off,' says Magda.

'She was supposed to take us in the water when she got back,' adds Evie, her voice trailing off at the end.

'Well, then what?'

'We went over to the rocks to catch fish.'

Hugo strides out toward the rough breakwater, Evie and Magda scrambling a little to keep up. There are three ancient black men fishing and Hugo feels incandescently white, overfriendly and jocular.

'How d'you do?' False, corncobby strains, accompanied by the flourish of a little bow. Why in English? Why an accent that's not his own?

He and the girls slip off their shoes before climbing onto the breakwater, Magda and Evie standing together on a large boulder, their own planet, buckets in hand, while Hugo stands on another rock beside them. The girls gaze at the submerged rocks below, turned green and gold by the sun's water-broken beams. Seaweed crusted with barnacles grows in a circle around each one, rippling with the gentle waves.

'See, I said it's like a monk's hair, only long and slimy,' says Evie. 'But Magda said a movie star's hair. She said her rock was Marilyn Monroe and I had to have Rosemary Clooney.'

'But then I said that game was *stupid*,' spits Magda, 'and I went to catch a fish.' And as though it's nothing, she dips her bucket in the water, sits perfectly still for a moment, then lifts the full bucket smoothly and quickly, something silver flashing inside. 'I like these ones that eat slime off the rocks. They're shiny but not very quick.' She reaches in the bucket and grasps the fish with both hands, lifting it out to show him its skin.

'The quincunx,' he breathes, grateful. Let his mind settle elsewhere for a bit.

'The *what*?' demands Magda.

'The quincunx. A quadrilateral diamond shape found in fish but also in plants: the diamond shape of the sunflower seed, those of pomegranates. And look,' he says, reaching into the water and pulling up plants from the ocean floor. 'It is in the roots of water ferns, in lilies. It is a design of nature, and it's everywhere.' Water drips down his arms, soaking the cuffs of his rolled-up shirt sleeves. 'Like the leafless decidu-ous trees you have never seen. Like the branched veins on the softer side of leaves and human wrists. The branches of rivers and tributaries are like veins also, carrying bodies, like blood, away from hearts. Or like ships, travelling up through the Caribbean, along the Gulf Coast and all the way to the St. Lawrence, to Canada.'

'But what does it *look* like?' asks Magda, his little inquisitor.

Has he been talking to them all this time and taught them nothing? Making connections no one else sees? He takes the slow-moving fish from the bucket and lifts it to their faces.

'The scales! See its scales? That shape is found again and again in nature. Everything is repeated.'

After a few minutes of having the diamond shapes in its silvery skin examined, the creature still thrashes.

'It's suffering!' Evie is nearly hyperventilating, begging for it to be spared. 'Maricota says that if someone suffers too much when they die, their soul can't be at peace.'

As Hugo tries to think of what to say, Magda lifts a rock above her head—the girl has the heart of a python!—but he snatches up the fish and tosses it back into the ocean. It sinks to the bottom and the men beside them look on, faces impassive. Nevermind the quincunx. Today's lesson: life's not fair.

*Are you there are you there are you there?*

'Papa, we're right here,' says Evie quietly, taking his hand.

He hadn't meant to say it out loud. But it occurs to him that soon they'll leave this place—Confederação, Rio, Brazil. And when they leave, they'll be leaving Luiza behind—and the pain of the realization is sharp and fresh. And if they return to visit, years from now, they still won't be able to swim in this sea, because she'll still be there, drifting on the ocean floor, debrided by urchins, hermit crabs. Taken but not claimed.

She told him once that until she was thirteen or so, it seemed as though life was illuminated—as if even she herself was lit up from the inside. 'But in the years since,' she said, 'everything has been leaching colour and I don't know how to retrieve that feeling, that sense of a world suffused I once had.' She'd lately become preoccupied with writing, and trying to express those sensations in words, but felt unable to.

For him it was the reverse—he wasn't really born until he came here to work for BrazCan, in his late twenties. He'd never known what it was to feel free until he found Rio. Free to feed his assorted 'appetites' away from Toronto's scolding, puritanical gaze; he liked to eat and fuck and dance and embrace, and sometimes he cried, overwhelmed by both the beauty and horror of existence. Such earnest statements didn't go over well at home but were considered downright charming here. Grey faces, grey minds, grey city—all left behind for Brazil's bacchanalia. Rio was a demented Eden, crackling with newness and feeling. It was Avenida Atlantica, passengers hanging out of trolleys on one side and pale sand merging with the sea on the other. Undulating waves of black-and-white mosaic tiles underfoot, carrying him toward Cassino da Copacabana, filled to the gills with those sequined showgirls, all happy little things, pretty and so young. Everything was *yayaya*: baccarat, champagne, the foxtrot. The first time he took Dora, they saw Errol Flynn at the craps table, and a month later, Lana Turner; he stood shoulder to shoulder with her as she dragged a heap of poker chips toward her, and drank in the scent of her hair. In Rio, everyone had appetites—the *Cariocas*, the celebrities, the showgirls. In Rio, he didn't stand out. Here, he was home. Here, he cheered watching games of *futebol*, and was embraced by the stranger beside him in the stands while the players wept and kissed one another each time they scored. Here, he'd seen a black man on the pavement, holding a rose and openly shedding tears after Vargas committed suicide; he'd seen grown men in suits climb telephone poles, crying and laughing as they waited for the Brazilian Expeditionary Force to return from the war after fighting the Italians. He danced with the *travesti* Juju, a fine-boned man who, in drag, made a strangely beautiful woman. Here, *below the equator,* as the Brazilians say, *there is no sin.*

But now he's eaten too much, felt too much, desired too much. Soon he'll be cast out, on a ship back to winter, graceless and deracinated. *Tchau*, Brazil. Surely, having driven her away, they, too, must go.

'This is boring now,' says Magda, and he sees that he is no longer touching them; he is standing apart, a few feet away on a separate rock, a bucket dangling from his hand. Magda has her arm protectively around Evie, whose eyes are red. They're smaller somehow. 'We want to go home.'

'Of course, of course.' Hugo busies himself gathering up the girls' shoes. 'Anyway, I suppose it's cooling off.' *Lit up from the inside*, that was just how she'd put it. How could someone that alive die? Back and forth, to and fro. He wishes he could stay with Evie and Magda for longer, but she's always there, pulling him away. And yet some part of him believes that in slipping further from everyone else, he's getting closer to her.

Back at their house, the girls ask if they can watch TV.

'Go ahead—as much as you like,' says Hugo. 'I'll ask the maids to fix your supper.'

But instead he wanders into his office, still feeling that some undiscovered detail is waiting to be found. He's learned nothing new today. What had he expected? Some clue or trace still on the beach after all this time? He must stop looking, stop waiting for messages or meaning to come to *him*. What if he were to write down everything he remembers, every conversation they had, every perfect thing she ever said? Surely something would reveal itself? The piece still missing, some aspect of Luiza he has failed to understand. These past months, he's been confined by grief—gelded and ineffectual. A perforated half-man. But now he must know—why did she leave him? He thinks of her, always of her. He must speak to her now while he can still conjure her, write to her now while he can. Yes, he will write her back into being.

He begins to rifle through his desk drawers, finding nothing. His notepads, pens—all taken. What was Dora thinking, letting the maids touch his things so long before they are meant to sail? Did she think he would sit and stare at the wall until she was ready to go?

And she insists on locking her desk, which shares his study, even though she almost never uses it. While normally he can find the key easily enough, today he's forced to hunt around, find a letter opener, molest the lock. Toward the back of the drawer lies a single folded page, hastily shoved in. He's broken into her desk countless times and is sure he's never seen it before. The paper is yellowing, the crease lines deep and permanent. Not new. It's something she must have extracted recently from some more hidden, more secret place. A letter. A *love* letter, he realizes quickly: How beautiful she is, how she's the only woman the writer has ever loved. How she deserves better. It is undated, unsigned—just a series of tiny Xs in the space where a name might go. He wrote her letters once, but never rubbish like this. He wonders briefly if perhaps she wrote it to herself, the trivial romantic diversion of a neglected housewife. But Dora is not the type, and the type is not Dora's; the top of the O always fills in on her old Corona typewriter, and these Os are perfect, clean circles, tiny holes for his heart to slip through. How could this person pretend to love his wife and take so little responsibility, providing neither date nor name, no place for him to direct his rising anger? Has it been kept in here for months, or years? Is it from a lover or just the infatuated teenaged son of a neighbour, for there have been several of those—she is still the most beautiful woman he knows. Perhaps it was a trifle, an oath from a lost soul, and being merely flattered, she kept it to remind herself that she was desired.

He buckles a little now and leans against the desk. *Why?* But another, bitter voice volleys back: *You know why.* A thousand times, a thousand different ways, he has absolved himself. For years, he hasn't wanted her to see him, *really* see him, so he slinked out of Dora's view, ashamed of what she had seen, his mind turned inside out. Instead, he wrapped himself in Luiza's uncomplicated admiration—her child's love, for a time unconditional. But he would not survive losing another beloved.

Doesn't she know? He was always planning to repair things, to show her how much he still loves her. He just needed to get better. He was always going to come back for her.

# DORA

The sand beneath Dora's feet is hot, covered by a thin crust where it dried after the tide went out. For reasons that she can't articulate, even to herself, she has been coming to the beach nearest their house every morning for the past five days since the ceremony—her first visits since Luiza disappeared. The beach is still quiet in the mornings, not like the beaches in the city, and only a handful of bathers are spread out on the wide stretch of white sand. Farther along sit a few tumbledown houses built into the promontory at the south end of the beach, part of the fishing village on the other side of the headland, and several dozen boats are setting out in the distance toward the horizon, where the sun has just risen, orange and dilated.

Dora told the maids that she needed a break from all the packing, the preparations, but there is something more drawing her here. Now up to her knees in the water, she hears a cry and turns sharply toward the sound. At the end of the beach, *her* end, a flock of birds wheels above a little wooded peninsula that juts out into the water and she smiles briefly to see them soar and dive. That point is at least a mile away and yet the birds seem closer, and she has to blink several times to understand why: they are very large and black, *urubus*—carrion birds.

It's their size that makes them appear closer. Their expansive soar contracts into a tight, agitated circle as their enormous wings beat the air before they drop down, vanishing into the woods. They have found something. Dora lets out a sharp gasp as she dives into the too-shallow water, scraping the fronts of her thighs and tasting salt. Worried someone might have seen, she tries to recover, and rather than stand up she propels herself deeper, pulling with her arms and pushing off with her feet until she is swimming. *No*, she tells herself. *No, it isn't possible.* After so many months. All the searches. The *urubus* have simply found some animal and she won't go look. She forces herself to swim instead, to keep moving.

She swims for as long as she can, heading in the direction everyone says Luiza went, though all they said was 'that way.' Really, she's just swimming out into open water. Why wasn't anyone watching? That is all she's ever done at the beach—watch her three girls, calculate the distance of each from the shore. Of course, Luiza was much older, so she got to swim out farther, but still Dora watched. And counted. One, two, three. She watched the sun glint off their hair and that's how she could always tell who was who. One auburn, one blond, one red. None of them close to Dora's own dark brown. Three little aliens. After each was born, Hugo would hold them up and laugh, asking, 'Where did you *come* from?' So why wasn't anyone watching, counting, assessing the colour of bright hair beneath sun? Because Dora wasn't there.

She swims until her sides hurt, until she begins to understand how one might just accidentally swim so far that it would be impossible to turn back. To get back. She feels the water pulling her down, like it must have pulled at her daughter. She feels her arms and legs, her tongue becoming liquid. She knows that if she doesn't turn back now, she'll soon be nothing but water. Maybe it *was* just a terrible accident. She couldn't go on. Just gave up. But then why not call out? Why not wave and cry for help, tread water until one of those strong men came, more than happy to oblige, to grasp her nearly naked body and carry her to shore? Too far, maybe. Or nobody heard, nobody saw. Nobody watching. And if the tide didn't carry her away? If she's still down there, beneath the very spot where Dora is swimming? She imagines a hand reaching up through seaweed, wrapping around her ankle, dragging her beneath the surface. She sputters and chokes and just barely makes it back to shore.

She collapses on the sand, gasping, not bothering to retrieve her towel from higher up on the beach, not caring anymore how foolish she might look, her legs stretched out in the water, her torso on land. Once she's able to breathe normally again, she feels her legs bend and contract beneath her, her body rising, propelled toward the peninsula. *Go home. Go home.* An incantation, as though she might invoke a lighted path to elsewhere, summon those great black birds to lift her away from whatever they're consuming. *Don't let me see.* But still she walks and soon stands at the edge of some scrubby bushes. The birds are surprisingly quiet, but she can see their heads bob and dip as they rip away at the flesh of the body they've found. Coarse twigs scrape her bare legs as she moves closer, and she can feel the heat and strength of their bodies, so large that they don't scatter like she expects, don't seem frightened by her at all. What if she can't see what they're tearing apart? What if she can? She stumbles and lets out a little cry and there is the low rustle of wing revolutions in sand, a stuttered whirring, and, finally, a lifting off, black feathered bodies ejected from the bushes, massive wings outspread against the sky. *Look down.* A few more steps. *Look.* Just beyond her lies the skeleton of a dog still sheathed in sinew, meat torn inside out. It could never have been her.


Dora walks back along the beach to where her clothes lie in a heap on the sand. She gathers them up and stands still for a moment, unsure of where to go. She knows she should go home, but home is chaos. All the things she should be doing—packing up the house, sorting through Luiza's bedroom, preparing for their annual cocktail party in a few days to kick off Carnival. It seems absurd to have a party so soon, but she promised her friends and it might mean something to the girls, to get to see all their old friends one last time.

But for now, she can't quite face going back to the house. Drained, she nearly lets her knees give out beneath her and lands heavily on the sand, then rakes it with her hands. This, too, she has lost: the seaside as a simple, perfect place, once the centre of their lives. Where she and Hugo fell in love, where they practically raised their children. She closes her eyes, tries to remember that night, the very first, when she and Hugo sat together running their hands through the sand just like this, more than twenty years ago. When they burned brightly, solar flares, leaving impressions more vivid and alive to her than who they have become. They went to a masked ball at the Copacabana. The men wore simple black masks while the women's were more elaborate—feathers and ribbon, sequins and velvet. Dora's had been peculiar, not pretty like the others: a velvet rabbit with sloping ears, elongated, slanted holes for her eyes, and sequin-trimmed gashes that stretched at an angle far beyond the line of her brow, mirroring the shape of the inelegant, padded ears. The mask was too large; where the other women's masks covered only their eyes, Dora's hid her nose and mouth as well, and when Hugo pushed it up to kiss her for the first time—a very quick, almost casual kiss after they danced, gliding together—her eyelashes bent against the velvet pile. Afterwards, she pulled the mask back down to hide her warm cheeks, her buzzing mouth.

As they left the dance floor, the band took a break and Hugo sat beside the piano player, a little round black man in a tuxedo who was preparing to play.

'What do they call you, my friend? *Seu nome?*' When he

spoke Portuguese, his accent sounded soft, not harsh like those of other expats she'd known.

'*Bola de Nieve.*'

'Snowball! Excellent. What are we singing?'

'*Yo soy negro social, soy intelectual y chic . . .*'

'*Yo soy negro social! Soy intelectual y chic!*' Hugo sang along beside him as everyone clapped and laughed, until Dora, also laughing, finally coaxed him back to their table, not realizing that would be the first of countless times she would have to pull him away, try to lead him back to somewhere familiar to her.

'What was I saying?' he asked her, not waiting for a reply. 'I think I speak Portuguese quite well already. Didn't I say I was black and intellectual and chic?'

'And a high-society negro!' she answered. 'But that was Spanish. He's from somewhere else. Cuba, probably.'

'Still, I'm doing brilliantly, don't you think? Let's celebrate my first show!'

Hugo ushered Dora over to the glass bar where he ordered a bottle of champagne, paid for two glasses, which the bartender said wasn't really allowed, and pocketed a handful of articulated straws. He carried the bottle and glasses in one of his large hands and took one of Dora's with the other. As they walked out onto the Copacabana's front stone patio, they faced the beach, the smooth-capped hills that lined the periphery of the horizon.

'Look at that, would you?' he said, as though she were seeing it for the first time. 'Right there, right in front of us. From the world's best nightclub to its best beach . . . minutes away. Like some outrageously perfect playground.'

They waited for a break in traffic and ran out across the road to its unmarked centre, cars whizzing past. Then across the black-and-white mosaic sidewalk, patterned in waves, and onto the white sand. Hugo poured champagne into each glass, which they sipped until Dora became too tired to sit up and stretched out alongside him, using the jacket he'd rolled up for her as a pillow. He placed a straw in her champagne glass and bent it to a right angle, tipping it toward her occasionally while pressing on the straw, every tiny movement allowing a few drops to fall into her mouth.

'What a place this is,' he kept saying, emanating a kind of quiet, thrumming joy. 'Like a collective dream we're all having. A tribal enchantment. A shared wish of a place.'

'Except that it's real,' said Dora almost inaudibly. She didn't always understand the things he said, but still she loved listening to him speak.

'For now,' he said matter-of-factly. 'For the lucky few. But dreams like this don't last.'

She pushed herself up onto her elbow. 'What do you mean?'

'You must have had a wonderful childhood,' Hugo said then, gazing back out over the water. 'I can just see you, a little golden creature scampering all over the beaches.'

'Yes, I suppose I did.' Dora rolled onto her belly so she, too, could face the sea. 'My grandparents had a beautiful old colonial house on a beach in Niterói, but we came down here as well. The mansions all faced the beach just like on the French Riviera, and there were little wooden cabins where you could change. My mother even remembers when women came to the beach in frilled caps and stockings. Garters and stays. But it was still so unspoiled when I was a girl, no buildings along the Avenida. I used to love to slide down those white dunes over there and help the fishermen with their nets and pick pitanga berries.'

'Let's go pick some right now!'

'Oh, those trees are all gone, I'm sure.'

As Dora's eyes began to close, Hugo was gazing out at the ocean, hungrily awaiting sunrise. *Never before*, he'd kept telling people earlier that night. He'd never seen the ocean until he came here. *Imagine it!*

'You probably can't,' he said to her sadly.

Triumphantly, Dora answered, 'I've never seen snow!'

He laughed and seized her arms, crying out, 'Snow is beautiful! At first you'll think it's the loveliest thing you've ever seen but you won't be prepared. You'll expect it to be warm like sand but then you'll touch it and it will be cold and you'll scream and then you'll grieve for this place but then snow will cover everything and it will be like a kind of lovely death and you'll be at peace.' This was how he was, how he spoke, as though he was willing imagined futures into being. Declaring to her, *You will come. You will be with me.*

When the sun began to rise, Hugo shook Dora's shoulder. 'No sleeping!' he exclaimed. 'Look!' It was an almost caustic pink, scattering its reflection across the gently breaking water like, he told her, a diadem of blossoms or the scales of an enormous mythical fish. 'There are no such colours in Canada,' he told her. 'Not of this magnitude. Maybe a flower, but not illuminated like this.'

This was not, he said, an earthly colour. This was the heavens bearing down on them. He was, she can remember thinking then, at once very young and very old. Like an unsettlingly precocious child, full of wonder but also dense with arcana. When, she'd wondered out loud, had he had time to learn so much, to absorb so many different ideas?

'You mean before there were fuchsia gods or chic negroes or exquisite women?' he asked, laughing, stretched out beside her. He turned toward her then and said seriously, 'Before, there was nothing. A grey, nothing kind of life.' But he couldn't lie still for long and soon pushed himself back up on his elbow, speaking in a whisper, not even really to her. 'I didn't know places like this existed.'

Her eyes were closing again, and sensing weakness Hugo scooped her upper body toward him.

'None of that! We'll have none of that. We're not mortal tonight. Where to next? I've heard of a place called Lapa, full of bohemians and ruffians and brothels. The kind of people who never sleep. Let's go there.'

Dora's words were coming out slow and syrupy now. 'We don't . . . Nobody goes there.'

Hugo also spoke more slowly, as though trying to adjust himself to her, filing down his sharper edges. 'Is that the royal we? All of us, or just you and me?'

'People . . . like . . . me.'

'Ah. The golden people.' There was a slight cut to his voice and she wanted to protest—she would not be wanted there either. *Cada macaco no seu galho,* her mother used to say. Every monkey on his own branch. But she had fallen into that liminal stage before sleep, where she could still hear but not speak, and images shuffled and mixed in her mind.

When Dora felt herself waking, her eyes still flickering, she was already moving. Being moved. Carried. She opened her eyes and saw first the sun, which had fully risen now, then Hugo's face, which was bright with sunlight, angled not toward her but at some fixed point in the distance. He was frowning slightly with the effort of carrying her, but not struggling— just concentrating on keeping her above the water.

Before she could manage any words, they were in the sea, which was as warm as the air at that time of year. Once they were chest-deep, Hugo began to sway her from side to side, creating an arc in the water with her body. She could feel the fabric of her dress fan out around her, swirling in the eddying waters.

Her eyes opened fully now, she asked him, 'What are you doing?'

'You fell asleep in the sand. You were covered with it. I thought you might be uncomfortable.' He continued to move her through the water for a few minutes, like a parent teaching a child to float on her back, then turned to carry her toward the shore.

'I can walk from here,' she said, breaking awkwardly out of his grasp, suddenly embarrassed and swallowing some water.

On the shore he helped her out of her wet dress and offered his suit jacket, the cuffs dangling past her hands. He faced the ocean and the curve of his back muscles swelled beneath his wet, white shirt. It repeated in her head like an invocation: *most beautiful*. To this day, however changed, however diminished, he remains the strongest, the most beautiful.

And so now, at the water's edge, Dora knows she still has not stopped loving her husband, cannot give up, as she sometimes wishes she could, because she remembers the jacket and the sunrise and the benediction. Somewhere in the back of her mind, she wonders: if she does everything right, everything she feels she should, might God (whom she doesn't believe in) give her back her old life? The old, normal life when her daughter was still here. The life Luiza always insisted she never wanted. As though Dora had forced it all upon her.

Dora lets a few more waves wash over her legs, then rises from the sand and walks in the direction of the path. The *urubus* have hurled themselves back into a loose congregation above the water, ascending indifferently toward the sun.

# LUIZA

## JANUARY 1961

The family was travelling to Florida by ship when, somewhere around Trinidad, Luiza and her father sat drinking black coffee in the ship's lounge with its panels of galloping Indians and orange polyester drapes. They were discussing all the things they could do during the four months they'd be living there (though she noticed he never mentioned the reason for their trip). She had ordered as he did, even though her tongue flexed against each bitter sip, and she tried her best to listen, a pleasant, encouraging expression fixed on her face, as he delivered the most recent catalogue of research gleaned from his dense, haphazard library. All the ways in which Florida might enchant them, the adventures they could have. There were mangrove forests—trees that grew in water!—and cypress swamps lurking with ghostly, long-throated egrets, their necks impossibly stretched and sharply bent in the middle. She wanted always to be the one person who affirmed him, a safeguard between him and those who couldn't understand his singularity, so she tried to smile as his list continued to tumble out—he was so very fond of reciting lists. There were also swamp oak branches closing over winding estuaries and growing into tunnels of vines, a thousand reaching arms, pocked with flowers.

'We'll weave through them with nothing more than a raft and a pole, alligators be damned. A passageway to the dark heart of America!'

His speaking like this, as if they were lost in a fairy tale—Hansel and Gretel together beset—had always comforted her father, and her as well. But lately she felt the stories, with their dark forests close and damp around her, inviting her, impossibly, back to childhood. And even he did not seem entirely convinced by his little speeches, smiling painfully as he proclaimed the Everglades, which she knew was nothing more than a poor man's slimy tropics.

'I have to go,' she said, abruptly getting up from the table and knocking over her cup. Her father half stood, reaching toward her with a napkin, his large body crouching awkwardly, causing her to take a step back. 'I have to get some air,' she added.

She left her drink upended, its dark, grainy puddle spilling onto the table, and hurried to the doorway. When she looked back, he was driving his thumb and forefinger apart above his brow ridge, leaving a bloodless trail in his skin, his thoughts unerasable.

As she made her way slowly along the ship's lower deck, Luiza prickled with envy as she watched the other passengers, some cheerily playing games, others reclining in canvas deck chairs, their limbs spilling languidly over the sides. Happy, relaxed bodies enjoying the ship's distractions while her own family twanged with anticipation. The journey to Florida alone would take nearly two weeks and her sisters were already pinging off one another, bickering, then emitting high-pitched squeals, shared jokes. Her mother had told her to think of it as a family vacation: a voyage on the famous S.S. *Brasil,* a visit to America. Yet the few times her sisters tried to enlist Luiza in some dull activity or other—shuffleboard, swimming in the pool, a routine for the talent show—she couldn't seem to focus for more than half an hour at a time before guiltily slinking away, saying she had a headache. The truth was her whole body felt taut, strained. She chewed at her cuticles as the base of her spine buzzed constantly—excitement or fear, she couldn't tell. They were off to find the miracle cure that could retrieve her father from his extreme states, and return him permanently to the flat, tenable space somewhere safely in the middle. But weren't those vagaries also his gift—the source of his pure, undiluted genius? And more importantly, weren't they an appropriate response to life—all the pain and joy and, as he often said, the beauty and horror of existence? And weren't they also so fucking exhausting?

Dora had first told her about the trip to Florida while arranging flowers—poorly—at the dining-room table for a dinner party. She seemed untroubled, almost blithe about the drug study, which made Luiza fight her harder.

'You just want to make him like everyone else,' she said. 'Average.'

'Up, down—we're always being pulled behind him.' Dora wouldn't look at her, and instead took up a small pair of kitchen scissors, snipping robotically at the stems in her hand, cutting them too short. 'Don't you ever wonder what our lives could be like if we didn't have to follow him? If we could lead our *own* lives.'

'I already know. Golf at the club. Dinner at Le Petit. Dancing at the casinos. The exact same life as everyone else we know.'

'If all that bores you so much, find something else,' said Dora, finally meeting her gaze before shoving three stubby gladiolus tops into the vase so that they stood, bruised and too upright, above the rest. 'You could have a completely different kind of life—whatever you want. For myself, I just want something normal! I want to know what's coming from one day to the next.'

'No one knows that.'

Her mother had snorted then and turned her back to Luiza to signal she was tired of her hazy philosophical truisms.

But now, on this ship heading toward the Gulf of Mexico, Luiza *did* wonder what a life of her own might mean. She was nineteen, but instead of thinking about going away to school (her father had always promised to pay) or dating boys (her mother was forever pointing out *nice young men*), she was accompanying her family to Florida as a glorified, unpaid nanny and caretaker.

'And what kind of life could that be if I'll always be stuck babysitting?' Luiza had asked her mother's back. 'Why can't we bring the maids? Why should I have to look after the girls?'

Dora clutched a handful of wilting stems in one hand and wiped the other on Maricota's old apron. 'What else do you have to do?'

As her mother's question came back to her, Luiza was struck by the realization that soon she might be able to—might *have* to—live on her own. Her breath caught in her chest. Would she even know where to go, what to do, how to be, if not in proximity to her father? If she didn't have to be his echo. What would it be like if she wasn't tethered to him, always calculating his distance from earth's flat surfaces, predicting when he might next wheel away or plummet. Then retrieving him, reviving him. Taking crusted dishes, stale underwear, empty pill bottles off his bed, unfolding his clean socks. Hope and dread—could there be a life in between?

*You're not responsible for him.* Even now she could hear her mother's voice. *It's chemical. Stop mythologizing a disease.* Dora always made it sound so simple, as though he was nothing more than the competing chemicals in his brain, which, if acted upon by some magical drug, could restore him to a neutral, unmodulated self. Without moods, without mercury. But to Luiza, the moods *were* him. His mind, his soul—could a drug act on those, take them too? Maybe it would leave him transfigured, a Frankenstein version of himself, patched together and only half alive. Or maybe it would take just the damaged parts, the suspicion and the glassy eyes and the worst, dead days. The part that could cut through them so casually; the part that had, on Dora's birthday a few years before, made a toast at dinner to her glorious cunt. (Dora should have known what was coming given the way everyone kept imploring him: *Slow down, Hugo. You're wearing us out, Hugo.* Now she and her mother have an arrangement, and such entreaties are Luiza's cue to make excuses, get him away before things requiring morning apologies are said.)

Later that infamous night, after their dinner guests had long gone home, she woke to find her father in her room, his eyes ferociously alive.

'I'm going to take you to the mountains and show you snow!' he said. It was three a.m. 'We'll drive for hours.'

But then he backed the car into a cedar tree on the sidewalk, so instead they rifled through the garage until they found their musty old roller-skates and skated down the street in the dark, Luiza shrieking with happiness because her body couldn't contain the feeling, and it spurted out of her in shrill, almost painful sounds that she hadn't known she could make. Then her mother came out, pleading in her see-through nightgown: a neighbour had phoned and said someone was screaming outside their house. But her father just took Luiza by the hand and they skated away. Outside the gates, she wasn't afraid as long as she was with him. That was back when she still loved him unequivocally.

But just a few months later he grabbed her wrist when she reached for one of his cigarettes, thinking he was asleep. 'You cost enough to clothe,' he said, his eyes barely open. Amphibious. Then he took away her mother's chequebook because he said she was giving the maids extra money for food, and Luiza had to steal the cheques back from him. Sometimes it was almost a relief when he sank so low he had to go into the hospital. She missed him, but at least she could breathe again. For a time. As much as she wanted to be absolved of him, she soon regretted it. Because when he'd taken her hand that night in the driveway and they skated away, when he described for her what snow would feel like, and she *felt* it, that was him too. What if the doctors stripped away his moods, then found there was nothing left?

Beyond the railing where Luiza stood leaning, gulls rose above the water, then dove, and for a moment she thought she saw something awful in the water—a grey, waving hand. Just a fish. Of course it was. And yet she shuddered, turning her back to the sea. Next to her, a couple had appeared, beautifully dressed and murmuring to each other, hushed and inward. The sun was setting and Luiza imagined they must be on their way to dinner, then maybe dancing in the ship's ballroom. Some part of her longed to join them, to be satisfied with fine meals and parties and conversations as light as soap bubbles. Shimmering, then popping, then nothing. But her mother's exasperated remark came back to her: she could have a completely different kind of life. Whatever she wanted. The truth was, she couldn't imagine what that might mean.

For years growing up had meant going downtown to Copacabana, attending parties, dancing at the casinos. But already the whole neighbourhood bored her, its contrasts harsher than she'd pictured, a simulacrum of her parents' photos from twenty years before, though those images seemed more real to her. Now, downtown was papered over with billboards, colonized by girls in short shorts, boys in rubber flip-flops. Where had she read that? A poem. 'Ai de Ti, Copacabana': *Be woe to you, Copacabana. Dark fish will swim through your streets and the fetid swell of the tides will cover your face. . . . Woe to you, Copacabana! The people from your hills will descend hollering over you.*

She knew the poem was overblown and humourless, that liking it only confirmed her earnestness. And yet the city felt that way to her sometimes, as though they were all thoughtlessly drinking Coca-Cola and smearing on lip gloss, playing *futebol* while somewhere—invisible for now but not far at all—a wave was swelling. It wasn't to her these angry words were written. She shrank from the new Copacabana, its radiant patina and too-bright sherbet hues.

These days, she preferred to stay home and read most nights to remind herself of the world beyond the eight-foot walls that surrounded her family's property. During the evenings, she often wandered outside and liked to sit against the wall farthest from the house and listen to the tinny sounds of her parents' parties— her mother's ukulele, aggressively jovial three-drink laughter, a glass shattering, family friends dancing. The same people she'd always known. Up close it all scraped, rang atonally in her ears, but from out in the garden it sounded almost joyous. Then, one evening Mr. Carmichael appeared from out of the gloom. He was gripping a book in both hands, pale-knuckled, his stance almost like a boy's. He was a friend of her parents', though not an especially close one—he and his wife occasionally came to their parties, or met up with them at the casinos, though Luiza had never made more than passing small talk with either of them.

She put her book down, suddenly worried. 'Is everything all right? Is my father—?'

'Oh, he's fine. He's quite happy, in fact.'

*Quite* happy. Such euphemistic kindness. And always the sense that others knew more about her, and her family, than they ought. She swallowed, the hairs on the backs of her arms rising into tiny barbs. 'Then is there something you need?'

'I just had to get out of there,' he said, looking beyond her now, smiling vaguely even as his eyes seemed to darken with a forlorn dissatisfaction she found immediately familiar—she'd felt it a thousand times. He stammered for a few minutes about the crowd and the heat, and how he was growing tired of it all—the nights out, the drinking. Was it a kindness? She had the impulse to reach out and touch his brow, smooth its crease, then was grateful he was too far for easy contact.

'I also wanted to give you this,' he said, holding out the shabby, leather-bound book. 'I've read it dozens of times, and I always see you out here with your little lamp, reading. I thought you might appreciate it.'

Grand, ancient myths free of irony. Overwrought, self-important, bloody. Beautiful. All these things Mr. Carmichael had given her when, a few weeks before she walked aboard this ship, she'd taken Ovid's *Metamorphoses* from his hand.

'This time in your life won't last forever,' he told her, barely smiling. 'I know it's hard to imagine now, but you won't always be here, feeling the way you do.'

'And where will I go?' Luiza asked, still trying to hide how startled she was by his attention. Though he seemed as aware as she was how unusual it was for him to be out there, talking to her.

'You seem like a clever girl. Where would you like to go?'

At the time, she couldn't answer, but the question kept coming back to her.

After he returned to the house that evening, she sat in the dark for several minutes longer holding the book he'd placed in her hands, warm from the substantial weight of it, and from the heat of his skin. Silly girl, she thought to herself now. She shouldn't be distracted by a brief conversation with a dis-affected, older man. She should be thinking about what to do with herself, her life.

Girdled by the ship's railings, she climbed now onto the upper deck and scanned the horizon. Maybe she would be a writer—hard, faceted sentences that would arrange her turgid, nagging thoughts into something manageable and serious.

Worthwhile. The way stress or fatigue deranged her senses, convinced her the natural world was encroaching on her selfhood, her psyche. How bright sunlight became a snaking shimmer across her vision, temporarily blinding her; how the dissonance of particular words—*slice, hiss, place*—turned everything red, their reptilian sibilance shooting a current into her neck. Imaginary bodies in the ocean. Couldn't she turn these into something beautiful?

And the persistent impressions—of places she's never been, people she's never met, snatches of conversations she's never had—writing them down was the only way to stop them repeating in her mind. It was how she kept herself company as a child, how she generated for herself the sense that someone else was always there, listening. *She lays out her dress. The light dances in her hair as she smooths the creases of its rustling fabric.* She did it almost unconsciously, without thinking it unusual. To remember that this other, the unseen listener, was imagined made her feel lonely. Nothing else was hers alone. Not faith (ruined), or madness (Hugo's), or beauty (Dora's).

But still, she couldn't quite see it, this other life. Surely it was dangerous to hope that her father might be helped by the treatment he'd receive in Florida. Wrong, even. Hope meant she wished for him to change, to be something other than the exceptional, beautifully alien man who never settled, never accepted a half-life. A man who couldn't hide from the full breadth of human feeling, no matter how agonizing or exalted. Who experienced everything.

But her own longing was a nuisance, turning her body to face south, to look over the open water, and to wonder how far they had travelled since leaving Brazil. A nagging calculation she couldn't fathom: How many miles between her and Mr. Carmichael? And how many hours, days, weeks before that distance would close?

— II —

# DORA

Dora stands outside Luiza's bedroom, her hand hovering over the door handle. It's only noon and somehow the maids have nearly finished all the preparations for tonight's cocktail party, so she feels like she should try to accomplish something before the guests arrive. Will anyone think it's too soon, she worries, just a little over a week after Luiza's ceremony? But she and Hugo have held this party to kick off Carnival every year since they were married, and this will be the last one. Of course, with so many things already packed, the house won't look nearly as lovely as it had for the goodbye party they threw last year, when their house was still a real house with everything in it, and there were flowers everywhere and Luiza was still here.

But the house is tidy, at least. It's good enough. Except for this one room. Dora closes her hand on the knob now, determined. It's up to her to sort through all her daughter's things and decide what to keep. Every little barrette and postcard from a friend, all her books and journals, those pages and pages she used to write. (Unkind thoughts about her mother?) Each thing touched by her, smelling of her. It will take hours, of course—does she really have enough time to make any progress today? But it's too much to ask of the maids, and Hugo would want to keep everything. It has to be her. Without warning, Dora's hand falls to her side, her remaining energy smothered by thoughts of everything she still has to do in preparation for the move.

There were once practical reasons for why they had to leave. Rational reasons. Hugo had condemned the way President Kubitschek spent like a madman. New industry, new roads, new city blocks. New city. But soon, her husband predicted, the money would run out, inflation would rise sharply, the Brazilian currency would become worthless. And now, a new president, Goulart—practically a communist! So officially, they are moving to avoid the impending collapse of the Brazilian economy; they want to be closer to Hugo's family, have the girls get to know their grandparents. Unofficially, they have no choice— they can no longer afford Hugo's treatment if they stay. Florida was a choice. A terrible one in hindsight—but how could they have known? Officially, there are better facilities in Canada, and talk of free health care. Unofficially, everything in this house is coated with the residue of what little their daughter left behind.

She can't put it off any longer. She reaches for the handle again, and the door opens now, though not by her. The unseen hand of a ghost? *Please, yes—come back to me.* No, a real hand. A fat, brown hand. The door creeps open and then Maricota is coming out of Luiza's room slowly and carefully, her eyes trained on her feet, as though the very act of staring down at them can stifle any noise she might make.

'*O que você está fazendo aqui?*'

The maid jumps a little and pats at her pockets without thinking, immediately betraying herself. '*Nada. Não estou fazendo nada, Dona Dora.* I am cleaning because you have to be packed soon.'

'*O que você tem nas mãos?*'

'*Nada.*'

'What were you doing in her room? What do you have?' Dora means to be encouraging, to show that she trusts Maricota to have a good reason for being in her daughter's room, but she cringes at her ugly tone. She extends her open hand as slowly and calmly as she can manage. *Me dá, por favor.*

Maricota places into Dora's palm a rosary, a bracelet, a pair of kid gloves. Sentimental things—cheap things. There are far more valuable items she could have taken.

*'Por que?'*

'To remember. Something to remember her by when you leave. We are all so sad,' answers Maricota without meeting Dora's eye.

'You know I would have been happy to give you these things,' she says to this woman who has been with the family since Luiza was a baby. 'Why are you sneaking around?' Dora feels almost ashamed to ask her these questions, as though it's a betrayal of Maricota's privacy, of her private relationship with Luiza. The daughter who they both know was more the maid's than the mother's.

'My mother has a shrine for her, at home. We put candles and flowers and photographs, and I want to make her spirit peaceful. I need something of hers and I know you don't believe in these things.'

But Dora wishes she did, wishes she could light some candles and arrange a few objects and believe she could be allowed something like peace. She takes Maricota's hands in her own. 'I still would have given them to you. You know that.'

Maricota lowers her head and says nothing, and Dora doesn't have the patience right now to keep scrutinizing so she changes the subject. 'Have you heard back from everyone about the party tonight?'

*'Sim, Dona Dora.'*

'Good. *Obrigada.*' Dora watches Maricota walk away, back bent with deference. Or is it pity? A kind of regretful disappointment in Dora from this so-called servant who wept openly when she learned the family was moving because, she said, she loves them so much it hurts. Or maybe it's really because Maricota has another woman's insufficiencies to atone for.

But enough of remorse, recriminations. Dora shivers as she turns away from Luiza's bedroom, trying to shake off the draining gravity of everything to come—the parties and the goodbyes. *The last* transcribed over everything she imagines. She can't deal with Luiza's bedroom today when there's so much else to do.

She knows she should be getting dressed but instead walks downstairs, where she mixes herself a gin and tonic. As she takes a sip of her drink, she's careful to avoid her reflection in the windows. She dreads looking in the mirror these days, where the once-fine lines have etched themselves deeply around her downturned mouth. The only way to hide them is to smile. Half their things are still missing, just as they have been this past year. Although they were only days away from leaving Brazil last year, she had insisted they keep the house exactly as it had always been right up until the day of the goodbye party, and only afterwards could the packing and dismantling begin. The next day, Luiza took the girls to the beach to get them out of the house while the adults packed and movers came to take the first, non-essential things away. But then Luiza vanished and everything stopped. The house was frozen for weeks in its half-packed state as they searched and held their breath and waited for news. Over the months that followed, some effort was made to put things back as they were; the maids redecorated with what was at hand in nearby boxes. But some things had already been sent ahead to Canada, leaving ghostly spaces throughout the house: the set of lacquered Chinese tables that fit inside one another in descending size like nesting boxes; the brass sculpture of a stern horse that reminded her of Magda; the rosewood sideboard and all the pretty matching teacups and saucers it held. These were all now sitting in a warehouse in Toronto.

She must really get ready for the party, because the guests will be arriving soon. Because it's been almost a year since Luiza disappeared and everyone says life must go on. Because they want things to seem normal for the girls. Because their friends insisted. Because it's what they've always done and they don't know what else to do. No one has told them what to do. Tonight they'll sing songs and try to laugh. Maybe she'll dance with Williamson (the best-looking of the husbands after Hugo), briefly forget the coming move to Canada, and feel not unhappy for a little while. But the moment will be brief and she won't be able to retrieve it. And then still more parties to come: tonight they'll go on to Cassino da Urca, and then on Tuesday, the night before Lent, the ball at the Municipal Theatre. Then, in two weeks, one last night at the Copacabana, the official goodbye. Because they promised. Because she has to.

She takes her drink outside and sits on the veranda, where Hugo is asleep. He hasn't been sleeping well—she heard him up walking the halls these past few nights. She still can't shake the sense that she has exposed herself in some irreparable way in front of Maricota, and she's momentarily glad they are leaving—and leaving the maids behind—so that all her shame, her weaknesses, will be hers alone and unwitnessed by those who are better at love. She hasn't yet bought Evie and Magda new socks for the trip, or mailed the cheque to the school in Canada. She hasn't learned how to cook or clean properly, or sew little dresses for the girls' dolls, which they're getting too big to play with anyway. She'd meant to. The truth is, she'll be lost without the maids. *Our Help*, she once wrote on the back of a picture of them holding Evie and Magda in front of the house. *Worth their weight in gold.*

And as though she conjured them, Dora now hears the girls' shrill, agitated voices bickering away long before she sees them. She watches them clamber up the embankment through the tiny flower-petal holes in the straw hat she has pulled down over her face. They are sunburned and filthy, their small eyes— bent toward her now—are intense and darting like their father's. Eyes incapable of stillness, always expectant and demanding something of someone—usually her. Evie's full of longing; Magda's full of reproach, because she thinks Dora doesn't notice her own daughters coming in an hour later than they were meant to. But she sees them. Sees them taking out the croquet game, knowing full well there was a time when the threat of mallets or balls near the windows would have sent her shouting, when they were expected to inhabit the margins, to play far enough away from the adults that they could be gazed upon from a distance: a happy, tranquil domestic scene. She often hasn't had the patience for all their exuberant clatter, the intrusion of their physicality, their bodily needs. But right now Dora finds their energy reassuring, a sign that they are still intact. And insistently, guilelessly alive.

Evie and Magda begin to wrestle for the only green mallet, which Magda argues should be hers, even though green has always been Evie's colour. Magda is ferocious, unrelenting. With Evie she'll never give in, and yet with some people she's the softest among them. She always gives money to beggars asking for alms because she empathizes with the maids and says she's embarrassed by all that the family has. Once, Magda actually scolded her parents for being spoiled, so Hugo half-heartedly spanked her as punishment. Of course she forgave him but never Dora because the child knew the punishment was at her mother's urging. There have been no spankings lately, no punishments of any sort. And though Dora still sometimes yells, she apologizes immediately afterwards, implicitly begging their forgiveness. Has it taken Luiza's death to make her into the kind of mother her other children could like? Maybe they'll love her better soon, in Canada, unfettered and alone. And there goes

Magda screaming after Evie with a mallet. Hugo doesn't stir. She should really get up and stop them.

Now Evie clutches her mallet with both hands while Magda tries to wrench it away.

Darlings, please don't quarrel over such silly things.

But they don't answer, don't even turn their faces toward her. They continue playing their game. Because they haven't heard? Or because she hasn't said it? These days, she keeps catching herself talking to someone in her mind, pleading for little mercies, and apologizing too. For what's been lost, for what she's failed to save. Gone are their sweet, daily rituals, their family habits and pilgrimages. The girls in their tidy, pressed school uniforms feeding scraps to the birds, the trips to Ipanema to visit her parents and to their little summer house in Petrópolis, outside the city. Trips to church with the maids, where she imagined they found—as she had once—warmth from a peripheral god. All the things that shape a child's life, make them believe that the world is safe and predictable. She catches herself promising to no one in particular—to them she supposes, or her not-God—that they first just have to do this one thing, just get *there*, and then things can go back to how they were before everything changed. But things have been changing for so long, which point on the chronological line of their lives is really *before*? And what was it like?

Yes. There *was* a before. She looks again at Hugo and thinks of that pristine and hopeful time when they glowed and were beautiful—in all the old pictures, they wore nothing but white. Once, they went up into the sky together. She can't quite remember now how they had ended up in the balloon with his colleague, an engineer and sometimes hot air balloon pilot. It was in those early, heady days when it seemed like Hugo could do anything, and convince her to come along. Sometimes that meant they ended up in a scandalous club with cracked plaster in Lapa, sitting on the bent knees of cross-dressers, everyone reeking of *cachaça*, though she'd sworn she'd never go to such a place. But that day it meant holding her hands over her ears as a large stainless steel fan filled the silk of a giant balloon with air. He kept saying how beautiful it would all be: gliding away from the earth with no sense of elevation or even movement, just the shrinking of the world beneath you. This was how he liked to seduce her, impress her, dazzle her: with new worlds. Things she had never seen. It was, at that point, still thrilling. Not yet exhausting.

'Think of it,' he kept saying. 'This is how we have our first accounts of what industrial Victorian cities looked like, what the Civil War battlefields looked like. We take it for granted, but before airplanes, they couldn't have known. These balloons changed the world, helped incite the French Revolution.'

And he told her that balloons were, by their nature, democratic because for the first time there was a spectacle in which no authorities could intercede, that ascension could not be sequestered for the private, privileged few. It belonged to the many. For the first launch, rather than risk human lives, they sent up a duck, a chicken, and a goat from Versailles and more than a hundred thousand people watched. And when that famous citizen balloonist, the physician Pilâtre de Rozier, launched himself into the air only to have his balloon swallowed by blue flames, he shattered on the rocks of Croy.

'Fifteen hundred feet, he fell. A foot separated from a leg. *He swam in his own blood*, I read.' As de Rozier's balloon came down, the gathered crowd reached up, extended their arms, as though by this involuntary movement they could, as one, halt the fall, push him back into the sky. Here Hugo's monologue slowed and he looked at her, rapt by the images he had summoned. 'He died so that we could experience this, so the populace could gather, spontaneous, ennobled, witnessing en masse a republic foretold.'

How beguiling these dense stories were to her then; his excitement and bravado punctuated by moments of fleeting but such earnest empathy. How large and capable and fearless he had once seemed to her. All his knowledge, the warmth of him, of his convulsing mind, radiating outward—his great strength, his muscles contracted and taut beneath her as he lifted her easily, pulled her up onto his lap, onto dance floors. So many expansive ideas, so much knowledge compressing inside him. Everyone was falling in love with him—her parents, her friends, waiters at the casinos, Bola de Nieve, the deviants of Lapa. The wayward and the divine. All eyes turned toward him and he seemed to emit a low blue light that sometimes flared, sometimes even threatened . . . not violence, but turbulence, rapid shifts in emotion. When had she realized that there was something more, something corroding his magnetic charm? Not then. Not when he danced one night with a *mestiço* man in a dress, all thin red limbs and thick, painted lips, then wept on his shoulder at the bar. He later told Dora that it was merely an act of compassion, and that he sometimes cried to disarm those around him so they might trust and feel connected to him.

'Isn't that a lie?' she asked.

'No,' he replied. 'It is a kindness. They feel less alone, less peculiar.'

And she, too, after enough drinks, enjoyed the company of misfits.

But as the balloon filled with air that day more than twenty years ago, she fell silent and thought how loud the fan was and how long it took for the fabric to inflate, and how everything being tipped on its side—the basket, the balloon—gave the impression of haphazardness, and all the many ropes appeared to be tangled as they trembled in the wind, and surely it wasn't safe the way the pilot kept wandering into the balloon, trampling on its altogether too-thin skin that would lift them into the atmosphere. And as Hugo gently pushed her forward, she could not bear to walk in, to further bruise the fabric. So they watched from the threshold, shoes in the damp grass, and he said how it resembled stained glass, the fabric billowing and translucent, the rising sun bleeding in from behind; and she thought how that was true and how beautifully he always put things. Flames propelled into the centre of the balloon through a narrow opening, licking maliciously at nothing. She thought for a moment of the *Hindenburg* on fire. How did the fabric not ignite? Tipped upright, the balloon was a fat upside-down tear shivering around a blue flame. She allowed Hugo to help lift her into the basket, but when she asked how they would come down and he answered that there was an anchor on board, she grimaced. He held each of her arms and brought his face down to hers and said, 'If you really don't want to go, we won't.' She was struck once again by the size and the strength of him, towering over her—Six-foot-four? Six-foot-five? She was too embarrassed to ask. Her father had been a slight man and she had no brothers—she'd never been so close to such a large, strong man, and the force of his body and his words seemed to physically repel the possibility of disaster.

'Let's go,' she said.

It was true what he'd told her—there was no bumping along the ground or feeling of surging suddenly, violently upward. Just a gliding, and the falling away of the earth, the shrinking of relative distance, and the disorienting knowledge that they were leaving the ground without feeling any movement. Gas roared above them, releasing and burning at intervals. His arms around her vibrated, giving off heat, and she thought about how the songs were all wrong: you do not fall. In love, you are aloft. Lifted away.

They have a photograph from that day, after they landed, the two of them standing in front of the basket of the still-inflated balloon. *You look like Fitzgerald and Zelda!* someone had once said upon seeing it, and Dora had been flattered—it mattered to her that people found them beautiful. But maybe it was an augury: they, too, were doomed.

She wonders now if there was something more in that story about de Rozier. Had Hugo tried to warn her? The balloon ride happened before there were any signs, before they even had children. Perhaps he wasn't strong enough for the stress and pressure and worry of being a parent, her sometimes-fourth child. She should have saved him too—lifted him back into the sky. Or maybe it would have happened no matter what, no matter who he was with, no matter where or how he lived. How will she manage him, get him on the boat, if anything happens between now and then? How will she keep them all together, pointing north? *Stop it.* She must think of the girls now, not him. How to help them through this. But he takes up so much space—in a room, in her mind. The sun to all their lesser moons. The girls still look at him as though he's the smartest man who ever lived. She wants to shake them, tell them he steals half of it from books and the other half is made up. But who could say which half? That's what he counts on. And then their little necks would hinge, deadheads on a stem, hearts broken like she broke Luiza's. Her tongue grinds at the back of her teeth, and now who's making that awful noise? Evie protesting, whining shrilly like a little girl.

'I don't care about the rules, I just want to try hitting. The. *Baaaall!*' She streaks across the lawn in front of Dora, grasping a mallet tightly to her chest and heading for the house, while Magda follows, brandishing her own mallet like a tomahawk. Poor Evie. Without Luiza to protect her, Magda is always after her, to torment her, to fix her clothes, to inflict some 'game' on her.

Dora calls out to them, 'I see you!' She really says it this time, out loud but too late; the side door to the house is banging shut behind them.

When they see her approaching, they freeze, startled by her attention. It catches Dora behind her ribs, how they sometimes stare at her, as though she's of some other, unwelcome species who lives only to frown and rebutton the backs of their dresses. But she musters herself and wipes their dust-streaked faces with her skirt. She wants to tell them she loves them, wants to gather them to her and say, I am your mother and I have shattered on the rocks of Croy, but I'll put myself back together, and your father *is* still the strongest, most brilliant man who ever lived and we will deliver you from limbo, we promise, and your sister isn't gone, she is alive inside each of us. Forgive us, we love you. Forgive us, please.

But there are no florid little speeches, no oaths of love. Instead she cries, brightly, and too loudly, 'I had a call from Judeetchy. Lambretta had her calf today!'

The neighbours in Petrópolis who want to buy their country house, their refuge. The place Luiza loved the best, where Dora can't bring herself to return. Where, in those early days after Luiza was born, they were almost innocent. That little house surrounded by owls and waterfalls and people they've known for decades; the neighbours with all their animals, which she never let her children have.

# MAGDA

'**Y**ou know,' their mother says, 'when we move to Canada, you can have a dog. But while we're still here, let's try to have fun!'

This is how their mother reminds Magda and Evie they'll soon be moving to Canada, just after she cried incomprehensibly about a neighbour's new calf. Now she bends down to clean their faces with the hem of her skirt, licking the fabric between each gentle wipe. Magda exchanges a quick glance with Evie, both crinkling their noses at the saliva but not wanting to protest this unusual tenderness.

'And remember,' Mama adds, 'tonight will be your last chance to say goodbye to our friends.' Then she walks away before they can say anything, and Evie wanders off to find the maids.

Magda goes to her room to change, imagining how she and Evie will have to stand at the door like they always do and greet the guests and shake hands. *How d'you do?* This isn't even a real party. She knows the real ones happen at the Copacabana, where children aren't allowed. Luiza used to tell her and Evie the gossip: the biggest musicians who played and who had flirted with whom, and who got terribly drunk and fell down. The parties at the Copacabana were *amusing*, Luiza said, but not really that special because nobody really listened to anything anyone had to say—everyone just talked over one another. And Magda isn't fooled: tonight is really just the same cocktail hour they have every year to mark the start of Carnival. Like their toy house or toy tea set, this is a toy party.

Once she is dressed, she goes into the living room and stretches her legs out on the window seat, feeling weary. So they're moving, for real this time—who cares? She hates it here anyway. She hates the dark upholstery of their furniture, and that crystal duck on the coffee table. She hates this whole house, with its starched linens and bunches of hard, glittering amethyst grapes sitting in a bowl on the coffee table, never eaten. She hates the heavy silver roosters that she used to chase Evie with, terrifying her, and the new white, broadloom carpets that her mother put in to make the house look nicer for buyers but which make Magda sneeze. She hates how the house is always quiet, always still, when really her family is caught in a tempest: the trees in the yard should be plunging, stripped of their leaves, the sinks filled with stinking water, maggots in the wet, rotting carpets. That's how it should be. That's how it feels. In her mind's eye, the garden is filled with uprooted plants, slimy flowers in smashed pots, insects' wings torn off their bodies. But really, the flowers stand upright, turning their bright faces to watch her whenever she walks by. And the sun burns on—never any shade—and grains of pollen drift prettily through its beams. And the birds still sing, and Cat, the then-kitten Luiza brought home last year, still stalks through the tall grass. Only the gardenia plant, forlorn and neglected, seems to have realized what's happened: its leaves film over with a black coating that Magda wipes off daily with a soft cloth.

Mama and Papa live on faraway planets. Their eyes are empty or pitifully sad, depending on the number of cocktails drunk. And Evie, little stray, always wandering, hovering right at the edge of this hole into which the rest of them have already fallen. Evie still sees flowers as they really are. She sees the sun, and it makes her feel warm. Some days Magda wants to push her back from that edge, take her away to somewhere bright and clean, feed her jam sandwiches. Other days she wants to yank the hem of her dress and bring her tumbling down like a rag doll, ribs snapping as she falls. Down here with the rest of them. With Luiza gone, and their parents barely here, Magda needs Evie in ways she can't say. Yet Evie seems changed somehow too. Even if their parents haven't, Magda has noticed the bruises on her knees, her scraped hands—how she's become more distant and reckless than usual, running off into the trees, wanting to be on her own. But Evie is always changing, always trembling like a weak wind or a leaf. She can't cope. She's told Magda that her body feels everything, every movement, so she changes with what-ever changes around her. But Magda keeps herself very still, so she's more like a tree trunk than a leaf. Instead of her body, it's her mind that grabs hold of everything. Evie remembers stories, conversations, people's faces, things they did when they were little, but Magda remembers information, place names, even dates. Important things. She is the Smart One.

Some part of Magda wants to move to Canada—soon, everyone keeps saying it will be soon—a blank, white horizon where everything will be new, where no one will know that Luiza's gone and their family is broken. But she can't picture it, this empty space; a world without Luiza, or the maids. Who will sing to her at night, or tell her stories until she falls asleep? Magda has always liked the old family tales best, especially the ones about adventure and peril, people travelling into dark, unknown places. Her parents tell these stories as habitually as prayers, so that even the maids know them all by heart. But lately Maricota has been telling Magda a story she hasn't heard before. Maricota says Luiza told it to her and she's been saving it until Magda was ready.

'Your people,' she whispered one night last week at Magda's bedside after Evie fell asleep. 'After they left America, they journeyed up the Amazon for days by canoe. The first night they slept in a *fazenda*, stretched on heaps of rice, rags around their heads to keep the grains out of their ears.'

But as they went on, they saw fewer and fewer homes— just the occasional hut thatched with palm leaves built into the steep riverbanks. *More like corncribs than homes.* So much living matter but so few people, and sensed all around them, beyond that dense veil of trees, creatures consuming other creatures. Invisible things being eaten.

Suddenly, a young mother grabbed the boat driver's hand and asked, 'But where are all the people?' even though he couldn't understand her. Then her little girl made a church with her first two fingers, then a steeple, and then she turned her little hands inside out and showed her mother her wriggling inner fingers. The woman hugged her daughter and said what a great adventure it would all be and never again showed her fear.

'The girl grew up to be fierce and smart and always knew which bends in the river were favoured by alligators and which months brought the worst rains.'

When Maricota leaned over to kiss her goodnight, Magda wouldn't let her go. All their lives, the maids have given them everything that mattered: love and church and time. Countless meals in the kitchen with Maricota and Odete while their parents ate alone or with guests in the dining room, living their parallel lives. The warm church pews where Magda and her sisters sat conjoined, pressed between the maids, heads hung and breathing incense; Magda knew all the prayers by rote even if she couldn't understand the words, their constancy making her still inside. All the maids' stories about their huge, devout, warm-hearted families: Maricota's tender mother with eighteen children, one who nearly died as a baby. She swore to God that if he spared her child's life, she'd never cut her hair, so now when she sweeps her dirt floors, her hair is piled impossibly high above her head, a thickly coiled braid. Because of the maids, their consoling tales, these are things Magda has always known.

And now, sitting in the window seat, Magda wants rain more than anything. So much rain. She wants rivers and floods. Black clouds, cracked branches, birds falling from the skies, horses trampling flower beds, Mother's fruit trees stripped bare. She wants the skies ripped open. And she wants fountains of water to shoot out of the ocean floor and spit Luiza up from its insides.

'Come on, darling.' Her mother has suddenly appeared in the living room and is pulling her away from the window. 'That's the doorbell. Our guests are here.'


As the house begins to fill with their friends, Mother does her best to transform. She thanks everyone for coming and kisses them all on both cheeks. The Langleys; the Williamsons and their son home from America for a visit; Colonel Fitzwilliam and his much younger wife, who brings an arrangement of flowers from her garden and wears a fox stole, even though it's summer-hot. The men wear suits, their hair smooth and shiny, and smoke cigars. All the women are in silk. They take their cigarettes from slender silver cases, light them for one another. Everyone perfumed, powdered, and pressed, as Luiza used to say. Some have brought their teenagers, who make the girls nervous now. Magda remembers how they all used to trail after Luiza like she was their queen, laughing and saying how pretty she was; how keen they were, her procession of scruffy disciples. Now none of them says anything, so Magda and Evie busy themselves serving drinks. The women trill as their husbands remark awkwardly on how big the girls are getting before looking away.

When the Cavanaghs arrive, they have a girl with them, a couple of years older than Magda—about fifteen. She is tall and thin with wild, frizzy red hair and pale, freckled skin.

'Magda, Evelyn, this is my niece Brigitta. She's visiting from America for the next few weeks,' says Mrs. Cavanagh, speaking in the sugary way of certain adults. 'Perhaps you three could play together sometimes.'

Brigitta crosses her eyes at the word *play* and Evie giggles as she and Magda curtsy, like they are expected to for all the guests. Brigitta claps her hands together as though it's all terribly exciting, and does a deep, exaggerated curtsy back at them, then reaches out to touch Evie's hair.

'You know, many people believe redheads have special powers. My mother always says that if my great-grandfather crossed a redhead in the road, he would have to go back home and spend the day in bed because he thought they were bad luck. And he was from Ireland, so you can imagine how that went! Anyway, I think we redheads bring good luck.'

Magda scowls, watching this new girl make a pet of Evie. But when she turns to push Evie back toward the bar, her sister is gazing at the odd-looking, pushy girl. Lovesick.

'Come on,' Magda says, shoving her sister as hard as she can this time. 'She's not even that pretty.'

At first Magda finds the party dull. She can't help but compare it to the goodbye party they had last year with Luiza. Everyone they knew was invited and there was live music and their parents' oldest friends gave toasts about how *remarkable* their family was, how beautiful. It was all so much fuller and lovelier and more colourful, even though she eventually got mad at Evie, who had walked around in a daze and refused to have any fun. And while she hadn't wanted to move then either, it was the last time their family was all together, the last time the house was normal—if she had known, she would have tried harder to make Evie join in. Also, there are hardly any flowers this year because Papa cut so many for the ceremony by the beach. Luiza always said a party was nothing without fresh flowers, and last year she had filled the house to overflowing with flowers from their garden.

'Isn't the party grand?' Evie asks now. Easily delighted, Evie loves to watch their parents, loud and cheerful, at parties. But Magda detects the slightly higher register of their voices; notices Mother's uncrinkling eyes whenever she laughs, which is often; sees their neighbours swallowing canapés in a single bite, exactly the way Mother has taught them not to do. She makes up a glass of sweet rum and juice, dividing it into glasses for Evie and her. After several deep gulps she feels better, almost light-hearted.

Mama is fumbling at the record player when someone calls out, 'Play for us, Dora!' and everyone hoots. The men whistle. Magda claps and can feel her cheeks turning red. She sees her mother falter, stuttering, but she craves a night like they used to have, when everyone got louder and louder and the polite conversation was drowned out by laughter and there was dancing and wildness and everyone was a child.

'Yes, Mama, do play!'

Her mother finally relents, hunts up the ukulele, and sings about knowing Suzie and Hard-Hearted Hannah. Magda had forgotten how pretty her mother can be, how much she loves attention, and how it can make her flushed and glinting and whipped up. Now Papa appears in the doorway of the living room, Mama's pearls tight at his throat, her homeliest brassiere fastened over his shirt. Bits of elastic puff from the straps like tiny hairs.

'I'm the Vamp of Savannah!' He loops a scarf around Mr. Langley's thick waist, pulls him closer, play-acting like he often used to. There are stamping feet, wolf whistles. Some of the other men put their hands on their hips and gyrate like cartoon women.

'Dance, my Evie! Smile, my Maggie!' His eyes are wet, black, moving. Still clean-shaven, full of rude jokes and attention—they love him like this. Now they're all dancing, laughing for real, even a few of the teenagers. Voices rise like birds.

Later, Tim Langley comes up to Magda and Evie, placing a hand on each of their shoulders, and says quietly, 'Some of us are going to go smoke outside.'

Magda can see that Evie is nearly hopping with excitement to be included in this way, and touched by an older boy, so she allows Evie to pull her out of the crowd and toward the back door, even though she'd rather stay and watch her parents dance. Once outside, they join half a dozen teenagers running toward the orchard, stopping at the pink cassia tree, heavy with blossoms, its branches so low that they almost touch the ground, because Georges, the gardener, has trained them downward to create a kind of canopy. As a few of the girls start to crawl under the canopy, Evie remains standing, frozen.

Next to her, Tim takes out a pack of matches from the inside pocket of his jacket, then lights a cigarette and holds it out. 'Do the good little girls wanna try?' he says, singsongy and unkind.

Evie's hand shakes as she reaches out, lifts the cigarette to her mouth, and inhales before she's even closed her lips around the filter, humming with a new kind of longing.

'Stop trying to act like a teenager!' Magda cries, knocking the cigarette out of her hand. 'No one here even cares what you do!' She starts yanking her sister by the arm back toward the house, but Evie's feet are rooted, her head rolling back and forth on her neck as though it were nothing stronger than a flower stem.

'Come on!' hisses Magda as the other kids begin to laugh.

'I feel dizzy,' Evie says. She drops to her knees and retches rum and bits of maraschino cherry.

Crouching down beside her, Magda remembers finding Evie by this tree once before, during last year's goodbye party, just sitting in the dirt. Like now, she wouldn't say what was wrong, and at the time, Magda had wiped Evie's face with her sleeve, stood her up, dusted her off, and led her back inside, a shielding arm around her sister's shoulder. Inside, Magda cut a slab of pineapple upside-down cake, but Evie said she felt too dizzy to eat, so Magda went to get some aspirin. On her way to the bathroom, she passed Luiza's bedroom and heard her crying in that ferocious way that sounds almost like choking. Hovering outside her sister's door, she was unsure what to do. Should she go in, or find an adult to help? She felt her heart beating, accelerated by the ugly sounds of adult sorrow but also a flutter of pity. Even as she remembers standing outside Luiza's door, she is pleased with her own generosity—by leaving Luiza alone with her sadness, she had protected her dignity.

Now, from her crouched position, Magda can hear Tim speaking under his breath to one of the older girls, 'Guess she's messed up in the head just like her sister.'

The girl lets out a little laugh, then tries to sound shocked. 'That's just an awful thing to say! Luiza was so pretty.'

'Well, she *was* very pretty,' says Tim, feigning expertise. 'But my mother says she was always a little bit off. She got it from the dad.'

Magda wants desperately to wound him, to rip his flesh in some way; there are rocks everywhere and shoes and sticks, and she can almost feel the sickening pleasure of his skin giving way if she were to drive something sharp into him. But Evie is shuddering now, her teeth chattering so loud that Magda can't hear what the other kids are saying.

'What's all this?' says a loud, breezy voice. Brigitta, the American girl, is suddenly standing before them, her hands on her hips like she's someone's mother. 'Do the big boys around here always pick on little girls? Because where I come from, that would make you a sissy and you'd get your little candy ass kicked!'

Tim's flock of girls gasp and titter, while he reddens but stays silent. *Ass.* Magda repeats it to herself, drawing it out. She can feel the whole shape of her face change. She knows the word but almost never hears it. Only now and then, when Papa is high, he might say something wonderfully crude, something she can then practise saying in her bedroom, alone. *Shit, ass, fuck.* For an instant Magda is grateful for Brigitta, but quickly grows angry again. *She* should have been the one to say it.

She wraps herself protectively around Evie and turns toward Tim. 'You'd better get out of here. I think I see my dad at the window.'

Tim puts his arm around the girl and leads her and the others toward the house. 'Raunchy,' he says, sidestepping Evie's vomit.

And then there is Brigitta, still standing a few feet away, studying the two sisters and smiling slightly, a frankly curious tilt to her jaw. Magda wonders how much of them she sees: herself, powerless, and Evie, all her need uncovered.


At the end of the night, Evie and Magda stand stocking-footed in the driveway, waving after the departing cars like they've done since they were children, watching red taillights snaking away.

'Can't we come with you to the casino?' Evie pleads. 'We never get to go anywhere!'

'Not tonight, darlings,' says Mother, reaching out to touch Evie's cheek unusually slowly.

'That means never,' Evie says as they watch their mother pile into the last car, finding a seat on Mr. Williamson's lap, slapping him lightly as she laughs at one of his terrible jokes.

Magda tries to push her sister toward the house, but Evie wrenches her shoulder out from under her hand and insists on standing in the driveway to watch the cars carry off their parents. First, it was the cigarette, and now, this. Why isn't it enough for her anymore, to stay home with her and Maricota and Odete? Lately she seems to want something more, something other than what they've always done. Magda almost expects Evie to disappear into the woods again, or run out the front gates, a pale blur in the streets.

Later, the maids put the girls to bed, even though they're old enough to go on their own. Maricota pins them into their beds with fiercely tucked sheets, while Odete, her face so round and familiar, recites a Catholic prayer they love because it is forbidden by their parents.

'*Boa noite, meus anjos*,' the women say, kissing each girl on the cheek.

'*Boa noite*.'

Once the maids have left, Magda hears irregular breathing from the bed across the room. There's the sound of kicking, mumbling, shifting, then the heavy swish of fabric hitting the floor. By the feeble hall light bleeding under the door, Magda can just make out the flat of her sister's back, the dented curve of her spine, her twitching arms. Evie already restlessly asleep.

# EVIE

P apa gives Evie handfuls of sweaty money and dances her about the room, singing.

They are downtown for the final night of Carnival, staying in a first-class hotel, and Papa is trying to convince Mama that Evie and Magda are old enough to go to the street festival by themselves, 'as long as you stay close to the hotel and come back before your mother and I leave for the Municipal Theatre tonight, deal?'

'It will be an asylum run by the inmates,' snorts Mama.

'Please, Mama-Mummy, *pleeeease*—' Magda pleads. 'We never get to celebrate with you because you always say we're too young to go to the ball. And this will be our last Carnival.'

Evie is full of admiration: Magda knows just what to say to make their mother feel guilty.

'I don't care one way or the other,' says Mama in her huff-iest voice as she takes out a lipstick from her purse in front of the hallway mirror, not looking at any of them. Lately, Evie has noticed, her mother seems very far away, a bit like Papa just before he gets grey and deflated. No energy to put up a fight.

'They can paint the town red,' Papa says, sidling up beside Mama. 'And we can stay here and get prepared.' Everyone is startled when he reaches out a hand and places it over Mama's—her parents hardly ever touch each other anymore—but then he pulls his hand back quickly, and Mama goes out onto the terrace, her cigarette dripping ash as she walks.

Then, remembering himself, Papa winks at Evie and Magda, saying, 'You're big girls now. Twelve and thirteen. Plenty old enough for a bit of fun. But, Evie,' he does his best to sound serious, 'you must listen to your sister. Stay close by her side, and no quarrels.'

They nod their heads, *Yes, yes.* Evie starts dancing around until Magda mashes her bare toes with a heel to still her.

As they ride the elevator down, they understand they've just gotten away with more than ever before, and it is both thrilling and sad. Evie knows that the real reason they're being allowed to go out alone is because Luiza is gone. Much as she and Magda miss their sister, they're careful never to say her name because it makes their mother go quiet. But just now, they said nothing and still she curdled. Retracted. Drifted out to the terrace, where she pulled leaves off a potted lemon tree and dropped them over the balcony, watching as they fell.

*But put your heartache away,* the song says, *tonight is Carnival!*

They peel out of the hotel, laughing and sweating in stiff polyester.

Outside the sun is low but bright, and the streets are clogged, the crowd moving in a leisurely, steady stream down the wide boulevard, sweeping Evie and Magda along. At the edge of this snaking mass, some people just stand and watch. There are babies and children dressed as cats, princesses, Pierrots—all carried aloft by their fathers—and dozens of Carmen Mirandas. And up ahead is a sequined guitar on someone's head bobbing above all the surrounding heads, glinting prettily in the sun. The streetlamps are strung with lights and globed paper lanterns in all colours. Evie notices a woman standing at the foot of a monument, knitting with the yarn looped around her neck; she scowls, looking all around but never down at her hands. Even the one unhappy person in Rio has come to see the show.

Despite the thousands of people—it must be thousands! Evie thinks—everything is calm and warm and unhurried. Everyone dances down the street rather than walking, many with their arms raised up. Several people seem weighted down in their hips, their feet just shuffling along, while others have crazy legs, leaping and skipping their feet about like *futebol* players, their torsos following behind, arms down low. A man beside her appears almost ecstatic, pulsing his hat above his head, singing as loud as he can. Whistle blasts pierce the air in time to music. Musicians advance in a cluster, large round drums slung over shoulders with straps while others shake tambourines or maracas. They are slow and sweet as caramel, walking and playing as though it were the easiest thing in the world. This is the kind of music Maricota and Odete like to play, so different from the smooth big-band music Mama and Papa listen to. It rolls down out of the hills that surround the city: dense and throbbing. Evie's eyes, ribs, and tongue itch and shudder.

Looking all around her, wanting to see absolutely everything, she trips and stumbles backwards at some point, suddenly noticing that Magda is no longer beside her. She is lifted up by strong, black arms, and a stark white face looms toward her own—kind, smeared with greasepaint, with large, pencilled brown freckles, an eye patch, and a huge red mouth painted on.

'*Coitada! Você está bem?*' asks the face. He is wearing a bonnet over his thick, red-yarn, Raggedy Ann braids, and a short-sleeved bolero tied over his nipples. The rest of his muscled chest and waist are bare. He helps smooth her dress, then pinches her cheeks. 'Sisters. You. Me,' he says, motioning back and forth between Evie's hair and his wig.

She realizes that he must think she is a tourist because she is so light-skinned and hasn't said anything. '*Sim*,' she stammers now. '*Irmãs*.'

His face lights up but before he can say anything, Magda appears suddenly at her side and shoos him away, which he finds hilarious. He blows exaggerated kisses and waves as he walks away, like a woman in a beauty contest. *He loves me*, Evie thinks. Everyone here loves everyone else; black, brown, red, white, men dressed as women, women dressed as men—it doesn't matter. No one cares. But Magda isn't interested in Evie's tender realizations—she pulls her forward, ever forward, always trying to get somewhere else.

A dirty, barefoot child, maybe a *favelada*, with nappy hair and a stained, shapeless dress, stands on the nearby street corner selling baby chicks that have been dyed pink, blue, orange. Evie wants so much to hold one, to rub it all over her face.

'Look!' Evie says to Magda, who has led her onto the sidewalk to buy them each a glass of papaya juice. 'Give me some money.'

'Are you crazy?' Magda yanks her away by the wrist. 'It'll get squashed. Besides, Mama would never let you keep it.'

Magda tries to distract her, saying she will buy them noise-makers, and anything she wants to eat. But Evie can't stop thinking of the chicks, how nice their feathers would look against her pillow at night, mixing with her hair. Farther down the boulevard is a man selling parasols and pinwheels that flicker in the sun. He has a small monkey on his shoulder; its eyes are black and glittering. When Evie reaches out to touch it, it screams. Tears prick her eyes and Magda is quickly beside her again, glaring fiercely at the monkey and the man. Laughing, he hands them each a paper trumpet.

Magda leads Evie to another vendor selling *lança-perfume*. She buys a can and sprays it on her arm, then Evie's, tightening the skin above their wrists. Then she sprays their dresses, and they breathe in the oddly appealing chemical scent. It smells almost sweet and clean, and makes them so dizzy, they begin to giggle. Then Magda drags Evie back into the crowd.

As the sun goes down, the mountains that surround the bay seem larger, emerging above the horizon like the lumpish, threatening shapes of sleeping giants. All around the girls stalk ever more curious creatures, disguised and unidentifiable, their contours sharper now. Passersby take pictures of mock high-fashion models in ski masks who tower on deeply muscled legs and rough feet in too-small heeled sandals, striking poses in the middle of street. A group of skeletons thrust white crucifixes toward anyone who looks at them. Behind them swarms another faceless pack all in red, their eyes winking through holes slashed in their peaked hoods. Evie hears a far-off yelping—a child or an animal? Or a voice saying, *Go*.

'How long have we been here?' Evie asks no one in particular before reaching for Magda's hand. 'I want to go home!'

But Magda shakes off her sister's sweaty palm. 'No way! I want to see the parade. That's the whole point.'

'But maybe we've gone this way for too long. Maybe we should go with them,' she says, motioning to the stream of people moving in the opposite direction, back down toward the beach where their hotel is. 'Maybe they're the good stream.'

'Come on,' Magda hisses impatiently, her big snake of a sister. *Irmãs*.

And Magda is off, Evie drifting alongside her again, almost light as snow but for her wrist, which is throbbing and sticky where Magda keeps pulling on it, pulling her, pulling the waves of bodies and light and colour that follow them. Evie wants to tell her that there are sparks falling from her dress, but it's all she can do to keep up.

It's almost dark now and people are lighting small torches that they hold in front of their faces like candles, but these have longer, blazing flames. Again Evie wants to ask Magda: how long have they been here? But before she can remember how to speak, the floats begin to wobble down the boulevard and she sees things she's only imagined or dreamt of until now. There are men painted gold riding golden camels, golden lions. Women in veils—*The Arabian Nights!*—blowing kisses. Gleaming urns full of flowers. Angels with harps. Spirals of stars. On almost every float that goes by sit women atop some kind of rotating pedestal, blowing more kisses; in wheelbarrows held up by winged, plaster cherubs twice their size, more women. So many women, so many kisses; Evie is awash in them and can feel them land, cooling her hot skin. Everything around them is gleaming now, alight with gold. Women astride a giant sphinx; a brass band in shirts of glinting fabric; spangles hanging from every moving part of the floats, which are edged in twinkling fairy lights. At the rear of the floats sit young boys manning machines that shoot sparks, smoke, phosphorescence, not bothered by the kaleidoscope of paper streamers and confetti that fall around them. *I am not afraid!* Evie thinks how much Luiza would have loved it, to the see the night so lit up.

Magda huddles around Evie, sprays more *lança-perfume* on each of their arms, which they inhale deeply. Magda begins to laugh again, the fumes from the can seeming always to relax her, but Evie can feel herself swerving without meaning to, careening into others with each surge of worry. Just a short time ago, she loved everyone—what has changed? Beside them a man wearing a toga and a ring of flowers on his head smiles and waggles his finger, *tsk-tsk-tsking* in aped disapproval, and Evie thinks his crown is almost like the one she made for Luiza at the going-away party last year. She wonders if he would give it to her, and is still trying to remember the right words to ask when she's poked in the back of the head. Behind her, a constellation of twirling parasols spin around and around like white planets. But when Evie reaches out to touch one, the woman holding it turns to face her. White face, black mouth, black eyes. A skull, a ghost. Another *negro* in white greasepaint.

Once more Evie stumbles, but this time no one helps and Magda is gone again. Her legs feel heavy as she tries to lift herself up, but the ground is littered with dirty paper and shards of glass from broken bottles and there seems to be no safe place to put her hands. Finally, she is up again but swooning. It's too much now, too chaotic, her insides are vibrating painfully from all the music and dancing and inhaled fumes. Too many boundaries dissolved—between men and women, black and white. It's more sinister now than beautiful, yet everyone here is smiling and laughing—at her? Maybe they want to trick her, or they think she's stupid for no longer being able to tell what they really are, for believing they are all magical, like Luiza: between two worlds. But really it's a joke and they're all just wearing gaudy costumes and everyone but Evie knows her sister is gone.

Then she sees it: a halo of shining dust, hair like points of light. Swaying down the boulevard, bright and terrible, its head on fire in the night. Everyone claps and cries out, but they see only a mulatto butterfly, neither man nor woman—or both—wrapped in cheap fabric and sequins. Evie sees it truly: a dark angel with cormorant wings. And it wears a flower crown, just like the laughing toga man. Like Luiza. Evie is queasy with love and dread.

'Take me home, Magda.' She means to shout but her voice is thin and weak. And Magda still isn't there. Evie looks around frantically and finally spots her sister on the sidewalk arguing with a vendor under tissue paper lanterns. Again Evie tries to scream—she knows if the creature sees her, she'll burn—but her throat is closing and nothing comes.

And now the bird-angel is right in front of her, leaning

forward, handing her a flower pulled from Luiza's crown. It can hear what she's thinking. It breathes her breath.

*Tchau, beleza.*

It exhales flame and rain, and Evie is clinging to the boulevard by just her fingertips, tiny hands grasping. Still the creature comes for her, inhaling essential parts of her—her heart, fragments of bone. She's nothing but a scorched twig now.

'Evie!'

The creature shrinks, drawing back into the distance, and soon Magda is once again dragging her away by the arm.

'That was a man, you know!' Magda sounds afraid, then angry. 'I don't know why men always dress up like women the first chance they get.'

Once they are free of the crowd, Magda turns to inspect her, holding her with two erect arms. Deciding she is unharmed, Magda looks at the paper flower in Evie's hand and holds up a similar one attached to a piece of wire.

'Oh great—then why did I spend the last of our money buying you this?'

Evie wants to tell Magda: that was not a human. It was animal, bird, lizard—all things but human. When it kissed her, Evie put her hands under the creature's skirts. Beneath its layers, she saw things from her dreams: huge black cats, giant waves rising out of the sea. Evie tried to reach her hands in, wondering if Luiza's crown of flowers might be there. But her fingers blistered and touched nothing. *Tell.* She hears again the ringing in her ears, remembers the bruises that came later, especially ugly on her stark white skin. Long sleeves in summer. *Don't tell.* The way he stood there, his face still and blank and big as the moon—he never even saw her. And then he reached out. The backs of her knees sticky with sweat, dirt. *I promise.* She knew what Luiza's secret was before tonight but she hadn't understood that it was important. Luiza kept saying it didn't matter, not to worry. Now, she can't retrieve the words.

Besides, Magda won't listen.

'We have to get *home*,' her sister keeps saying, striding forward, pushing through the crowd.

Home: sad, grey place where they'll never see such things again.

# DORA

At the Municipal Theatre ball on this last night of Carnival, Hugo and Dora sit at a table with their friends amid the fabric waves and painted, plywood boats, a dozen pairs of enormous eyes peering down from where the curved walls meet the ceiling. There are rows of tables like theirs, off to the side of the crowded dance floor, all covered in white tablecloths, fresh roses, open bottles of champagne, ashtrays crammed full. The brass band is excellent, as always, stationed behind two large pillars, metallic and candy-striped, that jut forward at an angle. Dora knows she should get up and dance—*Your last Carnival!* chime her friends again and again—but the energy she found for last week's cocktail party has long dissipated, and she refills her glass, vaguely hoping to retrieve some of it.

It was absurd to think that if she busied herself with parties, she wouldn't have time to collapse. To believe that if she did what she'd always done, surely life would somehow recalibrate, become recognizable. But now amid the frothy chatter, the giddily flung wrists, she is alone—even farther from Luiza and Hugo than before.

All around her twirl gladiators, clowns, and slinky cats, gashes of colour among the many men in white tuxedos.

Hugo used to love to dress up for Carnival, but tonight he wears the same tasteful uniform as most of the other men: white jacket and black tie. Dora wears an elegant white, V-neck gown with black gloves and a simple black mask over her eyes. It would have been undignified for them to dress up, but for a moment she is breathless, struck by a swift and sharp pang of nostalgia, remembering how they used to celebrate when they were first married.

Once upon a time, Hugo insisted they join the street parades, even though Dora said they were low-class. They went to a different ball every night—first to the Cassino da Urca, where they danced to Carmen Miranda before she started wearing all that silly fruit on her head, and then to the Artists' Ball, where most of the men wore costumes, and those who didn't were sweat-slicked beneath their short-sleeved shirts, unbuttoned almost to their navels, not a tuxedo in sight. Guests threw confetti into the air and grasped one another tightly as they moved in concentric circles around the huge room in a dance-induced trance state. And then to the beach, where everyone spread out, detritus of costumes lost in the sand, and Hugo's smooth shaven cheek and perfect hand pressed against her thigh as she slept. Then rest for a few hours, before returning to the frenzy of dancing, drinking, sweating—bacchanalia. He always had so much energy, and she did her best to keep up. Had she noticed it then, or were her memories imprinted retrospectively by what she knew now? He hadn't, even then, been encumbered by the physical needs of normal people. He never seemed to tire, and now she couldn't remember him ever taking more than a few bites of food before becoming distracted, clapping his hands, and seizing whomever happened to be beside him, proclaiming, 'Delightful! Have you ever tasted such manna? What wonderful people you all are!' She still misses it—the fever and delirium—before she knew enough to fear what followed.

'But you must admit, a certain elegance has gone,' some-one says over the bleating of brass instruments. 'It's fine in here, but out there, in the streets, it's all *pau-de-arara*.'

*Pau-de-arara:* migrants from the northeast who come to the city in uncovered trucks. Her friends still have the Rio of their girlhoods in mind, with its wild beaches and the sense that it belonged to them. 'There have always been the poor,' they say, 'but they used to be less . . . obtrusive.'

'The South Zone was *ours*,' they say.

Those with money, they mean. Those who are *claro*. Her friends sink into sentimentality when they mourn for those years they claim were untroubled. But for her, those same years were punctuated by chaos and regret. Perhaps it was better for them to leave these people behind, she thinks. People who have never lost anything.

'Speaking of lost elegance,' says May Buchanan in a stage whisper, 'did you hear about Ruthie's niece? Well, apparently she's got history. She's here because her parents had to fire her tutor. There was *something* there.'

'Wait,' Dora says, leaning forward now. 'Ruthie Cavanagh? What about the girl?'

'Her niece, Brigitta. Well you know her, Dory—wasn't she talking to the girls at your party? Lock them up, I say!'

'But what did the tutor do?'

'Oh nothing, I don't think. Ruthie even said it was all the girl's doing. They gave him two weeks' pay and a good refer-ence. Ruthie's sister wanted her somewhere far away for the summer, teach her a lesson to straighten her out.'

'I'm off to mingle!' Hugo says now, paying no attention to the conversation.

Is she the only one who notes the subtly higher pitch to his voice, Dora wonders, watchful as he retreats into the crush of bodies crowded into the theatre. Their friends, always so polite, pretend not to notice for as long as they can. But after all these years, all his so-called 'visits to Canada' whenever he was hospitalized while Dora remained at home with the girls, she's sure they suspect the truth.

When Hugo first got sick, Dora hadn't known what to do, who to call, where to take him. No one spoke about such things— such private matters—until they erupted, and sometimes not even then. At times the politeness and the reticence (for they were all still Americans deep down) was stifling: who could she have asked for help? His family was a continent away, and he barely kept in touch with them. Sometimes she almost believed him when he said he felt like he had been born upon arriving in Brazil, as though he had no life before. He made it clear he didn't want to remember or discuss his past. *Dull place, dull people—let us not waste our thoughts on them,* was usually all he said. *This is the only life I want. Let us live in the now, like the Buddhists say.* So when things escalated in those early years, and he spoke too much and too fast, or he was suddenly drained of colour and took to his bed, people made excuses. *Oh, Hugo—you know how he is. Probably had too much to drink.* And then they were all having too much to drink, so less was noticed than might have been otherwise, and even less was said.

His 'spells' (Dora had, at the time, no other name by which to call them) were relatively mild at first, marked by a seductive exuberance followed by melancholy, and lasted only a few days or weeks at a time. For a time, the spells made him a more brilliant, more appealing, more exciting version of himself. Nights when they stayed out until dawn and he took her to places she'd never otherwise go and they made love for hours. But soon small, knotted obsessions began to take root—Keats's poetry, Beethoven's concertos—and he would stay up all night even after they'd been out to the casinos, reading and listening to music. Then things would change; he didn't want to go out, to dance, to shimmer or seduce. And while his lows were defined, distinct, and harder for Dora to understand, there existed a word in Portuguese for his more melancholy moods. *Saudade.* A longing or nostalgia for a lost place or person, or something beloved that you once had, that you ached for still. So everyone said, *Oh you know, Hugo—so far from home. It's just saudade.* Not just a feeling but a collective temperament that marked the Brazilian people, who were a commingled diaspora, far-flung from their native countries. It was normal, wasn't it? It was even, perhaps, an act of empathy on his part. He was, in his heart, a true *brasileiro.*

Early on, there were breaks, plateaus, during which he was good and forthright, decisive and smart—himself. And enough time would lapse between each cycle of high and low that the last was nearly forgotten when the next arrived; too few and far between for a clear pattern to emerge. And the truth was, once his peculiarities—for still she had no name for them— became impossible to deny, it was really just a confirmation of what Dora had known for some time, that they were not just a quirk of personality but a *thing.* A condition. Something that should be named. And following the naming of it, what? She didn't know. It worsened while she was pregnant with Luiza, when he barely touched Dora and she was surprised by how much she missed him, missed the weight and heat of him, missed the way his thick, warm arms wrapped around her in the kitchen. Even that was enough, just an embrace as she made coffee, as though he *needed* to hold her. Needed *her.* Was it her naked, pregnant body that alarmed him? The livid, purple fissures spreading from her vagina toward her belly button, like inverted veins on the surface of her skin. By this time the war had started and she worried it would have seemed childish—unpatriotic!—to demand too much attention. She knew he was doing important things at work, drawing blue-prints for the Allies. So she busied herself playing canasta with friends and told them Hugo was occupied with work requisi-tioned by the Department of Defence. Top secret. Something to do with bridges.

Everything seemed fine, and if occasionally his laugh was particularly loud, particularly abrupt, or if he ran his fingers so roughly against his scalp that it left channels in his Brylcreemed hair, then she told herself it was the stress of the war, of not sleeping well, of his new executive position, of having a baby on the way. When the baby comes, she told herself, that will help focus him. He had always loved children. He was meant to be a father.

But after Luiza was born, things only got worse. She was a colicky infant, crying for hours every day for the first few months of her life. (Was it because she sensed what was coming? Silly thought, but Dora couldn't help it.) She noticed that Hugo became more distracted and withdrawn than normal, but so was she—they were exhausted, after all. Lack of sleep could make anyone feel crazy.

Until one night something inside him cracked in an almost audible way, as though his sane self ruptured and some other being was secreted. He was standing by the window when she entered their bedroom, and it startled her, the sight of him, so rigid. It had been almost a week since she'd seen his full height, seen him stand upright all on his own, and he seemed even larger somehow. She tried again to coax him toward the bed, but that night he wouldn't come. He didn't resist or get angry, he just stayed staring silently out the window, solid and inert as a granite block. Dora didn't know what else to do.

Eventually, she climbed into bed, resolved not to fall asleep in case he moved from the room. To keep herself awake, she listed in her mind the things she loved most in Petrópolis, where they would soon return.

When she shuddered awake, Dora immediately narrowed her eyes to see through the gloom. Hugo's place by the window was empty, as was his place beside her in the bed. Adrenaline surged through her. She was up quickly on the front pads of her feet, and when she opened the door of the nursery, she didn't expect to see anything horrible exactly, but she sensed something new, an unfamiliar vibration in the air. And there it was, Hugo's great, strong body, standing sentinel by Luiza's crib, his back to the door. He turned when she approached, looking toward but through her, his face inanimate but for his mouth, all affect drained. His voice was toneless, unmodulated.

'That hair, like the sun, I had that hair but mine was yellow also like the sun but the yellow sun not the red sun. That child I was with yellow hair, I killed that child and I can't find him. When we grow up we kill the children that we were, the purest versions of ourselves. We should instead age backwards and die as single cells, never knowing that we had died, having given birth to our own child-selves, and then for a time we'd all be children together and she would never be alone and never kill her most beautiful self. Where did that little boy go, that sun-haired boy? I killed him. This poor child. Who will take care of this poor, poor child.'

And though the small folds of Luiza's eyes remained closed, she began to squirm and become unswaddled. Dora had to get him away from the crib, out of the room. So she knelt before him and wrapped her arms around his trunk and pressed her hot cheek against his cool pant leg, for he was still dressed in his day clothes, and tried to pull him back from an invisible but definite precipice, draw him back into the shared secrecy of their little family. For the first time (but not the last), she was afraid that some vital part of Hugo had been irretrievably excised; he was blighted. She waited for his face to rearrange itself into an identifiable expression like it had the past few nights, the corners of his mouth turning strangely upwards as he wept, an inverted grimace, collapsed but familiar and, yes, like that of a child. But he remained somehow inflexible, even as he allowed himself to be led back to bed where, slow and susurrous, she tucked him in, remembering how much she'd always disliked street clothes touching bedsheets. Remembering when such things mattered.

After that night, she began sleeping with Luiza in the guest room and soon hired help. And now, when she remembers this time, before the maids came, it gouges something in her. Hugo's mind, his body—these, she believed, might be unrecoverable to her. So she wrapped herself around her baby daughter instead and absorbed the warmth of her rosy skin and listened for her shorter, infant breaths, trying to breathe in time with them. And when, years later, Luiza began to cling to Hugo whenever he left the house, Dora told herself it was because he needed their daughter more—needed more of everything— and Luiza was performing his need back to him, just like Hugo had once done for the freaks and the cross-dressers weeping in derelict bars. But still the amputation was shocking—the heat of Luiza's body pressed against her own in sleep, climbing onto her lap, gone from her now. Only Hugo could hug her, hold her hand as they walked along the shore. Hadn't she saved Luiza from her father? And then dutifully, as a mother should, kept that rescue a secret from both of them?

Someone takes the seat beside Dora at the table, and she comes slamming back down to the present, into the hard wooden seat at the Municipal Theatre, her ears suddenly filled with the crash of cymbals, some woman's light-hearted protests ('You never did and I won't hear any more about it!'), some man's low-throated chiding ('You know absolutely that I did'). A gold streamer has fallen across her lap. Her friends have all gone off dancing and Hugo hasn't returned.

'You're in the clouds tonight.'

The voice is muffled, stifled by a hideous mask with a monkey's fanged underbite and large, protruding ears. Still,

Dora recognizes it, but then she's known him since they were teenagers and everything about him—his voice, his movements—is familiar. But she waits, motionless and silent, trying to suppress a smile. They sit like that until Dora leans forward and gently pulls away the mask, looking around quickly as she does so: she can't see Hugo, or this man's wife. And there it is—this face she hasn't seen for almost a year, except at the funeral, where it would have been awkward to speak for the first time in so long, but where, touchingly, he had wept. Carmichael's face is lined around the eyes where the holes of his mask have imprinted the skin, but smiling and welcome.

'You didn't come to the party at the house,' Dora says finally.

'I came here,' he says.

She's aware of how close they're speaking, how careless he seems. There is whisky on his breath. 'I see that,' she says, leaning back.

'I thought it might be uncomfortable.'

'It would have been. Yet you came last year.'

He runs the palms of his hand over his face now, rubbing so hard the skin stretches. 'Yes, that was very uncomfortable.'

'Thank you for your condolences. Afterwards,' says Dora, handing him the mask, almost wishing he'd put it back on. 'That was very kind.'

'I should have liked to come see you, but I thought—'

'No, it's better that you didn't.'

He casts about for something to say. She doesn't help. Eventually he asks her, 'How are the girls?'

'Well. As well as they can be.'

'The service was lovely.'

'I saw you there,' she says, nodding slowly. 'It was good of you to come.'

More silence. 'And Evie and Magda, they're well?'

'They're fine.'

'Sorry. You just said.' Carmichael puts the mask back on. 'Well, this isn't goodbye. Alice said there was an invitation for the Copacabana in a couple of weeks?'

'Yes, that will be goodbye,' says Dora, meaning it as a caution but detecting a current of sadness running through her own voice that she hadn't expected.

He stands, takes her hand, and, bending toward her, touches it to the hard plastic mouth over his own.

As he walks away, Dora thinks of all those times Hugo left her with just the servants and the children—beginning that year he went to England for the war, when Luiza was just a few months old. So many husbands and fathers were going off to war at the time, she knew it was selfish to feel lonely, and he was only gone for a year—far less time than some. And *he* returned, unhurt. But then there were the times he went into the hospital, sometimes for a month or more—that went on for years. Being alone became unbearable, and she was often still lonely even after he came home. And then there was Carmichael—coaxing, bass notes—a physical approximation of her husband if she drank enough. They promised: fun and brief. A diversion. But it ended painfully when she insisted on their original terms—it meant nothing and no one would ever know. She held him ruthlessly to that promise despite knowing that she, too, had broken the rules. That she had loved him.

# HUGO

Hugo must get outside, must go and move and feel unfettered. He's attended the parties and balls. He has played along. But he won't forget Luiza, or the letter. For the past two days since they returned from Carnival, he has shut himself in the office as the contents of his house diminished around him, the maids packing, hovering occasionally at the door of his study to see if they can move any more boxes, as Maricota does now.

'Not yet, Maricota,' he says, beginning to undo the first few buttons of his shirt. He goes to the door, cuffs and collar open as he greets her. 'But here, would you like to take the shirt from my back instead? Here, have my tie.'

'*Claro que não!*' she says, then walks away, muttering under her breath. The best offence is a good defence. If he makes her uncomfortable enough, she'll leave him alone and he won't be discovered going through Dora's old letters, her desk. He locks the door behind the maid. *You deserve better.* He's said nothing to her about what he found—it's proof of nothing. Proof only that someone loved—or loves—her. So far it's the only trace. He can find nothing else and the air in here is stifling. The shafts of light that fall across the floor from beneath the half-drawn shades are too thin, their glow too meagre.

He shuffles the letters and documents before him, intending to confer some sort of order, align their edges into a tidy stack. But there is a bristling energy in his hands and three of Odete's potent *cafezinhos* in his blood, and the papers fan awkwardly in his grasp, their corners jutting at all angles like the points of a dangerous, asymmetrical star. *So go for a walk*, he orders himself. This is not the time to handle thin parchment or precious things. *Find the sun.*

As Hugo places his hand on the car door handle, it's like a miracle; the spotless chrome reflects the sun above and also the one growing inside him, for he has swallowed a star. It is still tiny, embryonic, and will most likely stay contained within him for days, growing but not too quickly. In a week or two it will almost certainly ignite, fluorescing sparks starting in his fingertips before spreading through his entire body.

As he slides onto the warm, white leather behind the steering wheel, the car suddenly feels like the wrong place to be, even once the top is down. He is too constrained, a man alone in a metal box. Instead he drives to the nearest trolley station, where he mounts a rickety streetcar and hangs off the side, gripping the metal handle, riding free and exposed into the city that made him. He glides above the tram lines toward the neighbourhood of Copacabana, the horizon before him vaster than what his eye can behold, and he has to turn his head along its axis to take it all in, to look past the beach with its wall of white high-rises, to the mountains that line the water's edge, then the open ocean, flashing and endless beneath the noonday sun.

When he dismounts, he imagines leaping gracefully but instead lands clumsily and stumbles, finally landing on his knee and one arm. Onlookers laugh from the streetcar, but

Hugo rises quickly with a little jump and takes a bow. Downtown the streets are congested and he feels the familiar rush of energy, the orphan thrill. Today the city feels pristine, more vibrant than it has in years. He heads toward the Rua Tonelero propelled by some internal compass that pushes him forward in no identifiable direction; just *that way*. Sometimes he crosses the street because he is suddenly and irrevocably compelled to be on the opposite side, but still he sticks to his route, ordained yet mysterious. And now he is here, where he was always meant to be, in front of this single-storey corner building, with its low stone wall topped by wide windows and a terracotta tile roof, ferns spilling out of the window boxes that line the entire facade below a red scalloped awning. Le Petit Club, where diners lunch on tiny portions of rich, fussy food in tribute to the Rio of the 1920s and all its early pretensions, when rich women wore French fashions and Mayor Passos imported sparrows so that this city's squares might echo with the imagined birdsong of Paris. But Hugo's memory of it is of squandered caviar, because when he and Dora brought Luiza here for dinner once, she squashed the iridescent red eggs with the back of her spoon. Dora said that if she would not eat what she was served, she should go hungry, but Hugo insisted they buy her a burger on the way home, which she ate happily. In every memory now, he searches for clues, for what might have signalled Luiza's disappearance, even though, as he reminds himself daily, hourly, it might have been a terrible accident. But it doesn't *feel* like an accident, and when he's like this, just barely starting to soar, everything is instinct.

*You deserve better.* Better than his ability to divine direction from the hot wind that gusts in from the ocean? Detect minute shifts in the air currents? Nothing is better than this.

Like his awareness now of too many bodies brushing past, creating a cool, slightly agitating breeze at his neck. He wants to keep studying the menu posted outside the restaurant, hoping he appears like a potential customer rather than a nostalgic supplicant, but there is the hum of constant movement behind him, the sense that he, too, should be moving. Aspirants and pederasts, Coca-Cola kids and the petite bourgeoisie, migrants and petty thieves. Hawkers, beauty queens, dope dealers. They are all blowing past him on the street. And the noise too; it assaults in a way it never has before, and goads him to keep going, as does the stench, a soup of food cooked in the streets, cloying perfumes, and the far-off but persistent smell of raw sewage from the neighbourhood's crumbling infrastructure. Before the city can spread any farther, before its buildings can grow any higher, before the whole damn place can swallow his past, he will retrieve his memories and go. Though his feet are stuck fast, his mind now wanders among the billboards, among the remaining colonial and art deco buildings, among the featureless high-rises filled with those trying to buy their little bit of *The Copacabana Way of Life*.

Still, his memories live in these streets—all those nights of dancing and drinking and swarming with joy—and the degradation brought with it a kind of decadence and seediness he has sometimes sought. But at times, the self-conscious glamour of *Anos Dourados*—the Golden Years, so named even as they were happening—had been stifling, and so he occasionally fled to the bohemian quarter, at first with Dora and then without. All those nights he left her so he could scrape away the posh, feel less bathed in manufactured auto-celebration. Had she, too, gone somewhere else? It had never occurred to him before now. And all the times he was away—the war, the hospitalizations. A life without him. He never thought to ask.

But sometimes he *had* to get away, from everyone trying to laugh louder than the person beside them, drained champagne bottles tipped on end in buckets of melting ice, women's pencilled brows smudged, erased in places. A tepid, fetal-looking shrimp snarled in tinsel and dropped into an ashtray. Eventually, he had to struggle to keep pace. Then, curtains drawn at midday. Sleep for weeks. Then back again. Copacabana was hedonism, miscegenation, but it was also more: the *most*. An escape from labour and reason and pragmatism. You could come and live a life entire, never leave because there was no need—it had everything. Until you died, that is, because there are no cemeteries in the neighbourhood. That would bring down the mood.

He commands himself, *Keep walking.* There can be no stasis when embarking on an odyssey. He strains one last time to see them again—Dora and himself, Luiza brandishing her tiny spoon—through the reflection of the huge, modern building that glances off the window of Le Petit Club, but they've gone. And then he, too, is moving, heading in a southwesterly direction, beneath the rubber trees that line the sidewalks of Domingos Ferreira, branches reaching toward one another to create a canopy above the cars honking below. Above the trees, air-conditioners jut from windows overhead, dripping condensation from apartment buildings onto the sidewalks below, onto his head. No matter. Soon he will be washed clean by the waves.

When he arrives at Copacabana Beach, its miles of white sand, bounded by the mosaic sidewalks in front and green mountains on either side, stretches out into impossibly blue water dotted with bathers. He has seen it thousands of times and yet today he can't see it, not really. He sees instead the beach near their house, the one that took her, superimposed on top. It's dusk now and he cannot see her well, but he can hear a woman splashing in the waves, laughing. He has to fight the instinct to jump into the water with her, just like that night when Luiza turned fifteen. At the time he could feel inside him the beginnings of a pleasant straining, that still-gentle effervescing, much like he does tonight. Not content to sit around the freshly polished silver tea service from India after dinner, he performed. He dazzled. But his laughter must have become too loud, too fierce, because Dora, glaring, finally said to him, through smiling, clenched teeth, 'Hugo, love—maybe you've delighted our guests long enough. You look so tired.'

It was the wrong thing to say. He was the opposite of tired, and he could feel the tension in his skin from just how very awake he was. It was Dora, he understands now, who was tired. *You deserve better.*

'Mother!' Luiza hissed at the time. 'Why can't you just let him be?'

But Dora knew better than Luiza what was coming.

'My dear wife,' he said, 'if you'd rather I leave you and this gathering of wholly mediocre minds you've assembled here tonight to bore our daughter and me senseless, nothing would make me happier. Come, Luiza, let us away.'

He grasped Luiza's hand then and pulled her, almost skipping, away from the dinner party so that she, too, had to skip to keep up. He noted rare tears forming in Dora's eyes, but there could be no turning back now. Luiza giggled as he lifted her high off the veranda steps and twirled her next to the azaleas before they unlocked the gate and sprinted into the dark.

They half ran, half danced all the way to the beach that night, and when she complained of blisters, Hugo crouched down so she could climb onto his back as he cantered along the dirt road, kicking up pebbles and dust. As soon as they reached the sand, he let her down, pulled off his shoes and tie, and made for the breakwater of large rocks. She had loved this beach more than any of the other famous Brazilian beaches they'd visited— Copacabana, Ipanema, Urca—because it had the softest gold- hued sand and seemed to stretch on forever, a headland at the far end that he couldn't imagine ever reaching. A few times they had tried walking toward them, walked for more than an hour, but the bluffs appeared no closer than when they'd begun.

Hugo held her hand and helped her clamber over the dark, slick rocks until they reached the very end of the breakwater.

The moon, not quite full, shone in pieces in the water, and they sat down, not caring that the seats of their clothes were soaked. He took a flask from his breast pocket and intoned mock-seriously that she was allowed to have *just a few sips* because it was her birthday after all and she was practically a woman now. But she took too much, so he pulled the flask back saying she should always remember that drunken women weren't appealing, never mind that he and his friends, the women included, were drunk most of the time.

But Luiza ignored his warnings. She flung her arms above her head, then around his neck—excited as she had been as a child, before terms like 'hypomanic' and 'psychosis' had intruded, colonized her vocabulary, her perceptions of him. When she used to tell him he was the funniest, the tallest, the smartest, the *most*.

'Do you remember when you used to throw me up in the air when I was little?' she asked. 'It felt like I might never come down again. I loved it and I was afraid at the same time—that feeling that I might just lift away.' He'd thought the same thing as she got smaller and smaller, and farther and farther away from him, with every throw. The slight burning as his flat palms connected with the reddening skin over her ribs, his long fingers against her back, his thumbs on the fleshy triangle beneath her sternum.

'That was before Mother started watching me all the time,' she said. 'Telling me I shouldn't encourage you.' Something in her tone, its precocious solicitude, made him uneasy.

'Well, she was probably right. I don't need it.'

Forcing a laugh, she asked him, 'What would you do if I disappeared?'

'What—right now? I suppose I'd hope that *I* was a drunken woman. I know I'm crazy, but I don't think I'm imagining things just yet.'

'Sure, right now. If I vanished into the water, what would you do? Would you find me?'

Mock-serious again: 'If you become a fish in a trout stream, I will become a fisherman and fish for you.'

It took her a moment, but then she smiled with recognition—it was a line from a book he used to read to her.

'But really, would it frighten you if I jumped in the water right now? I want to swim.'

'Then you'd be the crazy one. It's chilly and dark and you're not even wearing—'

But she was up and peeling off her cardigan, the poufy dress Dora had insisted she wear.

'Darling, please don't—'

He didn't try to stop her because he didn't believe she'd actually do it. It was August, winter in Brazil—too cool by Luiza's heat-loving standards to go in the water. Also, a classmate of hers had broken his neck jumping off these very rocks at night. But she went in with a loud splash and almost instantly she was treading water a few feet from the rock where he sat. He could make out her silhouette, the glint of the half moon off her teeth—she was smiling. She lifted her arm to wave and started to speak, but before he could make out what she was saying, she was being pulled away. Skimming across the water out to sea, away from the rocks and the broken moon, and away from Hugo, who dove blindly into the dark.

He swam ferociously, shouting, 'Swim back toward me! Swim as hard as you can!'

The water was incongruously calm on the surface, and swimming so hard through seemingly still waters felt like something out of a dream. But under the surface the current was powerful, dragging them away, apart.

They were both strong swimmers and afterwards he couldn't be sure if the riptide had ended or if, after a few chaotic minutes of swimming and shouting, they managed on their own to close the gap. But once he had her, he gripped her as hard as he could by the wrists rather than approach her body. He lifted her arms and spun her around, pinning both elbows behind her back so that she couldn't struggle or grab hold of him and drown them both, still somehow pragmatic through his panic and anger. He grunted as he forced her through the water, his one free arm churning like a machine. At the breakwater, he struggled to keep a foothold on a rock beneath the water as he pushed her up onto the rocks above, his head even going under a few times as he lost his footing. When he finally scrabbled up behind her, she embraced him.

'You saved me. You became the waves and pushed me where you needed me to go.'

But he just twisted her arms, stripping them away from around his neck, disgust distorting his face as she continued to speak.

'I would cut open the clouds for you. Free the water to wash away your tears,' she said, even though he wasn't crying.

Again he pulled her arms away, but this time he seized them both, his grip tightening until she cried out in pain. He shook her repeatedly. 'Stop this!' he shouted. 'You have to stop talking like this!'

It was only the sight of her head jerking unnaturally on the fragile stalk of her neck that made him go still.

Remembering that night now, he prickles hotly again with anger, in spite of himself—her childishness, her breathy, florid speech. But it must have proven something to her. For a time, throughout the highs and lows, she could still puncture the barrier of his condition, still get through to the part of him that was recognizable and basic and human. The part of him that was her father. A father who could still protect and save her. Once upon a time . . .

Because if she had swum away a few weeks later, when he was high, he might have jumped in and out-swum her, bellowing for her to follow. Damn the torpedoes. Or a few months after that, when he was low, his gaze might have remained fixed upon the barnacles as she slipped away. He never forgave himself for that night, or anything that came after. It was his fault. He was her father and it was his job to prove he loved her again and again and again. He should never have let her go.

Never again. He must never let her go again. Dora can make her plans, cross off her lists, hide her filthy letters. And he can pretend. But he won't leave Luiza—vapour or body— alone in this country. He'll find whatever's left of her. He'll go to wherever she is.

# LUIZA

## SPRING 1961

A few days after they arrived in Florida, Luiza and her sisters lined up in the driveway of the family's rented house in Pompano Beach to kiss their father goodbye. A taxi had come to take him to the hospital for the lithium study. He would remain there for eight weeks, after which he'd be allowed to come home for another eight weeks of daily outpatient visits for tests. As he stepped into the back of the taxi, Luiza saw his mouth tighten into the same crooked, uneasy line she could feel on her own face, meant to be a smile. He lifted his hand weakly and they all began to wave frantically from the driveway. Even Dora, having already climbed the porch steps and opened the front door, suddenly turned around and shot her arm straight out, her hand fanning the air. As the taxi pulled away, they all kept waving, watching as the rear window came down and his arm stretched out to wave back until it disappeared from view. Luiza imagined him, peering into the side mirror, seeing them all shrink until they vanished and he was alone.

And just like that—Luiza, her mother, the girls—they, too, were alone for the first time in their lives. Without help. Without a driver to take them beyond the unfamiliar boundaries of the neighbourhood, without the maids to cook, clean, and provide everything they needed. Dora had explained that four months was too long for the family to be separated—it was an important time and they should all be together. Soon everything might be different.

The house was located next to a drained marsh. It was spring when they arrived and there were froglets everywhere. They bred in the vacant lot next door, and their bodies lay crushed in the asphalt driveway, drying in the mud beneath their bedroom windows, trod upon in the screened-in porch. Their tiny shapes etched into the cool terrazzo floors. Luiza developed headaches from staring down so intently at the ground as she walked—she couldn't bear to kill any more. Whenever she felt another smooth, tiny form beneath her feet, she'd collapse onto the green porch swing and weep, both feeling and performing grief. Her mother said, 'Isn't it supposed to be locusts?' Then she insisted on cooking a roast for the first time in her life because they were *still a family*. An hour and a half later, Dora sat at the kitchen table weeping silently as smoke poured out of the oven door and Luiza shooed the girls into the living room and found Ed Sullivan on the television. After that night, Luiza heated TV dinners, spooning barely defrosted peas from a pot of tepid water onto their plates.

Since they would be in Florida for several months, the girls were taken to the local school by bus, and Dora—too anxious to drive beyond the grocery store a few blocks away—occupied herself with magazines and cigarettes, solitaire and letters home. Every day Luiza walked around the neighbourhood, then through a graveyard filled with victims of yellow fever and cholera, the coloured people buried on the far side of the cemetery, away from the whites. She hated going in, but if she didn't, she'd wake in the night tired and sore, jolted awake by dreams of bleached bones under her bed. So she went in and sat by the crumbling graves of children and read to them from Ovid—all those wonderful tales about Zeus and Demeter—and imagined that maybe she was the first person ever to read to them, and in this way gave meaning to her own shapeless days.

Outside the graveyard, it was worse. On her way home, in restaurant and store windows, even on filthy gas station bathroom doors, she saw blocky, handwritten signs: *Whites Only.* Had the maids come after all, how would they have felt? Unease clenched her stomach.

She tried to write in her journal, but it always came out sounding cloying and false. She found herself wondering what Mr. Carmichael would think of what she wrote, and sometimes let herself daydream, her jangly, unfocused energy subsumed by ascribing to him subtle feelings, imagined depths. How he had stood, bent over beside her as she sat against the wall that night in the garden, his eyes wide under crinkled brows. After that night she'd seen him a few times—more parties, more nights out—and though they didn't speak again, she sometimes glanced up to find him looking at her. Men always looked at her, but this was different. A sad, curious gaze, as though he were trying to both decipher and suppress something. It seemed to telegraph an inarticulate aching that she wanted so much to understand. Had he recognized something in her that she hadn't seen herself? And now, without him to look at her, to appear slightly puzzled and moved, she felt lonely. No one was watching her anymore. But it was more than just wanting attention. *Where would you like to go?* Only he had ever asked her this. Only he had asked her to consider a life outside her family.

When Dora came into the room, Luiza snapped her journal shut.

'Any word from the hospital?' she asked her mother, too lightly. The telephone hadn't rung in days.

'You know they won't tell us anything until the study is over.'

'I know.'

Dora tried to brighten then, crouching down next to the arm-chair where Luiza sat. 'By the way, what did you think of those creamed beans I made the other night, with the crispy top?'

'Oh,' said Luiza, unable to remember anything about their dinners other than how awful they were. 'They were good!'

'I can make them again tonight if you like. I want to get that dish just right for when your father comes home. The secret to their crunch is . . . potato chips!'

With her mother's face so close to her own, cheerfully beseeching, Luiza could see her grey roots and wilting curls, the lipstick bleeding into the feathery cracks around her mouth. But Dora seemed almost cheerful thinking of Father's return, and the promise of undemanding, housewife-friendly foods—maybe she actually *wanted* to tend to him, to housekeep, to fret over his quotidian needs. While Luiza brooded over his nature, his selfhood, Dora would roll his socks into pilled mounds, remember to buy the *TV Guide*.

And then one day the study *was* over, and Father came back to the house in Pompano Beach. He seemed well. Steady. Much the same as he always was during the in-between times. *Himself*, as her mother would say. That evening, they had a little party. Evie and Magda decorated the house with crepe streamers and bal-loons, and Dora burned another roast, and the girls were allowed to have sherry glasses filled with pink wine, warm and sweet. Father fumbled with the record player while Dora and Luiza set the table with cheap silverware, and soon velvety strings filled the room. Just as Luiza fussed with the placement of a polished steak knife, her father swept her mother into his arms, twirling her into the kitchen. All three girls froze—Luiza still with the knife in her hand—and held their breath, wait-ing for a harsh, sudden movement, maybe a wrist turned too quickly, bent and painful. But he moved fluidly, dipped Dora down gently, and kissed her on the cheek. As they moved together so easily, her mother laughing, Luiza remembered how as a girl she used to sit at the top of the stairs those nights after her father returned from one of his early hospitalizations, her knees against her chest so her parents wouldn't see her, and how they danced and laughed, two bisected bodies swaying. Their slow-moving, crisscrossed legs all that she could see. Luiza hoped her hot, red cheeks didn't betray that she felt almost as jealous now as she had as a child—touched to see them smiling together, but afraid that she'd be left behind once again.

During dinner, they chewed the tough meat and Father smiled, lay his hand over Dora's, and said it was delicious, then clinked his glass against each of the girls'.

'To good friends and long-legged women!' They all laughed and the girls climbed onto his lap, demanding bedtime stories.

That night, Luiza couldn't sleep. She rubbed her face against the rough, cheap pillowcases, frustrated that she hadn't been able to sit up with her father after dinner and ask him more about the study, without her mother anxiously insisting she not *egg him on*. Dora wanted to keep the mood celebratory, and probably wouldn't ask him anything real or want to know, truly, how he felt. Luiza wondered if she and her mother could ever both have what they wanted, or if what they wanted for him should even matter. He had not come home from the hospital dull and drained, as she'd feared, but nor was he fully himself, acutely charged. He had been subtly diluted. Made unobjectionable. But which was really his *true* self? Which could she lay claim to? And couldn't her mother—who had known him longer but *not* better, for there were many ways to know a person—wave her own map, point to the smudged lines of a different being, and swear the same: *this* is him, this is who he is meant to be.

Luiza was surprised, then irritated to find herself suddenly thinking of Mr. Carmichael and wishing he were there. He'd said, idly, that she was clever, which made him sound like a neutered uncle. But he also said something else: 'Rio, all the parties, the casinos—that's our life, your parents' life. When we were young, there was nothing better. But I don't think it will be enough for you. It's not enough for me anymore.'

'Then why don't you do something else?'

He tilted his head then, smiled indulgently in that particular way of his, the corners of his mouth scarcely lifting. In disbelief? Maybe he was touched by her artlessness. Or her foolishness.

But now, as she began to drift into sleep, she kept twitching awake, remembering this same feeling of frustration whenever her father used to come home from the hospital years ago. Suddenly, her parents were reunited, sharing jokes and private glances, and she was sent back to her own room to sleep alone after weeks of sharing a bed with her mother. Evie and Magda often slept in the same bed and her parents had each other now. Even the maids had only one room between them. In the whole house, only she was alone. Thinking of it now, she flinched. It was wrong, of course, to prefer her parents apart.

She was so tired, trying to decide how to feel about it all, trying to catch this green-blue hummingbird that kept disintegrating every time she reached for it, just as it called out her name, *Luiza!*

'Luiza!' Her mother's voice high and ragged, almost unrecognizable. 'I need your help!'

Her father was sitting in the bathtub, shirtless and panting rapidly, while Dora was on her knees in front of the tub. Luiza tingled with recognition.

'I can't breathe, I can't breathe, I can't breathe.' He sounded truly afraid, not remote and uninflected as he usually did when he slipped away.

'I don't know what happened!' Dora kept saying. 'He seemed fine when we went to bed, and then I found him in here like this.' Her father dug at his chest with one hand and pulled at his hair with the other using so much force that both were splotchy red. 'Stay with him,' her mother said. 'I'll go call the hospital.'

'No! I can calm him down.' Luiza tried to wrap her arms around him, but he kept clawing and tearing and gasping for air. 'Papa, Papa, tell me what happened.'

'I can't breathe, get it out. I can't breathe.' The skin on his chest was broken now, tumid white welts streaked with dotted red lines. 'It's rotten, get it out.'

'Your heart or your brain?' Luiza asked, crouching as low as she could, facing him.

'I can't breathe.'

'Nothing's rotting,' Dora said, standing just behind her now, talking over Luiza's head. 'You have to try to calm down.'

Luiza knew contradicting him only made things worse, made him anxious. Their language was unintelligible to Dora, who never learned to inhabit his worlds, not even long enough to try to bring him back.

'I can't breathe,' he said again, grasping at his chest.

Dora stood abruptly. 'That's it. I'm calling the hospital. Something's wrong.'

'No, I can talk to him. I can fix this! Go take care of the girls.'

But when he gasped again, Dora ran out of the room, and Luiza could hear her fumbling for the telephone in the hallway, then begging someone to come, to please hurry! And then, chaos. Worse than anything before: the girls, both wet-faced and standing in the doorway behind her, seeing their father smother in another bathtub as he continued to scratch at his chest, turning their twin nightgowned bodies to follow Luiza's every move. Dora's face pressed against the receiver, calling first Emergency then the psychiatric hospital. Then sirens split the night air, drowning out the frog-song, and out came the men in white coats. (They really did wear white coats!) Dora and the girls followed the paramedics down the front steps as they loaded the gurney into the ambulance. When their father began to thrash against the soft restraints that held his limbs tight to the stretcher bars, Luiza guided the girls toward the door and pushed them inside. She hoped her mother would stay outside while her father was driven away, but she came in behind them, the red lights still pulsing through the window on the opposite wall.

After the ambulance had taken him away and the girls were settled back in bed, her mother sat slumped at the kitchen table with a glass of straight gin—the only thing in the house to drink. Luiza registered for the first time that throughout everything that happened that evening, Dora's hair had been in the curlers she always put in before bed, and she wore no make-up. She seemed small and expended. Would she ever look like that? Luiza wondered.

'It's good that you were here,' Dora said, examining her own hands as she turned the glass in circles. 'You spared the girls the worst of it. He fought so hard at the end. I couldn't watch.' She got up then, kissed Luiza quickly on the top of the head, and left the room.

It sounded almost like gratitude, what her mother had said, something Luiza had always thought she wanted. Some acknowledgement that she knew him best, better than his own wife. But in that moment, even those few, tepid words washed Luiza's stomach with fresh regret. After all, this failure—was that how he would see it?—was partly her doing.

She took a drink from Dora's glass, swallowing down the pressure of her own vast selfishness. She couldn't forgive her mother for pushing him into this study, but Dora, at least, had believed in its value, that the risk was justified. Luiza was corrupt for never really having had faith in the study, for her own baseless complicity. She had dreamed of one day being free of him, his lassitude and delirium—the frenzy of their lives together. She had even let herself imagine a different kind of life. Now, an almost savage guilt cut through the gin. For having gone along with her mother's plans—no, for having helped her! By agreeing to come on this trip, by conceding that he should be tested upon, by allowing him to be taken alone to a hospital somewhere, febrile and toxic.

The little room in her mind where she sat alone, writing her fine sentences, that other life—it was gone now. Awful, selfish girl. And the girls *had* seen things, terrible things. They'd seen their father carried out tied to a stretcher by four men and, twice now, pathetic and wrecked in a bathtub. So what if they had been too young to remember the first time? The scene was nearly identical and it presaged the same ending: *someday, you will lose him.*

If she were to leave home now, she would be giving her father up to her mother, to a wife who couldn't contain the fullness of him. To rejection. Dora loved him, but only that middle strip, not the expanse of all his joys and burdens. And now he might feel compelled to seek a cure for their sakes, to atone for his brain's metabolic failures. *Him* trying to unburden them, pursued by their disappointment, spread wide behind him. And Luiza? Maybe she was just like everyone else, and as she aged and hardened, she, too, would want the same bland, uncorrugated comforts. Maybe that nebulous future life, the 'something more' she had imagined for herself—and lost—was really something less, and her father knew it. He knew everything— he always had. He had seen her aligning herself with Dora before Luiza herself had, and he knew he was alone.

Could he ever trust her again?

Everything she wanted that night, she could never have again: to be a child again, to be washed clean. To be forgiven, and to forgive them.

# MAGDA

In the days since the family returned from Carnival, Magda has watched the maids dismantle, pack, discard. All the best dishes, much of the art on the walls—they've all been repacked, and she senses a current of unease rippling through the house, across the increasingly bare walls. She walks through the house, enumerating in her head all the missing items she's known since birth, and reaches into the empty spaces they occupied. With her finger, she traces the outline of the absent amethyst grapes, the crystal duck she once despised, and wonders how it can be that now there is nothing where once, and for so long, there was everything. But Magda decides that it cannot be, because if she squints her eyes she can still see all the things that were there before, still feel their textures. And it's up to her to remember it all, because everyone else in her family is trying so hard to escape, to get away before they've even left, to pretend as though their lives here meant nothing.

Mama spent part of the afternoon drifting from room to room, moving the odd thing from one pile to another, before going out to the veranda, smoking and sipping a cocktail, staring at the gardens. Papa has been mostly shut away in his office, but he left the house early this morning and has been gone all day, and the maids cannot be enjoined to go outside or to the beach because they say there's too much to do. Even Evie doesn't want to play; these past few days, she's been sullen and withdrawn, wanting to be left alone to read on the couch among the half-packed valuables like some endangered aristocrat. Today, Magda pulled out tattered cards, the old backgammon game—more things they'll leave behind—but when she loomed over her sister to urge her to play, Evie squirmed off the couch and ran out the back door into the yard. When she came back a few minutes later, her clothes were dirty, her knees red and raw. It felt to Magda like a warning: even Evie could find ways to leave her behind.

And so now Magda sits beside Evie in the den, and when Odete stands in the doorway to tell them they should begin cleaning their rooms and sorting their things, the girls quickly become engrossed in old issues of *The Brazilian American* instead.

When the doorbell rings and no one answers, Magda flings her magazine toward the coffee table and gets up. She goes out the front door and down the walkway. Behind the gate: a family of beggars.

'*Pedindo esmolas,*' they say. Alms for the poor.

The man and the boy wear cut-off shorts, flip-flops, torn shirts, while the two little girls are barefoot and covered by loose cotton shifts, each with frizzy hair. A woman stands behind them all, looking down, a headscarf wrapped around her hair. But she has no bangles, no beads, no full skirts like the women who wore similar scarves at Carnival—just a man's T-shirt and a thin, shapeless skirt that ends above her dry knees. They ask only for a few *cruzeiros*, or some food. Magda tells them to wait while she goes back inside the house and up to her parents' bedroom.

When she returns, Evie is at the gate, asking the youngest girl, '*Você tem alguns pintinhos?*'

They stare at her blankly. '*O que?*'

'Chicks. Do you have any more of those little pink chicks?'

'It's not her, moron,' Magda says, swatting Evie aside. 'And they don't speak English.'

Magda begins handing over earrings, bracelets, a gold watch. Evie's mouth is an *O*, contracting and releasing but emitting no sound. Finally, when Papa's Rolex changes hands, she squeaks.

'You can't! I'll get Mama!'

Magda grips her arm. 'Don't you dare. We don't need all this stuff.'

But the family of beggars just stands there, equally shocked. They're still staring at one another when Papa pulls up to the gate in the Silver Cloud. Evie covers her face with her hands, but Magda is defiant, her arms crossed in front of her, hip jutting forward. Her parents probably won't even notice what's missing, though some part of her hopes they will.

Papa gets out of the car to unlock the gate and looks at the beggars, with their hands outstretched, each holding something gold, jewel-speckled.

'*Eu gostaria de ficar com o relógio*,' he says, carefully lifting the Rolex out of the young boy's dirty hands and winking at him as he slips it onto his own wrist. He pats Magda on the shoulder as he slides past her to get back into the Rolls-Royce and continues up to the house. 'They can keep the rest.'

Magda's shock soon bristles into outrage. He *should* let her give their things away. 'We have too much,' Luiza always said. Their parents are kind enough to the help, but it was Luiza who treated them like family, who took them gifts at Christmas. One Christmas, Maricota gave Evie a doll with a real dress that came off and Magda a soccer ball. When Luiza suggested they take their gifts to the maids that year, it was the first time Magda had seen where Maricota lived: the dirt floors, trodden so flat and smooth they were shiny. Every time she plays with that soccer ball, Magda wants to cry, thinking of how much money Maricota must have spent on them, even though they already had so many things. But she doesn't cry. She stops herself and thinks instead about how she'll work hard and get a good job and make all kinds of money so she can buy the maids each a house in Canada with real, shiny floors and their own maids. They'll never have to clean again.

The same night they took their gifts to Maricota, she led them down to the small bay near her family's house, filled with brightly coloured boats and villagers who dressed all in white. It was New Year's Eve and the crowd gathered filled little boats with flowers and candles, mirrors and lipstick, all offerings for Yemenjá, the mother of the seas. As the sun set, people's faces and hands receded into the gloaming and all that white brightened against the dark, seemingly animate clothing pushing a hundred points of flame into the night. Now Magda wonders, who will teach her how a person should be in the world? When they leave Luiza and the maids behind, who will pull her back from steep edges, keep her from ripping apart everything she sees?

Even as she thinks this, Magda imagines all the trouble she'd get in for what she's about to do. Back in the den, and watching her father's back as he stands at the window, she reaches for the ivory chess set, lifts the lid, and grabs a handful of pieces, relieved to see the red queen in her hand as she shoves them under the couch.

Her abdomen softens when her father returns to sit down on the couch, leafing through a magazine without pausing long enough to read anything. But when he gets up quickly, the sudden movement of his large, lean body is startling.

'To the garden, shall we, girls? Can't sit around inside with our thumbs up our bums on such a beautiful afternoon.' And he ushers them toward the veranda, where Mother is stretched out sleeping on a lounge chair. Seeing her, he hushes them theatrically and takes exaggerated mincing steps as though tiptoeing through high grass. 'This way!' he whispers, arcing his arm slowly in front of him.

Magda and Evie giggle quietly and burst into a run toward the garden, the same thought transmitted between them: *Mother is the troll beneath the bridge!* But Magda has to remind herself not to love him best of all when he's like this. Soon, he'll become someone else.

In the garden, Papa settles into his habit of fretting about the flowers. Though Georges does most of the work, Papa likes to poke around from time to time.

'What do you think, girls?' he asks, his voice booming and warm. 'Is the bougainvillea going to take over the whole damned wall? And isn't this hibiscus a bit vulgar, really? Something about the leaves, vaginal, and then that bloody great stamen poking out.' He'll tell Georges: cut back the bougainvillea and no more sexy hibiscus.

Magda and Evie tremble with suppressed laughter, still not wanting to draw too much attention to themselves, which they know instinctively is safest. Their father loves an audience and little clapping hands, but if they make demands he'll get confused, overwhelmed. He'll burn himself out faster.

'Think of all the work they did, you two,' he says, suddenly quite serious and looking them both in the eyes, a hand on each of their shoulders. 'Your people, when they came from America. Think of the work, to clear the land, go into the jungle. That's why I can't bear to see an overgrown garden, or let those trees there encroach on the yard. Someone worked so hard once to make this land habitable. Fruitful. Did you know they grew cotton and watermelon? Sugarcane, potatoes, tobacco. They brought ploughs. Brazilian farmers had only ever had hoes. Your ancestors were iron-fisted oppressors, perhaps, but they sure could turn a crop.'

He pulls a few rangy canes back from the wall, and it occurs to Magda: what will happen to the garden when they leave?

She suddenly notices Mother at the edge of the garden, squinting and shielding her eyes from the sun, her silhouette appearing tiny in front of the eucalyptus hedge.

'The girls should wash up,' she calls. 'It's nearly time for supper.' She gets up and goes back inside, not waiting for them to follow.

'Hear that?' says Papa, crouching down to Evie and Magda's ear level, conspiratorial and whispering again. '*Neah-lay* time for supper? Even their accents remain. Mosquitoes trapped in amber. Remarkable monsters.'

He tells them it's important they read everything they can so they don't end up with a 'myopic education.' He says that the American Empire will fall just as the Roman did, which is when her mother would usually accuse him of being a communist if she were within earshot, and he would wink at Magda, the two of them actually iconoclasts. (Whenever Magda repeats the things Papa teaches them, Mama says she's too young for such ideas—she finds Magda 'unnerving.') When Papa asks them now to name their favourite civilization, Magda chooses the Egyptians. Evie says the Babylonians, even though she can't defend her choice, and admits she just likes the sound of the name because it makes her think of gardens and flowers and rushing water.

'Hammurabi!' Papa cries. 'You're the reason we had to go to war!'

And Magda shouts, 'Bloody murder! Bloody murder!' and then they dance around Evie until she's about to cry.

Papa takes Evie's hand and says he's sorry but that she must learn: it won't do to be feeble like him. The world will be bloody to her. And her sock wants darning. He grabs her toe, then twirls her by the wrist and makes her laugh.

This time it's Odete who comes out, her face pleading. 'Dona Dora says please come in. Dinner.' English means it's serious. Papa begins to lead them in. But at the threshold of the door, he stops, tells Evie to go in, that he has something he has to tell Magda. Evie pauses, looks at them both, then moves reluctantly, still glancing backwards over her shoulder. Papa slides the glass door closed and crouches down so that his face is level with Magda's.

'These past few days, I have walked and walked. I've been to every place I ever took your sister. I even walked into the sea. But she wasn't there.'

This is how it happens sometimes: He stops being fun and free, and a heaviness settles over him. Her feelings get re-arranged. Magda begins to feel hot and slightly panicky, and turns to see Odete still hovering, now on the other side of the door. They can both feel the acute energy straining at the seams of his sweat-stained shirt, his creased slacks. Magda entreats with her eyes, but Odete just smooths her apron nervously against her thighs and turns away.

'And why would she be?' her father continues. 'Why would she stay in this crumbling, decadent place? She has set out, a dandelion seed on the ocean current. She is above the mountains now. Your sister is free. I can feel it.'

Until now, in spite of her determination to leave fairy tales behind, Magda has sometimes wondered if Luiza was taken by Yemenjá, the goddess of the sea. But she's grateful for a different story, a new story in which Luiza is in the sky rather than the sea, because in water, things rot. She wishes Papa could tell Mama this story too, but it would only make her angry. Poor Mama, always struggling to keep everything under control, to keep everyone around her spinning in their proper orbit. Magda can feel her mother fading, can feel everyone slipping away from her. Evie, and the maids too—Magda's losing them.

But *he* is here. When he wraps his arms around her, Magda goes rigid with disgust and leans away from him. But just like at the beach, her resistance quickly slackens, and she melts into his embrace. Papa takes her in his arms, a warm, yielding giant. Sparks come off him that don't yet burn.

# DORA

When Dora gets home from another morning at the beach, there is a rare silence, and all she wants is some sleep. To sleep and sleep and stop swimming after her dead daughter. She hasn't slept well in months, but today she remembers Hugo's discreet bottles with their different-coloured pills, and then she's in the bathroom, tipping two white ones into her hand before she can think better of it. *Luminal.* These are the ones that Susan Harris whispered about one night at the casino. She said they would set her right up—no one could survive all that Dora has without a little help. She takes them when she feels anxious—doesn't Dora have a few good reasons to be anxious? A small glass of sherry to wash down the pills and she'll sleep and sleep and sleep.

But even as Dora tries to lie still, she can't stop getting up to go to the window, looking for her girls. She can't quite remember where they've gone. Do they still exist when they're not together? She sees a bird with grass in its beak hop mechanically along the picnic table and fly off. Magpie! And her little pots of flowers— impatiens, violets—they're wilting from thirst. Laundry hangs on the line, shirts inflated by the breeze, bloodless bodies about to fly away. Luiza's white dresses have all begun to yellow. She climbs back into bed, feeling herself slowing inside, and picks up the bottle of pills. Two more. Sleep more. Hugo is beginning to make more sense. A dream hooks her cheek and pulls her through the mattress, a tidal pool dragging dust motes, cities, planets behind her. Her spine softens, a stew of dandelion stalks, the fragmented wings of honeybees. Jars containing preserved organs suspended in an amber fluid. Luiza.

But then there's shouting and when Dora opens her eyes, Maricota's face is a pale brown moon above her own.

'*Acorda, Dona Dora!*'

'I'm awake, I'm awake.'

'*As meninas chegaram em casa.* They shouldn't see you like this.'

Of course—the yelling is from the television, which the girls always turn up too loud.

Maricota takes the bottle of pills from Dora's hand. '*Nã não, isso de novo não, elas precisam da Senhora.* Not like Luiza. You can't leave them too.'

It takes her a moment before she realizes what her maid is thinking—she's always been overly dramatic. But Dora's too tired and groggy to explain that this was not a suicide attempt, just a brief flirtation with escape.

'*Não se preocupe, querida.* I'm fine. Just please go make me some coffee.'

'A man is here to see you.'

'I don't want to see anyone, Maricota. Please tell him to go away.'

'He says it's important. It's Mr. Carmichael.'


Maricota has made strong coffee, which Dora drinks silently as Carmichael sits across from her, gripping his hat. He appears bewildered in some way she can't identify, stooped in the shoulders, hair a bit too long. His boundaries seem blurred.

He was never good at small talk. This was one reason his adolescent crush on her had remained unrequited even though he was charming. When they were young, his quiet adoration had unnerved her. Later, when she was older and alone and it seemed like Hugo might be lost to her, for a time his devotion had seemed vital. She's felt ashamed ever since, but he saved her once.

Now she needs to move him along—the girls, the maids, they're all nearby. She used to fear he might do something like this, reach out in some awkward, dangerous way, but it's been almost fourteen years since their affair. He wasn't happy when she ended things, despite the blatant impracticality of it all. His wife, Alice, they could fool forever, but once Hugo came home from the hospital, there could be no more secrets. No complications. She told him she hadn't meant to hurt him, but it was all a mistake, a terrible mistake—all the worst clichés she could think of. He always saw through insincerity, and she hoped it might diminish her in his eyes, repel him. It was the rainy season when she ended things (of course it had to rain!), and she made him stand outside on the veranda with her behind the house as a torrent of water poured out the gutters that ran the length of the roof. This was where she always waited for him, watching as he came through the backyard after dark, once Luiza was asleep upstairs and the maids were in their bedrooms, in their separate annex of the house. She would leave the back gate unlocked, then wait for him outside so that he wouldn't have to knock, torqued with anxiety until he emerged from under the bougainvillea, occasionally cursing as he swept their hanging branches aside. Whatever feeling existed between them was deepened, she was sure, by the dim evening light that made him more lovely, and the hot, briny wind coming off the sea, the air charged with coming thunderstorms.

Those particular details, the manner in which they met— she sometimes wondered if the affair would have gone on so long if she didn't always encounter him in the dark, in a tangle of heady flowers and shrubs. She should have found them a seedy hotel room—it would have been over in a week. Instead it went on for nearly two months, during Hugo's second hospitalization. Sometimes they stayed downstairs all evening, just talking, laughing, dancing. On other nights, she led him to one of the guest rooms in the back of the house, far from the other bedrooms. In the early mornings, her beige underpants were a spoiled heap on the floor.

That last night, they had stood outside as just beyond them the rain fell off the veranda roof. He listened quietly, and as she spoke, she watched over his shoulder as the distant lightning jumped from peak to peak around the harbour.

'He has left you again and again,' he said at last, after she fell silent. 'One of these days, he won't come back.'

'He's sick. I promised—'

'You never promised to be alone.'

'I still love him.'

'You love me too. And I've loved you since we were children.'

'I don't. I'm so sorry. This has all been like a lovely little dream, but I need—'

He'd kissed her then the way he always did, with both hands placed on the sides of her face, which that night made her chest strangle. Finally, she pleaded with him, begged him not to be one more thing that shocked her awake in the night, that caused her knees to give as she descended the stairs. That had been the right approach after all. He'd always said he couldn't bear to see a woman cry. She can still picture him, slouching away under the scraping boughs, tearing off a handful of leaves as he went. Ever since, he has remained in their orbit just as he'd always been— work parties, cocktail parties, the casinos, even the occasional dinner at their house when it would have been awkward not to invite him. Still, he'd kept his promise never to speak of their affair, never to seek her out. Until today.

She places her coffee cup on the table carefully, as though trying not to startle a wounded animal, and says slowly, 'I think it would be best if—'

It all comes rushing out of him—the Dawseys' man, the one who looks after their gardens, the one who is simple?

'Yes,' Dora says cautiously. 'I know who you mean.'

'The Dawseys' man has been telling people that he saw a girl. He says he was at the beach that day, his day off, and he saw a girl.'

'Which day?'

'You *know* which day. The day she—'

'Yes.' Dora means to state it as a question—*Yes? Please go on*—but some part of her wants him to stop, wants to push him out of the house.

'He was at the far end of your beach, on the other side. He saw a beautiful girl, clothing drenched, hair drenched. He said she came out of the water like an angel with nothing but the dress she wore and a face like a secret, or something odd like that.'

'No.' Dora stands. She wants him out, needs him out before she runs into a corner and screams.

Carmichael stands too, moving closer to her. 'And she walked up the beach and away and never stopped once, never hesitated. He says she was like Sophia Loren in that film about the dolphin, soaking wet but even more beautiful.'

Dora tries to push him away, but Carmichael grabs her by the wrists, pulls her toward him, and speaks in a low, deliberate voice. 'I believe him. I wouldn't do this to you if I didn't believe him.'

'*He* said all that? Those were his words?' Her hands are still foolishly splayed, snared and useless in his.

'Yes.'

'Those are *ridiculous* things for a gardener to say.' She wrenches her hands away harder than she needs to and hits him in the jaw.

Rubbing his face and smiling gently, Carmichael answers, 'Even local halfwits go to the cinema sometimes.'

He was always able to make her laugh, and in spite of herself she aches for that now, for the simplicity of his company, the ease of it. For lightness where the swelling lump in her gut sits now.

'You don't believe me,' he says.

'She was at the beach, for Christ's sake. She wasn't wearing a dress. People like stories about beautiful dead girls. How dare you come into my house, use *this* of all things as an excuse to—'

'This fellow, the Dawseys' man,' he says, speaking over her, 'he's been telling the story to other maids, cooks, and anyone who will listen. Alice heard it from our weekend girl,' he says, finally drawing a breath.

'Why are you only telling me now?'

'I only just heard it myself. I couldn't stand it if you left without . . . '

Dora holds his gaze, but he breaks away and adjusts his shirt, which became untucked in their struggle.

'It just doesn't seem right somehow,' he says quietly. 'Her walking out into the water like that, vanishing without a trace. It seems impossible. And now all these rumours. What if she didn't drown?'

Hope claws inside her, because someone else has finally said it. Could it be true? Could Luiza still be alive? Would he lie so viciously just to be close to her again? He used to look at her sometimes, when they were alone, as though he were startled to find her in his presence, as though he couldn't quite trust in his own happiness. His forehead would crease with worry, then relax as a broad, warm smile spread across his face, altogether different from the brooding, slightly dissatisfied expression he wore at parties. It would sound old-fashioned if spoken out loud, but she believes he still desires her good opinion. No, he wouldn't lie. And the more he tells her, the less she hears, blood buzzing through her ears. *Don't hope.* These inchoate thoughts pulse through her mind, while another, louder word beats out the new rhythm of her heart. *Go. Go. Go.*

Her knees give way beneath her, just like those women in the movies. But when he tries to grab hold of her, she wraps her arms tightly around herself and falls to the floor in an awkward, half-seated heap. This man kneeling beside her, she thinks—so much like Hugo, but not Hugo. He's just articulated the thought she's struggled to push away for months. But that doesn't mean it's not true.

She waits until her breath has regulated, until the wave of nausea has passed, before she pushes herself back up to standing. Then, still ignoring Carmichael's outstretched hands, she grips her elbows and says, 'Take me to him.'

# EVIE

'*Parem de atormentar o gatinho!*'

'We're not tormenting him!' Evie shouts back to Odete. 'He likes it!'

All afternoon Evie and Magda have been dressing Luiza's cat in their old doll clothes: little white cotton bonnets and pinafores now coated in fur and pierced with claw-sized punctures. Evie likes to trap him under her shirt so that he's pinned against her as he tries to push his head out her sleeve, which doesn't hurt him. But Magda swings him up in the air fast, then pulls him in close to her body, terrifying him so that he'll grip her around the neck with his paws.

'Look, he's giving me a hug.'

'*Pra fora, anda!* Out!' Odete shoos them outside with a broom that tickles the backs of their legs.

*Poor cat. And poor Odete*, thinks Evie. They've driven even her crazy and she's never shouted at them a day in their lives. Evie knows the maids are terribly sad because they're leaving, and so is she. But it's more than sad—ever since Carnival she's wanted to cut up all her clothes and drag Cat's claws deeply across her thighs. A feeling she can't put into words. It seems like they've been getting ready to leave for years, talking about leaving, then packing to leave, but never actually going. The maids are always packing, the house becoming more and more bare. All the decorations, all the little knickknacks that she used to play with—the apple dolls with primitive clothes and the painting of dancing, silhouetted *baianas* with big bums and knotted headscarves—are gone. She pleaded with Maricota and Odete to leave a few things on the walls in the sitting room because it feels too strange to live in such an empty house, but they told her only what was absolutely needed could remain.

It's been almost a full year since she last saw Luiza, one week since the party, and there are still two more weeks before they leave. Evie measures everything this way, triangulating between when Luiza disappeared, when the last good thing happened, and how long until they sail away, spending three long weeks trapped on the ship. She tries to remember their old life, to imagine what is coming next, but 'now' is a horrible limbo, her heart always straining and itchy. She picks up a book to read to Cat but then puts it back down, worried that Magda will say it is childish (never mind that it was Magda's idea to dress up Cat). The truth is that Evie always feels pressed upon and hushed, but by no one or nothing she can see—by shifting currents in the air. By the faces of the dead at Carnival, secreted into this world. Now that they've seen her, they know where she is. So she goes along with Magda's games, hoping if she does, she won't feel quite so cold.

They are playing jacks on the front steps when a voice calls from the other side of the gate.

'Hey. You girls wouldn't want to entertain a lonely American girl lost in the jungle, would you?'

Brigitta, tall and wild, her hair gathered loosely on top of her head with a paintbrush. Dark red, almost auburn like Luiza's. Not pretty exactly, but almost better than pretty, with a long, lightly freckled nose and a broad, slightly upturned mouth; a permanent little smirk. Brigitta, who told Evie at the party that she's part Jewish and listens to jazz. Brigitta, pale and unhurried as she crosses the street toward their now-opened gate. (*I am not afraid!*) Brigitta, who saved her.

'Why look—your hero,' says Magda, scanning Brigitta up and down.

Evie rushes to speak before her sister can drive Brigitta, with all her gold dust, away. 'Thank you! For the other night. That guy was such a *bastard*.' The word feels thick in her mouth—she's never said it before. Magda's mouth drops open a little, but she says nothing.

Brigitta curtsies. 'Always happy to help a maiden in distress.'

'Let's *do* something,' Magda says, throwing her head back and fake-snoring. Evie goes pink. If Papa were here, he'd tell her to forgive her sister. *She has a Protestant heart.*

But Brigitta claps her hands together as though encouraging a small child. 'Yes, yes!' she cries. 'Show me what the *people* do here. I'm so eager to spend time with real Brazilians. My aunt and uncle are so *sedated*.'

Magda sneers. 'We're American too, you know. We have passports. We're the same as Mr. and Mrs. Cavanagh.'

But Brigitta just drapes an arm over Magda's shoulders and trills. How delighted she is to see them again! They decide they'll do sprints in the clearing at the centre of their property. Evie tries to protest that it will be getting dark soon, but the older girls ignore her.

'We have to run so we don't get fat,' says Brigitta, smiling back at her. By the time they find a spot they agree on, it's almost dusk. 'You be the marker, lovely girl,' Brigitta says to Evie. 'You go back to the edge of the trees and hold your arms out and whoever touches you first wins.'

Evie jogs to the tree line, then stands facing the other girls, the skin on the back of her arms tightening wherever it's brushed by some pale purple flowers that hang low on the shrub.

'We can still see you—go back farther!'

'No, you can't!' Her voice is like a little kid's, high and cracked. 'I can't see you.'

'Well, *we* can see *you*. Go back!'

She steps farther back until she trips over some tree roots, her ankles scraped and burning. 'Can you see me now?' No answer, so she inches slightly to the side, trying to make it look like she's going back. 'Can you see me now?'

Something brushes her calf. She wipes frantically at her legs, tries to pull off her shoes and loses her balance, stumbling backwards over a fallen branch. If they were in Canada right now, she thinks, lying out on bare ground, she would probably die from exposure. But it's too warm here so maybe something poisonous will come along instead and inject her, turn her insides to soup, and then not even bother to eat her. Or that rustling behind her will leap: a giant cat, disoriented and starving. Blows against the nape of her neck, skin in loose red ribbons. They'll find her here on the ground, her entrails unwound and spread out, reflected stars twinkling in her pooling blood. Magda's eyes will widen, her mouth will twist with regret. Brigitta will weep gently. Evie pulls her knees up to her chest to conserve the last of her body heat. It's coming now—what she's been waiting for all these months, just beyond unlit corners, just out of view. A kind of hoped-for emptiness. The end of her.

'You idiot, oh my god, we were looking for you, *puta*!'

She's pulled up by her wrist, wrenched and sore, and dragged along faster than she can walk. Magda pulling. Magda dragging. Magda ahead, always ahead.

They stop in the middle of the clearing and pull Evie's arms out to her sides, barking over and over, 'Straight. Straighter!' Even Brigitta is rough now, commanding.

'No, you know what? It's too dark here,' Brigitta says gravely. 'Let's go closer to the light.'

Evie lets herself be pulled from the clearing to the stone patio beyond the veranda, then be rearranged into a scarecrow. Then Brigitta and Magda both jog backwards about a hundred feet. Evie's arms sag a little, but she straightens up and shoots them out as far as she can when she sees them both sprinting toward her. Nobody even said *Go*. Magda's hand collides with hers first and sets her spinning. After Magda does this eight more times, Brigitta finally gives up. It's her smoker's lungs, she says, panting comically, head bent forward, tongue hanging out, her hands on her thighs. But Magda keeps running, keeps coming at her, a flame against Evie's hand. She rips up the dark.

With her hand numb and tingling, Evie speaks for the first time since they found her in the bushes. 'I want a turn.'

Magda spits. 'A turn to what?'

'To race. You've had about a hundred turns. It's my turn.'

Brigitta starts her little girl hand-clapping, foot-hopping again, then high-kicks like a cheerleader in an American movie. 'Sister against sister. I love it! I can rally for this. I can be your marker-thingummy. Just don't slap me silly when you come at me.'

As Magda jogs backwards beside her to the starting point, Evie watches only her new friend, and wonders if it could be her. Brigitta. Could she fill in all those empty spaces Luiza left behind? The places Magda's too sharp for. Maybe then, Evie could stop peering into corners, hoping to find someone who fits. Who stays.

Brigitta shouts 'Go,' and Evie explodes toward her, running so fast she worries one of her legs might break beneath her like a racehorse's. She doesn't dare look back, but she knows she's a fraction of a second ahead of Magda, and before her is Brigitta, her arms held out at her sides, one eye theatrically squeezed shut, the other staring right at Evie. A smile, urging her on. Even Magda wants this bright flare that is Brigitta, her beauty ruddy and slantwise. They are about to touch her outstretched arms when Evie drives her shoulder into Magda's body and leaves her crumpled at Brigitta's feet. As she keeps running past her house and through the gate they left unlocked, she knows she has saved herself from disappearing for one more day.

'Stop! Stop!' Magda screams behind her. 'You can't be outside the gates after dark!'

Under the dim pools of the streetlights, Evie runs faster now. Past every house on her street and for two more blocks until her lungs close up inside her, and she collapses on a stranger's lawn. When a car pulls up across the street, she's so busy tucking herself behind a bush that she almost misses seeing her mother climb out and Mr. Carmichael drive away.

# DORA

They sat parked in front of the Dawseys' house for twenty minutes before Carmichael finally coaxed Dora out of the car. She hadn't asked him any further questions about what he told her earlier and he hadn't said anything more. It seemed so strange to sit beside him, this man whom she had loved, and feel nothing. Scraped out. Eventually, she supposed, she would fill back up with some normal feeling, something like anger, or fear. But for now she was a casing of skin animated by invisible wire.

As Dora and Carmichael walked up to the house, Jack and Betty Dawsey stood on the porch waving awkwardly, trying to sustain tense smiles. Betty took Dora's hand and gave her a kiss on the cheek, though they'd only ever seen each other occasionally.

'I am so sorry again about your girl. What an awful thing.'

Dora remembered then that the Dawseys had been at the beach that day with their son, that they had spoken to her afterwards, told her what they saw and what their boy remembered after Luiza helped him bury his father in sand. (Nothing.) She didn't ask about him, feeling stifled by the smallness of her world, her public tragedy. More consolations were muttered, damp highball glasses pressed into hands, assurances given of what a lovely surprise it all was! Of course the Dawseys wouldn't ask the reason for the visit—it would be inelegant to ask questions of a poor, grieving mother—but their faces remained pinched with confusion.

'You have a man,' Carmichael said finally, uncharacteristically halting. 'A man who looks after your gardens?'

'Antonio?' Betty said. 'Yes. He's out back. Has he done something? It's not his fault, you know. He's not—'

'No, we'd just like to speak with him.'

As they waited in the Dawseys' sitting room, Carmichael sat on the couch while Dora remained standing beside it. It felt too intimate somehow to sit next to him, different than being in the car. Still, she was grateful for him. The anger, she knew, would eventually come, but for the first time since he'd arrived in her home earlier that day, she allowed herself to look at him, to really take him in. The grey at his temples. The deeper creases across his forehead. But she liked that. Young men seemed half formed to her now, too eager and cheerful and certain. Like Hugo, Carmichael seemed weary, more turned-down at the mouth and eyes—disappointed, she supposed—but still strong. Capable. Or maybe that was just what she needed to believe, because it meant that she, too, could still be beautiful. The grace of living through this.

The grown man Carmichael had summoned for her, while she was drained of both grace and words, limped in wearing only shorts, his face smudged with dirt. The Dawseys made their gardener take off his shoes, so he appeared almost naked amid the fine furnishings, standing with his hands clasped primly in front of him. Once Dora realized he was imitating her stance, she sat next to Carmichael, hoping it might make Antonio more comfortable. Without warning, she retched a little as her leg brushed Carmichael's, and when everyone turned toward her she said in a strangled voice that it was the drink, which was worse. Maybe it was for the best that

Antonio was simple—he didn't know enough to feel humili-
ated. Finally, Dora asked if she and Carmichael could speak
with him privately. The Dawseys kindly left the room, though
she could feel them hovering nearby. Everyone already knew
her husband was mad—so what if they thought she was too?

'You've been telling people you saw a girl, Antonio?' Dora
asked in Portuguese, speaking up at last. 'At the beach, last
March. A girl coming out of the water. What did she look like?'

'*Bela*. Like you, but beautiful. Younger. Same face. A white
bathing suit.'

'Where did the girl go?'

'She walked and walked, all down the beach, until she was
a spot.'

'Did she say anything?'

'*Nada*. She didn't see me. She was staring and not talking,
like a ghost. Or an angel. She was beautiful as an angel. I
wanted to follow her, but I'm stuck in the sand. Like stone. She
made me a stone.'

Dora held up the photograph of Luiza.

'*Sim!*' Antonio said, shifting excitedly in his seat. '*Sim*.
That girl.'

'You're sure you really saw this girl?' Dora pushed the photograph toward his face. 'Maybe it was a dream? Maybe you
wanted to see an angel.'

'Yes, it was a dream. I want that angel to come back.'

'But was she real? Was she a real girl, or a dream?'

'She was an angel, like the angel in my dreams.'

And he went around in circles like this until finally
Carmichael thanked everyone for their time and ushered her
out of the house.


Dora presses her fingers to her temples, Antonio's words
repeating like a litany in her mind. A dream, an angel, a ghost.

Dora's no longer sure herself that Luiza was ever anything more than these. After she disappeared, Dora sometimes had to interlace her fingers tightly until they ached to stop herself from going up to strangers on the street, in the shops. She wanted to grab them, shake them, beg them to tell her where Luiza had gone. Not her body, but her. If her body was dead, where was *she*? And why didn't they also need to know? How could they continue walking about, doing and saying everyday things? Didn't they know what had happened? Didn't they see the hole that had opened beneath them? But that is how grief ejects you from normal life—it tears a black hole in the world where most people still see sky. Her hands lock together now as they did then, praying to nothing.

'The way he described her,' Dora said afterwards in the car. 'He was just repeating what he saw in me.'

'But he was describing her, also. Why would he want to lie to you?'

'For attention, for money. I don't know. He might say anything.'

'He might not.'

'And if what he says is true, what will I do?' she asked. 'How will I find her? How does one go about chasing after a ghost?'

'Systematically,' Carmichael answered. 'We'll drive to the fishing villages that line the far side of the beach.' He was right—each village had only a few dozen houses, so that meant about two hundred people to speak to at most. 'You'll bring photographs,' he continued, 'and surely these people talk about everything they see, every scrap of news or gossip. A strange girl in a bathing suit—she can't have gone unnoticed for long.'

Again, she was grateful. Like Hugo, he was offering her a story, a better one than her real life could give. But they shouldn't be doing this together.

'I don't need your help,' she said finally, officiously. Yet he stood there waiting, saying nothing until at last she collapsed into him, her forehead sweating in the familiar crook of his neck.

Now inside her own house, Dora is met with silence for the second time that day. She sits on the couch, her hands upturned and loosely cupped in her lap. The maids made good progress packing today—there are a few larger items of furniture and some things hanging on the wall in the sitting room, but otherwise very little remains. Dora wonders if they might still be somewhere in this part of the house, cleaning. As she has so many times in the past several years, she waits for a few minutes, hoping someone will appear and tell her what to do. Then she goes into Hugo's office, which the maids have now been told to leave for last, and begins to look for more pictures of her daughter.

# LUIZA

## JUNE 1961

Moths, silverfish, mice. The house in Petrópolis was full of them, and even from her bedroom Luiza could hear Dora hectoring the poor local woman she hired to clean, demanding she deal with the mess *imediatamente!* And yes, she *had* sent word they were coming that weekend, she certainly had. Despite her mother's anxiety, Luiza was relieved to be there. Petrópolis was her favourite place, and now she felt calmer than she had in the past three months since they returned from Florida. She sat on her bed and lit a cigarette, balancing a teacup on her unbent knees for an ashtray, feeling brazen. If her mother smelled it, Luiza would put the blame back on her parents—they both smoked, after all. But her mother wouldn't say anything. Like her, Dora had also been seized lately by a kind of doomsday recklessness, drinking cocktails from coffee mugs in the middle of the day.

The door swung open suddenly and Luiza struggled to put out the cigarette and shove the ashtray under the bed as Evie burst in, slamming the door behind her and throwing herself onto the bed.

'Don't let her in. She's going to kill me!' Evie cried, burrowing under the blankets.

Luiza could hear the wood floor creaking outside her door as Magda shifted her weight, debating whether or not to hunt Evie all the way into their older sister's bedroom.

'Stop being a bully, Magda!' Luiza called out to the closed door. 'This room is Switzerland.'

The shadows of Magda's feet retreated, the thin crack of light beneath the door returning unbroken.

Evie, still red-faced, pulled the blanket off her head and looked up at Luiza. 'I won't tell that you were smoking, I promise.'

'I wasn't. Anyway, what have I told you about letting her ride roughshod over you like that? You can't let her.'

'I know, but she—'

'And remember Frog and Toad from the story. What are you supposed to say when she tries?'

'I am not afraid.'

'Louder!'

'I am not afraid!'

'Loudest!'

And together they shouted as loud as they could, 'I am not afraid!'

Evie laughed, then asked, 'Can I stay in here?'

'Fine, but you have to be quiet because I'm busy thinking very important thoughts. If you ask me nicely, you can come over here and I'll braid your hair. But still no talking, okay?'

Evie slid down the bed happily until she was sitting in front of Luiza, then leaned her head back. She remained quiet as Luiza combed through her hair with her fingers, because like her, lately Evie, too, seemed to covet time alone. Ever since the family had come home, everything had felt freighted and hopeless, pressing down on them but never discussed. The doctors later explained that the lithium study suggested the drug had a 'low therapeutic threshold,' which meant even a slight overdose could cause serious side effects: liver failure, heart failure, depression, paranoia. But for many subjects the drug was tremendously effective, unlike anything they'd ever seen before.

'That is, of course, the purpose of the study,' the doctors assured them in grave, pompous tones. 'This event could be very helpful in determining the correct dosage for Mr. Maurer. It might also be the case that your husband is one of those patients who simply won't tolerate the drug well.' But there would be no adjusting of dosages, no more experimentation. Her father had suffered a minor heart attack, and her mother withdrew him from the study immediately. She decided: they were going home. Across two rivers they had travelled, and a continent. A humid, sawgrass realm. All for a disaster. Maybe, her mother kept saying, some other treatment would come along.

Luiza exhaled loudly as she twisted an elastic around Evie's first braid. The silver bullet had failed, and she kept catching herself gnawing ferociously at her nails, the ends of her hair, ashamed of having allowed herself to imagine that her father might be 'cured'; that he would yield, become pliable, and a more manageable portion of himself, for their sakes. He was still recovering, but frail—*still a shade, still half himself*— and unable to have their usual long conversations, though he didn't appear angry with her, as she'd feared. Maybe she was even avoiding him, unable to bear his disappointment, and he was too kind to say anything. Hadn't he always known what she was thinking?

But they were here now for the June festival and she was determined to enjoy it. She had the feeling lately that she had to snatch up pleasure while she still could, before she aged and contracted like her mother and found herself forever making lists, planning what to get next from the shops. Without a true, beating heart. Dora hadn't wanted to come, but Luiza had pleaded and charmed, knowing that, since Florida, they both felt somehow beholden to each other. Her mother, too, lost something on that trip, and Luiza convinced her this was just what they all needed.

'It's *festa junina*!' she'd cried, seizing her mother by the arms and pulling her into a mock-*quadrilha,* like the country people danced at the festival. June meant it was chilly in Petrópolis, much cooler than in Rio, where there would be more spectacular celebrations, but the city parties had become too commercial and she wanted to twirl around smoky bonfires and watch the statues of saints paraded through the town square, hoisted on the shoulders of towns-people. 'Let us not fester at home and be grey, let us go into this winter filled with light!'

Dora had actually laughed then, and let herself be led like a rag doll around the kitchen, while the girls, excited now, also begged to go. Her father, thinner, hair newly shot through with bands of grey, applauded weakly from the couch where he convalesced wrapped in his old white robe. She wanted to kneel at his feet, to plead, 'Please don't leave us.' But her mother was smiling for once.

Just as Evie smiled now, running her hands over her neat, new braids, before she started at a voice outside.

'Butchie, Butchie!'

Luiza went to her window and saw Magda frantically call-ing after a neighbour's puppy that kept darting out of sight, into the long grass at the edge of their property. Her parents were outside too—Dora commanding the local gardener, Hugo dozing in a chaise longue positioned for him on the stone patio, still under doctor's orders to rest as much as possible. Evie took an old Nancy Drew book off the shelf at the foot of the bed and began to read, so Luiza reached for another book Carmichael had given her on her bedside table. This one was by Elizabeth Bishop, who, he told her, was American but had lived just a few miles from Petrópolis, and still had a house less than five hours away in Ouro Preto. She had lived for years there with an architect, a woman Carmichael knew of through work, because he'd long admired her designs.

After reading beside her sister for half an hour, Luiza finally stretched and rose from the bed. 'I have to get up and move around for a bit, pet. I'll come back in a few minutes.' She took her book of poems and was relieved when Evie didn't follow.

Outside, she made her way through the garden, reading as she walked, then sat beneath the jabuticaba tree, running one hand over its dense, dark berries. Berries that, rather than dangling prettily from stems, sprouted directly from the bark, the branches like tumours. Had Bishop written anything about these trees, the sweet jam they made? Her poems were exquisite, Luiza thought, and it seemed impossible that they could be about this very place. *Her* place. Someone else had seen it through her eyes: the lenten trees during the electrical storms and the hail that followed, *wax-white, dead-eye pearls* among the petals. *Wet, stuck, purple.* She repeated these phrases to herself again and again.

And because Carmichael had given her all these books, these beautiful, illuminating, even—yes—*life-changing* books, she felt sometimes like she could tell him anything. How, for instance, Florida had failed, and now she understood that this was her life, and it was all right, it really was. She would find a way to be content with her family, to be useful. She would be better.

'Failed how?' he had asked suddenly. But then he looked around nervously, rubbing the back of his neck. 'At any rate, we shouldn't be seen—'

Their conversations always ended this way, cut short by his interruptions, his eyes rapidly scanning the room for his wife, for Dora. She wanted to have the last word this time. 'I really don't think I should say too much,' she broke in airily. 'It would be a betrayal of his privacy. Besides, we don't have time—'

Just then, Lucy Baird hooked her arm through Carmichael's and pulled him onto the dance floor. 'You two are so dull and serious all the time. Enough talking!'

They had to be hurried, cautious—a few minutes at one of the weekly cocktail parties in Villa Confederação or at the edge of the dance floor in the Copacabana's Golden Room while everyone spun giddily just a few feet away. These days, she always went along with friends for the nights out, even though her father, and sometimes even her mother, stayed home. At the casinos, she could at least talk to Carmichael, however briefly. It felt lonely now, sitting by herself against the back garden wall.

And secretly she liked that this man who barely knew her was curious about her life. Concerned.

'What if we met somewhere else sometime?' she whispered quickly one evening. 'Just so we can talk more easily. It always feels so rushed like this.' She suggested Botafogo Beach, late afternoon the following day. A long tram ride away to an unfashionable neighbourhood, somewhere their friends and families never went. Their secret.

As they'd walked along the beach, he asked her again: What would she do now?

'Now I have endless things I can do,' she insisted, for this time she had thought it through, planned her answer. 'This is such a large, beautiful country, and I've barely experienced any of it.' Now that they were back in Brazil, there were so many places she wanted to see. The Meeting of the Waters, where the Rio Solimões and Rio Negro converge, cream-coloured waters mixed with black, eddying together like galaxies before being subsumed by the milky current of the Amazon; the two rivers were such different temperatures that fish became temporarily stunned at the confluence, easy prey for pink dolphins. Pink dolphins! The swarming Amazon Basin, with its otters and giant water lilies, carnivorous plants and tiny hummingbirds.

And the Flooded Forest most of all, where the waters of the Amazon rose until they spilled into the forest, fifty feet high, and piranhas swam among the treetops, fish ate nuts and spread seeds as red-faced monkeys screamed from wet branches. No dry land for miles as people teetered in huts on stilts, their chickens and pigs reared on rafts. An upside-down world. 'Just because I stay at home with my parents doesn't mean I can't go anywhere or do anything.'

'But why must you stay at home, with them?'

She told him they needed her help, and she wanted to be a better, less selfish person. And she could still find beauty, despite everything—this beautiful place! 'Maybe without having to worry about going to school or finding a job, I could write. I could still do so much, be more than The Pretty One.' She told him about a game she and Dora used to play when she was little. They would cut pictures from her mother's catalogues, each choosing one outfit, one best friend, one husband and three children, then glue them onto paper. Fragments of her perfect, future life, curled and soggy with paste, all over her bedroom wall. 'It's always been clear, what's expected of me. But the truth is, I don't think I've ever wanted that life. I still don't.' She tried to smile vaguely, like Carmichael often did, but now he was frowning.

'It's easy sometimes, when you're young, to get caught up in making all kinds of plans. You don't need to decide everything now.'

'I don't have to decide anything, as it turns out. It's a relief, in a way. But I could still help people. I could tell their stories.'

'How do stories help people?'

'You ought to know, the Great Reader.'

But the truth was, she had no answer.

Her paternal grandmother was born in England and used to tell Luiza wonderful stories about growing up on the English moors amid their dense fogs. *When I was a girl in England*, she liked to say, *we spent our holidays in the South and ate whelks on the pier.* As a child, Luiza imagined whelks as beautifully intricate, the shells you pressed to your ear to hear the sea roaring back. But then Hugo said they looked like clapped-out genitals. Eventually, Luiza found out her grandmother grew up in Acton, a pleasant but dull little suburb outside London. Perhaps it was in their genes: stories and lies. Like her absurd catalogue-life.

Carmichael become distracted then as he sometimes did when they were together. Did he want nothing more from her? To be nothing other than a family friend, a concerned uncle figure dispensing books and dry, chaste kisses when they parted?

Yet, now, with these exquisite poems in her lap, the stink of nicotine on her fingers, she decided again that, yes, there must be more to their relationship. She turned the pages: *tall, uncertain palms . . . your immodest demands for a different world, and a better life.* Inscribed in the margin: *made me think of you.*

But by that night, whatever feeling Luiza had of being lifted away and grafted to something other, something *more,* had left her. She was tied again to her family, who didn't want to go to the village to see the square dances—women in red wigs and freckles, men in straw hats and checked shirts—or applaud the country people dressed up as Country People. Her father felt too weak so instead they all bundled up in sweaters and wool blankets on the stone patio and watched the neighbours and the servants light lanterns, Bishop's *illegal fire balloons.* With each one that rose tenuously into the sky, lines from the book came back to her: *paper chambers flush and fill with light . . . flare and falter, wobble and toss.* And just as they headed for the mountainside, she saw them burst in her mind—phosphenes— *splattered like an egg of fire against the cliff.* Other, smarter people had already written whole swaths of her life, more beautifully than she ever could. What was left for her?

# DORA

They agreed that Carmichael would pick up Dora early the next morning, before Hugo was awake. As she was leaving, the girls were sitting at the kitchen table bickering about something when she heard Brigitta's name.

'I don't want you two playing with that girl, understand?' she said, crouching between them. 'She's got a reputation.'

'But—' began Evie.

'No buts. Just concentrate on getting your bedroom organized. I have errands to run, but when I get back, I'm going to check and see how far you've gotten, understand?' When she kissed the tops of their heads, they barely looked up. They're getting used to her absences.

As she walked down the street to where Carmichael was waiting, she reminded herself: it's for them, too, that she's doing this. They all need to know. Even if she finds nothing, she must do this so that she can return herself fully to them.

'There are only a few roads wide enough to accommodate cars,' Carmichael says now, parking at the outskirts of the fishing village, before making sure all the windows are rolled up. 'It will be easier to continue on foot.'

Dora sits for a moment after the engine has cut, taking in

a few deep breaths, but it's not until she sees Carmichael coming around to the passenger-side door that she stirs and tries to push the door open before he can do it for her. She must not give him opportunities for chivalry, which he has always loved displaying for her. She must not let him help too much. But when she's unable to get out of the car, he suggests a walk on the beach before they begin and her resistance dissolves. They've barely spoken since he picked her up, except to establish the logistics of the search. He must sense her agitation, that she's not ready. It makes her anxious, his close attention after all this time.

From the beach, the little village is pretty, its wooden shacks set into the lush land that slopes up from the harbour, surrounded by large green hills. Some of the stores and larger houses are painted bright colours, and a small, whitewashed colonial chapel rises above the other buildings. Small fishing boats scatter the harbour, and among them bob covered canoes, their frames like ribs fastened to tattered canopies. More canoes line the shore, raised up on wooden platforms, and nets lie spread out in the sun to dry. Across the harbour are more hills, more shacks clustered among them. Perfect places to disappear.

When Dora's breathing steadies again, they head away from the beach, along the dirt pathways, past a wandering pig and chickens scratching at nothing. They arrive at the first house at the farthest end of the beach, a ramshackle structure made from old bricks and a corrugated tin roof. A one-eyed cat skirts the shadows from the bougainvillea that climbs the walls. How lovely, that someone so poor has still taken the time to plant something beautiful. But the animal—mouldering, with patches of fur gone from its head and back—should be exterminated. Such thoughts drift in like the fishy stink off the water. She feels Carmichael place his hand on her back as they approach the door, but she shakes it off.

When the door opens, she holds up the photo, her hand trembling. 'I'm looking for my daughter,' she says in Portuguese, her voice too loud.

A deeply creased, elderly woman invites them in. The woman doesn't smile, and when she speaks Dora sees that most of her front teeth are gone. At this end of the beach, everybody is missing something.

She brings them each a cup of hot liquid that tastes like ash, grasses collecting at its bottom. She examines Luiza's photo for a long time, rubbing her chin. Finally, she says, '*Sim, sim*. I've seen the girl. She passed by here some time ago. A troubled soul.'

'My god,' gasps Dora. 'Was she wet? Her hair, was it wet?'

'Yes, from head to toe.'

Dora begins to tremble and leans into Carmichael, standing behind her, to steady herself, and he props her up easily, gently, without making too much contact.

'I'll get you some more tea,' the woman says and moves toward the small kitchen.

Then, seemingly from nowhere, a boy appears. Seven or eight—he looks malnourished, jaundiced; he may be older than his bony frame suggests.

'She knows nothing,' he says quietly.

Carmichael speaks now. 'I beg your pardon?'

'The old woman. She's lying to you.'

'Your grandmother?' asks Dora.

'She's not my grandmother. She keeps me for money. My mother is a whore and the old lady takes me out begging because the sight of me touches people.'

'You're a rude little boy,' says Carmichael. 'Off you go.'

'She never saw your daughter. She's saying what you want her to say so that you'll give her money.'

Carmichael coughs but recovers quickly and Dora realizes that the boy thinks he is speaking to Luiza's father.

'Off you go, boy,' says Carmichael again, waving his hand dismissively. 'Stop disrespecting your elders.'

But the boy doesn't move. He just stares at Dora—is that sadness or contempt? Indifference, she decides, seeing her own emptiness reflected back. She is swamped by a familiar shame, and wishes she could be the type of person who was immediately moved by these people. The type of person Luiza was. Suddenly, her clay cup hits the floor at her feet and her legs are spattered with black flecks, dregs of the revolting tea.

The old woman comes shuffling out and cries, 'It's broken! You'll have to pay me for that!'

The boy retreats calmly, cool and slow-moving. A lizard retreating beneath his rock.

Dora begins to fumble inside her purse for her pocketbook, but Carmichael quickly thrusts twenty *cruzeiros* into the crone's bent hand and pushes Dora out the door.


In the days that follow, Dora and Carmichael visit almost every house in the village. Most people are kind, some are drunk, a few won't speak to them, but no one says they have seen Luiza. Dora tries not to peer into the darkened shacks, their framed-up windows without glass, women sweeping dust out the doorways. How pointless it seems—these places could never be clean. On the third day of their search, she hears singing, wailing, and there are fumes from a slow-moving car somewhere up ahead. Someone tells them that a child has died in the night.

'These people, their pain,' she says to Carmichael. 'It never ends.' He nods slowly and begins to lift his arm to her shoulder, but she wraps her arms around herself, shivering despite the heat. 'But maybe that's why they don't feel it like we do,' she says. 'Maybe they've grown used to it.'

Carmichael studies her, cocking his head slightly to the side in the same way that Luiza sometimes did, as though Dora is some sort of inscrutable curiosity. But he, at least, is smiling affectionately as he does so.

'You know,' she says to him as they head toward the outskirts of the village, 'as a teenager I went to the same movie seven times—I don't even remember which one—so that I could watch the newsreel footage of the *Hindenburg* disaster.'

Seven times she watched it collapse into flames, the fabric eerily sloughing away. The first few times she wept, which was something she hadn't done since childhood.

'The year before it burned, the airship came here regularly—do you remember? It shuttled between Friedrichshafen, New Jersey, and Rio. The whole city was asleep that first time it landed, but I begged my chauffeur to take me. And when it came we laughed and laughed and were sure no one would believe us—just how enormous it was, and yet how still it seemed as it glided down.'

But later, in the dark theatre, Dora watched the ship's tail sinking lower and lower despite repeatedly dropping water ballast, its mooring lines tumbling down, the news announcer intoning gravely: *The* Hindenburg *appeared a conquering giant in the sky, but she proved a puny plaything in the mighty grip of fate. An airship destroyed in less than half a minute.* Flames swallowed the ship's nose, white against the black sky, spreading into a fire that quickly consumed the thin skin of fabric enveloping the frame's aluminium ribs. *It almost seemed as if fate had set the stage for this horrible tragedy. A graceful craft sailing serenely to her doom.* Sparks shot into the air and several people jumped, slamming into the ground. *An inferno which became a flaming tomb, a twisted mass of girders.* And even when she closed her eyes against the screen, the afterimage of the stark flaming cloth collapsing in on itself remained, her vision tattooed with white fire.

'I kept wondering, what if that had happened to me? What would I have done? I told myself it was instructive. By taking on other people's tragedies, consuming them, studying every imaginable way to die, I could inoculate myself. Maybe then I'd know what not to do. But there was no way out for those people. They chose to jump and die a second later on the ground rather than burn. For that one second they had hope.'

Hope. The only thing crueller being hopelessness. In hope lived *what if what if what if?* In hope she looks for Luiza because the search feeds possibility. Or might finally blot it out. Those people had jumped and deferred their hopelessness by a single second and at the time she told herself they would have wanted her to watch, to bear witness, to wish alongside them for that instant despite knowing how it would end. In that instant she imagined each time that someone would run up with a trampoline as though in a cartoon. *What if what if what if?* Would they really have wanted her to watch? She recalls how anyone who took too eager an interest in her own tragedy was revolting to her. But at the time, she could not stop watching—it was too great a catastrophe. It could not be true. Maybe the next time she watched, it would end differently, with the cartoon trampolines.

Carmichael remains silent, as though not wanting to startle her out of confiding in him.

Soon they arrive at the last cluster of houses, at the very edge of the village. These are even shabbier than the rest, with bits of mismatched wood for clapboards, tin siding, and a tarpaper roof. How can these people live just a short drive away from the luxury within her own gates? All her wealth and beautiful things.

A girl not much older than Luiza answers the door. When Dora shows her the photograph, she shakes her head. '*Não sei.* I work most days and don't get home until dark. I never see anything. But my sister just sits by the window. You can ask her. She doesn't talk, but she understands.'

The sister is monstrous. From the doorway, she appeared merely sickly and plain, but as they approach, her features warp. The far side of her head is bulbous and one eye is entirely clouded. It appears to lie unmoving in her skull while the other eye focuses sharply on Dora, who concentrates on the space between them and extends her hand. It doesn't shake. Not even beasts frighten her now. She and Carmichael sit on two nearby chairs with blistered paint.

'Have you seen this girl?'

The girl's good eye rotates slowly down in its socket, to Luiza's photo, and then back toward them.

'Outside your window, perhaps? Did you see her go by outside your window?'

She gazes past them for several seconds, then turns her gaze back to the window. Dora pulls a nearby chair toward the girl and sits so that their faces are level. She holds the photo closer to the girl's face.

Suddenly, the girl shoots her arms out straight, pointing out the window. She leans forward, following the trajectory of her finger. It points directly at another house. Dora stands and moves closer to the window, closer to the girl.

'Is that where you saw her go? Past that house? Over that hill behind?'

The sister sighs. 'She does that all the time. It doesn't mean anything.'

'But you said she understands things.'

The sister looks tired. 'She does. That doesn't mean she can help you.'

As they get up to go, Dora stares into the mute's milky eye for several seconds then reaches out to shake her hand again. She feels hers snatched up, then thrust out the window toward the exact same house as before. Something is alive inside this girl, Dora is sure—something she means to say, fighting to break out. When Dora turns back toward the sister, her face is blank.

'She can't help the tremors, ever since she was little.'

The giant-headed girl crumples against the window frame and Dora must use her other hand to unlace each finger. Once free, she allows Carmichael to guide her, trembling, toward the door.

They learn nothing more at the last few houses, each visit tiring Dora further until Carmichael has to support her as he leads her to the road where they parked.

Accordion music drifts up from somewhere closer to the beach. Someone is singing. Finally, Dora can't help asking Carmichael what she's been wondering all along, what she knows will make her sound like the bemusing artifact Luiza always considered her.

'Do you think, if she washed up here, she might have seen something to keep her going? Do you really think she kept going?'

'I do.'

'Why? Why would you think that? Everyone else thinks she's dead.'

'I think you're getting very tired, and we should come back tomorrow. There were those houses where no one was home. We'll come back to those.'

'But we've found nothing! This is a fantasy.'

'Neither of us believes she drowned, that she just gave up. We can't stop looking, but we need a break.'

'How can you be so sure? Maybe she really is gone and we're just chasing a ghost.'

Carmichael pauses, runs his hands through his hair and sighs, long and low. 'She came to me for help, Isadora. I didn't tell you because I knew—'

'What *kind* of help?' Dora says, backing away from him.

'Just advice! She was confused, overwhelmed. She knew how long I've known you and Hugo, and she was trying to understand things after Florida.'

'What did she say about Florida?'

'Nothing specific. Just that it was very hard. That things didn't go as planned. And she was afraid of moving to Canada. But she wouldn't say why.'

Because Canada meant the possibility of another failed experiment, Dora thinks. Only farther this time, and more permanent. She lets out a tight little laugh. 'No, Florida didn't go as planned. That is what she would say. That's what I told her to say.'

'But why? What happened?'

'You have no right to ask me that!' Flushed and sweating, she strides ahead.

'Dora, stop. Talk to me.'

She can feel him right behind her, nearly beside her, his voice almost in her ear. He is perfectly capable of catching up, but he doesn't. He knows to stay just out of sight.

'I thought he could be well again. But there's no cure, and we just hoped for too much. *I* expected too much.'

'And now he's making you leave your home, everything you've ever known, even though it's hopeless.'

'He's not making me do anything. He doesn't even want to leave. It was my decision. We have no choice.'

'You *do* have a choice. Do what you should have done years ago. Stay with me.'

Dora whirls around, her cheeks burning, and slaps him hard across the face. He touches his hand to his reddening skin but says nothing. 'What happened to her, after she came here?' she asks. She hates the pleading tone in her voice. 'Where did she go?'

'I don't know. She really didn't confide in me that much. Sometimes I think she just wanted to get away from Villa Confederação for a little while.'

'She was barely speaking to me that last year. Not since we got back from Florida.'

'Girls that age always torture their mothers. It's the natural order. Otherwise you'd never let them go.'

'She must have said something to you.'

'She sometimes talked about being a writer. And of being useful in some way.'

'No, no—' says Dora, batting her hand. 'I mean yes, she *said* that but she never actually did any writing. That was her problem. She was always dreaming. She may as well have wanted to be a unicorn. I kept encouraging her to pick a field, to look into schools. In Canada, she could study anything. I just wanted her to focus. To choose *something*.'

There is tension in his face, muscles clenching. He kicks at a loose stone. 'I think you're right. I don't think she knew what she wanted.'

'But did she tell you anything? Tell me what she said.' Dora's voice is low, strangled, threatening violence and tears. She pulls him to her now, gathering the open collar of his shirt in her fists. She tries to resist actually touching his body, out of disgust, out of fear. Because she might not let go. '*Tell* me.'

He exhales, grinding the fingers of his left hand into his forehead. 'She said that when she told you she didn't want to go to Florida, you insisted she had nothing else in her life. No better options. She said you made her feel as though she had no life of her own.'

Dora is silent now, staring into the mud, startled that Luiza actually listened to anything she said. But her words are barbed and layered now, in ways she never intended.

'I did this to her,' she says. 'I can't—I can't tell him. He'd never forgive me.'

'*He* did this,' Carmichael says, wrapping his hands over hers, still gripping his collar, though almost absentmindedly. 'He keeps doing this to all of you.'

But she's barely listening to him anymore. She was the one who failed Luiza, and in countless ways.

Somewhere in her sinews, her slackening ligaments, she registers his arms encircling her, pulling her up, closer. A sparrow lands in a puddle a few yards from her feet. Even here, there are sparrows. Maybe Luiza washed ashore here and saw this very one. Dora remembers that most of the people they've met in the village have been genuinely kind. Surely nothing bad would have happened to her here. Maybe she simply kept going. But Dora cannot hold off the fear, the terrible image of her daughter, vulnerable and without money, nearly naked, and these poor, hungry people eating her alive.

'Tomorrow,' she says, straightening. 'Tomorrow you'll take me. All the places you went with her.'

As she steps back, she feels his arms loosen, and it's a relief, to be released from the glut of his need, his always wanting more.

'Yes,' he repeats. 'Tomorrow.'

# EVIE

vie could tell that Magda was in one of her hungry, black moods. Luiza used to warn her to stay away from Magda when she was bored. *She'll eat you up.* But even when she saw those hunting eyes fixed on her, she couldn't stay away; when Magda is bored, Evie is all she has to play with. So now they are locked together in their toy house, with its scaled-down table and chairs and shrunken tea set, each holding a tiny teacup containing half a bottle's worth of aspirin so they can see who can swallow the most before throwing up. Everything is diminutive and insufficient. Even the pills are child-sized, pink and powdery, although Evie can already feel how they'll drag down her throat because they have no water and Magda pushed the key under the door so they can't get out. In here, Evie can't run or jump—she can barely move around. This is the first time they've played alone together since they ran heats with Brigitta yesterday, and all Evie can think about is how to get back to her new friend, where else they might go. But where else is there?

Soon enough, they'll be together all the time, with endless things to do. She had told Brigitta that once they arrived in Canada, she and Magda would be going to Aubrey Ladies College. 'It's the sister academy to the private boarding school where my father went to high school on a scholarship,' she said. She'd overheard her parents discussing it, found the colour pamphlet in their bedside drawer.

Then Brigitta said, 'I'll go too! My parents will be happy to get rid of me.'

It struck Evie that maybe her parents felt the same way: after all, they were sending her and Magda even farther away.

When they pledged their plans to go to Aubrey Ladies College together, Evie saw their faces alone grafted onto all the photos from the school's pamphlets: she and Brigitta at the Commencement Day garden party wearing white fluttery dresses, pinning corsages to each other's collars; Brigitta riding horseback and Evie laughing on skis, holding a rope attached to her saddle, trailing behind. She and Brigitta at graduation, wearing their caps and gowns, connected to all the other girls by that long, flowered garland but separate in their hearts. In those frozen, future moments, there were tear-streaked faces, oaths of devotion.

But first Evie must survive Magda. After she forces down her first aspirin (Evie always has to go first), she reminds Magda about the book Luiza used to read to them about a doll named Gertrude, who is beaten by her owner and runs away.

'Then she bought a little girl named Annie,' says Evie, 'at a store that sells children to toys who lead them about on leashes. Sometimes the toys have parties and eat heaps of ice cream and candy and give nothing to the children.' One night, Gertrude gives Annie a bath, but then she decides she's hungry and eats up all her dinner before going to bed. In the night, she wakes up quite suddenly and realizes she's left her child alone in the bath, and when she finds her, Annie is blue, her teeth chattering; she never called out or complained, not once. Gertrude sews her new clothes and takes her to a party. 'In the end, they agree children shouldn't belong to dolls, or dolls to children. But only after Annie is nearly eaten by a lion.'

'She never read us a book like that,' says Magda, her mouth still a flat line, even after four aspirin. 'We never even had that book.'

Evie doesn't bother arguing with her, even though she knows they did and Luiza used to tell her if she wasn't careful, she'd end up as Magda's child. Evie hadn't understood what Luiza meant. She'd always thought of herself as Luiza's child, or Maricota's child, or Odete's, because they were more like real mothers. They read her books and played games with her and never lost their patience or told her to go find something to do. Maybe she could be Brigitta's child now? Brigitta, who seems to know about distant worlds and who, as Magda ran into the twilight, whispered in Evie's ear that *she* was the pretty one. Brigitta, who she wishes she could run to right now. Because being Magda's child means she'll have to be nearly devoured before getting any mothering. But even when Magda hurt her, Evie always felt like they were almost one person. So Evie studies her sister now and tests her, silently asking, *Magda, why haven't you said anything? Why aren't we telling anyone?* And when there is no answer—just Magda pretending to pour tea from the tiny teapot into their teacups—Evie knows her sister can't hear her; they are separate people. Still, it seems impossible that she could know something Magda doesn't, that such a separation could exist between them.

Evie keeps hoping Magda will ask her—demand to know—because the pressure of holding what she knows inside her is too much. Luiza's face, white and puckered and awful, the flowers slipping over her eye, her fingers gripping Evie's shoulders, impossibly strong. Even stronger than Magda. But still Magda says nothing, asks nothing, doesn't even look up. *Tell.* Evie wants to, but it's all muddy now, shameful and red in a way she can't express. Luiza didn't want anyone to know, and Magda will not tolerate uncertainty.

Who will rescue her? With Mama gone every morning before anyone wakes up and Papa getting more and more wound up, and the maids preoccupied, she is trapped here in this toy house, pinned by Magda and her pitiless attention, while a whole world waits outside. A world with sky and sea and Brigitta and other, nameless mysteries. So Evie, too, sets her face, folds up into the smallest possible version of herself, and thinks about how to escape.

Finally, Magda speaks. 'Remember that time in Florida when that trashy girl called you a jungle monkey? And I saved you?'

'Not really.'

But that's a lie. When they had first arrived in Florida, children circled them on the sidewalk outside their rented house, asking all kinds of questions. The boy from next door was always chewing gum like an animal, and there was a girl with dirty feet who had a game of jacks but wouldn't let them play with her because, she said, they were *forun*. There was a queer girl in the neighbourhood who twitched and couldn't talk, yipping out the same sharp sound—*Nya! nya!*—as she lurched over warped legs. One day she limped by and the dirty girl threw rocks wrapped in candy wrappers at her. The nya-nya girl jerked around on her crooked spindles trying to pick them up and it was the worst thing Evie had ever seen, her face turning red as she wrapped her arms around herself, and that's when the dirty girl called her a stupid-jungle-monkey-crybaby. Magda went inside and came back out with Dora's jar of white rice. She removed her sandals and white socks, filled one sock with rice, and tied a knot in it. She began to swing the rice sock up over her head to build the necessary momentum, and the little boy went running, still smacking away on his gum, knowing what came next. The rice-sock hit the dirty girl in the head and knocked her out. The nya-nya girl was sitting now, still opening candy wrappers, while Evie just stood there crying.

'But you were safe,' says Magda.

That's one thing that has always been clear between her and her sister: Magda is allowed to torment Evie, but no one else could. That was Evie's thin bit of reward. And she has always tolerated Magda's occasional brutality because there was a sense of justice to it. No longer. Their world has gotten too small. Without Luiza, there is no one left to help draw Magda away. And now, new terrors: captivity.

'I have to pee,' Evie says, and Magda hands her the little teapot, white with pink flowers, her lower jaw protruding.

'First tell me that you remember.'

The windows—she remembers the windows. Evie jumps up and forces a handle with the heel of her shoe, and it opens just enough. Squeezing out of the little house, she feels gigantic, chalky aspirin rising up in her throat.

Magda is shouting that they're not done and grabbing at the edge of her skirt, her trailing leg, but Evie kicks at her with all her strength and manages to wriggle out the window. She sprints and only looks back once she's at the back patio doors. Magda's a giant now too, halfway out the window, Godzilla beating on the roof of their toy house.

Evie keeps running, heading toward the trees at the back of their property. But then she stops, pivots, and turns back. Magda isn't the only person who will protect her. She hurries through the narrow passageway alongside the house, then through the front yard toward the gate. Toward Brigitta.

# HUGO

n the morning, Hugo wakes early, but Dora has already left the house. Quietly, he goes into the office, locks the door behind him, and again forces open the drawer to retrieve the letter he first found almost two weeks ago. He heard her arrive home late last night, but she didn't come into his room like she usually did to say goodnight. They've been in separate bedrooms for several years now—it makes things easier, they tell themselves, when he has trouble sleeping, which is often—but he can usually count on a 'goodnight' at least, and a chat about the day, however brief. He shouldn't be surprised by her gradual pulling away—he'd all but dared her to do it.

Once, a few years ago, when she'd turned to him in the night, wrapped her arm around him from behind, and reached for his cock, he could only cry quietly. With all the medication, he was motionless, insensate, but he couldn't bring himself to tell her the truth. Instead, he told her to go ahead and find someone else if she needed to, never believing she really would. So many moments, he sees now, when he should have confessed to her, should have at least touched her, he absolved himself. Once his medication was sorted out, once his treatment was successful, he told himself, they would come back together. Once he was better. But then the doctors said there was no *better*, there was only *symptom management*. And so he pretended that if she did turn to someone else for a time, he could live with that—maybe it would distract her from his failings. But love? Did she love this man the way he said in the letter he loved her? He hadn't truly believed that possible. And he *is* surprised, he is. In all the years since he's been sick and the girls were young and a thousand tiny interstices widened between them, even during the periods of separation, he still imagined the other side. A future point when he would recover himself and she would again sit astride him, her skin blotchy and vivid, whispering *fuck fuck fuck*, a word she never otherwise said—

Suddenly, the girls come bounding through the doors of his office, waving sheets of paper in his face. Permission slips. A parent needs to sign. They want to attend a month-long day camp at the YWCA in Rio with the new girl—the one staying across the way with the Cavanaghs. She's related somehow. Can they? Can they? Today is the last day to register. They have to drop off the forms *today*.

'But you'll be leaving soon, my pets.' A slip. Be more careful. Say *we*. 'Do you want to start and then have to stop early when we leave?'

They stare up at him; equal parts silent challenge and indulgence. This is what they've been hearing for months: we're leaving soon. And yet here they stay, in Eden-cum-limbo. Now he must shine, be a giant to them, conceal all aftershocks.

'Fine, fine.' He whisks the papers from the girls' hands and holds them over his head as though taunting a puppy. 'I'll sign. But first you need to do something for me. Tell me, where is Mummy?'

'I don't know,' says Magda.

Evie echoes, 'We don't know.'

Magda is sullen, crossing her arms over her chest. He can tell she knows her mother is up to something, but she doesn't know what. Her lack of power in this moment disturbs her. Evie, on the other hand—she knows something more. See how she glances away, shifts her weight from foot to foot, fists the pockets of her dress. She doesn't want to betray her mother or set him spinning, but look how the edges of her mouth have begun to tremble.

'I know how much you want to go to this camp with your friend,' he says, fixing his gaze on Evie. 'And I *will* take you. Once you tell me.'

'I saw her get dropped off the other night,' she says quietly before Magda kicks her in the ankle. 'Ow!'

Hugo heaves her up into his arms like he did when she was little, rubs her ankle vigorously, and strides away from Magda, who follows but can't keep up. 'Yes, pet?'

'She always does that!'

'I know, love. I won't let her do it again.'

'It's not fair—she never gets punished.'

'How quickly you become little girls again. Magda'—Hugo swivels and faces her, Evie still in his arms—'go to your room.'

Magda's face is compressed with worry now, her anger gone. 'But she doesn't know what she's talking about. She sees these little things and makes up whole stories in her head. Like when you went for a walk the other day. She thought you were leaving us. Going to Canada without us.'

'To your ROOM!' The voice that comes out is deep, serrated, and frightens even him. Magda flies up the stairs. Evie starts to cry and buries her face in her arms, a jumble of bony corners against his chest. He traces her spine with his hand. 'I'm sorry. I lost my temper. I'm sorry. You can go to the camp. You don't need to say.'

'She was with Mr. Carmichael,' she says through her tears. 'He dropped her off down the street.'

Carmichael. That oily pretender. They'd been friends for a time, when they worked together at BrazCan, and he had helped

Hugo, covered for him at work. But over the years, Hugo has caught him staring hungrily at Dora now and then, and guessed that there were ulterior motives: an infatuation. Everyone other than his poor, sweet wife knows Carmichael is a skirt-chaser. But still, Hugo never thought much of it. He never saw Dora look back—she didn't even seem to notice. But maybe the absence of looking *was* the look, something masquerading as nothing. Maybe she is far smarter than him after all.

This, at least, is one last thing he can do for his family: rid them of this interloper. If he cannot defend his girls, he fears they will be forever beset by loss. Like their sister, Evie and Magda came into the world traumatically, and he's feared for them ever since.

As Evie continues to cry into his shoulder, all he can think about now is Dora, pregnant: she always became plump and he loved her that way. She was embarrassed by how she ate constantly, but it was endearing to him. The only time she allowed herself to lose control. He would come into the dining room in the morning, find her with crumbs on her dress, her fingers shining with butter or bacon fat, hurriedly wiped from the pan with her fingers. She was often uncomfortable, with aching hips and sciatica, but she would still place his hand on her stomach before bed, pressing his palm in harder than he ever would have. 'Hello, baby,' they would say, over and over. It moved far more than he had expected, ever-present yet alien.

The birth took too long. Three other fathers came and went, and occasionally a nurse appeared to say that things were not progressing well, the baby would not 'descend.' (Through his anxiety: the image of a tiny baby at the top of some stairs, a crowd of people in hospital whites at the bottom trying to coax it down.) In the end, Dora was cut open, which she said afterwards had been a relief—the drugs let her sleep. It seemed unfathomable—a human inside a human, the expectation that you could exit any other way but through a bloody, gaping wound.

The preposterous physics of it all! Two days later, the incision was still oozing. An anxious nurse called for the surgeon. Evisceration. Bowels protruding from muscle just beneath the skin. They said she would have died had they not caught it quickly. Died? A hundred years ago maybe, but not now. Surely not now. He'd never been so afraid as when they wheeled her back into the operating room. But the rupture was tidily repaired and once she was out of recovery, she held their sleeping baby for a full half-hour. Even through the subsequent infection, she only cried when she thought he wasn't looking. She kept saying it was all worth it. A few months after Luiza was born, he had to leave them both to go to war.

Later, two more Caesarean sections, too close together. More infections, scar tissue. When Evie came out, she was faintly blue. A week in an incubator. The doctor said no more; a uterus can only withstand so much. But that news came as no tragedy. Each time, he was more frightened than Dora—what if she left him behind?

He always believed they could get *back* to that first, unspoiled time when they loved easily. But has that time passed? No, he won't lose them both.

'Can we go to the camp now?' asks Evie while Magda stomps around upstairs.

'Yes, love. We'll get your sister, then let us rejoice in our Christian souls and jubilate before God! Magda?' Of course, she won't come now when he calls. He's betrayed their recent and burgeoning bond. He puts Evie down gently. 'Go get your sister. Tell her we're going to hand in the slips and tomorrow we will go on a great adventure!'


In the car on the way to the YWCA, Hugo puts the top down, and the girls let their hair tangle in the wind and seem to forget the ugliness just past. They sit back and listen to their father, who is fully charged, rambling, brimming with wind-muffled talk. Telling them how brave they are. Did they know? Did they have any idea how tough their ancestors were? How Dora comes from a line of flint-hearted rebels who would rather desert their homeland than live diminished. They'd travelled by ship, by makeshift steamboats, and, when the river became too narrow, by canoes manned by Indians with a paddle at each end. Imagine how terrifying, in the middle of the Amazon—*dark as Egypt!* And then the storms came up and lightning brightened the sky and that was worse, because now they could see the expanse of the river and nothing but jungle and water all around them. Great cracks of thunder, too, and rain fell harder than they'd ever felt. They spent nights on a *fazenda* and slept on heaps of rice. It rained steadily for days, but in most places there wasn't even room for a tent, so some of the women tied their petticoats from one sapling to another, too sleepy to fear the *onças*. These same women, only a week earlier, had blushed when some locals had proudly shown the Americans their hand-embroidered nightgowns. Now they slept beneath their own underwear, unafraid even of jaguars.

'These are your people,' he tells them. 'These are the women from whence your mother came. You are warriors. You could choke a black jungle cat with your panties in the night.'

And he thinks to himself how much better Dora's life should have been.

# DORA

The sun beats down on Dora's head from an unclouded sky. The air is humid but there is a breeze off the ocean. *Much* hotter than last week, agree the two women in front of the basilica when Dora and Carmichael squeeze past them, her thighs rubbing together uncomfortably. She turns her head toward her shoulder and sniffs quickly, afraid she might smell. *Even hotter than this time last year!* Dora feels a brief pulse of fear that they will tell her she can't go in, she doesn't belong. She has always felt this way in churches, as though she's looking in from a distance and they hold something just at the perimeter of her understanding. She had her transient religious education—two years at a Catholic school because it was considered the best in the country. Then, on weekends home, her hopeful, unformed beliefs were spoiled by her parents' contempt.

But here, now, there is stillness when they enter the basilica, cool and dark amid the quiet and blue-hued light of sunrays filtering through Mary's etched robes in the window. While Carmichael puts some money in a collection box, Dora sinks into a pew, drifting between comfort and unease. Or maybe just an old aching for faith. She hasn't been in a church for many years, and although she knows she should be repulsed by the gaudy cedar carvings that adorn the chancel, the twist of the ornate staircase toward the organist's box, the plaster woman kneeling before Christ and a little lamb, its front hoof holding up a crucifix—they soon become narcotic. Her breathing begins to slow despite a nagging reproach: she doesn't believe and so she shouldn't be here. Her peace is stolen from better people; those who utter devotions, pray for their families. She can hear her mother, reserved and rational, dismissing them as hypocritical, indoctrinated, naive; but perhaps, unlike Dora, they are also content. She closes her eyes. Maybe they wouldn't mind if she borrowed this silence for just a moment.

Eventually, she can feel Carmichael waiting patiently beside her in the dark. 'Why did you bring her here?' she asks finally, opening her eyes.

'She said she missed it. Missed God.'

'*Missed* it?' Dora forgets herself, then drops her voice back down to a whisper. 'She never had it! We were never religious.'

'I said that at the time, but she just got angry.' Then he rests his elbows on his knees and lowers his head, staring at the floor. 'No, that's not true. The truth is that I laughed and said that your family had always been agnostic, even her grandparents, so what was there to miss?'

She remembers now, the subtle intrusions, the insight he sometimes presumed to have. 'And what did she say?'

'She asked how I could speak with such authority about your family, why I thought I knew you all so well.'

'Oh, god—do you think she suspected?'

'I told her I had known you for most of my life and I'd worked with Hugo a long time, that he confided in me. It's true, you know—he did. And she did as well. You all seem to forget when it's convenient how much you've made use of me over the years.' As if suddenly aware of his plaintive, bitter tone, Carmichael tries to straighten up, but he is still leaning to one side, aggressively massaging his temples. 'It cost me, you know. I put in weeks of overtime at work, making sure his projects were finished, nothing left undone. I protected him, and you.'

Dora keeps her eyes fixed straight ahead, over the pews. 'I never asked you to.'

'You didn't need to.'

She looks at him now. 'Then why do you keep inserting yourself into our lives, if it's such a burden?'

'Because you're all such beautiful people.' His voice is acid. 'And because I keep being invited.'

Dora feels herself flush. 'There must have been something more?'

'She was curious about religion in general. She was always talking about your help. One of your maids had given her a book of psalms, and she was learning them by heart. I think she just needed an anchor. I mean, look at Hugo, barking mad. Then you're off to Florida and back, then it's on to Canada. I tried giving her books, but she needed more. She said she was tired of stories, she wanted to understand *real* people, find out the truth. Her life was a mess. She wanted a map for how to live a better life.'

'The truth!' Dora scoffs. 'That means nothing. It's just a different set of stories.'

'There was more,' Carmichael says now, and Dora can hear his throat constricting, that he's having to force out the words. The books of myths he gave her, she read them all. She said she realized that her father's life was a tragedy, and that like those fallen heroes, his best feature—his brilliant mind, his expansiveness, his visions—would also destroy him. She needed a different story. Someone else to worship. To love God, she said, would be a perfect, unrequited love of the highest ideal, the object of which could never leave or hurt or disappoint you. Incorruptible. As humans, she said, we want too much, feel too much. Instead of trying to have everything, one could choose nothing, and be content with that.

Dora is quiet for a long time. Is it just a fatigued sadness she detects in his voice? Or admiration?

'She was right,' she says at last. 'You say too much. You think you know us. You don't.'

Carmichael falls to his knees then, a supplicant before her. He lays his head in her lap and she permits it, her hand hesitating in the air above his head. When she lets it fall, she feels the familiar warmth of his neck, the soft hollows at the base of his skull. Her joints unlock. How long has it been since she's touched anyone but the girls? An unexpected relief, which is something like grace.

But Carmichael, this church—comfort poached in the dark, she knows, cannot be preserved. In a few minutes, they will go back out into the world, to the midday sun, almost white, and a damp, hot wind. And the hush and feint of this moment will be unprotected.

— III —

# MAGDA

Their father wakes them at dawn.

'But it's so early,' Magda protests, only able to make out his shape in the dim light, his face a grey smudge. 'Why do we have to get up now?'

'Just please do as you're told,' Papa answers. Something pleading in his voice quiets her, and she gets herself dressed and then helps Evie—still sitting on the bed yawning, eyes half closed—into her clothes. He brings them a breakfast of hot dogs left over from the night before and pink lemonade from the bottle, then he makes them wait in silence, hunched on their beds in the gloom. After they hear the front door open and close, he ushers them into the hallway, down the stairs, then leaves them in the entranceway while he gets the car. Outside, they hurry down the walkway and into the Silver Cloud, where they wait a few minutes, giving Mama a chance to walk down the street and get into the car that is waiting for her at the end of the block. Papa unlocks the gate and pulls out slowly, hanging back, her mother just a tiny, moving spot turning the corner to the next block, and suddenly Magda knows what they're about to do.

'Please, Papa—no!' For all her barbs, she can't bear the thought of real fighting, real anger. Thumping Evie from time to time is necessary, but following her own mother feels like trespassing into the muddy, confusing world of adult secrets. 'Maybe she's just running errands for the party tonight.'

But he ignores her, and for a moment she admires how carefully he follows, how patient he is and how far back he can stay while still keeping Mr. Carmichael's car in sight. She knows it must be agony for him to move so slowly and deliberately, especially now.

She tries again: 'Why don't you just ask her where she's going? Why do we have to follow her?'

'Your mother is a skilled dissembler,' he answers. 'She's doing this in secret for a reason. She won't cop to it just because I ask. We need proof.'

'But why do *we* have to come? It's just going to make her angry.'

'I want to come!' Evie chimes in, as if they're going to the zoo. Magda pinches her arm, but Evie pinches back—she'll do anything to hold on to this newfound attention from their father.

'It's the element of surprise,' Papa says, 'and the element of adorable-yet-sad little girls. A jealous husband can't pack the same punch as disappointed children. Now hush.'

They follow Carmichael's car to downtown Rio, which is thrumming, even this early in the morning, and finally to Avenida Atlantica, where they park several car lengths behind and crouch down while her mother and Carmichael cross the street to the beach.

'The beach?' cries Papa. 'We can't very well start striding along the beach. They'll see us for sure.'

'Can't you just go up to her right now?' pleads Magda, aware that she's sounding more like Evie than herself. 'Isn't walking on the beach together bad enough? I'll pretend to cry if you want.'

'No, this could all be explained away. He's a friend, after all. She could say they're just talking.'

'But they are just talking.'

'Take off your dresses. Are you wearing those funny little bras your mother gave you? We'll take off our clothes and if they look back from far away it will seem like we're wearing bathing suits, like we're just regular people at the beach.'

'No!' Magda and Evie say in unison, more frightened than outraged, though there is also the cut of betrayal—their mother has discussed their breasts with their father.

'They're getting too far ahead. Do it NOW.' The same bass, guttural voice as yesterday, the voice that shocks them all. The girls, pink with shame, pull off their dresses and hand everything to their father, who carries them in a jumbled ball. They then follow him, stripped to his briefs, darting through the swaying palm trees and across the two-lane avenue.

For almost an hour they trail far behind Mama and Carmichael, the only fully dressed people on the beach, one red dot and one grey up ahead. At first Magda and Evie huddle together to try to cover themselves, until they realize it's true— no one seems to notice they're in their underclothes and not swimsuits. They begin to relax a little and Evie even pauses to pick up a few seashells, filling the shoes they've been carrying. At one point Magda is tempted to call out, alert her mother that she's being watched, save them all from this humiliation. But then she notes how Mama and Mr. Carmichael sway slightly together, a little closer than they should be, then apart. Her voice smothers in her throat.

Eventually, Papa pauses, holds them back. 'They're turning. They're coming back this way.'

He wraps his long arms around the girls and leads them away from the shoreline, up toward the clumps of bathers under beach umbrellas. But then he spots the *lambe-lambe*, a travelling photographer with an old-fashioned, upright camera that looks like an accordion. The man is out on the sand taking a picture of a young couple while a woman is positioned several yards back beside a large box on three legs sheltered by a large umbrella. Twine hangs from its spokes, covered in clothespins that hold the drying photographs. Papa squeezes Magda and Evie into the umbrella's shade, and while he begins to ask all kinds of questions about the development process as a way of stalling, Magda examines a photo of a woman standing alone in a bikini, her arms folded behind her head, one leg bent—a real cheesecake pose. How had she had the nerve to stand in front of that man like that for so long, Magda wonders, wishing she could be half as brave and beautiful. Now Papa is peering over the girls' heads at Mama and Carmichael, who pass by unaware. After a few minutes, he hands the woman some money and leads Magda and Evie tentatively back toward the water's edge to have their picture taken, even though they won't be back to collect it. Even in his frenzied state, Magda admires how he can't bring himself to take up the woman's time without paying her something.

When Papa deems it safe to follow Mama and Mr. Carmichael again, he weaves them back through the crowd of sunbathers, splayed and idle. Magda hears a low whistle and feels the painful snap of elastic against her bum. She looks back and sees a man, potbellied and leathery, laughing and eyeing her underwear. Her fists close tightly as her jaw contracts, and inside her ears a high-pitched tone sings up from her teeth. Her father could destroy this old man, but she only glares silently; in the state he's in, he probably would. Or, too consumed by his strange hunt, he might not do anything, which would be worse.

Eventually, Carmichael leads Mama toward a café—a small empty patio outside with stairs leading to a gloomy room below. With his hand on her back, he gently guides her down the steps. Inside, on such a beautiful day? Not her mother. More secrets. They hang back awkwardly on the pavement, pulling on their clothes, pouring shells and sand from shoes.

Evie shoves a few of her best shells into their father's pants pocket. Now what? Papa finds a window around the side of the building, a tiny, grimy little aperture that allows a partial view of the bar and the open floor in front of it. They wait several minutes, but the pair must be sitting at the edge of the room, somewhere in its margins. Eventually Carmichael crosses the floor, disappears, then returns to its centre, directly in view of the peepers at the window. He waits a moment, faint strains of music begin, and then she goes to him: wife, mother, nucleus, who these past few days has been quietly splitting off. *The centre cannot hold.* Papa used to say that sometimes when he was getting depressed, and Magda never knew what it meant before. Now, she watches as her mother dances with this man—stiffly, but still she dances.

Magda puts her arm around Evie, her tired old gesture of protection, but it's too late to hide from any of this. Mama has some other life, doesn't need them. Papa is unwinding again, can't care for them. Maricota and Odete are at home working like slaves, not coming for them. Magda feels an unfastening inside, the presentiment of more shifting. Breakage. What now? Now that they've been made to see their parents as dishonest, lonely, uncertain; now that they understand. How can they ever go back to who they were before?

# DORA

Dora and Carmichael walked along the beach in Copacabana for nearly an hour, waiting for the café to open. The light on the water was gentle at that time of the morning, and she gazed out at the same mountains she had seen all her life, trying to imprint them into her mind. She wonders what she will forget, if she's stamping her memory with the correct images. But it's not as if she will never come back! This interjection heckles her, suppressing her melancholy mountains. There isn't time today for such restless longing.

She had to leave her house early again, before anyone else was awake, or she wouldn't have had the nerve to go through with it, to keep lying to them. She likely won't see Hugo until just before they leave for the casino tonight, but thinking of it all—him, the goodbye party—makes her vibrate with anxiety. She doesn't know how she will get from *here*, a clandestine meeting on the beach, to *there*, a jumpy, disorienting party she'll have to pretend to enjoy. Still, as she and Carmichael trailed together along the sand, she kept these thoughts to herself.

Now, inside the café that Carmichael has told her is the last place he went to with Luiza, she can hear the strain in her voice as she says, 'This seems like a strange place to bring her.'

'It was her idea,' he answers. Too quickly?

'And she didn't say anything to you? Nothing out of the ordinary?'

'She was . . . a little unsettled. I think she was anxious about the party. Something about wishing she could be around real people.'

'We weren't real enough, I suppose, our crowd.'

'All too real, I'd say.'

Frustration, unexpected but familiar, rises up in her chest, the same exasperation she often felt with Luiza's heightened emotions, the way she would latch on to some notion, or a sad story she'd heard or read, then be overwrought for days. She remembers now how Luiza kept taking to her bedroom during those days when they were meant to be packing. Her 'bad spells' and headaches. It sometimes felt to Dora like everyone else let themselves fall apart around her because they knew she never would. But it isn't fair, and she mustn't get upset. It must spread ugly forces out into the atmosphere somehow, to feel anything but love and sadness for her lost daughter, as if anger could repel Luiza farther away. She wouldn't have run away over a bad memory.

'You know how she could be,' he continues. 'Girls at that age get so worked up.' His voice drops, quieter. 'And she didn't know about Hugo being fired, which I let slip. I'm sorry for that.'

Dora bristles at his hushed, intimate authority—his tone almost paternal—and because Hugo didn't want any of the girls to know he'd lost his job. But she still needs him. She's not sure she could keep up this search alone.

'And I suppose she seemed—' he struggles for the right word, running his fingers through his slick hair in that way that always reminded her of her husband. 'Well, she seemed a bit lost. A bit unsure of what to do with herself when you got to Canada.'

'She never said anything to me,' says Dora, almost inaudibly.

'She did say once she felt she couldn't discuss the move with you, how she felt confined. You would just say how lucky she was. She could have anything.'

Dora's skin prickles. There is a faint hint of triumph in his voice, she thinks, at having again exposed a breach between her and Luiza. 'We had no choice but to move. She knew that.'

'Of course she did. And I did try to tell her that she could do any number of things, what with women being so much more ahead up there. But she just said she couldn't *see* it. All Hugo ever told her of Canada was how cold it was—the place, the people. He had made her afraid of the very idea of it.'

'There must have been something more.'

'I don't even remember what else we talked about. We made conversation. We danced a little.'

'Where did you dance? Show me how. Do everything again.'

Carmichael sighs and gazes at her, a defeated half-smile stretching out the corners of his mouth. He goes over to the barman to request a song, and then stands in the middle of the room, arms stiff at his sides, waiting for Dora to come to him. Only when she raises her own arms do his slacken a little, mirroring her movements. The space between them closes. As she lets herself embrace him awkwardly, she looks away, over his shoulder, and feels him exhale, his body relaxing, maybe because he no longer has to meet her gaze.

Yesterday, in the basilica, Dora had been lulled, faintly seduced into feeling for him as she had during their affair. Back then, she'd thought at first that he was a bit like Hugo; he could be charming, often quoting from books. But he soon began to seem muted and indistinct by comparison, and she suspected those little memorized passages had been acquired just for her, entreaties uttered hopefully. And then sometimes that look that belied his smooth charm, an expression of such sudden, unexpected gratitude, as though he wondered how he had come to be there with her. To her, he was an attenuated, uncomplicated version of Hugo—like getting a vaccine instead of contracting the virus; you might be flushed and shaky for a few days, but it wouldn't last long. She never wanted to be unkind, never told him what he really was to her, even when it became clear that he himself had lost control of his own guise. He loved her.

She tries to push this thought away, and also the unwelcome realization that he was, for her, some kind of surrogate for Hugo; an anodyne version who wouldn't suddenly transform or cloud over. All those nights when Hugo was in the hospital, and Carmichael would come, she felt benignly comforted, amused. He always said the same thing, played the same song, kissed her the same way. But now she remembers how he reminded her of the worst parts of herself too, of how she briefly considered staying with him, abandoning her sick husband, and the uncertainty of their future together. And even though she knew he loved her, she never doubted that he would eventually disappoint her, and her disillusionment would embitter them both. Hugo, for all his terrifying, complex mutability, could not pretend; he was the rawest, least concealed person she'd ever known. She knows—has always known—that both she and Carmichael are too easy with deceit to ever be together. They could never trust each other. She doesn't trust him now.

So now this song, with its big band trumpets and clarinets, and this man she almost loved holding her in his arms—they feel newly threatening. Where has she heard it before?

'You played her this song?'

'Yes.'

'But this was . . .' Dora begins, remembering all the nights they danced on the veranda, out of view from anyone in the house. He had to go inside to choose the record—a small show of masculinity that she'd thought little of at the time. Every time he came over, he chose this same song: that old jazz hit from when they were young, 'Avalon.'

'But we used to dance to this song.'

He drops his eyes to the floor. 'Yes.'

'You lied to me. You weren't trying to help her. There was something more between you, wasn't there?'

He tries to hold her closer now, suddenly dropping his voice, which falters in his throat. 'Whatever you think of me, I'm grateful the last thing I did was dance with her because now we're here together.'

Dora pushes away from him, her arms rigid. 'Tell me. Did she love you?'

'No, I really don't think she did. I think she was . . . entertained by me. Just like you.'

'Maybe you're the reason she ran away. If she ran away.'

'She didn't need any more reasons.'

'Did she know about us?'

His face reddens, a colour filling his cheeks. 'It was you. Whenever I was with her, I saw only you.'

Dora takes a few steps back, her arms still straight out in front her as if they might push away what he's just said, what she now knows for certain, even though he's still too cowardly to say it. She stumbles, then rights herself, and runs out the door.

# HUGO

Hugo stands abruptly when he hears Dora crying, ready to burst into the café to rescue her. But it's not her cries he hears through concrete and glass—of course he cannot hear her.

'It's okay, it's okay,' he says, crouching before the girls, wiping their tears away with his sleeve. 'Mr. Carmichael is our good friend. No harm. Sometimes Mama just needs someone to talk to, and I know where to get the best orange ice cream in the city, just a few blocks from here.'

If Hugo were well, if mania were not once again cutting his moorings, if he could watch this entire scene from above, he would see that it is all unfolding as if in a farce. He would recognize that his daughters—clutching each other and crying—would still follow him anywhere, forgive him almost anything, but not for much longer. Somewhere inside he knows this, some ugly voice is telling him that he's running out of time, but it's drowned out by the compulsion to follow, to rout, to win back. He looks at his girls, silently begging them: *We are on the verge of learning something crucial to our survival. Don't abandon me now. I won't make it.* Their contracted brows convey their deep concern, how much they understand, and consent.

As he leads them away from the window, the breeze on the avenue dries their faces, and he buys Magda and Evie everything they see: ice cream, popcorn, kites, and marionettes that clack against the pavement, their painted heads twitching. There is a man selling papayas, which he's hung from short lengths of string from a little clothesline between two slender poles attached to his cart. When people pass by, he blows a little bugle and motions toward his fruit.

'All your papayas,' says Hugo, making a sweeping gesture with his arm. 'I'll take all your papayas.'

The girls clasp their bags, stuffed with food and oddities, but still they snuffle and cringe and something must be done. Some penalty must be exacted. Carmichael has taken everything, sacrificed nothing. Hugo pushes the girls toward the car.

There is a beat now, and then the stench of rubber tires on asphalt, bleating horns, Magda gripping the upholstery of the Silver Cloud and Evie squealing, delighted. In the car, Hugo flies with the girls along Viera Souto with the top down so they can breathe in the salt air of Ipanema, see the chain-shaped mosaics rippling along the sidewalk. He tries to take deep breaths, move and speak normally, so as not to startle them; he hates that he sometimes frightens them, but when his impulses roar up inside, it feels like a freight train about to burst out of his chest and the only way he can keep from exploding is to say, do, move. Keep moving. But now, having seen Dora with Carmichael, he feels strangely subdued. Their interactions looked so uncomfortable, perfunctory. He has always considered Carmichael half a man. He's even sensed, at times, that Carmichael was almost *impersonating* him, as though the cadence of his voice was shifting, adaptive, and that he was adjusting it almost imperceptibly when they were together. And now he knows why. The bastard has been insinuating himself into their lives for years—befriending him at work, helping him with his projects, 'checking in' on Dora when

Hugo was in the hospital. But hadn't he asked Carmichael to do this? Why hadn't he guessed?

They're outside the city centre now, back in Confederação. From the back seat, Evie leans toward him. Thinking she means to kiss him, he reaches back with his hand and tousles her hair, too roughly, he realizes, when he sees her wince. But Evie motions for him to lean back, which he does but only barely.

'What is it, pet? Speak up.'

'Is that why Luiza was so angry at Mr. Carmichael, and dropped all my flowers?' She's crying again, and beside her Magda squeezes her sister's thigh, trying to quiet her with a terrible shushing sound. 'Because he loves Mama too?'

# EVIE

Papa has stopped the car on the side of the road and told them to both get out. Evie realizes now that her father hadn't known Luiza's secret. But maybe now he can scrape away all the mud and flower petals, dig up her body, find out what she could not; what Magda never knew. Understand what happened to Luiza. She doesn't dare look at Magda, who she can feel is puzzling, who keeps elbowing her in the ribs. Instead she wipes her eyes and just stares straight ahead, sending her sister silent thoughts. *I have to, I have to, I have to.*

'Tell me what you saw,' Papa keeps saying. 'You must tell me.' *Must* with his mouth tight around the *m*. He's trying to be gentle, but his fingers are digging into her upper arms.

'She didn't see anything,' says Magda. 'She just wants attention.'

'I *did* see something,' Evie shouts. 'It was the evening of the garden party, right before Luiza disappeared.' Hot, red waves ripple through her. She fights back tears, and wishes she could bite Magda's knowing smirk right off her face as she tells Papa about how she sat for hours hiding under the cassia tree, with its branches that hung down as low as her knees. The ground was carpeted with pink flowers she had gathered in handfuls, plus a few white ones from the gardenia. She tells him about how their stems were so thin that it took all afternoon to make a crown and she worked very hard on it, even when she heard Magda calling her to come help with the bar. The crown was for Luiza and, though a few of the flowers were a bit bruised at the edges where she'd held them too tight, it looked so pretty. When the party started, Luiza came out to the garden and stood by the cassia tree, and Evie crawled out from under its branches to give her the crown. Luiza said she loved it and promised to wear it all night, even if their mother got cross. But then she kept feeling inside her pocket, where Evie could see the outline of her cigarette packet.

'She said I should go help Magda before she came to find me, so I left. But then I remembered that I'd left my book under the tree, and when I crawled under again to get it, I saw that the school I'd started making wasn't finished and I just wanted to poke a few more holes in the ground and catch a few beetles and give just one last lesson.' Here Evie reddens, trying not to see Magda's sneer, and angry at herself for forgetting to make up something that sounded less childish. 'I was little then,' she says, staring at the ground, but Papa gives her shoulders a gentle shake, which brings back the memory with sickening freshness.

'I know,' he says, rubbing her trembling arms. 'You're a young lady now. What happened next?'

So Evie takes a deep breath, for she's about to betray the adult she loved the most, the one she still believes loved her the most, and who she now imagines reaching back through space, smelling of cassia flowers and sea water, gripping her arms until they bruise. *Don't tell.*

Evie was still under the tree when a man came to talk to Luiza, who wouldn't face him. He had his back to Evie.

'I couldn't see him very well, just his back and his legs,' she says to her father now, worried she's mixing things up.

'That's fine, pet. Go on.'

'Then she said he was disgusting and worth less than a madman.'

Her voice had sounded strange, high and fake, and she kept turning her chin in a funny way and shutting her eyes.

'Then he said something like he was growling, and he did something—I think he hurt her—but I couldn't see because he was in front of her.'

'He hit her?'

'No, he barely moved, but she fell down on the ground and she was crying so hard and he just turned around and walked back to the house, and then I saw that it was Mr. Carmichael.'

Her father says softly, 'Carmichael?'

Evie worries that she's in trouble, and doesn't say how funny Luiza had looked wearing the crown while she got angry at Mr. Carmichael, and how when she lay on the ground, her face was puckered and ugly. And then the way the crown had come apart in the back after Luiza slid to the ground, covering one eye; how she didn't take it off or try to move it; how it *did* look childish, and awful, and sad.

'I wanted to take the flowers back but—' Evie chokes, noticing that Magda is trembling beside her.

'*That's* all you cared about?' demands Magda. 'The stupid flowers!'

Her sister shoots hate from her black eyes after Papa tells her to wait in the car, that he and Evie have more talking to do in private. Magda sulks off and Evie knows she'll catch hell from her later, but she doesn't care.

'The flowers were very special,' says Papa, blinking hard, still rubbing Evie's unbending arms. 'And you were right not to waste them. You can keep going.'

But Evie is too tired to say the rest, to say that she didn't care about the fucking flowers—she wants to say the forbidden word to help expel some of her frustration and grief, but it

won't come. No words come. She only wanted to take the flowers back so that Luiza wouldn't look ridiculous as she cried,
but it didn't matter—it was too late.

Papa lets go of her arms and kisses her on the head. He
waits until her shudders have slowed, then says she's to tell that
very same story to Mrs. Carmichael.

'But I think it will make her feel awful.'

'I think you're right.'

'Then what will we do?'

'All these months; has it been a year yet?' he says, taking
Evie's face in his hands. 'I've wondered why. Why did she leave
us? Now I know.' He crumples against her.

Before he stopped the car, Papa had driven faster than ever
before, the trees above them a patchy blur. When Evie tipped
her head back, she imagined the branches overhead as arms
stretching over her, reaching down, about to pluck her from
the back seat. This is her father now, the heavy, smothering
boughs of his arms, the crushing weight of his trunk as he sobs
into her hair, lifting her off the ground. Then he straightens—
his body, his tie, her dress. He takes her hand and leads her
back toward the car, smiling queerly.

'Your sister loved you, Evelyn. I know she did,' he says to
her now. 'Everything that happens from this point on is necessary, for her.'

# HUGO

ugo stands on Carmichael's porch, holding Evie's hand and peering down into her now-smiling face. She is so pale and slight, so receptive to everything, trusting everyone. Her sister is suspicious, but this one can be bent and led. She needs so much. He has pressed the bell and soon there will be chaos. In this moment, however, she keeps hold of his hand and beams up at him, tethering him to earth, imparting the clarity of mind he requires to avenge Carmichael's violation of Luiza. Grief: later. Sadness: after. Even rage must wait. Pedestrian emotions will subsume him soon enough. But presently, everything is crystalline. The great gift of his 'disease' is manifest: a surge of power and meticulous focus as he crests upward, transcending normal human feeling, deferring all weakness. Yet there is a thin voice inside him that he bats away like a fly: *I am sorry for you, my little human girl. For what you are about to see, forgive me.*

Carmichael's wife, Alice, opens the door, glass in hand and almost falling out of her swimsuit, clutching some low celebrity rag. He grips his youngest daughter by the hand. Daddy's girl. She's a confection in her smocked blue dress, and Alice is grinning foolishly, enchanted already.

'Hugo, Evelyn! What a pretty pair you make. Do come in.'

Hugo knows Alice means to dazzle him with the blond sun flare of her porcelain bobbling head, her too-white teeth, her veined, jiggling tits. No. Crouch by Evie and draw her out; she doesn't like to injure people, but she wants to please him most of all.

'Evie, tell Mrs. Carmichael what you told me.'

It is a curious gift of the child, thinks Hugo, that she, like a savant, is able to recall the minutiae of all she sees, even things that happened months before: the exact pattern of Luiza's dress, that it was white with blue flowers and the sun shone through it while they argued; the precise wording of his cruel attack ('And you're just as heartless as she is'); that the cassia blooms fell upon his black leather shoes, and it was Luiza's right leg that buckled under her when Carmichael—what? Pulled her toward him, or grabbed her somehow? One last attempt at counterfeiting intimacy with his daughter, who, it appears, was being used as a proxy for his wife. Hugo himself hasn't absorbed it, even after listening to this second telling. Something inside him is forcing it out. It's as if his insides are tight, impervious, like water-filled balloons, pushing his revulsion back to the surface, to skin level, so that he can function, enact his plan, not be incapacitated by sorrow and hatred and grief; until later, when he will just shrivel up and blow away.

For now, he watches Evie, lost in the memory and the tiny details. She doesn't acknowledge Alice's shock, is insensible to the rigid set of the woman's mouth. Hugo begins to see everything Evie sees, and he questions whether she is such a skilled mimeograph or if she has accessed his very thoughts—a vision he had, or a dream—had he really been there, after all? And now the lines of Alice's mouth are turning down like those of the marionettes that sit in the back seat of his car, but the child keeps tapping out a facsimile of the scene, the curve of the petals, their brightness against the green grass. There were so many shades of green that day it began to hurt her eyes, and she had to crawl back under the tree to cover them. Hugo, too, has known every shade of green, and he recognizes now that after so many years of being enamoured of Luiza as his spirit child, it is Evie who is just like him. She can perceive such various hues of a single colour yet doesn't notice the tears spilling from Alice's small, red eyes. Eyes that he himself barely notices because he is perfused with love for this perfect child, who now says, 'I'm sorry, Mrs. Carmichael. He'd get so . . . worked up if I didn't tell you.'

At the sound of that name, Hugo is restored to his purpose. 'Carmichael, you son of a bitch, get out here. Get him out here, Alice.'

But as she turns toward the house, the bastard comes to the door, feigning surprise, wiping his hands on dirty pants. He then raises them in a self-protective gesture disguised as greeting.

'Maurer, good of you to stop by.' He is all limp obsequiousness. 'I was just puttering in the garden.' Lie.

'Do you have a crowbar back there?'

'Sorry, a crowbar?'

'A crowbar, please.'

'I think I might have a hammer . . . ' And he is so determined to preserve his sham performance of ignorance that he skulks back into the house to fetch a hammer.

Alice follows, shrill and agitated behind him. 'What have you done? For god's sake, don't bring him that thing!'

Hugo can feel them, even after he can no longer hear them, the thin vibrations of their muttering, their determination to rid themselves of him and his genius daughter. Recalling that he's not yet taken out his golf clubs from the trunk, he returns to the car. Magda's still sitting in the back seat watching him intently. He gives her a look: *stay*. He opens the trunk and the polished wood of his clubs gleams in the sun. Inside him, a red tsunami swells and yet his movements are precise, deliberate.

Sane. He's not an animal. He lifts up the bag with ease, then selects his nine-iron. He must maintain control and yet move quickly before any more plotting can take place within the house, before a gardener or a driver or benevolent neighbours can be mobilized. Something inside him is pulsing, threatening to break through. Don't frighten the girls; say it's a game. But the strident emphasis he places on *game* makes Evie flinch, so he sings it out instead. 'A *game! A game!*'

He strides over to Carmichael's Buick (peasant) and raises the club above and behind him like a baseball player (Robinson).

'Ready?' he says to Evie, who nods.

*Play ball!*

The windshield of Carmichael's car cracks but holds, the filaments of a spider's web spreading across the surface. A second crack shatters the glass with a loud pop, and there is a pleasant tinkling as it collapses in on itself and covers the seats in glinting, ice-like segments.

*A game!*

The back window implodes. He doesn't feel like the beast he must appear to be, more like a mechanized entity, compelled by an exterior force to continue. But that self-awareness is eroding with each slap of frothing blood against his ribs. With each smashed side window, even when the glass doesn't spray but only curls over the car doors in crackled scrolls. *A game!* He doesn't have to think to raise his arms; they raise themselves again and again, robotically, and he is free to watch Evie, who only starts a little with each crack and doesn't cry because she knows this is what must be done. Each side mirror. Alice is in the doorway, weeping and wringing her hands in an exaggerated, stagey way, while Carmichael hovers by a window, ducking as the blows land.

It feels insufficient to address the windows alone, so Hugo swivels the club and uses the handle to puncture the taillights. He is momentarily pleased by the sight of the machine's remains, so often has he seen Carmichael preening about in it as though it's an extension of himself. But too quickly the assault starts to feel like a tiresome pantomime. He's become a caricature of rage, Alice's mouth a grim line, Evie's arms still stiff at her sides, and Carmichael, in the background, deprived of nothing more than his beloved car. Hugo drops the club—it would wound Evie too much to see someone beaten with a weapon, and now he's peripherally aware that Magda has arrived to shield her sister. There is a commotion in the back-yard; Alice has run out like a madwoman. Soon, her screams will draw people from their homes.

Evie and Magda are sobbing now. Why are women around him always weeping? He has terrified them again. He wraps his arms around the girls and inhales deeply, breathing for all of them, uncoiling their awful tension. Then he leads them away from the carcass and back across the street, toward his own perfectly intact car.

Driving home, he is acutely alive. His hair is not hair, but vibrissae, alerting his nervous system to the slightest tremor in the air. His ears stretch out into thin appendages like antennae, sensing the flight paths of insects. His eyes are those of flies, faceted and jewel-toned, seeing hundreds of feet down the road, seeing what hasn't even happened yet. The wind enters him, envelops his heart, crushes his lungs. He leans back, sees the trees reach over him like arms just as Evie said they would. He sees eight shades of green rippling through the grasses. Now nine, now twelve, now too many to count. He has the eyes of a child. He weaves back and forth across the centre of the road and Luiza's laughter—for yes, he can still hear it, she is here with them now—her laughter is the peal of bells.

# DORA

When Dora gets home from the café, Hugo and the girls aren't there. Odete tells her Hugo took them out early in the morning, and Dora's stomach contracts. *Where are they?* But she doesn't have time to ask. She has to get ready for one final night at the Copacabana Palace Hotel, one last night of goodbyes.

'Please be sure he gets ready quickly,' she tells the maid. 'And make sure he dresses appropriately. He should be home any minute.' She can almost feel the knots of anxiety tighten around Odete's eyes. As if she, a plump, little, coloured woman, could control him. Dora could wait for him, but she can't bear the idea of being trapped in a car with him, spreading his hands along his pant legs again and again, thrumming as he leans forward to ask their poor driver, Bechelli, a thousand questions. So she leaves without him, and now they are driving slowly into the city, the chauffeur humming quietly to himself. She closes her eyes, focuses on the soft, tuneless vibrations around her: the car, Bechelli, something inside herself. Soon they'll pull up to the Copacabana, and she'll have to face that grand, grand place, where it feels as though she has lived half her life, free to laugh hoarsely from the back of her throat, touch sweat-dampened skin, drift prettily across the dance floor, buzz with liquor and soda and nicotine. But after running away from Carmichael, she isn't sure how she'll manage the goodbye party—what to say, how she'll pretend.

Once they arrive, Dora thanks Bechelli as she emerges from the car just in front of the revolving doors, but then she takes the wide side steps on the left to one of the two large, tiled terraces that flank the main entrance. As she walks past the café tables and leans against one of the glass-globed art nouveau lanterns that rest atop the marble balustrade, she gazes out upon the very beach she walked with Carmichael earlier today, the same beach she and Hugo dashed across the street to reach all those years ago. This is the last time she'll stand here and have a cigarette while looking across to the sea, the last time she'll appear regal and favoured, swishing through the doors of the Golden Room. While it seems absurd to try to celebrate on a night like this, to have to hide what she now knows, if they don't make an appearance their friends will wonder, want to come by, and she can't play hostess right now. For tonight, paste on a smile.

'Dora!'

It's Carmichael, about thirty feet away, thrusting his keys at the valet, unfamiliar car door ajar, wearing dirty chinos and a T-shirt.

'Dora, wait!' He comes running toward her, sweating, his hair falling into wide, desperate eyes, taking the steps two at a time. She's so startled to see him, she doesn't move.

'I tried to call you but your girl said you'd already left. Is Hugo here?'

'No.' She starts to back away, embarrassed. She's never seen him like this before, so agitated, and there are people entering the hotel door beside them, everyone staring. 'I mean, I came by myself.'

'You should leave. You have to leave.' Carmichael tries to guide her down the stairs as he speaks.

'No! Don't touch me. How dare you come here after—'

'It's not about that, it's Hugo. He's wild. He destroyed my car today. Alice was there. And the girls! He made the girls tell Alice about Luiza. They saw everything and were terribly upset and—'

Dora is beginning to tremble, thinking of Evie and Magda out of reach, near Carmichael. 'Where were you?'

He drives his uncombed hair back from his eyes with his fingers, rigid and white. 'I—I was in the house.'

'So how do you know what happened?'

'I watched—Alice and I watched from the window. What could I have done? He had a golf club. I thought he was going to kill us.'

'Where is he now? Where are the girls?'

'He drove off with them, I don't know where. But it's not safe for you here if he comes, you need to go.'

Dora feels herself being guided down the stairs from behind, his slicks arms pressing against hers, dampening the silk sleeves of her dress. His chest is against her back. She can feel his heart pound against her spine.

'Get off me, get off!' She's feral, almost unable to speak, as she realizes they are already halfway down the stairs and no one has stopped to help as she struggles against him. The heat of his body, the weight of him wrapped around her—she's almost ready to scream when suddenly he is gone and she is free and cool and light again. But where—? When she whirls around he is tumbling backwards, arms twin propellers, a fall in a comedy routine except for his terrified face. And behind him, a giant, pulsing and triumphant. Hugo. Hugo, who can destroy cars, whole buildings if he puts his mind to it. Even her.

Carmichael is in a heap at the bottom of the stairs and now Hugo is upon him. One, two, three. Three swift punches, one in the face, two in the gut. Strong but not devastating. Sickening but not damaging. Hugo in his best suit.

'You get away from her, incubus,' Hugo growls, pinning Carmichael into the corner of the stairs, up against the railing. 'You go back down to hell or I'll have you arrested. She was a *child*.' This last word Hugo spits, leaning his face into Carmichael's, and for a moment Dora fears he might kill him and no one would do anything. But then Hugo stands up, smooths his jacket, straightens his tie, and takes Dora by the arm.

'Dora, he'll hurt you,' coughs Carmichael, his lips lined with blood.

She turns her back to him, a crumpled doll with legs apart, still sitting in the corner, and allows herself to be led through the spinning glass doors.


As they make their way toward the Golden Room, they pass great white columns in pairs and floor-to-ceiling mirrors the length of the hallway. Above them, glinting crystal chandeliers—she may never walk beneath them, or through these magnificent archways, again. Already she catches the scent of wilting orchids and heavy cigar smoke, the bleating of brass instruments, drifting down the hallway.

Hugo speaks low into her ear. 'Tonight we dance and drink and pretend to laugh and soon we'll be gone.'

But passing through the doors into the ballroom, she glances quickly back down toward the corridor and wonders, who saw? And those people just there by the bar are whispering—about what? When Hugo is like this, she's always afraid.

She is still shaking from the fight outside. At first she was grateful to be rescued, for Hugo's animal strength. But Carmichael's fear for her was genuine, and she feels infected by it, as though she can't quite catch her breath. They find their friends—the Williamsons, the Langleys, the Bairds—people she's known for decades, and yet in the past year they have all but faded from her consciousness. *Abraços!* Kisses on both her cheeks. She feels so cold.

'Dory, you're trembling!' exclaims Lucy Baird. 'Dick, would you pass that champagne? This poor thing needs a drink.'

'I'd like a bourbon,' Hugo announces, rising from the table.

'No!' says Dora before she breaks into a wide, painful smile. 'Champagne. We're celebrating, remember?' The statement, she knows, is ridiculous, but she can't risk letting him wander. So they sit with the other couples in the Golden Room, where an elevated balcony lines the walls, lights on delicate metal stems sprout in clusters, and a chandelier descends from a golden dome set into the ceiling. Tables covered in white linen fill the raised perimeter of the room while couples dance across its centre.

Dora gulps at her champagne, watching as Hugo knocks back drink after drink, though he's likely eaten nothing for days. He won't meet her eyes. She doesn't have much time. Even amid the crush of bodies, she can feel it. Hugo is humming now, magnetic, flush with energy. The women—even the men—turn to him, heliotropic. This is that incandescent sliver of time: Hugo ascending. Just before he frightens or offends. Or, worst of all, extinguishes altogether. A sallow, cowering body in an unwashed dressing gown. These people here tonight, they've been upset by him, but they've never been afraid. So, good: let them remember him like this.

The band starts to play 'Chica Chica Boom Chic' and everyone begins, with Pavlovian swiftness, to shake their hips.

'A classic!' Hugo calls out. 'Dora, remember when we went to see this?' He grabs Lucy by her birdlike wrist and spins her around. They stand side by side and rotate their forearms in and out at the elbows, their hands at the wrist, just like Carmen Miranda in *That Night in Rio*. 'Boom chica boom boom boom boom!'

As Hugo dips Lucy down, Dora feels her own spine curving treacherously, her head hung back and growing dizzy, her own uncertainty: is he strong enough? Gentle enough? Will he pull her back up? Will he injure her when he does? They had danced like that in this very room, more than twenty years ago, on that first night. The night of the sunrise, and the piano player, and her awkward beach baptism, when he lifted her so easily as she slept that she woke in chest-deep water, already in his arms. That night that became the next morning, and he never slept, never ate, never needed anything. He was both supernatural and more human than anyone she'd ever met. Could she have known then? Maybe she would have walked away, had a different life. But her girls . . .

Dick appears with tumblers in each hand. 'I just saw a fellow I know at the bar who told me Carmichael was here, outside. Apparently got his bell rung.'

Lucy, now disentangled from Hugo, is almost breathless with twin thrills: flirting with Dora's husband and now violence. 'Who was it?'

'Some angry madman, he reckons. He didn't see it himself.'

'An angry husband, more likely,' says Lucy.

Knowing smiles all around, and Dora is, again, sickened. She and Luiza—just two of many. He had lied about that too. She was never the only one.

She's pulled out of her thoughts by the cold, sharp sounds of metal and glass. Dora scans their corner of the room to see if it's Hugo, knocking things over, breaking something, dancing on tables. It wouldn't be the first time. But all around her, their friends are clinking spoons and forks against champagne glasses.

'Speech!' someone calls out.

'Yes, speech, speech.'

Hugo runs his fingers through his hair, loosens his tie. He's moving in that particular way he does when he's cresting, about to soar out of reach—as though he's straining against his own skin, too tight to contain him. He leaps onto a chair and pulls off his suit jacket, throwing it to the ground. His eyes are bright and still focused as he scans the group, meeting each person's eye, making them feel singular. Chosen.

'My friends, I extend felicitations to our South American relations!' Now he sings, again swaying his arms like Carmen in the movie. 'May we never leave behind us all the common ties that bind us!'

Applause. They are all delighted. Amused. But as the clapping dies down, Hugo's gaze moves to the back of the room, as though he's trying to identify something far off, beyond the walls of the casino. When he speaks again, his voice falters, grows quieter.

'Soon we leave. Leave the only place I've ever considered home. I'd never known what it was to feel free until I came to Rio.' Tears gloss his eyes now and Dora goes to the edge of the chair and reaches up, hoping to persuade him down with her own urgent gaze. But he doesn't reach back, doesn't even look down.

'We can't stay in the country that swallowed our girl. That holds her in its gut and exhales her ghost. *Tchau, amigos. Tchau, terra infestada.*'

Even his Portuguese is failing, thinks Dora, and she tries again to ease Hugo off the chair. This time his body gives. His toast has, however briefly, consumed his energies. Some of their friends stare at her, doe-eyed and exuding unwanted sympathy. Most of them just glance past her, begin their chatter again, light each other's cigarettes. Someone drops an exhausted champagne bottle into a bucket of ice. Gently, she pulls him toward a seat at the table, but then feels him quicken, reanimated.

'Let's dance!' says Hugo, his eyes dilated and wet, darting across her face.

'I'm so tired, love. Why don't we just—'

'Dance with me. When will we have another chance? I won't take no for an answer.'

Already he is leading her to the dance floor, and as he holds her there is another slight shift, tremors only she can feel.

His body tenses, and he digs his fingertips into her spine and the back of her hand in that way of someone trying to fight the impulse to hurt, to crush.

'Today was a big day,' he says cheerfully, and Dora laughs in spite of herself. But then he pulls her even closer and whispers in her ear, 'That beating was for you. For both of you.'

She feels herself retract, trying to create space for herself within his tightening grasp. Is she supposed to be grateful that he still thinks of her? That Carmichael, pathetic, spitting blood, was some kind of offering? A dead rabbit laid at her feet. She wonders how he found out, after all this time, yet knows she cannot blame him. Together, they broke him.

'I don't hate him.'

'He took her from us,' Hugo says quietly, and again he's entreating her, begging her to believe him.

'We did that,' she says quietly, afraid that if she says what she's thinking he will finally enfold her entirely and smother her. 'I think . . . we pushed her away.'

'No.'

'We . . . we were so—'

'Shall we call it a day?' he says, straightening up, speaking at full volume. 'I swore to myself I'd never leave here, but I don't want to hurt you. I've been breaking things—cars, faces—and I've enjoyed it immensely. I might not be lucid for much longer, and I want you to be safe. I could leave you, go back to Canada on my own, get "help." You don't have to come. You could stay here with everyone you've ever loved. Because if you come—shh. Hush. No crying. If you come, there will be times when I'll piss myself and you will vomit orange blossoms and someday we'll carve up those sweet, good girls, Solomon be damned.'

She tries to push away from him, but he holds her tightly, his fingers pressed into her ribs, her hand squeezed and aching inside his, the vein in his neck pulsing against her cheek. She's insubstantial, a hollow-boned bird, but she doesn't want to attract attention by struggling.

'It has been years now but I still remember when your cheeks ignited, flaming peonies, every part of you sweated, even your ankles and the insides of your wrists. So I will pretend and you will pretend, in this casino by the sea. I'll pretend that you do not still smell like Carmichael and I didn't almost have the Andrews boy just now. I won't tell you how he pleaded with me to follow him with that look I'd forgotten. If you press me, I'll say—' She begins to push harder, to beat against his chest ineffectually with the palm of one hand, hoping to quiet him. But the words keep coming, relentless, like an incantation he has rehearsed and cannot stop. 'I'll swear he didn't make sounds you haven't in years and I won't tell you that I quite suddenly remembered—at an unfortunate moment indeed—that he once took Luiza to a dance and so I choked him just for a minute until his eyes popped a little and his skin began to light up from the inside. But I stopped because it's to you, in the end, my mind still speaks. Did you know that? Luiza never comes. Instead, I'm haunted by the living. But all is beauty now, it was beautiful to wreck your lover's face and the Andrews boy, well, I'm sorry for that. I apologized. So now we dance. The boy is still weeping in the washroom and a wind is whistling over our daughter's grave.' He squeezes her closer the faster he speaks and now it's becoming difficult for her to breathe. For the second time tonight a man is trying to envelop her, and she pushes him away with all her strength.

'Enough!' Dora cries, breaking away at last.

Hugo's grip loosens, but he hooks his arms slackly again at her waist and slumps onto her shoulder, finally quiet and momentarily exhausted.

'I'll call the doctor tomorrow,' says Dora, now leaning into him, gripping him almost as tightly as he'd held her. 'We can take you back to Renaissance for treatment before we leave. You need help. You frighten the girls. You'll never survive three weeks on a boat like this. You have to go. We'll delay our trip.'

'For how long?'

'For as long as you need.'

'I can't take that drug again like I did in Florida.'

'Not that one. The usual ones.'

'Do it soon then. Tonight, while I'm still willing.'

'Yes.' She lays her head on his chest, where she can hear his heart. It surprises her sometimes, to be reminded that he's as human—mortal—as she is. 'I want you to know, it ended years ago with Carmichael. These last few days were just . . . goodbye.'

'Thank you.'

As they continue to hold each other, the music ends and onto the stage struts a dancer wearing a bikini made from wooden beads. She wears enormous hoop earrings and a headband and unsoled foot coverings like thongs, also made from beads. Her hair is long and thick and uncombed, and she's dressed in armbands and a loose skirt made from some kind of coarse grass that looks like seaweed. It swings between her legs as she begins to sway, making Dora think of pubic hair, and how unsuitable this country is for tragedy.

# LUIZA

## DECEMBER 1961

Luiza had arrived early, yet she kept looking down the path for Carmichael, anxious to finally have someone to talk to. It was another hot, clear day, just two weeks before Christmas, as she waited in front of the fountain in the Botanical Gardens, studying its four sculpted muses, holding a bag containing a wrapped book for him. *The Waves* by Virginia Woolf. Her ears prickled and turned red thinking about how long she'd spent composing the inscription. *This made me think of you* echoed what he'd written in the book of poems he'd given her when she returned from Florida: thoughtful, possibly even intimate, yet discreet. Friends think of friends all the time. But it might sound like she couldn't come up with her own ideas. Then *Yours, from the Underworld*. Meant to be funny, but could be read as too heavy-handed. In the end she had simply signed it *From your friend, L.* Her initial in loose, hastily written cursive loops. Equivocal.

How silly, she thinks now, to have spent all that time obsessing over the order of these few words, when in a few months she would be gone. Three weeks at sea—crokinole and talent routines and dinner with strangers in the great hall—but this time to Toronto, gelid Protestant city of her father's birth;

the anguish he endured until, he said, he was reborn in Rio. A place where people barely touch, and the land is cold and bald, with spiny trees punctuating the sky. A blank space she couldn't envision. Life there looked like nothing.

But now tears slid out from under the frames of her sunglasses and she wondered how people hide the fact that they're weeping in Canada, where half the year its pallid faces are laid bare. Then a warm, tentative hand grazed her shoulder and she gave a little cry. He was here, in a short-sleeved linen shirt, a golden cast to his skin.

'You've gotten some sun,' she said, wiping her nose with the back of her hand. She clutched the book to her chest, noting he carried nothing. Nor did he remark that she'd just been crying. She wished suddenly she hadn't brought the book, hadn't revealed herself in her unwritten sentences. She wished, again, that she couldn't hear her own nagging, humiliating thoughts.

'Alice and I were at the beach all weekend,' he said, and her stomach seized. 'It was so hot—there was nowhere else to be.'

'Yes, maybe going to the orchidarium was a silly idea. Should we just go for a walk instead?'

They walked along the alley of giant imperial palm trees, fifty metres high, which almost seemed to close over them. This wasn't how she'd imagined it. He wasn't supposed to have come up behind her; he was meant to walk *up* to her, to have seen her from a distance wearing her oversized sunglasses that he said reminded him of Audrey Hepburn. Then, once he was directly in front of her, she would have lifted them off her face and he would have seen her puffy, tired eyes, and concern would have clouded his usual queer, abbreviated smile, and he would have demanded to know, why? *Why so sad, sweet girl?*

Now the news wouldn't be uttered in the hushed tones of forbearance, but would burst out of her, abruptly, shrilly, sharpened by her rising panic.

'We're moving to Canada!' she said, exhaling loudly. She felt something in her uncoil, and she was relieved that he seemed so surprised, distressed even.

'What? When? Not permanently.'

'In March.' Awkwardly, she thrust his gift at him. He took it without even glancing down.

'But that's so soon—that's not enough time to do anything. What about your house? Where will you live?'

'The company's going to take care of all that after we've gone. Apparently they already found a house for us there.' She stopped and wandered off the path to lean her back against a tree. 'I know. I can't believe it. My mother's lost her mind.'

He turned to her but hung back, the book still wrapped, still tucked under one arm. He stood silently rubbing his jaw, and the air between them seemed almost to ripple with tension. She wanted to pull him closer but kept her arms pinned to her sides.

At last, he asked, 'She's agreed to all this?'

'It was her idea! But I can't talk to her about it. She just goes cold and says it's all for my father's sake. What can I say to that?'

When her parents had sat her down to tell her about the move (they wanted her to know before the girls), she noticed how orphaned her father seemed, leaning back against the sofa as her mother spoke, his eyes staring. Silently begging Luiza to agree it was the right choice, to make it seem tenable.

'It's not how we planned it,' Dora said crisply, a tight smile setting her face. And because her mother's feelings had been dulled by years of disappointment, Luiza was just meant to ignore the acute tension in the house, the impossibility of leaving behind everything they've ever known. As a Canadian veteran, her father was eligible for free health care in his home country, which had better hospitals and a stable economy—their future, she was told, would be secure. For these practical advantages, a lesser, transactional kind of life. These towering, humid trees, her oceanside city and all its abundance, exchanged for sedate, beige waiting rooms and favourable rates of inflation. She'd swallowed her undigested sadness for him and agreed, Yes, they should go. It was the best thing for the family.

Carmichael placed a hand over his mouth and rubbed it slowly back and forth. Luiza imagined he was pressing his lips shut, holding back all the things he couldn't say. All at once, he seemed very far away. She returned to his side, and they continued to walk along the path, the towering trees like columns on either side.

'And you'll go with them?' he asked, his eyes fixed on the path.

'I don't feel like I have a choice.'

'Well, it is up to you. It's your life.' His eyes were damp and he kept clenching and unclenching his jaw and looking up, as though something had materialized in the corner of his vision.

'I have no education, no money of my own. Girls like me don't just *live* here, alone. I suppose I should have listened to my mother and found a nice boy, then I could have just moved from one man's house to the next. But you're married and—'

'Me? I wasn't suggesting . . . '

She hadn't meant to say it out loud. 'I just keep thinking of all the things I haven't seen yet,' she said, speaking quickly. She passed her hand over the bark of a palm tree as they walked past and listened for the shrieks of marmoset monkeys that lived in the nearby trees. Here, there were wild animals loose in the city and two-storey trees. Here, there were acres of gardens at the foot of the mountain, watched over by Christ the Redeemer, his arms spread wide. 'The jungle and the north and Ouro Preto! I—I wanted to go stand outside Elizabeth Bishop's house and just see it, just once. And I keep thinking of what the beach was like when I was a child, and what I'll be leaving behind, and it's too much, my mind can't contain it all.'

She wanted to stop talking, to reel back her nervous, un-important remarks, but she could feel her chest shudder and Carmichael still said nothing, still ignored the book she'd given him.

'Did I ever tell you how I used to visit my grandparents in Ipanema?' she said, her voice lower. 'I'd wake at dawn, the house still silent, then walk out past the *praça*. I used to run past the end of the tramline to where there was nothing but white sand dunes and a few grand, old houses. I picked pitanga berries—they were so sour and good—then went down to the water.'

Sometimes, she told him, she would ask the fishermen, 'Do you have any whelks?' But they only laughed and let her help haul their nets in and spread them out to dry, and then she watched as they covered them with tiny squid. The skins were stretched tight, like a membrane of jellied wine. Somehow, they stayed clean of sand, as if the nets were borne aloft, never touching the ground.

'That landscape, that beach—it was paradise. And there were no high-rises—just those beautiful mansions that faced the sea like in France and—'

He stopped short in the path. 'Wait, where do you mean? Here in the city?'

'Yes, when I was little.'

'No high-rises? Luiza. There haven't been houses on that strip in over forty years. Even the casinos were built in the twenties.'

'I know, but I remember—'

'You must be thinking of another beach outside the city. Copacabana, Ipanema—the beaches downtown haven't been anything like what you're describing in decades. Maybe when I was a kid. Long before you were born.'

'But I remember it, vividly. It was here.'

She knew he must be right—the details of her memory were, of course, impossible. But where else could it have been?

In her mind, she could see the coves on either side of her and the hills that stretched out into the water for miles. She saw the exact silhouettes that she would see if she left this garden and went to sit on the beach right now. There was no *futebol*, no paper coffee cups, no car motors. Just the shrieks of seagulls and the greetings of fishermen, creased and smiling broadly, waving to her as she ran across the sand to them. *Tchau, boneca!* This memory, not hers. Scaffolding giving way.

It was unlike him to argue with her over something like that—her stolen memory—so trivial to him. He kept clearing his throat and shifting the unwrapped book from hand to hand as they walked. She wanted to draw him back to her but she didn't know how. For months she had tried to push the thought away: she might never have anything of her own. Even her memories weren't really, reliably hers. But maybe she could take this one thing for herself. That tuneless, high-pitched tone between them, calming her whenever they were together—she could have that, at least, for now.

'I'm sorry,' he said curtly. 'I don't know why I'm so surprised. I guess you've caught me off guard. I think I'd better go.'

As they stood before a stone archway, she took his free hand, pulled him off the path toward the cover of some smaller trees, toward her. Her parents' shrinking lives, Carmichael's pained smile, their diminishing expectations—enough of all that. 'Please don't,' she said. 'I'm sad too. And so touched.' She pulled his face toward her and kissed him. For a moment he seemed to pull away, but then his hand lifted to her face, his fingertips on her cheeks. She felt something like pain and told herself it could be love.

# DORA

Dora sits on Luiza's bed, turning over a pair of kid gloves in her hands, Luiza's favourite. They had belonged to Dora's mother, but Luiza liked to wear them to parties, despite—or because of—how old-fashioned they looked. There is a stain inside the wrist of the left glove that wasn't there when Luiza commandeered them, something that once would have upset Dora. Luiza always so inattentive, even with old, precious things. Cleanliness, propriety—they once gave Dora a sense of order, a scrim between her and the world.

But last night, Hugo had called out 'I'm not crazy!' as she turned to leave his hospital room, the nurses preparing to sedate him. 'Just haunted. Beset by a secretion from the numinous space between life and death where our eldest daughter dwells!' His voice echoed after her as she hurried down the hall. Yes, her husband was a 'madman,' and things might go on like this forever: hospitals, drug studies, stuttering hopes. But containing it, hiding it—she couldn't do it anymore. Afterwards she didn't even plead with her chauffeur not to tell anyone, like she used to. She hadn't the energy to worry anymore who might find out. Bechelli had waited while she wept silently for a minute in the back seat before taking her home, and when she nodded into the rear-view mirror, giving him the signal to go, she saw that he was crying too. All these good people—she would never know them again. She reminds herself they have no choice: Hugo has had another breakdown, and if they stay, soon they will no longer be able to afford his care here. They can't go on like this.

But when she told the girls this morning that their father would be in hospital for at least two weeks, there were no tender, dignified tears. Evie wailed and Magda stomped and the question of why—*why was she doing this to them?*—still rang in her ears. Why now, if they were moving to Canada so he could get treatment, and why couldn't they bring the maids, and why was she ruining everything? Sitting here on Luiza's bed, turned down and with perfect hospital corners, she almost cries again remembering how upset they were and all that's still to come. All the things she'll have to do by herself once they arrive in Canada: cook meals, do the laundry, manage the accounts. Until those few months they spent in Florida, Dora had never even made a bed. She had tried to learn to cook, but after a few burned dinners they lived off frozen, prepackaged meals from the Piggly Wiggly. They all became unmoored somehow, during those months without Hugo at their centre, their sun. The younger girls, at least, had school to fill their days, but she and Luiza wandered and sighed, watched hours of television, scratched at crossword puzzles, and made idle circles in the rattan swing, staring out at all the tidy driveways, leading to houses with saner families inside. Luiza went for walks sometimes and Dora did the shopping, but mostly their lives were left to stall, held by that half-furnished house smelling faintly of mould.

At the time, she thought Florida was hell. But it would be worth it, she told herself, if the drug could bring Hugo back to himself, unbeholden to the extremes of his disorder. Now, Dora understands that Florida was merely purgatory. Hell is now. Hugo lost to her again and again, penitent one minute, brutal the next. On the way to the hospital, he was agitated, running his splayed hands up and down his pant legs, seeming trapped in the car, in his body. Then he held her face in both hands, told her softly that she was a frivolous person who had endured something terrible. That he and Evie were artists who could make their suffering an act of beauty, while Magda was ferocious and would claw her way out.

'But you,' he said, 'what will happen to you?'

First, jealous rage, then remorse, followed by casual malice. The usual treatment—Thorazine—will put him somewhere in between. Manageable, until the next time. He had to go.

Absentmindedly, Dora leafs through a photo album, Luiza's last scrapbook. Halfway through there's a picture of the maids and the youngest girls in front of the house when they are about four and five, Odete holding Evie, Maricota holding Magda, and the girls each holding a doll nearly as big as they were. Though the picture is in black and white, Dora recognizes the dolls. Each doll matches her owner; Magda's is blond with a red dress, like she always wore. Evie's doll has red hair and a green dress, just like her. Luiza always wore blue. It seemed so simple once. Auburn, blond, red. Blue, red, green. Pretty, smart, nice. Had she ever really believed that was all they needed to be? Constrained to familiar, amenable borders—within and without. Her three lovely, little dolls. Shut up in this white house, with its eight-foot walls and barred windows. The fortress, Luiza called it. It looks better and brighter in the photo, but it was a different house then. An acre of land! And inside those walls, how they ran and ran. She'd once believed that kind of life was enough. And what of the house they're moving to—split-level, ranch style—already arranged for in some place called Willowdale, where there are no barred windows, no shattered glass embedded atop foot-thick bulwark, but also no orange trees in the yard, no clamour of bougainvillea, no scent of eucalyptus upon waking. There will be a few pretty things in spring and summer, and then all those dormant months inside, waiting. Skeletal trees out back, deciduous shrubs in front. They'll have to gather all their colour in such a short time. *Hell is here, without you. Hell is your father, without you. Hell is Canada, without you.*

She keeps flipping through the pages: photos of Luiza at seventeen, eighteen on the beach, in the garden, always surrounded by friends, by boys. She'd nearly forgotten Luiza's expression of weary petulance, as though bored by all the attention and admiration. It wasn't long after these pictures were taken that Luiza seemed to lose interest in her friends, and Dora knows now it was because of Carmichael. She wonders if, like her, Luiza fed on the attention only someone like him could provide; if her daughter had used Carmichael for some of the same reasons she herself had. If, when this reserved and brooding man broke down for her, she felt as though she'd won. Disgusting idea. What if Luiza can hear her? Feel her mother's unkind thoughts like a cold wind, wherever she is. Alone. She wants only to remember Luiza like everyone else does. Beautiful Luiza, melancholy Luiza. *Such a sensitive girl!* But the more Carmichael told her about her own daughter, the more she remembered of those last painful years, their thousand brittle exchanges. Luiza had been lost to her long before she disappeared.

Dora turns the page and finds another photo of Evie and Magda, playing in the driveway. A few days ago, she came back from the beach to find the girls riding their bikes, Evie with a whole raw chicken wrapped in a doll's dress inside her bike basket, turning circles in the driveway. She said she found it in the sink, where the maids must have left it to defrost before disappearing to some other corner of the house to pack and clean. Dora's been asking too much of them lately. So she took Evie and the chicken inside and washed her daughter's hands, then cleaned the damn thing herself. She worries that Evie is regressing in some strange way; she seems to be getting younger while Magda hardens and ages beyond her years.

But these small, absurd moments belie the serrated edges of their lives. The girls have seen and heard things they shouldn't have, things they couldn't possibly understand, things she herself doesn't understand. Nights when Hugo cried out, terrified by visions. Together, she and Luiza did their best to protect the girls from the worst of it. But what about Luiza?

Following a few sporadic hospitalizations when Luiza was still a child, several years passed when Hugo seemed steadier. Then one night, shortly after Evie was born, Dora woke to the muffled sound of gasping in another room. For days before, Hugo had paced the house in silence, and she herself had been anxious, her body waiting, even in sleep, for some burst of chaos. She rose from the bed, steadied herself on the nightstand, then tripped on the bassinet in the corner of the room where Evie lay asleep, momentarily forgetting it was there. Evie squirmed a little but didn't wake, and Dora, still confused, wondered how she might cover the baby's ears. Eventually, she followed the sound, her head heavy and full as though stuffed with saturated wool, until she found him fully dressed, curled up, and sobbing in the bathtub. When he saw her, he began to moan.

'Nothing, oh god there's nothing, oh god god.'

She knelt beside the tub, reaching for him with heavy arms, weakly trying to pat his head with one hand while using the other to cover his mouth, stuff his desperation back in. 'Sssshhh. Shush, shush.'

The previous times, he had retreated into himself, depressed for weeks. But this was a crude anguish, different from before. She pressed harder against his mouth, surprised that he didn't struggle, and couldn't think of anything else to say, she was so thick and uncoordinated with fatigue from Evie's frequent night-wakings. Her upper body was now half in the tub with him, one leg still bent beneath her while the

other stretched toward the door as she tried to push it closed
with her toes. Then the door pushed open against Dora's foot
and Luiza squeezed in holding one-year-old Magda, who was
whimpering in her arms, pressing her eyes shut against the
light. The pain of sharp-edged wood scraping over her toes
focused Dora enough to make her cry out.

'Out! Get her out of here!'

'God, please, there's nothing. Nothing. What have I done.
Oh god.'

But Luiza, stunned and staring at her father in the bathtub,
remained frozen. Magda began to wail.

Dora's voice grew more strained and panicked as she yelled
at Luiza to take Magda back to bed. Then the sound of more
cries, sharper and more insistent, from her bedroom.

'Evie,' said Dora, finally lowering her voice and raising her
hands to cover her chest. Her nightgown was suddenly damp
as breast milk soaked it quickly and thoroughly. After three
children, it was still a shock that her body could act so inde-
pendently of her will.

Luiza began to hand Magda to her, saying, 'I'll get the baby.'

The thought of a frightened child holding a tiny, pulsing
infant propelled her forward. 'No!' said Dora, pushing a still
screaming Magda back toward Luiza while trying to stand on
her crushed toes.

Luiza stood motionless, holding Magda in one arm while
covering an ear with her free hand. 'I don't know what to do.'

Two babies crying, a grown man sobbing *nothing, nothing,
nothing*—it was impossible to think, and Dora wanted to hold
her oldest daughter most of all but there was no time. She worried
about waking the maids in their separate part of the house. At that
point, she was still managing to hide the worst of it from them.

'Take Magda into my bed and I'll get the baby.'

Dora climbed into her bed and nursed Evie, then gathered
Magda (quieter now, just the occasional snotty shudder)

toward her with her other arm. She began to sing—*Hush, little baby*—and looked up to find Luiza standing stiffly beside the bed, her face still so uncertain, still waiting for instruction. Dora nodded toward the door. She'd simply meant for her to close it and then come back into the bed so they would all four be together as they waited for Hugo to calm down. She hadn't meant for her daughter to leave, hadn't meant for her to go to him. But Luiza went through the door and shut it behind her.

Once both babies had fallen asleep again, Dora put Evie back in her bassinet and Magda back into her crib in the next room. She tiptoed to the bathroom and opened the door slowly and quietly, holding her breath just as she had when she used to walk into Luiza's nursery and find him there, standing over the crib, and the question would penetrate her mind painfully: had he hurt her? But she was always fine. And she was fine this time too. Luiza lay with him in the bathtub, asleep, her body draped over his, arms embracing him, legs folded in front of her. Two curled embryos, one on top of the other. Dora thought he must be crushed, the full sleeping weight of a ninety-pound child resting on his hips, his ribs, pressing him against the hard cast-iron tub. But he was quiet at last, his eyes open and staring straight ahead. He didn't move when she placed a bath towel over them and walked out leaving the door open, the light on.

And this, or some variation of it, was what they did for years: Dora took care of the babies and Luiza took care of Hugo, and that was when she began to lose her eldest daughter. Because her focus had to shift to her father, and she was just a child, after all; she had to choose. To become his nursemaid, devote all that care, mimic adult duty to such a degree—it was too much. Yet Luiza insisted, and in some private corner of herself, Dora was relieved. And she had allowed it.

She knows she should have left the girls with Luiza and gone to him herself, but it never seemed to help; Luiza was better with him. And so she hadn't retrieved her daughter from the bathroom all those years ago and lain there with her husband herself; she hadn't protected her. And in failing to, she had blunted Luiza, and her capacity to live a normal, starry young-girl life. How could she ever leave them—her mother, so diminished, and her father, broken?

It was several more years before he was diagnosed. And though they went on in this way, tenuously, and somewhat uneasily—listening for uninterrupted sentences, oddly inflected, or the screech and topple of a chair too quickly thrust back— they were often quite happy. There *was* a good life between poles. A golden life! Until Florida.

'I could have saved the girls from the worst of it,' she remembers Luiza saying now. And Dora thought then—but never said—that Luiza was also worth saving.

How else to explain her sad, ragged search in the village, the basilica, the café for dingy lovers. The last, forlorn act of a mother trying not to succumb to despair. Running about like a March hare in those hills, infected with fantasy, a side-effect of too many years living with a madman and a dreamer.

She continues to leaf through the scrapbook slowly, finding nothing but photographs and the expected bits of ephemera— dried flowers, postcards, ticket stubs from films and a concert Hugo took Luiza to for her birthday. Dora flips back to the beginning and turns the pages more slowly this time. She scans the book again and stops at the last page: a picture of a church she's never seen before, whitewashed with terracotta shingles, with a bell tower and a crucifix perched above the centre scroll-work. She gently pulls it from the black page, pieces of which stick to the photo where it was glued down. But she can still read a few handwritten words on the back: *Convento. Ana Claudia.*

When Maricota comes back from grocery shopping, Dora is sitting at the kitchen table with the photo in her hands. She's not nervous exactly. She has, over these past chaotic years of Hugo's highs and lows, learned to contrive a state of calm within herself, a detached interest that allows her to observe everything while feeling little. She feels later, in private, when the cloudburst has cleared and she can tend her emotions alone. She cries at kitchen tables, after everyone is in bed, or quietly, in cars, with kind chauffeurs. Luiza used to say her calm was unsettling, unnatural, and it's true that Dora sometimes fears she feels less and less. But for now, it is useful. Her hand is steady as she passes Maricota the photograph. It's important to Dora that she not pointlessly upset this woman who she knows has grieved almost as much as she has, and who they are leaving behind.

'I found this in Luiza's scrapbook,' says Dora. 'Is it yours?'

'*Sim*. It's from my sister.'

'When did she send it? Recently?'

'*Ela está morta.*'

Of course. From meningitis years ago. Maricota took the week off. They both look down to avoid facing the fact that Dora has forgotten.

'Why would Luiza keep this in her scrapbook? She only kept family things in there.'

'*Não sei*. She asked me for it a few weeks before—'

And here is the difference between her and other people, Dora notes; Maricota's eyes fill with tears, the hand holding the photograph trembling until Dora closes her own two hands over Maricota's wrist, trying not to bend the photo. It feels like an awkward gesture, but the crying stops and eventually the woman is still.

'I told her once about my sister, about the convent, about how much I wanted to go there. How it's a beautiful place of peace and worship and the sisters spend their days in prayer. And they make these little things—nice things—candles and rosaries and dried flowers. I always think about what a nice life that is. Making things. And Christ. And so much quiet.'

Dora has to suppress a laugh then, having already appeared inhuman enough for one day. That this poor woman who yearned for a life of quiet contemplation and handicrafts should have ended up with them. With Hugo. Who once threw the steaks Maricota was defrosting out the kitchen window because he was convinced they were cross-sections of a human thigh. But here she remains, her sweet, fat hand held out, gripping the photograph, apologizing for telling Luiza about God.

'She kept asking me what it is to believe, and she asked for the picture. I thought it was okay, just Luiza's *tristeza*.'

Dora assures her it was harmless and asks for more details about the convent. She asks about Maricota's sister and her life there, and smiles at her stories, and sits perfectly still, all the while hiding the shuddering inside.

# HUGO

ugo paces in front of the window in his hospital room while the nurse pours water from a plastic pitcher. They call it a 'recovery centre,' but it's full of doctors and nurses and machines and pills. A hospital for misfits and lunatics and those who won't co-operate. But it is the 'best' in the country, Dora always reminds him, so he gets his own room, with a door that locks from the outside. Out on the rolling, green lawn, automata glide, unfocused jelly in place of eyes. These, he thinks, are his final days, and that nurse is laughing at him.

They want to scour his brain, dig out the girl at the core of it, the star of the fruit, the one in the middle. The midst. *I get midstsy*, he sings. Hopeless as a kid lost at sea.

*How purple!* says laughy nurse, and the window behind her shatters, exposing more humanoids slumped in wheelchairs, silently pushed along. His ears are weeping blood and his very thoughts show themselves to her, raised red welts on tumid skin. Purple indeed! What would life in any prison be without extravagant thoughts?

*You're conspiring to leave me.*

A corona of light pulses around her head. She recedes with each cry, then surges forth, brighter, more awful than before.

Eyes platinum, tears of molten silver, cheeks stained with pomegranate.

*Take me with you! My heart is singing.*

Atomized, his daughter scatters on the south wind. She says it's not time yet.

Today, she's trying to dope him up with a handful of Dora's Black Beauties—they would have him disintegrate in this place. *Never mind, you duchess of nothing, it fortifies me, trifling with tarts like you. Come, come, merkin, don't run off— it's this meandrous limb of mine, indifferent to my virtue.* (But she is gone, and he's alone again.) That one's not to be trusted. Scent of dying flowers: alyssum, pasques, love-lies-bleeding. All gone, all rotten. *Garçonete, cauterize this spoilt portion of my meat!* He was a sophisticated man once. Evie, Magda? What is that racket in the hallway? Is it his daughters? Or Dora, spreading anxiety wherever she goes? *I wish it were my best one, my Luiza, my gone one.* Gone on the wind. She quick-churned into a dancing stream, broadcast on the ocean, far-flung. Abandoned? Drops of her still come out the taps, even here.

*I'll dance with you soon.*

He is dilating. Stricken with a cursed languor. But meiosis begins to contrive within him, until there is enough matter hatched to make two of him, then four—an army of Hugos! Gemini, with golf club rising. The feeling of glass cracking, giving way, shattering as I wailed. And later, his organs, shifting beneath my fist. Even on a plate, they would make a sad offering in exchange for all he took from me. Hear our name resound. Hugo! they will say. But even the old king stinks of mortality, while I moan and die.

*Ow! Watch it with that fucking thing.* Needles now. Pills too pedestrian. She whispers, *Sleep now, Papa.*

— IV —

# EVIE

As they stand side by side brushing their teeth in the bathroom, Evie is aware of Magda watching her in the mirror. Her sister spits out a mouthful of toothpaste and holds her toothbrush aloft as she says, 'It's your fault Papa had to go back into the hospital, you know.'

Evie tries to protest through a mouthful of foamy saliva, but it drips down her chin as she answers. 'It's not—'

'And now he's going to be there for weeks, and we'll have to unpack and then pack everything up again. You should have just kept quiet about what you think you saw. You don't even know what you saw.'

Evie wipes her mouth with a face cloth. 'I do know. I just didn't understand it before.'

'You know he can't handle stuff like this. You had to wait until the worst possible moment, when he was high as a kite.'

*High as a kite.* This was something Mama sometimes said, always under her breath, to the maids or over the phone to her sister in Santa Bárbara. Magda goes back to brushing her teeth, as though whatever Evie says next is of no consequence to her. Then suddenly, a spray of white over Evie's face in the mirror, a wet glob of white marbled spit over her reflected eye, two rabid Magdas, one beside and one in front of her.

'But what if Mr. Carmichael *did* something? Shouldn't Mama and Papa know?'

'Did what? Did he force her into the water? Did he make her swim out too far? He wasn't even there. She did that herself but no one ever wants to say it!'

Evie won't allow herself to think about what Magda has said. Magda, the Angry One. Angry even at the dead. No, instead she'll think about how Papa's golf club flashed in the morning sun, all that glass coming down like rain, gleaming in the grass. And how, even though Magda cried in the car on the way home, Evie was not afraid.

'You're just jealous because Papa made you go wait in the car.'

Magda places her toothbrush back in its cup, wipes her mouth delicately on a hand towel, then wheels around and lunges forward. Suddenly Evie is on her back, Magda's full weight holding her down, Magda's whole hand against her face, pressing the flat of her head into the hallway floor. She can feel the rough carpet fibres against her neck, fingertips gripping her cheeks and forehead, a palm painfully squashing her nose. Evie lies pinned for a moment, listening to their uneven breaths. When she feels her sister's body relax, she wriggles out from under her and sprints toward the stairs, bracing herself on the banisters and jumping down three steps at a time.

'Where are you going?' Magda shouts, coming down the stairs after her.

If she doesn't get out of this house, Evie knows Magda is going to kill her. And with Papa in hospital and Mama 'away' for a few days (supposedly to visit a sick aunt) and the maids always busy packing, unpacking, repacking, cleaning, her body probably wouldn't be found for days.

As she runs out the front door, she remembers Luiza telling her a story once of a woman who came over to Brazil with their ancestors nearly a hundred years ago, when people were expected to die. The woman's husband broke off from the larger group and led some people south to Juqiã, where he named the colony Lizzieland, after her. It says in their family letters that Lizzie's death caused the colony to fail but it doesn't say why. Losing her simply broke him, Luiza said. When Evie heard the story as a child, she thought nothing of the man's sadness—who had feelings that long ago? But she'd loved the idea of a place named after oneself. She imagined a fairground, like the kind she knew they had in America, and all the games would be just for the girls, and they'd all be named Lizzie for the day. Dozens of little girls running around calling out, 'Hello, Lizzie!' 'Hello, Lizzie!' And always the uncanny sense that the real Lizzie was there, a ghost or a giant, her pale face gazing down from above, all-knowing. Evie can still see the scene so clearly in her mind's eye that she thinks she must be trapped in a place like that now: a dreamscape of mirrors and tent flaps and wide, grassy avenues. She wants to call out, 'Luiza! Hello, Luiza!' She wants to see her sister's face in the sky. There are moments when a presence grazes past her, something cold with hummingbird wings, but when she looks up, Luiza is never there. Luiza, who would have told her, once, what was right or wrong. Which secrets to keep.

But now Evie is outside and everything inside her is strung too tightly. She runs down the path from the house toward the gate and jumps, hurtling herself forward. She hits the ground, breath knocked free, and lies unmoving. For now, she is lighter.

Later, in the car, after they pick up Brigitta on the way to the old, stone Y WCA building for their second week of camp, Evie chews the dead skin on her lips and wonders if it really is her fault that Papa is back in the hospital. The last time he'd been admitted was two years ago, in Florida, when men in white uniforms had come to the house and he fought so hard they had to stick him with a needle. Seconds later he went still, collapsing in on himself, like a puppet with its strings cut. Then Luiza pushed her and Magda back inside the house.

Evie's almost sick from it, the idea that she's the reason her father has to go away again, and she lingers now in the car as Magda and Brigitta hop out. As Magda sprints through the doors of the Y, Evie leans forward from the back seat and whispers in Bechelli's ear, asking him to wait. She can't stay here.

'Brigitta!' Evie calls out the car window. 'I need your help!'

As they drive away from the YWCA, Evie knows that trusting her sister not to rat on her for skipping camp is risky, but maybe Magda will forgive her later? After all, they both know now: parents lie. They love you, but they lie. They leave in the middle of the night without explanation, without even saying goodbye. They keep secrets. Children should have their own secrets, too, and their own world with its particular, unspoken children's code. But for now Evie has to save her father, who sometimes crosses over into their world, because he sometimes forgets how to lie.

When they arrive at the hospital, Brigitta nods her head toward Bechelli, humming in the front seat. 'Tell him just to wait here,' she says, suddenly taking control.

They sign in at the front desk and a nurse points them toward the elevators. 'Room 322, third floor,' she says in Portuguese.

But when they get to the third floor, Brigitta ignores the floor map and pulls Evie down the hallway. 'I've never been in an insane asylum,' she says in a stage whisper.

'It's not an asylum, it's a recovery centre.' But Evie's voice sounds small and far away, even to her. Brigitta is walking two paces ahead, her neck craning forward, stopping only to peer through the small round windows set in each of the doors, Evie following behind her like a puppy. 'Anyway, what are you looking at? We should find my dad.'

'I just want to see . . . there! See? This is exactly what I expected to find.' Brigitta stands on tiptoe squinting through a window, even though she's tall enough to see in. 'That poor man, left in an institution and forgotten. Doesn't it just look like he's imprisoned in his own flesh, fighting to get out?'

'No!' Evie squeaks, seeing Brigitta's hand close over the doorknob. But the door is opening and she is being pushed inside the room and the young man in the chair by the window turns his head toward them, these twin intruders. Evie feels shrunken and prickly, her ears straining to detect footsteps coming down the hall.

'Hello,' Brigitta says, sitting on the bed opposite the man, her knees touching his lightly. He flinches when she takes his hand.

'Brigitta, you shouldn't—'

'The problem with these people,' Brigitta interrupts, sounding sharp and imperious, 'is that they drug them to the point where they can't feel anything. If they could just experience normal, human feeling again, they would be okay. Not vegetables.'

'My father says it can be awful when you feel *too* much, feel all the time.'

But Brigitta ignores her and rubs the man's hand, turning it over in her own, slowly tracing his punctured, blue veins. 'What did they do to you?'

'You don't even know why he's here. Let's just leave him.'

Brigitta places the man's hand on her thigh, stroking just above her knee and below the hem of her skirt. Evie shivers, suddenly cold, immobilized by Brigitta's cool curiosity, the pushy way she leans toward this man, peers at him as though he's an insect she's trapped. He moans softly, but it sounds more like pain than pleasure, and his mouth is contorting into a livid, red-blue smear. The sound builds in Evie's ears: a siren, escalating rapidly, filling the room, the hallways. And any minute, she knows, the room will be full of people—nurses, security guards, outraged visitors. But as she pulls wordlessly on Brigitta's shirt, fear rippling through her, she realizes no one is coming, because what she hears is only the memory of a sound—the one Luiza made in the garden after her fight with Carmichael. Evie covers her ears reflexively just as she did then. After a moment, she yanks as hard as she can on Brigitta's sleeve.

'Come on!'

'All right! Get off already.' Brigitta pulls her arm away and they are out the door.

Evie walks as quickly as she can to her father's room without drawing attention to herself while Brigitta, languid behind her, hums Bechelli's little tune. When they arrive at room 322, Evie pushes the door open slowly so as not to startle her father, then fixes a smile on her face. But the bed is empty, and there are no shoes paired neatly beneath it, no jacket hanging from the hook.

'Come on,' she says again. She wants to find her father but is certain they'll be in trouble if they linger too long. 'We have to get out of here now.'

In a mirror on the wall, Evie sees her own red hair, her ghost-white skin stutter past. She pushes through a set of doors marked EMERGENCY, only realizing as it swings open what she's done. An alarm sounds, real this time. But then Brigitta is right behind her and they soar, leaping over half-flights of stairs. For the second time today, she is flying. *Hello, Luiza!* Then there is sky, and trees, and Bechelli with a newspaper. She begs him to start the car and go, and when he asks what's wrong, she says she's crying because her father was so upset to see her leave.

# MAGDA

*T**hwack!** Magda stands in the backyard, knees apart like a batter, holding her croquet mallet, which she just found, forlorn and leaning against the garden shed. They're not allowed to bring the croquet set with them when they go. ('We can get new things in Canada,' Mother said, 'better things.') She strikes the jacaranda tree and trembles with a fierce and perfect sorrow as purple blossoms carpet the ground. It was Luiza's favourite tree. Next she walks over to the pink cassia tree, covered in the flowers Evie most loves to hoard away, to weave into her silly crowns. It's not normal—a twelve-year-old girl who still believes in ghosts and fairies. She should mention it to their mother, she thinks, if she ever returns from her mystery trip. They woke up on Monday morning to find her gone again, only this time the maids said she'd be away for four or five days. (A sick aunt. More lies!) The real goodbye party at the Copacabana was last Friday, and they were supposed to leave at the end of this week, yet here they all are, still stuck, possibly for a few more weeks. Waiting. *Thwack!* A heap of pink flowers. Magda raises the mallet overhead and pounds the petals into a sweet-smelling mass, imagining Evie when she finds them. Will she cry? Will she officiate another melancholy little funeral?

*Here lie some flower petals that would have died in a few days regardless.* Evie doesn't care about anything important. She skipped camp the other day and Brigitta forged a note for them like it was nothing. Magda was tempted to tell on them, but to whom? Her parents both absent and now the maids—betrayers. Magda has devoted herself to the Y, to sport, to excellence, but no one ever asks about the gymnastics exhibition she's been rehearsing for the end-of-camp showcase in two weeks—which she can now attend because Mother has delayed their departure yet again—or about the special synchronized swimming routine that only she and a handful of other girls were selected for. The best, most athletic girls.

She moves on to the flame tree, beloved by Odete, its boughs outstretched horizontally as though reaching away, covered in bright orange blossoms. Showy, thinks Magda. Tasteless. This time, pound the trunk *and* the branches. The blossoms drift like many-pointed embers against the darkening sky, the petals a soft explosion of red spikes. Carnage.

At last, the frangipani. This will hurt. Its crown has been pruned into a perfect arc that casts, in late afternoon, the perfect circle of shade. Here they sat, she and Maricota, for endless afternoons, as Magda read out loud, digging her bare feet into the grass. When she grew tired, she would lay her head in the woman's lap and close her eyes. Maricota liked to cluck her tongue, tell her not to be lazy, to read all she could, *because* she could. Magda would stick frangipani blossoms between her toes, yellow centres fading into white, and try to walk on her heels. Maricota always laughed, and Magda read until her mother arrived home, looking out anxiously from the veranda door, wondering wordlessly why no one had started dinner.

She steadies herself, perfects her stance, lifts her mallet. Hasn't Maricota's betrayal been the greatest of all?

That morning, Magda had stood in the kitchen with her hands outstretched, the three ivory chess pieces she'd stolen growing heavy and sticky with her sweat, as Maricota and Odete, her lovely ones, indulged her, exchanging glances in that way of adults who are deciding the best way to lie to a child. Or break their hearts. Finally, Maricota took the pieces and placed them in her pocket and, for a moment, Magda felt hopeful.

'I'll put them back,' Maricota said in Portuguese, address-ing Odete. 'I know where the box is.' Adults conferring, making their own plans. Children an afterthought. When they turned their attention back to Magda, even their amazement, she thought, was phony.

Odete, always the softer of two, teared up, while Maricota took Magda's hands in her own. '*Querida*,' she said, frowning. 'We can't come with you. Those little things aren't worth enough to get us to Canada, though that's not the reason.'

'But they're ivory! And if these aren't enough, I can get more. Mama has so much jewellery, and Papa leaves money lying around all the time.'

Their mouths compressed, their eyes moist with pity. All her newly toughened muscles unwound. She tried to retract her hands from Maricota's, but not very hard.

'We have families, other people who we love very much. We belong here.'

They live *here*. They have families of their own. Of course they do. Families who live in houses with dirt floors. Families with eighteen children and a mother who never cuts her hair. A mother who prays to God and has her prayers answered. Magda has jumped over brooms with them and placed lipstick in their little boats, an offering to their goddess Yemenjá. And yet she hadn't even thought of them. Hadn't imagined they might be more important to Maricota than her.

'Please?' she added, as though she could extract what she wanted by asking nicely. These most patient, substitute mothers—they loved her, she knew they did. Yet there were others, near strangers to Magda, who they loved better.

Now, with her knees still locked before the frangipani tree, mallet hanging limply from her hands, Magda doesn't want to feel sorry, doesn't want to understand. She wants to be angry. She wants to feel, again, the appalling, satisfying thud of wood against tree. She wants to see the blossoms rain down, gasping uselessly as they fall, begging for mercy. Mercy she will not grant. She lifts the mallet for the third time, determined. Now: vengeance. But shame simmers inside her. She's no better than Evie, with all her childish wants.

Soon, there will be another life in Canada, with only her parents to show her how to be—she can't grasp it. She reaches out and touches nothing. Maybe there's nothing there? Canada, where her parents imagine all their cobwebby sadness over Luiza can be swept away—Luiza, who hadn't expected enough of herself. Who left them all behind. Magda, too, wishes sometimes that she could be with Luiza, could swim away from all the adults charged with caring for them—distracted, impotent—who don't understand they're still needed. But she doesn't know how to give up.

In Canada, she and Evie will be sent away to Aubrey Ladies College, with its colour photo brochure scenes: a pool, horseback riding, tennis. Soon, there would be starched uniforms and the day punctuated by bells. The medicinal smell of chlorine lingering on her skin long after she breached the water and showered. The earthy scent of a horse's flanks as she soars on its back over rails. Sanctioned grunts of rage as her racket slams down, thrusting back balls. A chance for her to be distinct. There, she could be their family's envoy, the one who thrives, plunged out into the world to prove they aren't broken. She will display the same excellence that led to her being singled out earlier this week for the swim routine. Evie and Brigitta would probably laugh if she described the program planned, when in fact it's punishing and very physically demanding, her skin now scaly from so many hours in the YWCA pool.

The mallet seems to fall from her hands and Magda stumbles backwards, loose-legged, gasping. Reflexively, her knees lock and she rights herself, her shoulder blades squeezing together, her arms shooting out like wings, as if poised for flight. Her heart begins to slow. She takes three deep breaths, then tumbles forward, completing a perfect somersault before landing in a lunge. Next, a series of somersaults, ending with a round-off, which is a little wobbly but still well executed. It's getting darker all around her but she fights the impulse to go inside. Has anyone ever actually told her she shouldn't go into the garden at night? Maybe that was just an unspoken warning she absorbed. Maybe the maids instilled fear in her to keep her safe and now she has to stamp it out. Or maybe she just imagined it. Luiza always said their house was a fortress. Who could get over *those* walls? Her body feels flexible, small yet strong, meant for something more than anger and fear. She split leaps, then punches the ground as she lands. She leaps again, her limbs extended, points on a star in the fading light.

# HUGO

Around and around the halls, Hugo walks. He craves the sun, but after the Thorazine injection, his body feels heavy and stalled. The sedative effect was immediate, and it's taken days for his thoughts to clear, for feeling to come back, especially in these brightly lit rooms with plants, games, a television—all provided to help patients relax; but even medicated, he cannot sit still. He begged Dora, made her swear to instruct them: *Not too much. Bring me down, but don't wipe me out. I won't be any trouble on the boat, I give you my word.* She turned away when he pleaded, but she promised.

Another condition he stipulated: since he had voluntarily committed himself, he would be allowed to sign himself out, go for a walk, leave whenever he wanted. He tells the nurse at the front desk he likes to walk to clear his mind, but the truth is he has something he still needs to do. The nurse takes his day pass, makes a call to the ward upstairs, then gives a nod, and he is buzzed through the automatic doors and walks into the sunlight of late afternoon, his shadow stretched long and thin behind him. To the beach, to the water, always the water. The ocean, he thinks, will pull at him forever. When he was young he used to go down to Toronto's waterfront to see the ships and look out, dazzled by the sun shining over frozen Lake Ontario. Could he ever go back to a mere lake?

The hospital is near the seafront, and he is at the beach in under twenty minutes, this time at the other end of Copacabana Beach, opposite Marimbás, where he ended his last walk. Today he's coming from the other side; he'll meet her in the middle, where he wanted to arrive last time but did not, could not. This time he will ask her what he needs to know.

The middle was where he and Luiza ended up nearly three years ago, on her eighteenth unbirthday, after their drink at the boat club.

'Just like Alice in *Through the Looking Glass*,' he said. 'We'll fête you 364 days a year instead of just one.'

They were celebrating a few weeks late because he'd only just returned from another month in hospital, and Dora had taken all the girls to Petrópolis for Luiza's real birthday while he was away. His small way of making it up to her. He promised a bottle of their best champagne (for her, just one glass!), but when they arrived at the club that evening she was charmed by a ridiculous pink cocktail poured into a perversely curved glass, topped by a kebab of orange segments, strawberries, maraschino cherries, and spiralling rinds of a lime. They sat out on the balcony overlooking the darkened beach, lights around the bay reflected in the water.

'This is the perfect drink for an eighteenth birthday, don't you think?' Luiza said as she held it up to the light, grinning. 'A splash of rum for my burgeoning adult self dressed up in every little girl's pink-princess dreams. I am between two worlds.'

These little speeches of hers sometimes made him nervous—they were affected, as though performed just for him. But so much had been expected of her at a young age, and for too long she had feigned maturity. Had he done this to her?

He raised his glass. 'To my daughter, on her eighteenth birthday. Or thereabouts. There's no rush.'

She tilted her head, furrowed her brow, then burst out laughing. 'Not one of your better ones, Papa!' But she connected her glass with his, their cold clink hanging oddly in the air.

Hugo cleared his throat. As close as they had always been, she was becoming the only person who could make him uneasy. Evie and Magda were still too young and absorbed in their children's world to understand much about his condition, but Luiza knew—had known for years—that he was ill. And yet she still adored him. Unlike Dora, who was often suspicious and fatigued by him, Luiza was still enchanted by his energy, his caprice, even what she witnessed of his depressions before he was sent away. But disillusionment would be healthier, and he felt he had to disabuse her; she was, he sensed, becoming infatuated with the idea of instability, of a life lived in extremis.

'I confess I have another reason for bringing you here,' he said before he gulped so much of his martini that he choked. Again Luiza laughed, and he thought how much she looked like her mother, and how sorry he suddenly was that Dora wasn't there, with them. When he'd asked her, she insisted she didn't want to go—that Luiza would take the news better from him. But it felt wrong suddenly, their distinct little team of two, and he was struck again by all the damage he'd done. 'No time to drown,' he muttered under his breath.

'Pardon?' Luiza said, leaning toward him.

He reclined away from the table. 'Nothing, nothing. I wanted to tell you—' he was straightening up now, his voice hollow and loud. He tried to modulate his voice, soften it to a normal pitch, but it dropped back down to just above a whisper. 'I wanted to tell you that we'll be taking a trip.' Luiza's eyes lit up, so he added quickly, 'All together. As a family.'

'Oh?' she said, primly putting her drink back on the table and interlacing her fingers. There it was again, her simulating adult gestures and inflections. He felt tears in his eyes.

'There's a study in Florida. For a new drug. Lithium. Apparently it's done wonders for some tragic folks in Australia.'

'What does it do?'

'Evens you out, I suppose.'

'And do you want to be . . . evened out?'

He could barely stand it, the way she was speaking, slowly and cautiously, like the nurses at the hospital.

'You have to stop this, my darling, you really must stop acting like all this is normal.' He was speaking very quickly, avoiding Luiza's searching gaze, waving his hand for emphasis. 'I want you to stop pretending like this is something you want for me.'

His voice was rising, and when he finally met her eyes again he knocked over her drink. A pink puddle spreading toward the edge of the table. Hugo was suddenly on his feet, grabbing at napkins from nearby tables to sop up the spill.

'Waiter! Another one of those pink drinks for my daughter!' The urgency of his voice, the desperation—ridiculous man, he thinks, remembering it now.

When he looked at Luiza again, she was still seated and blotting her skirt with a napkin. Why hadn't she stood up to avoid the spill? Why was she moving so slowly? Whatever they'd done for him in the hospital wasn't enough—he always seemed to be moving at a different speed than everyone else.

He stabbed roughly at her dress with a fistful of napkins.

'Now it's ruined,' she said, and at last she sagged into her chair, lip trembling, arms hanging limply over the armrests, soggy napkin balls on the floor beneath her. At last—the child he recognized, that he needed her to be.

Hugo sat down, leaning toward her now, trying to pull her chair closer. 'It's not like you think it is, being this way. Not any longer. I'm tired. Your mother is tired. Something needs to change.'

'But I love you this way! Why can't the world just allow for people like you? You're going to end up becoming whatever's easiest for everyone else. You'll be just like the rest of us.'

He should not have told her; he should never have described
to her the way it could be during those first warm and irresistible
surges of mania, when his blood rushed with the immaculate
connectedness of all things, and he was enchanted, his senses
heightened and his mind tentacular, reaching out and grabbing
ideas, pristine and preformed, from the air. Utterly cogent, spar-
kling ideas flying around his head like comets, which, when followed, only led to better, brighter ones; and all of them discrete
yet connected, like the threads of a perfect web. But he'd told
her, too, what eventually followed, when the lines blurred and
once-perfect ideas muddied and congealed, and that dreamy
sensuality and euphoria were replaced by an escalating, exhausting wildness. And about the anxiety that inevitably set in: what
had been said, and to whom? How great was the damage? How
much money spent? In the early days, apologies could still be
made, friendships salvaged. But for how much longer?

'I want to be like *you*,' he said then, clearing away the bits
of orange rind and strawberry hull from her spilled drink. 'I
want to be with all of you. I don't want to keep leaving for
weeks every time I crash. I'm tired.'

'But you have visions,' she pleaded. 'Such wonderful, other-
worldly visions. In some cultures that would make you revered,
a shaman. Genius has a price.'

He had tried to corrode her overly romantic ideas about his
disease, yet he believed some part of her still wanted it for herself. He tried to tell her that she misunderstood. Those beautiful hallucinations, those showers of stars—those were
undeniably beautiful, preternatural. He was grateful he wasn't
like other people, because he'd seen things other people only
imagined. It had been enough, for a time, to make all the
rest—the anxiety, the depression—worthwhile. But sometimes
those weren't even the worst aspects of the disease.

'Don't you remember,' he implored her now, 'all those weeks
I believed the CIA was following me, hunting me? My body

actually cramped up from the fear. But those delusions, this condition—sometimes it protects me from something worse. When
they pass, I'm left knowing that in fact no one is tracking me. No
one is listening in, or watching, or thinking of me at all.'

She said then, very quietly, 'But I'm always thinking of you.'

And in that moment, he knew: that was what he had done
to her, bequeathed to her the myth of their reciprocal devotion,
a predestined twinning. Never when he was 'flat' of course,
but when he was high, he had said such things. *In you, I have
geminated and borne my most pure and unrealized self.* Such
grandiose, cruelly burdensome things.

After one last garish pink drink and another martini,
Hugo promised Luiza that the treatments were improving all
the time and would only take away the worst parts of him, the
parts none of them could go on living with. As though it were
surgery, as though they could extract aspects of his self, of his
mind, and leave the rest intact. Of course the doctors in Florida
made no such claims, and without the lightning-strike cure
they hoped lithium might be, he saw the years yawn open
before him, sedatives alternating with antidepressants, one
spitting water on a forest fire, the other a flutter-board thrown
to a man already submerged, five fathoms down.

Luiza had bravely tried to smile and said that she trusted
him implicitly, and he covered his mouth as he winced a little.
After he paid for the drinks, they went down the spiral staircase to the beach and stood on the sand, dull and white in the
moonlight. Luiza eventually asked if they could sit for a few
minutes—the cocktails had gone to her head. So they turned
back toward a set of stairs that led from the beach to the brick
road, then followed the tree-lined sidewalk away from the
beach. They sat on one of the little wrought-iron benches that
faced a stone retaining wall and looked out over the water. It
was completely dark now, and they took turns pointing out
ships on the horizon, dotted with pinpricks of light.

'Maybe you're right,' Luiza said, resting her head on his shoulder. 'Maybe Florida will be a nice change. Everything here is becoming so crude and crowded, and there are so many more buildings going up. It's decadent and cheap all at once.'

He laughed then, but felt sad more than relieved. He could hear her trying, lying—she was pretending again, for his sake. He had made her that way—sentimental, melodramatic, often awkward—then abandoned her for one of two extremes, private planets of light or dark he alone could inhabit. What was she to do? Who else could she have become? People like them weren't fitted to the world. All she wanted that night years ago when she jumped into the water was for him to save her, to prove he loved her. On how many beaches would he lose her?

Hugo rises now from the sand where he's been sitting, staring at the water. He wants to understand; he wants an answer. He can feel the distance between them rapidly expanding, can feel himself letting go, feel her slipping away psychically as well as physically—that thin gold thread that always shone between them is dulling. Soon, it will snap altogether.

'Come back.'

He walks into the water, feels it fill his shoes. 'Where are you?'

His pant legs are wet to the knees now, wrapping around his calf muscle with each wave. Now his thighs, back pockets, hips, belt, waist—all soaked through.

He leans into the waves, shouting, 'Come back to me and we'll face the sun.'

The waves slap higher against his chest, then his chin. He swallows water when he opens his mouth to speak again, quieter this time.

'Come back and we'll never leave.'

# LUIZA

## MARCH 1962

'No nap today!' Dora had warned her, over-enunciating as she strode briskly into Luiza's room, pulling open the drapes. One must never be allowed to rest on the day of *a party*, thought Luiza as she lay on her bed, flipping through her old scrapbook.

'Oh, Luiza,' Dora sighed. 'I asked you to sort through your things. You haven't started packing at all.'

'You said the movers weren't coming until tomorrow. I'll start now.' Luiza made a move toward her dresser and began listlessly sorting things into piles until she heard the door shut loudly behind her.

Alone again, her whole body craved sleep. Today was a day of goodbyes, and yet she had been hiding out in her bedroom for most of the morning. She was meeting Carmichael for the last time today, and she still had to make up some excuse for leaving the house before the party. She'd also promised her father she'd help him pick flowers from the garden, but outside, the colours were too vivid, and the intensity of the light gave her headaches. Small sounds amplified in her mind and took on physical shape: if she dropped a spoon on the floor, its clatter reverberated for several minutes; when her father rubbed a wet finger around the edge of his wineglass to amuse the girls, it divided the hemispheres of her brain, thrumming in each side. When Evie pointed to rabbits among the clouds, Luiza saw only turds. Worst of all were Hugo's delicate orchids. She'd helped him coddle them, but they were vulgar to her now, transforming into inverted ears, a spleen, sections of occluded rectum centred on the table at dinner.

Her mother didn't want to hear about any of it—the naps, the headaches, the 'so-called' images, these psychic encroachments from the natural world. She cautioned Luiza not to indulge herself. In a few days, they'd be leaving for Canada. There wasn't time for her to *carry on*.

Luiza left her room and went downstairs and out back to the veranda, inhaling the humid air. These days, Dora always seemed harried and put-upon, as though she herself would have to do all the packing and handle all the preparations alone, rather than simply bossing the maids around. Here she was again, scolding Luiza from the back doorway.

'Luiza! Answer me, will you? Take this to your father.'

Luiza took the crystal glass of sherry from her mother, and was briefly mesmerized by the points of light that flashed in its cuts until she tripped a little and had to lick the sweet liquor that had gathered in the space between her thumb and index finger. But there wasn't time for meditating on prisms today. As she walked out toward the garden, she wondered if her father would be able to detect her preoccupation on her face, how she kept thinking of Carmichael, how she'd been lying to her family for months now to hide the fact that she was having an affair with a man twice her age, slipping away to hidden, marginal places: the city's northern beaches, unaired hotel rooms—places no one they knew would ever go. But she liked it, the dirty feeling that came with knowing they were living a life apart, the hushed details of secret meeting places, the sneaking around. Channelled into Carmichael, her hopelessness induced an oblique sort of pleasure. He needed her.

Still half expecting her father to read her mind, she fixed her face into wide-eyed stillness as she approached him, but he remained down on one knee, shirt sleeves rolled up over elbows, as he took the glass and sipped without looking up, murmuring his amateur gardener's litany of self-recriminations: Really, he ought to have had Georges put the tomatoes beside the marigolds. And the geraniums weren't really dead; they just needed a good cutting back. This year's attempt at cantaloupes was a bit of a dog's breakfast, he feared (and she did see in their withered skins something unwholesome: the extracted brains of infants or small animals). He could go on in this pleasant, preoccupied way indefinitely, that is if Dora didn't come out and interrupt them like she usually did. Luiza used to think it was simply her mother's childish envy at seeing them enjoying a calm moment together, but now she understood that these periods when he was relatively steady were, in some ways, the most frightening of all; they felt like a held breath. Her mother was watching for signs, preparing herself for what his next cycle might bring. And after Florida, even Luiza had to admit that while her father's plateaus were contracting, the poles of his moods were growing farther apart, each becoming more extreme than the one before. These days, the glint of hope they'd had in Florida was too dangerous to remember. In Canada, they would return to the familiar, old pattern: hospitalization, sedatives, antidepressants. *Symptom management.*

But for now, they walked side by side through the freshly mown grass, which was safe from her perverted perceptions as long as they were together. Clusters of large, soft-bodied flies billowed up from underfoot, their long, fine wings segmented in iridescent green and blue.

'I think these are the ones,' said her father, gesturing his spade toward the cloud of insects, 'that only live for one day.' He said they must get it all done—mating, reproducing, the entire cycle in a single day.

'Are they the same ones that mate for life?' Luiza asked.

But he pointed out that two such exigencies forced on a single variety would be too cruel, and surely would have wiped them out long ago. So they agreed: probably more of a Roman approach.

Her father made a long face when they came to the bird of paradise plants, saying they looked very poor indeed and also needed cutting back. Some were fragrant and strong, but some had the blight, their blossoms rotting and stinking on their stems. Together they selected the best, her father laying the long stalks across her outstretched arms.

The flowers now neatly arranged in the basket, they sat for a few minutes on the garden bench and, at last, Luiza felt her heart beating at a regular rhythm, the breeze cool on her neck. She felt neither wild nor empty, nor even conscious of her own skin. This was why one lived: Love. Wind. Red. But think it and the moment's gone, a saturated and irretrievable snapshot.

'Pensive, poppet?' her father said, gazing at her. She'd been speaking to him in her head again but hadn't actually said anything out loud for some time. He seemed to be returning to her for the first time since Florida, and he was physically stronger than he had been for weeks. But she just smiled. No use in saying it: how tired she'd become of her own voice, her own thoughts.

'I was just thinking about your beautiful gardens. What will happen to them when we're gone? What if the new owners plant ugly things?'

'We'll have a new garden. Things do grow in Canada, you know. We're not moving to the Arctic.'

'But only for such a short time.'

'We'll pick the flowers with the prettiest names. Alyssum, pasques, bleeding hearts.' He took her hand then and spoke very earnestly. 'You wait. There's nothing like spring after a long winter. It shocks you every time. Every year you think it can't possibly come—nothing will ever live again. And then it does and you breathe with new lungs.'

She wanted so much to believe him, but she knew too well it was a confidence game. Her father could make anything sound beautiful, but she believed him less and less. Only seeing Carmichael could rearrange this day, relieve the pressure building behind her ribs. From all the numbing tasks she had still to accomplish, he would divert her. She just had to get to him.

'A game, a game!' Evie and Magda came running through the grass, launching themselves at Hugo's pant legs. 'We want you both to play a game with us.'

They all walked to the playhouse, Evie and Magda bickering about what to play.

'Not bowls again!' Evie wailed.

Her father snapped a flower from its stem and tucked it behind Luiza's ear. Then his smile inverted, and he clapped loudly and broke up the girls, who were shoving each other now. '*Boules*, ladies,' he said, pushing them apart. 'Let us say *boules*. Let us not be vulgar.'

The cloth bag containing the small wooden balls was found, and they walked toward the green behind the house. Her father scooped Evie up and peeled her hair away from the dirt-streaked trail of tears, and it struck Luiza that at last he was strong enough do this. He was alive again.

'Come, come, Evelyn. No crying. We'll give Evie the mat, will we?'

Evie was pacified by this small gesture and aligned the jack.

'You know,' he said, 'this is a venerable and subversive game we're playing. It goes back to the thirteenth century, conjecturally even the twelfth. In his biography of Thomas Becket—'

Luiza tried to listen as she pulled the flower from behind her ear, inhaled its scent, and wiped the golden powder from its thin stamen, coating her palms while her father's voice distantly sketched out medieval London. At the centre of the blossom was a tiny black bug that repelled her with its rapid, writhing movement, so she tried to rake it out with her nail and crush it without damaging the petal—'. . . *holiday amusements for young men . . .*' She peeled open the flower only to discover a swarm of the same tiny bugs—'. . . *leaping, shooting, wrestling, throwing of javelins and casting of stones . . .*'— then killed them all by crushing the flower, and dropping it down in disgust, while Magda barked, 'That one's dead, Evie, you don't get to chalk it!' '*In jactu lapidum . . .*' Her fingers coated in flower juice and dead insects. 'But it touched!' '*Jactu lapidum . . .*' 'It did not!' '*Lapidum . . .*'

'What did you *say*?' Her voice was harsh. She hadn't meant to say it so loud.

'That is what they called it—casting of stones. *In jactu lapidum.*' It was the jolt he needed and he was off again. 'But the game was banned in the reign of Edward the Third, along with many others, of course . . .'

The catching on words, their compulsive iteration—her throat tightened as she noted the early signs of oncoming mania: soon there would be unopened shopping bags everywhere, slurred tributes to women's body parts. A private, internal voyage to a fictive star. '. . . *worried it interfered with the practice of archery so vital in battle, the war-mongers . . .* ' Then, inevitably, several weeks in his 'winding sheet,' the blinds drawn.

'Let me show you something,' he was saying to Evie now, placing a ball in Evie's hand and her hand in his. 'Have you heard of a forehand draw?'

'You can't help her!' Magda, outraged.

Luiza knew she should stay, play their little game, be with her family—*want* to be with her family—stop pulping tiny insects. But the truth was, she couldn't wait to get away from them.

# DORA

The bus heaves through the countryside, and Dora sits stiffly, unable to sleep, absentmindedly expecting the luggage stuffed into racks overhead to begin falling into the aisles. Outside, rain pours down so heavily that sections of the flimsy shacks that line the road wash away, bits of tin and wood mixing with garbage, all running into the cataracts of water that overwhelm the gutters and rush downhill past the bus. Staring out the window, Dora sometimes cannot see a road at all. A thirty-hour trip with nothing to look at but water and poverty.

She has never travelled alone until now, never been on a bus. She has left the girls alone with the maids a few times before, but this time feels different, as though she's abandoning them somehow; as though during these few days away, they could be lost to her. It's Evie she worries about most of all. She's drawn to that low-class girl, Brigitta, in the way of adolescent girls who, for a time, fall in love with one another and turn inward, involute as the whorls of seashell. No one else matters. Magda sees through Brigitta, and Luiza would have too, but Evie is pliable, with a vacuum of wanting inside her since losing Luiza. Girls like Brigitta can tend want. Naive longing. Until they grow bored. She told the maids, 'Make sure they get to that camp every day. And make sure they come home. No sleepovers. That girl is *indecente*.'

As condensation fogs the windows and the structures outside the bus blur into vague grey shapes, Dora watches tiny rivers branch apart against the glass, the wipers pump against the windshield. This is what she has begun to wish for at home in Rio, with its perpetual parties, its ever-hanging white, tropical sun—for the landscape to mirror her grief, to show her some fucking sympathy. Sympathy for her, of all people. When the *Confederados* arrived in Brazil, her father told her, they found cockroaches the size of a fist, and mosquitoes carrying dengue, malaria, encephalitis. A third of her ancestors died; a third went home, and accepted Northern rule; a third stayed, thrashed and coaxed the landscape. And now she, their descendant, can do almost nothing for herself, by herself. Some part of her is grateful that Canada will be hard. Perhaps all that labour will wash away the slick sheen of her advantages, the way Luiza had said it would, when she was trying to be keen.

'Maybe it will give us *character*,' she said. 'Like pioneers, or tradespeople.'

'It's not the frontier, my darling,' Dora said dryly. 'Toronto is a city with cars and highways and tall buildings.'

'But it's very cold, isn't it?' Luiza asked hopefully. 'We might suffer terribly!'

A convent. It was both impossible and somehow natural. Her poor, unhappy girl—what had he *done* to her? But there was always some unnamed transgression Luiza seemed to want to atone for, even before Carmichael—some imagined sin she felt they had committed, simply by existing.

'Because we take too much,' she used to say. 'We have so much more than we need.'

At the time, Dora had refused to feel guilty. Cockroaches, mosquitoes, dengue fever. Her people, she told herself, fought for everything: for her and her friends, who played hours of golf each day, and never once changed a bed. Never boarded a bus.

A cloud of dust falls on Dora's simple cream-coloured dress as the taxi pulls away the next afternoon. What was she thinking, travelling in a light-coloured fabric? For several minutes, she brushes herself off, feeling fixed to the ground. There is dust on her fine, heeled leather shoes, and she bends to wipe those as well, licking her fingers. Something Luiza would do. Standing in front of the convent from the photograph, she wonders if her daughter could really be inside. But going in and finding nothing would mean her search is finally over. Nothing left to do but sail. The whitewashed building before her is larger than she expected, with small terracotta tiles curved and overlapping on the roof like rows of scales. Above the door is a little recess that houses a statue of Christ, framed by two large windows. If she allows her vision to blur a little, it looks like a face, the mouth agape. There are black, threadlike stains spreading across the white facade from the rain, and except for some scrollwork around the edges of the roof and a pretty little bell tower with a rooster-topped weathervane, the whole building is quite austere.

When a nun comes out and asks her what help she needs, Dora realizes she's trembling, unsure whether she's been standing there for minutes or hours. She explains that she's looking for Luiza, and the nun tells her there's no one here by that name, but she should go see the postulants—the new girls who come for a year and receive vocational guidance without having to make a commitment to the convent. If her Luiza is here, she'd have to be among them.

The nun introduces herself as Sister Medeiros but asks no other questions—perhaps, Dora thinks, it's not so unusual for people to hide here. As she's led down the arched, marble hallway very slowly, she has to fight the urge to break into a run ahead of her guide. And where would she run to? There is door after door, and Sister Medeiros continues to plod past each one, expressionless. These must be games the mind plays on anyone who's ever lost someone, truly *lost* them. Never seen the proof of her body lowered into the ground, never seen her lie still as she is covered with dirt. *Maybe she ran away, maybe she has amnesia, maybe she was stolen. Maybe.* The refuge of every mother of a soldier whose body is unrecovered, or whose child has disappeared. Finally, the sister pauses and opens a door.

Dora scans the row of postulants bent over pews, thinking she sees Luiza in each of their faces, and starting every time as if to run toward them. But it's not her, not her, not her—she is seasick from her tiny abortive movements—and it's still not her again and again and again until it is. It is. It's her. It's her pale face frowning into the prayer book. It's her auburn hair tied back sloppily but still so lovely. It's her body, alive and dry and sitting as calmly wrapped around a book as it so often was at home. Dora starts then stops again because it can't be her— she will not clutch and slap and weep all over some other woman's child. But it *is* her, and Dora finds she runs like she's in a dream, too slowly. When she finally reaches her, she doesn't clutch or slap. She falls to her knees, crumples, thanks God, and sobs into her lap.

Dora lets her hair be stroked for some time before she straightens up and allows herself to see what she already knows—that she has, after all, been crying into the lap of some other woman's child. And as the girl holds her, Dora wishes so much that Luiza *had* come here because this is a place where they embrace strangers who weep in their laps.


After a few minutes, Sister Medeiros gently gathers Dora up, unpeeling her from the young girl who is not Luiza. She offers to give her a tour of the convent, but all Dora can do is stare ahead, her mouth incapable of movement, as she is led toward the door.

'The Poor Clares are contemplative, and our mission is to serve God by being ever prayerful.'

As the woman speaks, Dora feels grateful for Sister Medeiros, grateful for the heat of her rounded body beside her, for the certainty of her step, for the conviction in her voice. Grateful that she seems to know where she is going and that she's taking Dora there. The sister clearly believes what she's saying, and maybe it's true. Dora is grateful there are people in the world who still believe things. They stop before a painting of a saint holding a lantern.

'By the grace of St. Clarissa's prayers,' Sister Medeiros says reverently, 'the convent in Assisi was miraculously saved from the plundering Saracen hordes. And so we all follow her example, and remain poor. All day and much of the night, we are vigilant sentinels who sit in silent contemplation of God, in adoration of the Blessed Sacraments.'

Next they go to a room full of women sitting at tables, hunched over handcrafts. They're making the kinds of little trinkets Maricota likes to give the girls—dried flowers, embroidered handkerchiefs.

'One of our tasks is to make sacred vestments, liturgical robes and stoles,' the sister continues, seeming to register Dora losing focus, her waning ability to execute movement on her own. 'Thus we celebrate the Word, the Eucharist, and the sacraments with works from our own hands, made in the glory of God as an act of supplication, adoration, and love. Today Sister Araújo is making candles. You can join her. You see how you do it? You take the wick and dip it in the wax, just a thin layer.'

And now she is sitting Dora down, taking her hands and manipulating them so that they dip a length of wick into the beeswax, a coin tied to each end for weight, then plunge it into cold water and dip again. She does this a few times, then hangs the wick on a broom balanced between two chairs, leaving two very thin candles to dry. Wick, wax, broom. With the woman's arms still wrapped around her, Dora wonders if maybe she can stay here, if she could be led through her days by the ringing of church bells and the thick, warm arms of women who believe they are loved by God.

Eventually, Dora feels Sister Medeiros back away, leaving her to dip her candles again and again, moving like an automaton, soothed by the simplicity and repetition of the action but still thinking. Always thinking. No, she couldn't stay here because she could never stop thinking and if God had anything to say to her, she'd never hear it. Will she have to wonder forever about Luiza? Maybe pills will make it stop, or a lobotomy, or the shock treatment Hugo hated so much. She'd rather feel nothing than live with never knowing. What did it say that she had been so willing to believe that Luiza could be here, that she would have left them, let them grieve? She remembers her daughter's long stare, how she always seemed to be looking beyond them, unable to locate within reach whatever is was she needed. And yet, something in Dora, even now, still thinks Luiza could have done it after all. That she could swim and swim away from them and toward these hundreds of mothers.

But for Dora to have left her family now, with Hugo in the hospital and the girls practically feral, all because she could not let go. How will they ever forgive her.

*Thank you, sweet girl. For taking him from me. For lying with him in bathtubs and deciphering all his strange phrases. Or pretending to. Thank you for staying.* All these things she had wanted to say countless times, but the closest she came was in Florida: 'It's good that you were here,' she had said, turning a tumbler of gin in her hands. 'You spared the girls the worst of it.'

At the time, Luiza said nothing. She sat and had a drink with her mother, until Dora finally left the room.

But later, on the voyage home, it seethed out: '*You*. You did this to him. I never wanted to come here. I helped you talk him into it because I believed you. You did this.'

She closes her eyes and takes a deep breath. Wherever Luiza is, Dora tells herself now, at least she's free. Like Dora's, her life was claimed by men—a madman, a sick man—before it had really begun. But Luiza got away.

Sister Medeiros comes back to see if Dora would like dinner. When she says no, the sister asks if she would like guidance. Dora blushes, says no again, *obrigada*, but asks instead if there's somewhere quiet she could sit for a little while, until she's ready to go. She's ashamed to ask for rest but can't imagine beginning the long journey back into the city feeling this way, turned inside out, nerves peeled back and strafed, yet somehow numb at the same time. She's led to a beautiful garden and wishes for a moment Hugo could see it. The sister helps her to a bench, and just as the woman is about to go, Dora asks her if there has been a girl here with hair like the other one, the one she embraced, that unusual deep auburn hair. Sister Medeiros says no, no one like that here, but she could give her the addresses of the other convents in Bahia.

'*Não, obrigada mas não precisa*,' Dora says. 'She would have come here.'

# HUGO

ugo faces the shore, then kicks his legs, turning back out to sea. He's not sure what he was expecting. Not her, of course—the drugs have extinguished any hope of holy visions—but at least a feeling, words transmitted to his mind, an electric thrust to his heart. But as he treads circles in the water, a few people have begun to gather on the beach; curious, concerned, they huddle and confer. He sees himself now through their eyes, a grown man, fully dressed, swimming fifty yards out and shouting at nothing. He wants to tear off his clothes, swim out farther, be surrounded by the sea, consumed by a body larger than he can conceive of. But he could strip off his own skin and still not get down to the place where he went wrong; he could swim forever and still never find her. Because she's not here.

He is tired of alarming people. A voice says, *Go back*. His own. He swims toward the shore until he stumbles onto the sand and waves at the group of people higher up on the beach; some wave back before they disperse. Then he walks on for a few minutes until he finds the spot in the sand, the very spot they stood the night of Luiza's belated birthday celebration. They had watched gulls bob on the water and Luiza said each bird should have a name: Miguel, Felicity, Gordon. Something silly like that. Eventually, they'd gotten up from the sand and walked the thirty minutes back toward the Copacabana Palace Hotel, as he is doing now, and their conversation turned to books, as it often did, because they were usually easier to discuss than life.

'I just finished the diaries of a woman from São Paulo. *Children of the Dark*,' Luiza told him, staring off toward the mountains on the other side of the bay. 'She lived in a *favela* with three children all by herself. She collected paper in the streets to sell, and some days had no food at all. She talks about a little boy who was so hungry he ate bad meat and his whole body swelled up.'

'Did he live?'

'Of course not.' She stopped then and turned toward the mountains, the *favelas* that line their peaks. 'How can all those desperate people be up there, with nothing, and we're down here with everything, and everybody just stays where they are?'

'It's like that everywhere in South America though, isn't it? We have no special problems here.' Hugo knew that this was a ridiculous thing to say, but he was tired, and too agitated for one of her heartfelt laments. Normally, it was one of the things he loved about her, but at that moment he felt hollow, scoured out—typical of his 'in-between' periods.

'I think we need a revolution here,' she said, still transported, still staring off into the distance. 'It's a wonder they don't come down from those hills and kill us all in our beds.'

'At least they have a nice view . . . usually it's the other way around, and the rich people have the panorama.' She looked at him then, not with the disgust he knew he deserved but saddened. Something had shifted between them, and now she was the one earnestly asking questions while he was insincere and glib. 'Anyway,' he continued, more quietly, 'don't wish for revolutions. They are often bloodiest to the poor. Reform is the best we can hope for.'

She snorted a little, in that way of young people who must endure the tepid aspirations of the middle-aged. Even she had begun to tire of him. This, he thinks now, must have been why she preferred him when he was high. If he'd been high that night, he would have dropped to his knees and drawn out battle plans with her in the sand. For too long he had depended on her admiration of him because, he sees now, he had lost that of his wife. Dora did not want him ill, and Luiza did not want him well; in her eyes, he was better, smarter, more beautiful when he was sick. Maybe he was just one of the tragic, marginal people she liked to imagine herself fighting for. Or was she right—by agreeing to treatment was he giving up the best, most essential part of himself? Again he feels the pull toward the water, toward his promise that if she were to come back, they would stay. Stay in this golden town and never leave.

But instead he walks, and imagines what he might tell her, what might interest her. Would she be excited by what was happening here now? There were no revolts, no riots in the streets, but there had been some faint rumbles of dissatisfaction: students protesting, unions organizing. He had sometimes mused in the past that the same perfect climate and genial temperament that made Brazilians so warm and open also made them ineffective. There was a joke: *No one fought in that revolution—it was during the rainy season.* But *now:* a barely perceptible shift in air currents, a palpable unease among the moneyed people. *His* people. Somewhere, lately, a serpent's egg has hatched, and the collective intangible energy of millions of hungry, dissatisfied souls is keeping it warm at night. Another thing he has to leave behind—something was changing in this country, some current beneath the surface. She would have wanted to see this—she never would have wanted to leave.

She, like him, always saw traces, bits of ephemera, strange things in the margins: a headless chicken in an alleyway tied up in red string, an empty bottle of wine beside it. Witchcraft, someone would explain casually. Maybe *macumba,* or voodoo. Things other people seemed to ignore. And if he pivots in the sand, he can see the apartment building where a friend of hers lives, facing the beach. Luiza told him she'd once stood on its fifteenth-floor balcony and saw something red and glowing in the sand. Something radioactive had washed up, she feared, or maybe it was just a new breed of phosphorescent jellyfish. But she could not stop staring and finally took the elevator down, walked between cars and across the street and onto the sand. A single red candle placed in a hand-dug pit. More voodoo. It unnerved her for days. 'Why can't they keep it up in the hills?' Dora had sighed. 'That used to be such a classy neighbour-hood.' *Every monkey on his own branch.* He jerks around now, sure he will see that same candle, sure that his memory has conjured it, but there are just some people stretched out in the sand smoking and laughing, others fifty yards away play-ing a game of *futebol* in the twilight. Beyond them he can see the hills that overlook Guanabara Bay, and still, even now, wet and tired and drugged, he sees the threads, the connections between things—Luiza and this city and the people who came before them and everything he'll leave behind.

'It's true,' he says to no one. To her.

It's true we are all steeped in longing, and wish for that golden time. That is the curse they brought when they came, Cabral's men, who sailed from Portugal in search of gold and coffee, sugar and rubber. They entered the bay in January and thought it was the mouth of a great river. They called it Rio de Janeiro. The River of January. And they gazed upon the Tupi people and were themselves warmed by their naked, red, sun-covered bodies. And they wrote letters home, wrote of the beauty of these people who felt no shame, and their generosity, for the men gave freely of their weapons and fruit, and the women laid down with them (they said) and fucked them sweetly and were

not dishonoured. And as darkness gathered over Europe, reformations and counter-reformations, these men attained in this
bay a paradise here on earth for which they neither had to atone
nor die, and after they learned from the men and impregnated
the women, they enslaved them and then longed forever for those
first, innocent days, free and without shame. This is what he
should have told her, that night on the beach.

So the masses come now, down from the hills and from the
drylands of the northeast, and they want back in, want their
little bit of the beach, and they edge out *The Copacabana Way
of Life*, just as she would have wanted, and he is a monster to
ever grieve for it because it was always its own kind of lie, and
maybe something better, something more will corrode the
golden sheen and replace it, red and seething and alive. But he
does, he does miss it—like Cabral's bloody conquerors, he
aches for the time *before,* their before. Before he was ill, before
she saw him pull his own hair from his bleeding scalp, before
he broke her heart. Before she was gone.

He could keep walking, past the hospital, beyond the city
limits, into the mountains. Away from the harbour and its
waiting ships. No amount of speaking to Luiza in his mind has
brought her back, but maybe this is not the right time—he is
medicated. His senses, his receptors, are dulled. If he ran from
the hospital, hid in the hills, waited until he was high again—
maybe then he could hear her.

But before the next high there will be a low. When this
nascent clarity clouds over, he will begin to slide downward,
and on his way down he will have just enough time to feel it: a
perverse nostalgia for this moment right now. For this moment
of understanding, at last, that despite all his futile seeking, she
really is gone, and soon he too must leave. And for his grief, for
the capacity to miss and love Luiza in the normal, human way.
Grief, after all, will eventually respond to solace. Grief can be
consoled by love, by literature, by the childish belief that they'll

be reunited someday. But depression will follow eventually, and when it does, he won't be able to grieve for her. He'll barely be able to imagine her. The once-dazzling ideas will be too numerous, come too fast, crowding out the light until they suffocate and there is nothing. Frenetic, confused, feral, he'll pace the halls at night, trying to remember her face. Trying to retrieve this deep, aching feeling of mourning her.

# DORA

Dora wakes to the sound of bells and sunlight flooding through the white curtains. She feels groggy and bloated—she's overslept. It must be late. She's embarrassed, even though at first she can't remember where she is. But soon images take shape, arrange themselves into a memory: last night, one of the sisters making up a bed for her, though Dora can't recall any arrangements being made, any discussions had about where she would stay or for how long. She doesn't even know when she left that perfect garden. She does remember being desperate to stop thinking, stop feeling, and then quickly swallowing a sleeping pill from the bottle in her purse while Sister Medeiros pulled back the blanket and sheets at a perfect angle and laid out a clean, white nightgown for her. Dora had to resist the impulse to ask her to stay and tuck her in. She thought then of her years at Catholic school, how comforting the routine had been, bells ringing out, rationing the day. It startled her how grateful she was, almost thirty years later, to again feel voided of autonomy, guided by a reassuring pattern of actions and rituals.

'There is always a sister available for counsel if you should need it,' the sister said, taking her hand. 'Day or night.' Her palm was dry and warm, and Dora held it up to her cheek for a moment while the woman kindly said nothing.

'Luiza.' It comes out of her mouth before she's even formed the thought in her head, before she has time to remember that she didn't find her. Then something cold floods her spine, her stomach. Now, she tells herself, let go. Collect the girls, discharge Hugo, embrace the maids, Bechelli, even Georges. Say goodbye. But how will she get back home? She sits immobilized on the bed and waits for someone to come and show her where to go next.

And soon someone does come. There is a gentle knock at the door and Sister Medeiros pokes her head in, speaking softly. '*Senhora?* Could you please come with me?'

'*Sim, sim.* I'm coming.'

The sister waits outside as Dora rises and dresses quickly, too relieved to have something to do to ask why.

Fifteen minutes later, Dora sits on a lacquered pew, alone now, late-morning light spilling in through the chapel's stained glass windows. Despite the bright rays of light, she feels herself slipping away again. The sleeping pills have made her fuzzy, unable to keep her eyes open. There is something damp around her mouth. Drool. Wipe it away. Then a shape. Female. Blood orange sun behind her, multicoloured spots going by like tiny comets. They shrink as Dora's eyes adjust to the brightness, but the shape is still there, faceless, the filtered light a corona behind it. *She will be our angel.*

The last one had the right hair but the wrong face. This one has the wrong hair but the right face.

This one says, 'Hello, Mother.'

Dora doesn't shout or cry. She just reaches out to touch Luiza's face, to make sure it's real. But the touch doesn't reassure her, because her hand doesn't feel like it belongs to her body. They sit like this in the chapel for several minutes, her daughter's hand lying over her own, still cupping her cheek, until Luiza begins to shift uncomfortably.

'I don't think I can explain it all now, but I promise I will.' Luiza gently slides a thumb under her mother's eye, wiping away tears Dora hadn't known she was crying. 'Will you come with me to Midday Prayers?'

Now Dora is in another room, full of people. She is shivering, being touched, Luiza's warm hands on her upper arms, guiding her. Now she is being manoeuvred into another hard, shiny pew, as Luiza takes her place at the front of the room with the other sisters, facing Dora. Now they are singing, Luiza's mouth a perfect, untrembling O.

*I will praise you Lord . . . I will wake the dawn.*

Psalms fill the chapel and Dora feels something knotted inside her loosen. Watching Luiza sing, standing perfectly still, not even looking at her, Dora has trouble breathing and has to close her eyes and focus on the singing until she can hear her own thoughts again. She has everything she wanted now, she tells herself, everything she needs. She has her daughter back.

# EVIE

'What do you mean, *bust him out*?' asks Magda, riding her bicycle back and forth along the sidewalk just outside their front gate. She's too prickly from boredom to bother hiding her contempt for Brigitta, who either doesn't notice or doesn't care.

'Like you bust someone out of prison!' says Brigitta, with the bursting energy that, just a few days ago, Evie had wanted so much for herself. Maybe Evie is misremembering Brigitta's prodding gaze upon the mute man at the hospital, her fitful kindnesses, how her eyes have turned cold and hard as enamel. Brigitta is the only one who imagined they could get her father out of hospital, who is brave enough to do it. Doesn't that prove she still wants to protect people?

'E. and I saw this poor, dreadful man there. I bet they're all getting shock therapy. Haven't you read *One Flew Over the Cuckoo's Nest*? It's basically torture.'

Evie cringes every time she thinks of the man—the boy?—at the hospital, with his collapsed face, his silent cry. He may not even have been as old as Luiza. They left him alone in that room, disoriented and raw, to fight against his own body. Did he scream inside? Beg them to stop? How much damage had they done?

'We'll pretend we're just going to visit and then we'll bust him out!' Brigitta continues. 'He *is* your dad.'

'I *know* he's my dad,' says Magda.

'Well, I would do it for my dad.'

Magda looks startled, like Evie, by the thought of their father suffering some violent electric treatment. Shock therapy. She doesn't actually know what that is, but it does sound painful and wrong, and like a lie—shot through with lightning like Frankenstein's monster in the movie they saw, deformed and terrifying. Terrified. Like he was in Florida.

'And when I told Brigitta about how we saw Mom with Carmichael, she said it sounds like Mom's just shunting Dad off so she can have our last weeks here all to herself.' Even as Evie says it, she can feel herself blinking too much, not believing it. But she needs Brigitta to inflame Magda, and herself. She needs Brigitta to make the plan and Magda to come along, to protect her and their father as they all move, perfectly and powerlessly, toward his rescue.

'Okay. Fine,' says Magda, folding her arms across her chest and leaning back on her bicycle. 'But you don't get to talk to him. He doesn't even know you.'

At lunchtime, Brigitta forges another note and this time their counsellor barely glances out the window to make sure Bechelli is there.

On the stairwell landing, Brigitta swings out her arms, stopping Evie and Magda before they can head toward the exit. 'As soon as we get down the stairs, we peel out of here for dear life, okay? So your driver doesn't see us.'

'Wait, why?' demands Magda. Brigitta hasn't said anything about avoiding Bechelli before now.

'We need to do this on our own. We can't keep relying on the help. Besides, how will the chauffeur react when he sees that your dad is escaping? Even if he were willing to help, wouldn't that get him into trouble?'

'Fine,' says Magda. 'We'll just go the other way. He always reads the paper while he waits anyway.'

Evie gapes at her sister. 'What happens when we're not here at pick-up time? Won't he get in even more trouble? And what about Maricota and Odete? They'll flip.'

But Magda's jaw is set and Evie knows she's already lost. 'In a couple of weeks, we'll never see Maricota and Odete again. We have to think about Dad first, not them.'

Once they exit the building, they turn quickly away from the parked Silver Cloud. As they walk, they match up their strides, each leading with her left leg, and together count out their lunch money to pay for a taxi, which they hail on the tree-lined street on the far side of the YWCA building. Evie vibrates inside—this is so forbidden and foreign and thrilling.

'Can he take the scenic route?' asks Brigitta. 'My aunt and uncle never want to bring me into the city. Ask him to take the scenic route.'

'*Você poderia pegar o caminho mais bonito?*' asks Evie, and Brigitta gives her arm an approving squeeze.

'It's like you're a different person when you speak Portuguese. Like having a whole new friend!'

The windows are rolled down and Brigitta leans her face out. Soon they find themselves on the coast, driving once again along Copacabana Beach.

'Is it far from here?' asks Brigitta urgently. 'Ask him if it's far from here.'

Evie asks and the driver answers, gesturing with a loose hand. 'He says it's at the other end of the beach. It's a pretty long walk.'

'Tell him to let us off here,' says Brigitta.

'No way,' says Magda. 'It's a *really* long walk.'

'Don't worry—we won't have to walk.' Brigitta is looking toward the beach, and once out of the taxi, she strides ahead of them, across the mosaic sidewalk, and onto the sand. 'It's so strange,' she says, stopping to pick up some sand. 'Don't you think it's strange, that the sidewalk ends and the beach just begins? No dunes, no parking lot, just street and then beach. I've never seen that before.'

Evie and Magda don't answer because to them it doesn't seem strange. But Brigitta's attention has turned to some women playing *peteca*, hitting a feathered shuttlecock with their hands. She jumps up and down excitedly for a few minutes until someone bats the shuttlecock in her direction and she flails about wildly, uselessly trying to get it back into the air. Laughing, one of the women walks over to retrieve the *peteca* from Brigitta, who gives her a hug, making everyone laugh. Evie has never met anyone like her, someone who seems both older and younger than she really is, who, like Luiza, cares so little about what other people think. And now she remembers how it feels to be on the precipice of loving her.

Brigitta is standing in front of a long row of bike stands holding dozens of bikes. She finds the man who is renting them out and then gestures for Evie. 'Ask him how much for three. I think I have enough. Can you really ride them? Ask him if they really go on the beach.'

But Evie just points at several people biking away, across the sand, which must be different from American sand because Brigitta seems so flustered and excited. Evie takes Brigitta's money and translates the negotiation of the rental—two hours—and as they mount the bikes, Brigitta is shaking a little, smiling and red-faced, and even Magda lets out a shriek of laughter as her bike wobbles in the sand. As Evie rides easily, smoothly past them, she sees the gravity and disapproval lift from her sister's face, sees a girl she recognizes, the child Magda once was.

A voice echoes behind her. *Hello, Luiza! Hello!* But the voice is quieter now, landing lightly in Evie's ear, then ringing out into silence. When she glances back, Luiza still isn't there. But there is something familiar, something or someone propelling her to pedal harder.

Brigitta is here, and Magda, and they all labour against the packed wet sand until their revolutions become more steady, more sure. Evie leads the way, heading for the green hills on the horizon, her father an invisible beacon somewhere at the foot of them, pulling them toward him. As slow as they're moving, she knows what they're doing is necessary—he needs them. He needs her.

In Brazil, Evie has been shrinking, disappearing into tree-tops, too thin and pale and quiet to stand out amid all the colour, this endless sunshine. But here on the monochrome beach, she shines like Magda. Like Luiza. No longer skirting the margins the way she has for months, a nice, no-one girl. If Canada is all grey and white—snow shrouding the school campus, she and Brigitta arm in arm in twin charcoal blazers—maybe she will shine there too.

# LUIZA

## MARCH 1962

After she helped her father gather the flowers for the goodbye party, Luiza gave up looking for an excuse to tell her mother and simply snuck away to the tram stop. Taking the tram especially pleased her because it was something her mother would never do—she drove or was driven everywhere. Luiza found a seat and leaned into the open window, lulled by the repetitive sound of metal against metal. The constant clicking reminded her of going to the beach in Ipanema during those long summer months she spent with her grandparents, a memory that gave her no comfort now, unsure of how much of it was hers and how much she'd absorbed from others.

But one thing she knew for certain: as a child, she had been indulged. Tap-dancing lessons, horseback riding, Girl Guides, ballet performances at the Municipal Theatre. And yet it had felt very grave at times, being a child. *Like some rough gale, blowing me all about . . . while I blaze and swoon*, she'd once written to Carmichael. She blushed now, humiliation surging through her again when she remembered the stolen phrases scattered throughout her letters to him. *My talents, I know, are thin.*

The air around Luiza soon changed, cut by the smell of sea water. The tram was now rolling down Avenida Atlantica,

approaching the expanse of Copacabana Beach, green mountains on either side and swarmed by surfer boys and bikini
girls. They'd better not be going to the beach, she thought.
Carmichael hadn't said to bring a swimsuit. Their time together
recently had felt strained. He was often distracted and never
asked her to stay, and there were often long silences, periods
when she hoped he might say the kinds of things he used to,
that proved he was paying attention. Still, it felt exciting to go
somewhere downtown she'd never been, some place her parents wouldn't want her to go. She imagined how he would look
at her, eyes just wet but not tearing, and how he'd say he never
meant to fall in love with her—it was all supposed to be good
fun—but he *had*. And she would answer that she was sorry if
she hurt him, she'd never meant to, but what else could she do?
They were her family and they needed her more.

And then, as though she'd conjured him, there he stood,
waiting for her at the next stop, his perfectly smooth hair
combed back and shining in the sun, watching people go by
with his particular mix of bemusement and disdain. There he
was, promising something else.

He led her to a small underground nightclub, practically
deserted on such a beautiful, sunstruck day. Before sitting down
at the sticky table where he had pulled out a chair for her, she
took off the white kid gloves she wore to annoy her mother.

'My hands, at least, can be washed. These are antique.'

'A bit seedy, I know,' he said without glancing up from the
menu, 'but tucked away. And don't worry. They'll still put an
umbrella in your drink.'

Once they had ordered, Carmichael folded his hands on
the table in front of him, as though she were a business associate he was making a show of deferring to.

'So, how is the mood at home?'

'Oh, tense I suppose. The maids are running themselves
ragged. Mother is directing. I haven't even begun to pack up

my room and I emote whenever I get the chance. My father is . . . gardening. I suppose he's the only sensible one.'

She wanted so much to seem detached and sophisticated, but she could feel the tears at the corners of her eyes and was paralyzed trying to decide which was the greater humiliation—to wipe them away or let them fall. Ever since she found out that the family would be moving, she had cried every day. For Carmichael, for her family. For the blurred outlines of the coming life she couldn't make real in her mind.

'Hey, hey. No tears allowed.' Carmichael reached over the table with a napkin, which he handed to her, rather than wipe her eyes himself, as she'd hoped he would. 'Maybe this will be good for you. No, I mean it. There are fascinating things happening in North America. Civil rights. Shouting in the streets. All those things you're interested in. Have you decided what you'll do there?'

'What do you mean?'

'Well, everyone's always saying they're so much more advanced than we are. Women up there can do all sorts of things.'

'Everyone's always saying that, but nobody ever says *what*. What sorts of things? What should I do?'

He gave a weary little smile, the one that always made her feel defenceless, infiltrated in some way. She thought sometimes she wanted him to really *see* her, but not this part. Not this girl, suspended at the edge of adulthood and weeping despite having, as people kept reminding her, *every advantage*.

'You could go to school! You're *very* smart. All those books I gave you—you understand them better than I do.'

It was as though he were talking to an especially precocious child, offering admiring blandishments tinged with pity (for smart children always suffer). She had expected more, some frantic last-minute petition for her to stay. A few grave, stifled tears, at least. Not this embarrassing, abridged sympathy. She was about to leave for the ends of the earth, and he was being kind again.

'I guess that's what I will do,' she said, trying to dab inconspicuously at her eyes with the rough napkin. 'But I feel like I'll be missing something here, I don't know what exactly.'

'Luiza—' She looked up. He almost never said her name. 'Nothing will change here. You could come back in twenty years and the same handful of millionaires will still be running the country, and all those people you say you want to help will still be scrabbling to survive, and those few of us in the middle will be just the same. Go do something for yourself.'

They were quiet for a long time and finally Carmichael put his hand over hers, for once unconcerned that someone might see. Maybe he was coming back to her at last. 'This place is changing so fast,' he said. 'It's getting more and more crass. You're better off going to somewhere new. Somewhere clean. Some part of me wishes I could leave too.'

Then he pulled his hand back again. Urging her to go.

She struggled to keep her face calm. 'I don't know. My father left Canada for a reason. He always felt like a misfit there. Here, he fit in.' If they stayed here, her father could live unashamed, unrestrained. 'I think people here barely notice. It's my mother who is forcing this on us.'

Carmichael watched her intently, then picked up her hand again, slowly, before enclosing it in his own. 'People notice. They just don't say anything. Luiza, your father lost his job. I suppose they told you he retired?'

Luiza nodded. 'To get treatment.'

'Well, the company has been generous and he'll get his pension, but with the inflation here it won't be enough. Your mother is just trying to protect you all.'

Her neck felt suddenly blotched and itchy, and she scratched at it, unable to stop, in what she knew must be an ugly way. Her family exposed again. New, abrading truths: the money, the public fact of her father's madness whispered about behind their backs. And again more thoughts of herself, always her tiresome, unavoidable self: she had hoped that he would ask her not to go, or that she would find the courage to stay, alone. But there really was no choice. Their money was nearly gone. In Canada there would be free care, maybe some peace—life viewed through a telescope, circumscribed. These were the best her family could hope for. She had to go.

Carmichael stood up abruptly. 'Things are getting too solemn around here,' he said, suddenly loud. 'I think we need a song.'

And he was off to talk to the barman, bantering about music in that hollow, confrere way he dialled up with other men. He returned to their table and led her to the dance floor as the music began. Trumpets, clarinets, an up-tempo song that for some reason they slow-danced to. A voice that sounded tinny and far-off: *I found my love in Avalon, beside the bay.* She saw her own scraped knees and, behind them, her parents' bisected bodies; headless torsos with languidly shuffling legs that had hypnotized her at the top of the stairs when she was six years old, folding her legs up uncomfortably high in front of her to avoid detection. *I left my love in Avalon, and sailed away.* She remembered her mother's body swaying, legs intertwined with her father's. The two of them moving in and out of her field of vision, her mother always laughing in the same way, his finger tracing and retracing a line back and forth across the small of her back. *Every morn' my memories stray, across the sea where flying fishes play.* That particular laugh—throaty and warm—had become a kind of touchstone in her memory: when she heard it that night, sitting there on the stairs, even as a young child she knew that it was a sound she hadn't heard in a long time. *And as the night is falling, I find myself recalling, that blissful all-enthralling day.* She had loved that laugh, soothed by how easily her father could bring out her mother's lightest self. (Though, thinking of it now, she wasn't sure she'd heard it since.) *I dream of her in Avalon, from dusk till dawn.* Maybe she'd laugh now, emulate her mother's warm, quiet joy, try to force herself to feel carefree. But unease was creeping under her skin, which tickled unpleasantly, recognizing the familiar line traced on her lower back before she did. *And so I think I'll travel on, to Avalon.* Then the collapse of space between what she remembered seeing and what she now felt against her skin, her hand reaching behind her to push Carmichael's away until he stepped back. *Close to my heart I pressed her, upon that golden yesterday.* He stood facing her now, in the same way her father used to stand before her mother after they danced.

Luiza studied the line of his mouth, tired and turned down, set into a face so aged by disappointment. By her. He was bewildered, then genuinely concerned as she began to tremble violently. All these years, she had grafted her father's head onto a body whose face she never actually saw. This body: Carmichael's. She heard herself gasp, and static filled her ears. But the shame was as loud as the shock. She couldn't let him decipher her bald reaction, to see any more of her.

'I have to go,' she stammered. 'I'm sorry. Something at home.' She turned and hurried out the door.

Now, in the chapel, Luiza struggles to stay upright and keep her gaze fixed at the back of the chapel, avoiding eye contact with her mother—who is staring at her from the front pew—so she doesn't fall apart. *Mother is here. She is here, she is here, she is here.*

After the service, the sisters file out while her mother continues to wait in her seat, unmoving and staring blankly. She must be in shock to have sat still all this time. It will be awful, Luiza thinks, when she finally comes out of it.

All through Midday Prayers, she thought only of her parents, of Carmichael. Of herself. Did she even sing? She can't remember. Studying her mother, she reddens with an old shame. She's been here almost a year, and after the endless hours spent in prayer and meditation, still she can't be a better person. Can't rinse herself clean. She was still ugly inside, still angry. Maybe she was a fraud, after all; did it rise off her, a brackish stink? Could everyone tell? The same thoughts loop endlessly, and some days she finds she's more tired than when she first arrived. She prays: *When you lie down, you will not be afraid; when you lie down, your sleep will be sweet.* But it always feels like begging.

Luiza unfastens and refastens the scarf she wears to keep her hair back, then hesitates for another moment before going to her mother, still hoping some pure feeling, some truth, will purge her, before all the questions begin.

# DORA

Standing outside the doors of the chapel after Midday Prayers, Dora watches Luiza carefully, half expecting her real daughter to burst through the body of this changeling. But Luiza is motionless and silent—a contrived calm—as though waiting for her mother to speak first.

Dora doesn't protest as she's led, once again, out to the gardens behind the convent. She follows Luiza, unsure of how her body can be moving even though she is empty. What is propelling her forward? She watches her legs move in front of her, but they don't feel like her legs. They can't be. A little voice is telling her that she should be shouting, she should be thanking God and shaking her daughter and embracing her. But she is too numb to do anything but follow. Her body craves emotion, waits for it, but nothing comes.

The air outside is cooler and damp, fragrant with orchids. Pennywort climbs the plaster walls, its leaves like tiny lily pads, and purple passion flowers tangle behind the concrete bench where they now sit. Luiza seems older, inelastic somehow, more austere, a newly boyish haircut framing her face. She keeps staring at Luiza's hair, thinking how short and dark and strange it is now, and how vain she used to be about its beautiful auburn colour.

'You'll come home,' Dora says finally, with such sudden force that, for a moment, Luiza looks startled, as though she might believe her.

Luiza touches her mother's arm tentatively, then says quietly, 'I can't.'

Dora slaps her hard, but her tingling palm, Luiza's sharp intake of breath, the pink stripes across her child's cheek she now reaches up to touch—none of this brings relief. Luiza limply tolerates the strangling, minute-long embrace that follows, but just as Dora is about to let go, Luiza holds on to her so tightly that she feels hopeful. Everyone else is attending to afternoon chores inside, so the grounds around the convent are empty, but soon Luiza disentangles herself, seeming embarrassed and claustrophobic, and pulls Dora up by the wrist. She begins to lead her around the orchard, nervously pointing out the monkey banana and maracock trees, and how well tended they are and how their fruits are the same kind they had with breakfast this morning. But Dora pays no attention because she's focused on Luiza's hand holding her own, absorbed by its network of veins, its thin tendons. This real hand, intact, with blood moving through it. Not waterlogged or decomposing.

'You'll come home,' Dora says again. 'We'll find a way to explain it all.'

'I know how awful I must seem to you,' Luiza says. 'But I did this for you. For *all* of you. For Evie and Magda most of all.' Her arms stiffen at her sides, just like they did when she was a child and had something terribly important to proclaim. 'I'll hurt them,' she keeps saying, her skin splotching red in places. 'I'll hurt you.' Then realizing she's pulled a handful of leaves off one of the wild cherry trees and crumpled them in her fist, she lets them fall to the ground, astonished, all her affected serenity exhausted. 'Look what I've done,' she whispers now, almost to herself. 'Everyone here loves these trees.'

And though her daughter stands before her, unquestion-
ably alive, spattered with a hot rash, Dora can hardly recognize this woman as her own child. She wonders if her daughter,
too, has been subsumed, like Hugo. If Luiza was somehow
driven to this place, to cruelty. To another kind of madness.
What if Carmichael lied? What if he hurt her in some other,
more permanently wounding way he couldn't admit to? *What
if what if what if?* Those two words have tormented her for a
year, and now their register, the breadth of their possible
answers—it has all changed, and it should be beautifully so.
She doesn't need to wonder *what* happened to Luiza anymore,
only *why*, a question that will, in time, be answered. No more
imagining, again and again, lungs filling with water. Maybe
now she'll stop dreaming about Luiza's body rotting in a tangle
of seaweed, nipped at by fish.

*Deus, in adjutorium meum intende.*

The windows of the chapel are open, and chanting comes
pouring out. Something bristles in the small of Dora's back and
tiny quills rise up all through her body. She allows herself to
imagine that they are singing for her before turning back to
Luiza, who is gazing at the open windows.

*Gloria Patri, et Filio, et Spiritui Sancto.*

'I know about Carmichael,' Dora says.

*Amen. Alleluia.*

After a long pause, Luiza says, 'You don't know everything. And he's not why I left.'

'Then why? What makes you so special, so very threatening, that you're unable to live with your own family?'

'There's something wrong with me. Just like Father. I
wanted to protect you.'

'Don't be ridiculous,' says Dora, louder now, almost spitting.

'I've done ugly things. Things that frighten me . . .'

Luiza begins to speak in that way Dora remembers, that
mannered, heightened way that has always tired her, sending

the heel of her hand to the contracted space between her eyes, trying to erase the confusion. The frustration.

There is something dark and clotted in her blood, Luiza says. She *swears* it. The same dark moods and hypersensitivities as her father, but also, at times, the same utter indifference to people's feelings. There were days when her eyes felt enormous, compound—magnifying everything to the thousandth power—and days when the tiny hairs on her arms seemed able to detect every shiver of breath emitted by another human being. She could feel what they were feeling, sense the wind brush over some tender spot on *their* body. When Odete furrowed her brow as she polished the silver, Luiza could feel the maid's anxiety, and was herself drained by it. But there were other times when she felt desolate. She *knew* others were suffering, but she didn't care, content to merely observe, remotely, as if she were a scientist. *Poor Mother. She's just realized yet again that her life will never be the same.*

'I had to leave before you all hated me.'

'We have *grieved* for you. We never hated you.'

'You would have.'

They've left the orchard and are standing in the courtyard by the bell tower. Luiza seems depleted again. Her eyes keep wandering back to the convent behind her, and Dora tries to glean what she is thinking; perhaps how odd it is that there is a weathervane on the roof above the bell tower—an authentic one, which would matter to Luiza, with a rooster and arrows and a little moon, all silhouetted sharply now against the low afternoon sun. It's the highest thing on the building, higher even than the crucifix directly above the entranceway. Dora keeps watching her, wondering what her daughter is so afraid of. Because she believes nothing Luiza has told her so far.

Another voice now: Had she planned it, knowing they would all mourn her forever? Planned it without considering how the human brain tortures its host: images of Luiza, grey and bulging, shedding skin on the ocean floor. *Don't think these things*, Dora chastises herself. *Don't be angry. You got the impossible. You got her back.* But something is eating through the relief like an acid.

Dora can feel herself constricting, shrinking again, like she has all these years beside Hugo after he's made another scene, upset another friend, claimed to have traversed another galaxy. An animal instinct to protect herself. Maybe, without meaning or wanting to, people like Hugo and Luiza give everything, but they take as well—all the sadness, all the beauty, all the air. They cry a sea of tears, then swallow it all back up, all that love and empathy, and leave everyone else floundering in puddles. Dora tried for years to contain them, lead them where she thought they should go, and now she's caught again in the belly of a whale, in the dark and still alone.

'I've never thought that you have your father's disorder,' Dora says, her voice cold. 'Though it seems some part of you wants it. But even after the disappointment in Florida, even after we thought we'd lost *you*—he never left us. Did you think about what he might have done to himself? I still worry about it. Every day.'

'He wouldn't—I was protecting him. If I had come with you, it would all have been ruined.'

Dora holds her gaze, and she can see that something in Luiza's face has changed. The entreating, the fear—they've vanished, replaced by something harsh and confrontational.

'You must have known I'd find you. You wanted me to find you.'

'You were supposed to have left a year ago!' Luiza's voice rises, then quickly lowers again. 'I was trying to make it easier for you to leave. Make him *want* to leave. Have to leave. I was helping you. Why are you *still* here?'

Dora studies her, trying to decide whether she's lying or not, then says quietly, 'To find you.'

Again, Luiza says nothing.

Dora looks down at her hands, now folded in her lap, the tears gone. 'You're *not* responsible for him, but you did break his heart. You did do that.'

'You weren't supposed to stay.' Petulant, and thin. It's all Luiza can manage to say.

Dora pulls her daughter to her and holds her close, breathing into her hair. She can feel it happening again: Luiza sliding away from her. Slipping below the surface. Where will she go this time?

# MAGDA

itting in the hospital waiting room, Magda watches
Brigitta as she picks up and examines anything she can—
pamphlets, a box of tissues, a telephone, some spider
plants, and a family of little plastic deer on fake grass. Brigitta
pokes at their forever-open eyes, seeming almost disappointed by
how clean and dull everything is. No patients running naked up
and down the hallways, no zombies left propped in wheelchairs,
abandoned in corners. Everyone appears cared for, but a bit
dazed and fuzzy. The nurse is friendly and says she'll take them
up to see Mr. Maurer in five minutes when visiting hours begin.

'This is what they want you to think,' Brigitta whispers as
they walk behind the nurse. 'They make it seem like everything's fine, but then behind closed doors they're performing
lobotomies, cutting out people's true selves.'

Magda shoots her a dirty look but silently tries to reassure
herself: he's only been in hospital six days. Not enough time to
erase someone.

'You should really read Ken Kesey's work, both of you. It's
a revelation.'

Then the nurse arrives and tells them they can follow her.
Brigitta pulls Evie up, linking their arms, leaving Magda to

follow behind. But Evie hangs back, her wrist hooked limply over the girl's forearm, and gives Magda a wide-eyed glance. Brigitta, too busy trying to peer into every room they pass to notice, continues to drag Evie, her sour doll-child, down the hall.

When they get to their father's room, they find no restraints, no bandages, no scars. No thrashing or toneless muttering. He is just sitting in a chair by the window, his hands in his lap, a blanket over his legs. Evie seems briefly embarrassed—as though some part of her wanted the crackling father who Brigitta would be delighted by; the father who once hired a barefoot young poet he met in Lapa to come home with him and write them all sonnets. But Magda rushes over to him and bends to give him a hug, and he hugs her back, weakly but warmly. Not a madman, not a poet, not a vegetable. Just a tired, middle-aged man, faded but still so handsome. Of that, even Magda is proud. Evie hugs him too and so does Brigitta, and he gives an abrupt, bemused laugh at being embraced by this strange girl.

Evie leans toward him and murmurs, 'Brigitta said Mother wanted to shunt you away.'

'You mustn't blame your mother for this,' he says. 'We won't do that anymore. Come with me.' He leads them to a large picture window in the central recreation room and points inland. 'See that? Up there, on the way up to Corcovado, is the hotel your great-grandfather built, where your mother spent her summers as a child. Down there is Cassino da Urca, where we used to go dancing. It sits almost at the edge of the water, and one night people came in boats to watch us.'

He looks at a point in the distance as he speaks, but his voice is steady, unbreaking. He tells them how he and their mother were once very foolish, and they had danced and shown off to the people in those boats, imagining themselves admired from afar. Thoughtless as children.

'But then I left her alone with your sister again and again, for more than a thousand days and nights. She changed, but she stayed. And she is losing more than any of us, because even though this family matters more to her than anything, she's losing the life she was promised.' He stares out the window for a long time, his lips moving slightly, as though counting, Magda thinks. Enumerating all the things Dora will leave behind. 'Carmichael,' he murmurs, moving his lips so minutely that Magda wonders if she'd imagined it. Then, 'Luiza' last of all.

'We won't blame her,' he says finally, clearly, and meeting his daughters' eyes. 'She's the only one who takes care of things, who keeps us safe.'

And Magda can see that he believes it, that their mother will save them.

Brigitta, who has been absorbed in some puzzle pieces laid out on the ping-pong table, suddenly whirls around. 'We've been so worried about you, Mr. Maurer, and wanted to make sure—'

But Magda pushes her aside. 'We'll take him outside.'


Evie and Magda follow their father as he makes his way slowly to a picnic table. Giant trees line the grounds, swallows wheeling above them. Patients and their visitors are starting to trickle outside as visiting hours begin.

Once they find an empty table, Papa turns to Magda and whispers, now quite audibly, 'But what are *you* doing here, my girl? You're much too sensible for this sort of thing. You need to get your sister away from—' and he jerks his head in a stagey nod toward Brigitta, who's just gone skipping off across the lawn, an idiot wanderer.

She wants to tell him about Maricota and Odete, about how thoughtless she was to imagine she could be more important to them than their own families. Instead she says, 'I had to make sure you get out of here.'

'I *will* get out. I'm not a prisoner. They make sure I get rest here, but I'll be home in a few weeks.'

'Can we stay a little longer?'

In a few minutes, Brigitta comes at them with a wheelchair, but when Magda moves to push it away, remarkably, her father eases into it.

'Go on then, take me for a spin.'

Together, the three girls take turns pushing him on the bright green lawn, while they gossip about the other patients. Her father tells them who howls at the moon at night and who thinks she's Queen Anne. None of it is true, they understand, but they laugh anyway, and when visiting hours are over, they all three labour to push him back over the grass.

'I can walk, you know, but I quite enjoy having underlings.' Some things are not *the disease talking*, as Mother would say. Some things are him.

There is a narrow concrete ramp leading up to the door. Evie and Brigitta walk ahead and hold the door open so that Magda can push him up by herself. At the top of the ramp she turns him around, but instead of guiding him into the building, she lets go. The slope is gradual, so the chair rolls down slowly, then rocks forward only slightly as it hits the grass. But he emits a stuttering sound as he goes down, and she's not sure for a moment if it's laughter or fear.

'Again,' he says, his voice younger and lighter than before. And so they push him back up the ramp and release him again and again until an orderly says it's nearly dinnertime and they have to go in.

# DORA

L uiza's bedroom is narrow, with just enough room for the bed, a small side table, and a desk in the corner opposite the bed, though there is a large window. The bed is also narrow, so they must lie close, the lengths of their bodies touching as they stare up at the ceiling, which is unusually high at over twelve feet. And yet despite the actual dimensions of the room, there is a feeling of spaciousness, of openness. All the furniture, doors, and trims are made from lustrous wood, and the walls are off-white and calming, and as they lie on the bed, some part of Dora finds herself understanding the pull of this place. To have your spaces so clearly defined, so circumscribed, your choices almost entirely made for you.

They've ended up here because they don't know where else to go. Some incalculable distance has been traversed and even though there are still moments when rage flashes through her, Dora wants only to be beside her daughter, this warm body that was once her baby, her child—more familiar and real and precious to her than her own. When Luiza was little and bumped her head or scraped a knee, Dora used to tease her, 'You be careful with that little body! I *made* that body!'

All those times when Hugo went away for treatment and she used to let Luiza sleep in her bed. *Let* her—she needed her there. She wanted her child so close that she could reach out and wrap her fingers around Luiza's ankle, remind herself that she was safe. By morning Dora always ended up curved around Luiza's perfect, little body. An ear within an ear. But when Hugo came back, what happened then? She can't remember. Luiza must have gone back to sleeping in her own bed, alone. Pressed against her daughter now, maybe she can absorb some understanding of her, see past the queer expressions that keep settling on her lovely face—haughty, sympathetic, aggrieved. All tried on. All fake. All meant to push Dora back to the threshold.

On the walls are a few small statues of sublime human bodies, eyes upturned in ecstasy. Convenient, she thinks, that there are no ugly saints. Believing what these women believed meant you could spend your days in quiet reflection, making things with your hands, singing, praying, gardening—devoted to a clear, singular purpose. If you believed. She envies them. Will she spend her life seeking what they already have? It doesn't seem possible for people with lives like hers. Imagine always knowing what to do next, believing that one's actions have worth and beauty and grace—a perfect kind of peace. Free of constant, plaguing doubt, wondering if you've done the right thing for your family, wondering if you've been good enough. But now that she's had her children, she can't imagine another life, a life without them. She can't wish herself backwards. She can only nudge herself forward with her mind, try to heed that low, hissing voice: *Get them out. Save them.* But which ones?

Suddenly she's up on both elbows and shaking Luiza from her sham sleep.

'You know these places were tombs for women, don't you? The Portuguese, the plantation-owners—they sent their daughters here to keep them pure, to keep them from committing adultery or losing their virginity. Or if their fathers couldn't afford to marry them off, this is where those poor girls came. You think your father is the only one who knows anything about history, but I'll tell you something about your precious cloister. It was just a place to bury women alive. And whether it was by their fathers or their husbands or their church, they were all hidden away. Made to disappear.'

Luiza pulls herself loose from her mother's grasp and lies back down on the bed.

'Why did you come here? Really?' demands Dora.

Luiza's eyes are open, but she just stares at the ceiling, her arms crossed over her chest, already adopting the position of someone mummified. 'Tell me a story,' she says finally, when their breathing has returned to normal. 'Something about our family.'

Dora understands her daughter is telling her that they are *not* going to talk about Carmichael. Overtired, she starts to tell her old favourite, about how her parents met: how her grandfather was an entrepreneur who started a company that ferried cargo from large ships to shore. Then, a jute factory, a diamond mine, a hotel on Corcovado Mountain where the wealthy spent their summers, almost airborne, lifted above the heat and filth and the crowds. He became rich. His daughter came home from school to visit in 1891, set to travel from the train station to his house by horseback. But just as she arrived, it began to rain, and she arrived at her father's house wet, *soaked through to the bone!* A family friend was visiting, a young dentist, and just as he entered the darkened central parlour off which all the rooms adjoined to light some lanterns, a door suddenly burst open.

'And in ran my mother, your *vóvó*, stark naked,' said Dora. 'Running from one room to the next to get dry clothes. She never even noticed this young man standing in a corner in the dark. The next day he threw a rose through her bedroom window. He never told her what he'd seen, even after they were married. But he told me.'

'No more family myths,' Luiza says. 'I'm so tired of myths. Tell me something real about *our* family.'

A relief because Dora, too, is tired of these stories. 'Myth' sounds so grand and gilded, almost supernatural—how she herself thought of them not so long ago. But now they feel sticky and vestigial, secreted into her mind even before she could think for herself. A residue she can't scrape away.

'Tell me about when you and Father met.'

Her daughter has heard this story countless times already, even more than the rose story, and it sounds just as make-believe, just as apocryphal. She used to work as a translator at the American embassy (she had once taken dictation from Truman!), and there were always two copies made of each translation: one original, for the Americans, and the carbon that she had to burn in an old sugar tin after transmittal. She always insists on telling this part of the story even though Luiza seems impatient with it. Dora wants her to know: she had another life once.

But today Dora skips ahead to the part Luiza wants to hear, about how, when Hugo stepped into her elevator at the embassy, she immediately thought she'd never known until that day that a man could be beautiful. And when he stepped off the elevator at her floor, she took the hand of her co-worker, a sweet woman named Betty, and whispered to her, *That* was him. *That* was the man she was going to marry. The doors closed before they could get out and they were too caught up to press the open button, so they had to walk down three floors, giggling the entire way. Everybody loves the romance of this story, but what it reveals embarrasses Dora now. Her naiveté, her caprice, her shallow attraction to a man she didn't know. Those few brief moments have become myth, but the truth that followed from them is what now sounds to Dora like something from a fable. Or a warning. Could she bring herself to tell her the truth? That she married a man because he was so very beautiful. He spoke pages from books but moved like an animal beneath his clothes. His tastes, his smells; she craved them, and marrying him was the only way to have them. Thank god the world is changing and her daughters will never know the pressure of having to make that choice: to have to marry someone just to experience their body, to learn they are broken. But she says none of this. What she says instead, her voice breathy and false: 'And then I turned to Betty and said to her, *That's the man I'm going to marry*. And so I did.'

How hollow and comical the story rings in her ears now that they've been with the same man, now that she's been so exposed. She rolls onto one elbow to look at Luiza, her anger, for the time being, drained away.

'Carmichael . . . we didn't know what he was. I think he must be sick, and it was him after all who did everything, not us. Maybe it doesn't matter.'

'It matters.'

'But maybe it won't when we leave here and we're in a new place and we don't have to see him.' Dora hears her voice grow thinner rather than lighter. 'Maybe we won't even feel like ourselves anymore. We'll be new people, Canadian people. We'll be stoic and hardy. We can still hide what you've done. Come up with some story. I know we can fix it.'

'You left too. Can we fix that?'

'I never left! I never—' She can't pretend she doesn't know what Luiza means.

'When Father was in the hospital and *he* started coming. You may as well have left.'

But Dora can't answer, can't acknowledge what she knows to be the first, the smallest heart broken in all of this. She lies back on the bed. Hoping feebly to exploit any feelings of love and nostalgia for their family that the elevator story might have inspired in Luiza, Dora tells her about the ship they'll take to Canada, tears sliding into her ears. There are performances every night, and a full band and a swimming pool. They'll bring you breakfast in your room with a single rose in a doll-sized vase. But as she speaks, Dora hears herself listing off the kind of diversions that could only please the child she lost years ago, so then she tells her the truth: as you move out into the deeper water and the land behind you disappears and you see nothing but water for weeks, something in you changes. You feel distilled, reduced to your essential self, and lesser things fall away. You moult, leaving your old, shedded skin behind you in the waters.

'And what about when you arrive? And you have to move in, and unpack, and fill out hospital forms and school applications. What then?'

Dora can think of nothing to say, so Luiza answers for her.

'I love you all so much, I do,' and here her voice catches and Dora knows that, for now, she's telling the truth. 'But I already have a new self here. Or I could. But I don't think I can keep hold of it if I leave.'

'And when you tire of this,' Dora says finally. 'What will you do then?' She asks this matter-of-factly, almost robotically, without any accusation in her voice.

'I could be different. Better. I could do some good.'

# LUIZA

For what feels like hours Luiza and her mother lie together on her tiny bed, arguing and explaining and tiring themselves into a long silence that Dora finally breaks.

'Are you awake?'

Luiza doesn't answer. Her neck has seized up from curving into the crook of her mother's, but she tries not to move. She can hear the prayers carried through the open windows, and she feels both trapped and like she's surging inside. Wide awake. She came here to get some peace. All she wants is for her mind to stop for a while, to be still. Even if she doesn't yet believe what the sisters believe, couldn't she live as they do? Meditate, pray, contemplate. Be content making candles or helping a poor child? Wouldn't that be a better life for her?

Dora asks her again, 'Are you awake?'

They both know she is, but Luiza remains silent. She wants to ask about the girls, about Evie especially—is she all right? Or has she changed, been permanently damaged in some way—but she can't bring herself to ask. The shame still sits in her throat, undissolved. Eventually, Dora turns her back to her. She doesn't feel those first little twitches of sleep in her mother's body, but at least there won't be any more talking for now. She almost wishes she could have thought up some dramatic story to tell her mother, an awful lie about Carmichael—rape, impregnation—something that might make her flight to the convent more comprehensible. Some tale that would reassure her that Luiza was innocent—that someone, in all of this, might be innocent.

She rises quickly from the bed, unwinding her mother's arm from around her shoulder. 'I have to go for the Antiphon of Our Lady,' she says quickly. 'I've missed so much already. I have to go.'

Luiza kisses her mother's hand in a hurried awkward way, then asks her to stay and rest until she returns in an hour.

'I'll bring you some dinner,' she says, still not meeting her mother's eye. 'You can sleep in my room tonight. I'm sure they won't mind.'

As she leaves the room, she sees her mother, hollow-cheeked and bewildered, staring at her from the bed.

Luiza manages to arrive at the chapel a few minutes early, and watches the sisters file in; so many creamy brown, smiling faces, like those of Maricota and Odete. She wonders if her mother thinks she's a monster. What else could willingly abandon its own family?

But what Luiza hasn't told her mother is that she's haunted by them, even here. In the convent orchards live Evie and Magda, running wild, hanging from trees that, if she unfocuses her eyes, almost become the trees behind their house. She thinks of Dora whenever she makes anything—how Dora would do it better, more precisely. More beautifully. Of course, she misses her father most of all, but she pushes those thoughts back. She repeats her own prayer, *Not forever. Just for now.* She'll find him again one day, she tells herself, and maybe he'll be only the best parts of himself. She tries to imagine her family as little figurines she takes in and out of an imaginary dollhouse, shrunken down and manageable, unchanging, never ageing. But at night they unspool, balloon back into their real, cumbersome human shapes and sizes, crowding her dreams, their faces etched by grief.

Already her borders are dissolving, and everything she's done to safeguard herself is slipping away. Soon she'll break down and be reabsorbed by them. Her family, seething with need.

Luiza had convinced herself that she'd never see Carmichael again. After her awful realization at the café that afternoon, surely he wouldn't dare seek her out. Once they left Brazil, she could begin to forget him and try, in time, to face her mother again but never, ever tell her the truth: That she couldn't even have an affair without following in her mother's footsteps! It was too perverse, too shameful to think about. For now, she busied herself helping the maids prepare for the goodbye party and carefully avoided looking at her mother. There had been more tension between them as their departure date approached, allowing Luiza's guilty hostility to slide beneath the troubled surface unnoticed.

She was still arranging the long, thick stalks of bird of paradise in a vase when she saw Carmichael calmly crossing the threshold of the front door, handing his jacket to Maricota, and smiling indulgently as Magda, always tasked with greeting guests, curtsied. (And where was Evie? She was supposed to be helping.) He appeared as bored and insolent as ever; it had never been sadness, or a turbid inner life—she'd only imagined a better story for his empty face. But as Dora walked up, apologizing for not being there sooner to greet them, his face relaxed, became a new face. Why had Luiza never noticed it before? And poor, meek Alice standing behind him, folding her coat neatly before handing it over. Luiza's hands closed into fists, the stiff tongue of the plant's blossom digging into her palm. It was clear to her now that he'd always go back to Alice—he probably even loved her, in his way. Maybe he would have left her for Dora, but from that point on, his affairs were just shallow cuts in a dreary forever-marriage. Luiza was just another girl, unseen, unheard. Waiting for a man to notice her.

Try as she might to dismiss Carmichael as a scrap of material for later use in a book about dead marriages and miserable, used-up people, Luiza knew that he *saw* her. Her vanity and her *effort*, trying to play at adulthood and sophistication. She had liked having a secret, liked seeing Alice at parties and knowing something about her husband that his own wife did not. But an ugliness soon sprouted from her, some greedy, entitled outgrowth hidden from everyone but her. It demanded things—that was how she thought of it; it wasn't really *her*. And Carmichael, too, played a part, seemingly unable to resist her, even though he kept saying it was all so wrong.

Together, Luiza and Carmichael had been negligent. They'd never gotten caught, but she knew their lies had wounded people. The tissue between herself and her parents, between Carmichael and Alice, was damaged. All because she'd wanted to grasp a few thin pleasures. And then she'd begun to care for him, assigning qualities and depth to that opaque hole at the centre of him. That Dora-shaped hole.

The stem of the bird of paradise now lay bruised in her hands, and she did her best to hide it in the vase behind the other flowers. When Luiza glanced up again, Carmichael was staring at her in such an uncharacteristic way, his face softening. Open. He seemed so sad, so sorry—was it all calculated? She went to change the music to something upbeat and then danced, too eagerly, clapping her hands until they stung and trying to shake her hips like the girls on American television. The guests had to move back to make room for her. As she danced, she tried to see out of the corner of her eye if Carmichael was watching, but he was gone, and the living room was getting crowded now. She couldn't find him in the kitchen. Maybe the garden. Luiza went to the glass doors that opened out onto the veranda and looked out.

Yes, there he was. And her mother too.

They chatted politely, but then of course they knew that anyone could be watching them, as she was. Was her mother leaning back slightly, uncomfortably, or was Luiza imagining it? Yes—almost undetectably. Trying to get away from him. Not even wanting him. Luiza slid the glass door open as quietly as she could and strained to hear.

'Yes, still *so* much to do,' her mother said, still leaning away from him. 'In fact, I should probably get back.'

'Well, then. I won't keep you.'

He had to reach forward to take Dora's hand. He kissed it, then curled it into his own. When he let go, the white corners of a note poked past the fleshy web of her closed fist. Her mother seemed to shake her head at him, then stopped herself and shoved both hands deep into her skirt pockets. An audible intake of breath as she moved toward the door and saw Luiza standing there.

'Hello, darling,' Dora said as she pushed past her. 'Enjoying the party?' And then her mother was gone, absorbed into the crowd inside.

As Carmichael went to follow Dora back into the house, Luiza put her hand out to stop him, knowing how dangerous it was. When he turned to face her, she raised her eyebrows, begging him to deny it. But as he squeezed past her in the doorway, his mouth was a white line, shut tight, denying nothing.

Smearing away her tears, Luiza headed to the back of the garden. She found a quiet place behind an orange tree and took out her cigarettes and lighter, then startled when she heard a small voice. She dropped a cigarette and ground it into the grass with her heel.

'I made this for you,' said Evie, crawling out on hands and knees from under the branches of the pink cassia tree. There was a crown of wilted pink and white flowers sitting slightly askew on her head. 'It was very hard because these aren't the right kind of flowers,' she said, taking the crown off her head and placing it on Luiza's. 'You can't pierce their stems, so I had to sort of braid them together.'

'It's so pretty. Thank you, baby girl.' Luiza forced a smile, though she wanted so badly to be alone. (Why couldn't she ever be alone?) She repositioned the crown slightly on her head and kissed Evie on the forehead. 'There we go. Now I'm a real princess. But you had better go help Magda with the cocktail onions. You know she hates the smell, and she'll come looking for you soon enough.'

'But now you've made it *crooked*,' Evie said, reaching her hands up. 'It's supposed to be like this.'

'It's *fine*. Just go now.' And as she swatted her younger sister's hand away, she saw disappointment film over her eyes. Careless, she thought. She was becoming a careless person, but she didn't know how to stop. She repositioned the crown uncomfortably low on her forehead, as Evie demanded. 'There. I fixed it. Now run along. I promise to wear it all night, even if Mother gets cross.'

Evie seemed placated and skipped off, and Luiza went in among the orange trees again, angling her body so that her back was to the house and garden. She lit a cigarette and was inhaling deeply when a voice behind her made her jump.

'Miss me?'

When she turned around, she saw Carmichael's tall, easy stance and his full, scornful mouth, and for a moment she had the impulse to kiss him. Instead, she brought her cigarette to her lips again and then, exhaling, said, 'You're vile.'

'I'm sorry about just now,' he said, reaching for her, muttering consolations, but she pulled away. 'You know I couldn't risk your mother seeing.'

For research into the post–Civil War migration of the *Confederados* from the American South to Brazil, I relied on *The Confederados: Old South Immigrants in Brazil* (edited by Cyrus B. and James M. Dawsey), Eugene C. Harter's *The Lost Colony of the Confederacy*, and Ricardo Orizio's *Lost White Tribes: The End of Privilege and the Last Colonials in Sri Lanka, Jamaica, Brazil, Haiti, Namibia, and Guadeloupe*. Some of the Maurer family stories were inspired by first-person accounts related in these books. The fictional community of Villa Confederação is based on the real municipality of Villa Americana, located outside São Paulo.

Two memoirs by Kay Redfield Jamison, *An Unquiet Mind* and *Nothing Was the Same*, were crucial to my research on bipolar disorder. Both are penetrating and empathetic studies that were particularly helpful to me in developing the character of Hugo. Several of Mills Baker's posts on Quora.com were also very valuable in deepening my understanding of bipolarity. David Healy's *Mania: A Short History of Bipolar Disorder* provided me with historical context for the treatments available in the 1950s and '60s. Other useful books include Maria Carolina de Jesus's *Children of the Dark*, Michael Greenburg's *Hurry Down Sunshine*, Kathleen Norris's *The Cloister Walk*, and Simon Schama's *Citizens: A Chronicle of the French Revolution*, which inspired Hugo's speech about hot air balloons, democracy, and the French Revolution.

In a few places in the novel, which is set in 1963, I have deviated from the historical timeline for artistic reasons. For example, Richard Strauss's *Gertrude's Child* wasn't published until 1966, and Arnold Lobel's *Frog and Toad Together* wasn't published until 1971. Also, while gambling was outlawed in Rio in the 1940s, many *Cariocas* (or at least my grandmother) continued to refer to the fashionable nightclubs as "the casinos" in later decades.

A very smart person once said, 'In art, the details do not need to be accurate. They just need to be convincing.' I have tried to use the research outlined above to make this novel as convincing as possible, but it no doubt contains errors, inaccuracies, and omissions. In some cases, I have knowingly taken liberties with the truth, and in other cases, when facts could not be found, I have simply made things up. In the end, this was an act of imagination, and a love letter to the Brazil conjured by my family's stories.

16–17 **Star of the sea, pray for the wanderer. Pray for me . . .** Lyrics from the Marian hymn "Hail, Queen of Heaven, the Ocean Star," by Father John Lingard (1771–1851).

25 The story Luiza tells Evie is adapted from "The Girl Without Hands" by the Brothers Grimm.

37 **filled to the gills with those sequined showgirls, all happy little things, pretty and so young. Everything was *yayaya*** The description of the Cassino da Copacabana is adapted from the September 2011 *Vanity Fair* article "All Havana Broke Loose: An Oral History of Tropicana," by Jean Stein.

55 **'Be woe to you, Copacabana . . .'** Adapted from the poem "Ai de Ti, Copacabana," by Rubem Braga, as translated and quoted by Beatriz Jaguaribe in *Rio de Janeiro: Urban Life Through the Eyes of the City* (Abingdon, Oxon: Routledge, 2014), 155.

68 **'This is how we have our first accounts of what industrial Victorian cities looked like . . .'** Hugo's monologue about hot-air balloons, the French Revolution, and Pilâtre de Rozier are adapted from several paragraphs in Simon Schama's *Citizens: A Chronicle of the French Revolution* (New York: Vintage, 1989), 123–7.

95 **'The South Zone was *ours*'** Adapted from Paulo Francis's memoir *The Affection That Ends*, as translated and quoted by Beatriz Jaguaribe in *Rio de Janeiro: Urban Life Through the Eyes of the City* (Abingdon, Oxon: Routledge, 2014), 165.

99 'That hair, like the sun, I had that hair but mine was yellow also like the sun but the yellow sun not the red sun . . .' Adapted with permission from a post on Quora.com by Mills Baker (https://www.quora.com/What-does-a -manic-episode-feel-like/answer/Mills-Baker).

110 'If you become a fish in a trout stream, I will become a fisherman and fish for you.' From Margaret Wise Brown, *The Runaway Bunny* (New York: Harper & Row, 1942), 3.

132 lightning jumped from peak to peak around the harbour. Adapted from Elizabeth Bishop's *Prose*, edited by Lloyd Schwartz (New York: Farrar, Straus and Giroux, 2011), 187.

151 *wax-white, dead-eye pearls. . . . Wet, stuck, purple.* Adapted from Elizabeth Bishop's "Electrical Storm," in *The Complete Poems, 1927–1979* (New York: Farrar, Straus and Giroux, 1995), 100.

154 *Tall, uncertain palms. . . . Your immodest demands for a different world, and a better life.'* Adapted from Elizabeth Bishop's "Arrival at Santos," in *The Complete Poems, 1927–1979* (New York: Farrar, Straus and Giroux, 1995), p.89.

154 *Illegal fire balloons. . . . Paper chambers flush and fill with light. . . . Flare and falter, wobble and toss. . . . splattered like an egg of fire against the cliff.* Adapted from Elizabeth Bishop's "The Armadillo," in *The Complete Poems, 1927–1979* (New York: Farrar, Straus and Giroux, 1965), p.103.

159 *The* Hindenburg *appeared a conquering giant in the sky, but she proved a puny plaything in the mighty grip of fate* . . . Adapted from the British Pathé newsreel "Tragedy of The Hindenburg" (1937).

204 His hair is not hair, but vibrissae. . . . His eyes are those of flies, faceted and jewel-toned Adapted from Kay Redfield Jamison's *An Unquiet Mind: A Memoir of Moods and Madness* (New York: Vintage, 1995), 3.

231 *I get midstsy* . . . Hopeless as a kid lost at sea. Adapted from "Misty," lyrics by Johnny Burke. (First appeared on the Johnny Mathis album *Heavenly*, released by Columbia Records in 1959.)

232 **She quick-churned into a dancing stream** Adapted from Maurice Sendak's *Outside Over There* (Boston: Lothrop, Lee & Shepard Books, 1981), 26.

266 **But he could strip off his own skin and still not get down to the place where he went wrong** Adapted from the film *Michael Clayton*. Directed by Tony Gilroy (Los Angeles: Warner Bros., 2007).

268 **Somewhere, lately, a serpent's egg has hatched** Adapted from Zuenir Ventura's *Cidade Partida (The Divided City)*, as translated by Beatriz Jaguaribe in *Rio de Janeiro: Urban Life Through the Eyes of the City* (Abingdon, Oxon: Routledge, 2014), 158.

268–9 **a headless chicken in an alleyway tied up in red string, an empty bottle of wine beside it. . . . A single red candle, placed in a hand-dug pit.** Adapted from an anecdote in Elizabeth Bishop's *One Art: Letters*, selected and edited by Robert Giroux (New York: Farrar, Straus and Giroux, 1994), 243.

270 **And as darkness gathered over Europe, reformations and counter-reformations . . .** Adapted from a passage in Peter Robb's *A Death in Brazil: A Book of Omissions* (New York: Henry Holt, 2004), 65.

280 *Like some rough gale, blowing me all about . . . while I blaze and swoon* Adapted from Virginia Woolf, *A Writer's Diary: Being Extracts from the Diary of Virginia Woolf*, edited by Leonard Woolf (New York: Harcourt, 1982), 176, 180.

284–5 *I found my love in Avalon, beside the bay . . .* Adapted from "Avalon," lyrics by Al Jolson, Buddy DeSylva, and Vincent Rose, 1920.

286 *When you lie down, you will not be afraid . . .* From Proverbs 3:24 (New International Version).

311–12 *Mother benign of our redeeming Lord . . .* Lyrics from "Loving Mother of Our Saviour" (originally composed in Latin as *Alma Redemptoris Mater*) by Hermann of Reichenau (1013–1054).

# DORA

As she rushes through the darkening streets of Salvador, Dora is grateful for her prescriptions: one to help her sleep, one to keep her awake, and the one she's just taken to quell the electrical storm beneath her skin. This one makes everything feel like a dream, like it's not really happening to her. Everything is more colourful somehow, but also so much gentler, and the babble of people in the streets is familiar and comforting. Soon the enormity of what has just happened is going to hit her, and the ground will give way again, but she's not ready. Not yet.

She walks the steep streets, past farmers packing up crates of watermelon, bananas, *maxiera*. Past multicoloured buildings and gilded seventeenth-century churches; the thought of their many carvings, their baroque and dimly lit interiors, make her feel queasy. Then through the market, with its stalls filled with flour sacks of beans, a man selling hot peppers spread out on newspaper and wedges of squash. And the black women wrapped in shawls and wearing big tiered dresses, colourful fabric wound around their heads—they are here, just as she's seen in photos, at Carnival, on tea towels, at the borders of neighbourhoods she never goes into.

She wonders if somewhere behind one of these painted doors is a scene like the ones she saw in a magazine years ago, of women with shaved heads in dresses of white cotton and lace, armbands made from cowry shells and twine, wrists covered with silver bangles, white dots painted all over their brown skin, a single feather tied to their foreheads. They were being initiated into Candomblé, a kind of fusion of Catholicism with indigenous and African religions. In some of the pictures, they were covered in blood and feathers from a sacrifice, and in others they simply sat with their heads tipped forward, their eyes closed, appearing unearthly and at peace. The pictures had caused a stir—Brazilians as savages, the brides of bloody gods and all that. Dora wishes she could find them now, have them perform some sort of reverse exorcism on Luiza. In the convent, as soothing and alluring as it was, Luiza had already seemed less embodied, less alive. Her daughter wanted to believe she was being restored, even transfigured, in some way, but she already seemed less of a person than when she'd disappeared. The Candomblé initiates had looked, Dora remembers thinking, as though something had been put *into* them, not taken away. They looked full, serene. Whole. Or haunted? Filled with ghosts. Luiza would probably be angry with her if she said any of it out loud. So much of her own country remained a mystery to Dora.

How can she leave her here? In this old, cluttered city, teetering on high cliffs above a bay. It startles her, the force with which the conviction comes—she has to.

Even now Dora can see her, Luiza as a small child, not even three, running on the beach. Of course they went often, but on this day Luiza behaved as though it were the first time. She ran and squealed, her face widening, seeming to expand as if to hold all that joy, the white shine thrown off the waves. She pulled off her clothes and ran, crying out to no one, *I go far!* She ran until she was a pink dot on the horizon, where the water and the sky became indistinguishable, hazy and golden.

How can Dora hold these two things inside her at once? This memory and the acute, painful love she feels for Luiza thinking of that day, and the simultaneous conviction that she must leave her behind? Because it is necessary, she tells herself, to save the girls, and Hugo too, and because she will come back. She will come back for her child, whom she loves, who she knows is suffering in some unutterable way. All of her daughter's justifications—she hadn't believed them. There was still something Luiza wasn't telling her, but Dora couldn't stay. A small fissure had opened between them years ago. She has to leave before it is a complete rupture. At some point it will hit her, all they've lost. But right now, there isn't time. The weight of the rest of her family, the pressure of them waiting, waiting as they always did for her to decide, to tell them what to do— she can feel it. Hugo, Evie, Magda, all in unsteady orbit around her. How far would they spin out with her gone? No hospital doors could contain Hugo if he really wanted out. *We are getting away!* repeat shrill, wild voices in her head. Voices, terror, madness—is it all catching?

Hugo must first be stabilized before he can spread any more chaos. But if Hugo or the girls were to find out Luiza was alive, none of them would ever agree to go to Canada. And how many people can she drag across two continents, resenting her for it every step of the way? No one can know, not yet. Once they have a new home ready for her, a new life that is gentler and real—then she'll come back for Luiza.

For now she has to go to them, collect Hugo from the hospital, get them all on the ship. Sometimes, she imagines them aboard without her: Hugo giving the girls one of his 'lessons,' moving like an unstrung puppet, a parody of himself, silent though his mouth is moving. And yet when she pictures them now, they are just three—Hugo, Magda, and Evie. For almost a year, whenever Dora has seen the three of them together, she would focus on the empty space beside them where Luiza ought to have been and wonder for a moment where she was. Now, just as flesh can heal around a foreign object, they've grown into other versions of themselves, shaped around her absence.

Brazil is the place where, for years, they've been stuck, unspooling, radiating grief. Maybe once away from here, Dora can gather her family back up again, shape them into a single cord, trembling and alive.

— v —

# EVIE

At home, everything is finally, truly packed. The furniture is gone, shipped ahead of them. The walls are bare except for some nails.

'Remember,' Mama has reminded them in a tired voice. 'Just one suitcase each for the trip.'

Since Mama's return, over a week ago, she has been different, kinder yet also further away. At times, she has followed Evie and Magda from room to room, startling them with suffocating hugs. But she has also spent whole days sitting on the veranda, chain-smoking and sliding a thumb up and down her thigh, just below where her skirt meets her flesh-coloured pantyhose.

Yesterday, as the maids finished cleaning and Magda ferociously rehearsed her gymnastics routine in the backyard, Evie had drifted about the house with no one to cleave herself to. For a long time, she stood watching her mother on the veranda from the back doorway, as if by hovering so close she could silently absorb some understanding of her. She sensed she shouldn't interrupt, but then Mama suddenly spoke.

'Once we leave, I'll be better.' Then, still without even turning to look at Evie, she added, 'I promise.'

Evie hadn't known she could see her, and retreated quietly, leaving her mother pinned to the bench, her stocking puckered with runs at the knee.

When it was time for the family to say goodbye to the help this afternoon, Mama seemed more like herself, and actually hugged them all goodbye: the maids, Bechelli, even Georges. She also gave them lovely gifts and said they were from the girls. Evie cried so hard her throat hurt, her arms wrapped around the maids' doughy waists, bodies she once felt were almost her own, more familiar to her than her own mother's. Magda, who had been sullen for ages, held on to Maricota for so long that Mama had to come up to them, lingering alongside, murmuring gently that they were running late to pick up Papa from the hospital.

'We'll come back!' Evie and Magda promised, waving frantically as they climbed into the car. Maricota and Odete echoed them again and again. 'You'll come back!'

Tonight, the family will spend a night in a hotel near the harbour in Rio, and tomorrow they will at last set sail for New York City. From there, they'll take the train to Toronto. But first, they have to attend the final exhibition for Evie and Magda's day camp.

Outside in the back field, all the girls spun in circles with transparent scarves, Evie twirled around a maypole, and Magda performed her tumbling routine. As Evie joins her parents in the stands around the swimming pool to watch Magda, her mother says, 'You were pretty as a picture,' and her father kisses her on the cheek. The air in the bleachers around the pool is warm and humid and caustic-smelling, harsh in Evie's nostrils. The men unbutton their collars while the women roll up their sleeves and slip off their shoes.

Magda comes out in her shiny blue swimsuit, all rigid muscle and stretched skin, a mantis behind her goggles. She parades to her starting block and positions herself. The Wilson twins, to her left, were the prettiest girls at the camp, lightly tanned with long, blond, natural curls. They are good at everything, but maybe their excellence has been diluted, portioned out between the two of them, because today Magda looks electric beside them. When the whistle blows, she enters the water a full head in front of them and finishes first by three full seconds. All the adults go crazy, clapping and cheering, slapping the backs of their plastic chairs. It's been so long since Evie has seen her parents like this, excited, or at least trying to be. At last, they are trying again.

Next is the backstroke, which Magda also wins.

'Bravo, my girl!' shouts Papa, suddenly animated, jumping to his feet with his fist in the air. 'You devoured them!' When he sits back down, he breathes dampness into Evie's ear. 'Your sister is vulpine. She absorbs the spirits of her enemies like Caesar upon his execution of Vercingetorix. Their extinction is her animus.' Bright parts of him are sparking, Evie notices with relief. He's not all gone.

A few minutes later, the overhead lights are switched off so that it's almost completely dark but for a cluster of five candles that emerges from a corner before gradually spreading out into a perfect line across the pool. Evie can see nothing but points of candlelight shimmering on the water, and she's transfixed as she watches the flames move apart and bob back together, then form a constellation of five swimmers that rotates in circles. A quincunx, she thinks.

Papa grabs her hand in the gloom. 'Alight,' he says. 'Not merely living but lit up, brightly. Alighting, there, like birds upon the water.'

Everyone seems to hold their breath, the wobbly constellation throwing gold scales onto the black surface of barely lapping water. All those days she goofed around with Brigitta, doing nothing, tormenting that poor man at the hospital, Magda was absorbed with others, a perfectly synchronized part of a whole, making this, the loveliest thing Evie's ever seen.

The lights go down, then back up to dim, and there is Magda with the other girls, all swimming upside down in the pool, ten feet pointing up into the air, then flexing.

'How lovely!' her mother cries. 'What did they do?'

Everyone is clapping as the lights come all the way up and the swimmers climb out of the pool. Magda glances up at her family and waves, and even smiles slightly, her candle strap sliding a little across the front of her bathing cap. Evie sees how their father looks at Magda, amazed, and she, too, is warm with pride. She thinks how she might never astonish anyone; she'll scribble little grey horses in the margins of her school notebooks, forget to pay attention in school, and remain resolutely average. But then Papa turns to her, takes her face in both his hands.

'You girls. You two are bright stars.'

Before she can think of anything to say, he is pulling her by the hand to find Magda in the crowd.


As they wait for Magda to get changed, Evie tells her parents that she's exchanged addresses with Brigitta, then instantly regrets it. They both smile tightly and say nothing. But it's as though she can't stop talking, telling them all about how sophisticated her new friend is, and how she's read the complete works of Byron, and how she, too, wants to go to Aubrey Ladies College. Evie wants so much for it all to be true, this version of Brigitta.

'To start a little losers club of two?' Magda is behind them, her hair tied in a fierce, wet knot.

'Shut up,' says Evie. Tumbling, swimming—excellence makes her mean.

'She's such a phony. All the other girls hate her. You know that, right?'

Evie knows. That Brigitta pushes and provokes helpless

people just to see what will happen. That Brigitta never loved her back. Even so, when she speaks she's just a dumb kid again. 'Drop dead.'

'Now, girls,' says their father, but he's waving at someone across the pool, distracted now, while their mother pushes them all toward the exit.

Evie reminds herself that it's all the better for her character that she should suffer, and thinks of everything she and Brigitta promised each other that was good: They would be loners. They would not associate. They would take art classes, despise all jocks, and disdain 'school spirit.' So something like a day-dream was lost when, a few days after their visit to the hospital, Brigitta told her that she wouldn't be attending Aubrey Ladies College after all. She said she couldn't *bear* the idea of being so stifled, so conformist. And though Evie had known for days it was all just a story they made up, she still felt sad that someone else decided how it would end. Maybe she wasn't really as brave as she thought.

Now, when she sees those scenes from the school in her mind again, she is alone, and yet she senses someone else is there. Luiza is gone. Magda is indeed a separate person. Brigitta has abandoned her. But she's never truly alone. There is the residue of everyone who has loved her, and the brightness of Magda, and her parents, cheering. Straining and fumbling in too-loud voices, but still crying out: *we are here*.

So for now, Evie lets herself imagine all the best things she might do, she with her family, she with her ghostly, conjured friend—such lovely things!

# HUGO

*utiny on the Bounty*, thinks Hugo, is a strange film to show on a ship. The girls have seen it three times already in the onboard theatre, and now they're off to listen to the jukebox in the 'teen lounge.' They seem to bounce happily enough around the ship all day, and find their parents at mealtimes. As Hugo and Dora continue on their daily walk about the ship—Dora's idea—he wonders if weeks of travel might be a gift. Goodbye by a thousand tiny degrees, unlike travelling to Canada by plane: a rupture too sudden and shocking to consider.

It's been almost a week since the top of Sugarloaf Mountain disappeared in the humid fog that hung over the city, obscuring the tops of buildings and Christ the Redeemer. Next vanished the city's smaller, jumbled peaks, and the tall lamps in the harbour, their hazy lights receding, dimming, then extinguished. Soon, the wheeling, flattened V-shape of gulls circling the boats was gone, then the contours of the shore, until finally there was nothing left of Brazil to see. Eventually, the muddy waters of the Amazon merged with the blue-green of the Atlantic, and from the promenade deck, they inhaled salt air and the white paint freshly applied to the corroded railings and blistered iron shell of the ship. Their voyage barely begun, Hugo already found himself suppressing swells of nausea from the sway of the boat. From leaving Luiza. A few times he's caught himself imagining her tangled in the ship's rudders, hair and skin and sinew churning in their wake, following them all the way to Canada. The ugliest part of his mind is still the quickest, and has the habit of horror. But his medicated brain doesn't hold on to these thoughts the way it used to: they streak through, then just as quickly evaporate. He can't hold anything for long. So he thinks of other things. He feels the breeze on his skin. Looks into the sun. Hears the crackle of a woman behind him fondling her packet of chips. These are the moments when he almost feels free.

Hugo and Dora spend their time on the ship stretched out among the other idle bodies on chaises lining the promenade deck, or joining card games, drinking cocktails, staring out to sea. Since his treatment, he doesn't have much desire for alcohol, but he drinks to join in, to keep Dora company. She is frequently distracted, often staring out into the distance, drinking more than usual. Yet she stays close by his side, as though pulled there. But even as they were embarking at the dock, surrounded by families weeping, embracing, she kept looking around, then over her shoulder as they boarded, a mass herded up the gangplank. Had she hoped he would come?

Now, as they walk around the ship together, she keeps her hands curled around his upper arm. Little is said. Nothing of consequence. He moves carefully, his arm pressed gently at her back. He doesn't want to startle her.

'It's cocktail hour in the ballroom,' Dora says to him now. 'They're going to have music of some kind.'

And so they go, and for a while it is the usual big band with some samba, some jazz thrown in to make the passengers feel more adventurous. One giant entertainment, this ship: buffets, a show every night, a swimming pool, shuffleboard and crokinole and bridge tournaments on deck. The saxophone player comes toward the microphone, his face glistening with sweat.

'And now, what's new?' he says slowly, enunciating carefully and lingering on sibilance. *What'sss new?* He gestures to the piano player to begin as he turns and wipes his face and the back of his neck with a cloth, sweating under the bright stage lights.

The music is warm and smooth and hazy, and when Hugo asks Dora to dance she looks almost as pliant and transported as he feels. By the time they reach the dance floor, a shadow has crossed her face and she is scowling, preoccupied again. They dance in silence, until he feels her body shudder slightly against his.

'Look now,' he says, suddenly awkward. His own wife and he doesn't know what to do with her pain, what to say. Remote, he had sometimes thought her; but it isn't that she's cold. She's determined, sometimes afraid. Careful not to feel as much as the rest of them, never to fall apart like they have, because then who would hold them up? But now that she's crying he is like a child seeing a parent cry. Unsure what to do. He tries to lift her chin so that her eyes meet his, but she won't let him, so he speaks into her hair.

'That man was nothing to us,' he says. It doesn't matter if it isn't true. 'I won't mention him again.'

'I won't either.'

'And when we get to Canada, it will be so cold your tear ducts will freeze, so you won't be able to cry anymore.'

Here she laughs a little, then lays her head on his shoulder. 'It's not cold there all the time, you know.'

'I know.'

A thin, high-pitched whining escapes through her clenched teeth. She might split open; she's fighting so hard to get something out. Or keep something in.

'There's time,' he says, holding her tighter now, holding it in. 'When we get there, once the girls are in school. We'll have so much time.'

'Yes.' A release of breath now. She leans into his lapel and the saxophone player goes on: 'Georgia on My Mind.' 'Misty.'

'Do you remember, when we were young,' he says, 'how much we loved to dance?' He lifts her chin again and this time she meets his gaze, nods, then shuts her eyes once more.

'We went to that masked ball for Carnival once at the Copa. I remember thousands of people.' As he says it, he knows that can't be true, but that's what he sees in his mind. Translucent waves of fabric hung from the ceiling and crested onto the walls above people jammed around small tables. Silhouettes of boats were mounted above crowded balconies, streamers spilling over their edges. Giant stars hung from the walls, and large pillars topped with lanterns protruded from the floor at an angle. The men were in white jackets with plain masks while the women wore lace, cat ears, peacock feathers.

'You wore that velvet rabbit number. All the other women wore the prettiest masks they could find, and you looked so bizarre, with those ears that kept nearly poking me in the eye. I loved it, how you were willing to make yourself ugly, when you were the most beautiful one there.'

For years, they've been drifting farther from one another, their lives bifurcating, but he promised her he would come back. And perhaps they could still recover something elemental, those cardinal lines on the map where they still cross. Elsewhere.

Outside the ballroom windows, he is surprised to see only the slate-coloured sea, the deepening blue sky. The ship is an amusement park, but the world outside is nothing but air and water.

They had danced all night at the masked ball, and then as now, she lets him hold her up.

# LUIZA

**S**he sits on the bed in her tiny room at the convent, hold-ing her mother's note, reading it again and again. *We sail in two weeks. I'll get everyone settled. I will come back for you.*

Luiza had said everything she could think of to get Dora to leave her at the convent. Everything but the truth. Now her mother is gone and it hadn't even taken the worst parts of her story to frighten her away.

The truth was she hadn't planned it. The day after the goodbye party, she couldn't wait to get away from home, from thoughts of Carmichael, her mother. She had promised to take the girls to the beach so that her parents and the maids could deal with the movers, and all day she longed to feel surrounded. Salt. Sand. Sky.

It was unusually bright that day, a silvery mist over the sea whitening the horizon. Their usual spot was crowded with people they knew—the McMullans, the Dawseys—and Luiza sat with her lunch amid the jumble of blankets and folding chairs, chatting slackly with neighbours while Evie and Magda played on the shore. She tried to read for a while, but became hot, agitated, and finally put her book away and let the girls bury her legs in the cool sand. Evie decorated Luiza's sand-covered legs with stones as she always did, took a bite of her sandwich, protested when Magda wouldn't release some spiny creature from a bucket. But how could she really be fine? Maybe she was just pretending, for Luiza's sake.

'Here,' Evie said at one point, holding out a leather-bound book, its pages forced apart by sand. 'You dropped it again.' Luiza reached out her hand but looked over Evie's shoulder, painfully into the light. She couldn't meet her sister's eye.

'Just stick it in my bag for me, would you, pet?'

She smiled at the dentist from Santarém sitting nearby, made some excuse for her poor treatment of literature. *Tacitus! Too hot, too dull.* Soon after, she must have dreamed restlessly for a few minutes. When she startled awake, the world around her seemed subtly rearranged, its textures indefinite. Gouging at the sand, scooping huge handfuls from around her legs, she was suddenly desperate to get in the sea. At last, she stood, slapping at the sand still clinging to her legs. She quickly kissed Evie on the forehead, thanked the girls for staying close by, then caught Mrs. Buchanan's eye before going in the water, hoping a swim might wake her up. The older woman nodded but didn't smile, and Luiza was sure she was judging her somehow: sleeping when she should be minding her little sisters, then oddly abrupt and frantic in her movements, too selfish even to take the girls swimming with her, too caught up in her own world. That was what these people thought of her.

Luiza headed for the water, trying to shake off her unkind chorus. She had to shield her eyes as she waded out, blinded by the midday sun over the water. She imagined she would swim then turn around to face the beach, see her sisters playing with no notion they were being watched, their faces strangely serious. When she did glance back, the dark shapes of people dotted the beach, but they were ringed in a harsh, erasing light and she dove to escape it. She would swim. Swim until she was clean again. She slid underwater above the sand for as long as possible, then drifted toward the surface and stood waist-deep in the water, splashing around. Then she jumped in with her arms in an inverted V-shape, diving shallowly, just like she used to as a girl, trying to retrieve some feeling other than regret and disgust. Sorrow. A forgotten image kept flashing by, a fish at the edge of her memory, trying to take its full shape, to form itself into words in her mouth. But again it slipped past.

She stood and tried to catch her breath. Then, that familiar, hesitant touch. Carmichael's hand on her shoulder. A clammy chill shot through her as her stomach dropped away, like expecting a step that isn't there. She moved unsteadily backwards. For a moment she wondered if anyone could see them. He must have walked in behind her, perhaps entered the water a few hundred yards away from everyone else, unseen against the dazzling light by her sisters and their various neighbours, including Mrs. Buchanan, who stood by the rocks, watching solicitously over the girls, her hands on her hips. Maybe she should scream. He might truly be dangerous—he'd touched her in that disgusting way, made her hurt Evie. And now he kept moving slowly toward her. She continued to step back, but really she wanted to withdraw from knowing she'd ever loved him, from the shame of inhabiting this same, expended skin. He appeared thinner, almost wasted. He had lost weight in just these past few months. Had she done this to him? Of course not. Dora had.

'It doesn't matter why,' he said, still moving toward her in his black swim trunks. 'Why we . . . came about. It matters how we are now. Leaving out yesterday. I was awful.'

'You took her from me.'

He frowned, briefly puzzled, as though the idea had never occurred to him. He answered almost as though asking a question. 'I loved her.'

'I loved her. I was a child. My father was gone. I needed her.'

'He took her from both of us. Your father changed her. Yes, you were a child, but I remember. I watched it happen. He broke her, again and again. It wasn't his fault, I suppose, he was ill. But for all the times he left you, he should have stayed away. I would have taken care of you.'

As she watched, he appeared to shrink before her. Becoming more pathetic and helpless. In all of this, he, too, had suffered. But it was draining her again, all her ineffectual empathy. She wouldn't give in to him.

'And at what point would you have traded in my mother for me? Or would you have remained a good man in your version?' She took a few more steps back. 'And my sisters? In your little fantasy, they would never have been born.'

'I could have been a father to them. A better one.'

'He took that too?'

'Yes.' Carmichael was trembling now, sinews taut, and Luiza worried briefly that he was cold. 'Even after your sisters were born, he should have left. I would have taken care of all of you. I would never have expected you to give up your life. He's always been selfish.'

'You've been fixated on my family for so long, but deep down you hate us.'

'Not you,' he slackened and reached for her in a way that was almost comical, as though he was paralyzed above the elbows and able only to extend both forearms. Another hopeless act. 'Never you. Not even them. In my own way, I loved you all.'

As she stood there facing him, Luiza saw a shard of her life there in Brazil, the one she might have if she stayed. There would be no grand adventure, no pink dolphins. Now, a shift: turn all boats toward the future. Uneducated, unattached to family, she would end up in a tiny kitchenette apartment overlooking Copacabana Beach, a cell in a beehive Carmichael would pay for, where they would both grieve quietly for her mother, for a time when they'd been whole. An unconsecrated pact: each of them a secondary consolation for the other, time stretched out shapelessly before them.

She knew her mother was right. In Canada, there could be more: university, a husband, a home. A family. But there would always be the possibility of her own inherited madness waiting in the margins, until one day—a tear at the seams. All the damage she could do. Carmichael shrank before her, pale concavities reflecting on the water where he stood, almost as weak and stunned as Evie the night before in the garden. Her child's body, thin and yielding in Luiza's rigid hands, head tipping back and forth violently on her white neck, then the distortion of her face as she fought back tears. That memory was worse than all the lies, all the shame. It was the worst thing she'd ever done. Could ever do. What was she becoming?

'Whether he stayed or left, it wouldn't have mattered,' she said, gazing at a bird on the horizon, its distance incalculable. 'She didn't want you anymore. And neither do I.'

She felt the tips of his fingers graze her rib cage as she turned her back to him, and there was violence in them, in that briefest of connections. But she dove cleanly away and began to swim, imagining herself receding, merging with that far point on the horizon.

How long did she have to swim before someone squinted into the distance, asked themselves whether or not that figure was really her? Before murmurs of concern rippled through the adults on the beach? Before Carmichael realized she wasn't simply playing and stopped swimming after her? Perhaps he was marvelling right now at how fast she was. A little farther. Soon she would turn back, but it was as though the water propelled rather than resisted her, as though some outside force was pushing her away from shore. Just a few minutes more.

But then water, not air: an awkward turn of the head, a miscalculation when she took a breath, her face a few centimetres closer to the sea than it should have been. She kept expecting to choke, but instead she swallowed more water. Twist, head up. She tried to right her body, get her shoulders above the water, but she kept slipping under, tied to that darting fish in her mind. Pulled under. It took more and more energy to get her mouth above the surface, to take a single breath, and yet she had time to think about how she wasn't doing the right things, wasn't drowning in the correct way. She should be waving, calling for help, but she couldn't. Somehow she was already mostly underwater, climbing an invisible ladder that kept sliding out from under her, and soon there were so few breaths and so much pressure in her head that she couldn't remember how to move. When the water closed completely overhead it was almost a relief. She wouldn't have to struggle anymore. She felt herself drift down through the deeper, colder water, her vision darkening and smudged at the edges. The blackness branched and spread through her vision. Then, a bite. A monster on the ocean floor. She realized later it must have been a crab, but the contact flooded her heart with adrenaline, jolting her back from near-unconsciousness. With both knees bent, feet flexed against the sand, she shot through the water, then swam upwards into the air.

At the surface she gasped and spluttered, then swam as hard and fast as she could without even thinking about where she was going. Not back necessarily—she didn't think about getting back—just away from the horizon, away from the vastness, the emptiness. Just get to the shore, catch your breath, then go back. Go back before they get too frightened.

Once she reached shore, she collapsed on the sand, throwing up sea water. She dragged herself up high enough so the waves barely touched her feet, sure that at any time the water could still drag her back in. She wanted to stay there, fall asleep on the sand, but soon they would notice how long she'd been gone. They would come looking for her. She'd washed up at least a mile away from where everyone was sitting—she could only make out a tiny, indistinct clump of bathers off in the distance. But here there were cockleshells and sand dollars and the vague sense of what this place might have been like once, before her people brought their shoes and ploughs, their piti- less endurance. And their wonder. She didn't think it through, didn't know then where she would go. There was only that voice inside her, saying, *Go. Walk. You're not like them. You won't survive a second time.*

So she walked a little farther, and still a little farther, until eventually there were narrow dusty roads, then people, then a man selling bright dresses and rubber flip-flops from a stall, some of which he traded her for her silver ring. A taxi, then a bus. More jewellery bartered. The convent. Maricota said it was such a peaceful place, describing how the women there sang and prayed and grew flowers and made pretty things to sell. Just for a little while, she thought, and then she'd call home and tell them she was all right. She could pretend she'd hit her head and couldn't remember, lost a few days. She could just be quiet for a while, alongside peace.

But she did not call home.

What could she have told her mother that would have satis- fied her? Luiza didn't understand herself why she'd stayed away. That was a cruelty she couldn't explain. Except that it saved her. She told herself she wouldn't survive her family. They wouldn't survive her, the ugliest version of herself. It would have been selfish to return. Better that they believe she was gone than have to watch her slowly degrade, or be wound into her chaos. How many tragedies could a family withstand? And which is the greater catastrophe—an accident or self-destruction?

The truth was, it was lonelier being with her family than apart from them. But she hadn't planned it, hadn't mapped it out in advance. She went down, into the dark, into the underworld of the ocean floor and something happened to her there. A sea change. Some part of her froze over, unable to return to them.

And now here on her bed in the convent, holding her mother's letter, it closes over her once more, the sea, everything she's left behind. And taken.

She stands up so suddenly she nearly falls over, the forgotten letter dropping from her hands. Her family will be gone soon, to the white shores of an unknown place, and perhaps one day she will go there too, and live. Earthbound.

But not yet. She'll stay in this gentle, sunlit place a little longer. And before she leaves she'll swim again like she swam that day, before she slipped under. She will turn onto her back and stretch out her arms, borne by waves until the mountains seem to topple in on her, the sky wider than in any dream.

# ACKNOWLEDGEMENTS

My deep gratitude to the many people who have helped me during the writing of this book:

To my tireless and brilliant editor, Anita Chong at McClelland & Stewart, for her commitment, insight, and attention to detail; to my wonderful agent, Samantha Haywood, for her faith, vision, and help with early drafts, and for holding my hand throughout; and to my U.S. editors, Amanda Brower, for her passion, invaluable edits, and for the title of this book, and Carina Guiterman, for taking on the project midstream with such warmth and enthusiasm; to the teams at McClelland & Stewart and Little, Brown for helping to bring this book into the world; to copyeditor Heather Sangster and proofreader Catherine Marjoribanks, for their careful readings; and to Kelly Hill, for her beautiful cover design.

I gratefully acknowledge the support of Arts Nova Scotia.

I've been so fortunate to have many thoughtful teachers and dear friends who read early drafts of this novel and provided feedback and support: Terry Byrnes, Stephanie Bolster, Kate Sterns, Catherine Cooper, Maureen Green, Mary Catherine Karr, Susan Paddon, and Jocelyn Parr.

A special thank you to Edward Carson, Johanna Skibsrud,

Rebecca Silver Slayter, and Amy Stuart, all of whom read closely and also helped me navigate the practical aspects of publishing a novel.

Love and thanks to my family for their support, especially my cousin, Georges Cunningham, for his translations; and my aunt, Jean Faber, for her excellent recall and fact-checking, and for sharing her memories. To my *vóvó*, Lucy Faber, and my mother, Susan Faber, both emigrated to another star, I miss you. Thank you for telling me your stories and inspiring so much of this novel. And to my father, Paul Vincent-Smith, for reminding me not only to see but to *look*.

Above all, I'm grateful to my husband, Oisín Curran, for his boundless encouragement and for reading almost as many drafts of this book as I have. And to our children, Fianan and Neva, for so much joy.

# NOTES AND SOURCES

I am indebted to the work of several great writers and artists that enabled me to write a book set in a country I've never visited and during a time before I was born. I cannot name them all here but a special thank-you is owed to the following works.

The prose, poetry, and letters of Elizabeth Bishop written during the years she lived in Brazil were invaluable. In particular, my descriptions of Petrópolis were informed by Bishop's letters, collected in *One Art* (edited by Robert Giroux), and her poetry collection *Questions of Travel*. For a deeper understanding of the people, development, and landscape of the Copacabana neighbourhood, I owe much to Beatriz Jaguaribe's fascinating *Rio de Janeiro: Urban Life Through the Eyes of the City*. Peter Robb's *A Death in Brazil* is an absorbing book that helped me better understand the complicated, often violent colonial history of a beautiful, complex country. His descriptions of Bahia and Recife informed some of Dora's descriptions of travelling to and walking through Salvador. Several passages in the book were also inspired by *Chroniques Brésiliennes*, a beautiful collection of José Medeiros's photography of the Brazilian people in the 1940s and '50s.

She touched at a speck of tobacco on her tongue, imagining it made her appear harder, uncaring. 'But I saw you.'

He gazed at her, confused. Always that same weak smile. But then his hands fluttered up in an uncharacteristically sincere gesture of supplication, and she held her breath.

'It was because of gestures like that,' she said, now shifting her body away from his, 'that I've sometimes believed I actually care for you, that I might matter to you. But you already know that. The effect you have.'

'You do matter to me,' said Carmichael, yanking on her arm, trying again to get Luiza to face him, which she finally did.

'Well, you disgust me. You're a sad, middle-aged man who can't let go of a woman who finished with you more than a decade ago. You're worth less to her than a madman.'

His face scarcely twitched but she saw it—deflation. His body registering that she knew the truth. Then, a slight flush of colour in his cheeks.

'And you're just as heartless as she is,' Carmichael spat. He thrust his arms out violently and grabbed her at the waist with one hand and between her legs with the other, pulling her toward him as he did. It hurt more than she could have imagined and she gasped, tumbling into him, grabbing his shoulders to steady herself.

He spoke into her ear, clear and vicious, 'But she tasted so much better than you.'

Her whole body seemed to fail her, and she buckled, sliding to the ground, surprised by the sound of her sudden, dry sobs. She watched his legs step back from her—a ruined animal—slowly and deliberately, and turn to walk toward the house. Even as she lay heaving in the dirt, there was a part of her that wanted to call him back. Wanted to stay in Brazil and be her mother's deficient surrogate, to cease to be herself. If she remained there long enough she might extinguish, breath by breath, until she vanished altogether. Despicable thought. She was willing herself up off the ground when two scraped knees appeared before her, two feet enclosed in scuffed Mary Janes. Evie reached out a trembling hand to help Luiza up.

She sat up quickly, trying to wipe her eyes and smooth her hair and brush dirt from her dress all at once. 'Hello, pet! Don't cry . . . we were just play-fighting. Just playing a little game.'

'You have to tell Mama he was mean to you. She'll make him leave.'

'No! Evie, you can't tell anyone. Promise me? Don't tell.'

'But she'll get angry at him. So will Papa. He was so mean to you.'

Luiza rose up on her haunches and pulled Evie down roughly so that the girl knelt before her, still trembling in the face of her sister's clouded, staring eyes. 'Mother can't know about this. She'll get hurt. Promise me. Don't tell.'

Evie looked down, and Luiza knew the child was incapable of keeping a secret. Her little sister always wanted to please, and every feeling she had flickered across her face, intelligible to anyone who knew her.

'Promise?'

Still, Evie said nothing and Luiza forced her chin upwards so that they were face to face, Evie screwing up her face so as not to meet her eyes.

'Evie, promise me!'

'No!'

Evie tried to push away, and something awful rose up in Luiza then, from the floor of her stomach into her head and hands, which became rigid and ferociously strong as they dug into Evie's upper arms, seizing her, holding her there, then shaking her again and again, longer and harder than Luiza herself could understand, because it was as though she was watching it happen rather than doing it herself. It was someone else growling through jaws ground tightly together, *Promise me*. It wasn't the sight of Evie's head rolling back and forth on her little neck that made Luiza stop, but the strange, almost soundless staccato of forced breaths her sister pushed out her nose, like the faint snuffle of a pig. Not a human sound. When she let her go, Evie crumpled to the same spot where Luiza had fallen, in shock and silent now. Luiza waited, nauseated, for Evie to seize or vomit, but she just lay there for several minutes as Luiza rubbed her back, saying, 'I'm sorry' over and over again.

Eventually Evie sat up, bleary-eyed. 'I promise I won't tell anyone,' she cried before running away.

Gratitude washed over Luiza: Evie was lucid. But also a sickening relief: her parents would never find out about her lies and perversities, the violence that exceeded even her own worst memory of her father, how upset he became the night she swam out, how he'd gripped and shaken her. But not nearly as violently as what she'd just done to Evie.

Who could hurt a child? Only the worst kind of person. She could no longer pretend to be the martyred caretaker; she was brutal and bitter and even more guilty than him for having no disease to blame for her anger. And Evie, poor Evie—some day she, too, would be dismissed as too sensitive, too sentimental. People like her felt things more deeply, and Luiza wondered if her attack on Evie would stay with her sister forever. What if *this* was the critical moment that shaped her, that arrested her in a damaged state? She had imprinted a child, this child she loved and who was so much like herself, with fear. Because now Evie knew that Luiza was a person who would rather break her little sister's heart than tell the truth.

*Mother benign of our redeeming Lord,*
*Star of the sea and portal of the skies,*

The sound of their voices rises—it is bells, it is birds, it is a vibrating cord pulled taut.

*Unto thy fallen people help afford*
*Fallen, but striving still anew to rise.*

Voices layered upon voices, as half of the singers reach out with their throats and the other half answer back. The first group leans slightly forward as they sing, then back as they're responded to, the second group now tipping gently toward them. Gentle inhale, exhale. Together, they are the breath of a sleeper's lungs.

With them, communion. Gone now.

She can't slip under into peace and relief, because there is still so much more to say. There is more she needs to tell her mother, but there is water all around, closing over her. She's disappearing.

'Mother!' she cries out into the quiet murmur of women leaving the chapel, and some of them look at her sadly, unsurprised.

Luiza pushes through the sea of black-draped bodies and rushes down the hall, nearly breaking into a run. She bursts into her room, pushing the door open wide. But the room is empty and dark, except for a white piece of notepaper left on the bed.